I0785012

The Dragon's Maw

Book Two of "The Soulbound Song"

C.A. Chaplin

Edited by R. N. Barbosa and YarnWyvern
Formatting by A. E. Cosby
Cover art by Prokaryarts LLC

1st edition 2025

To those who can never go home.

Table of Contents

Author's Note & Content Warnings

This book is essentially a grimdark love story; dark romantic fantasy combining subgenres of dark and monster romance under the overarching umbrella of the fantasy genre. It is not capital-R Romance genre, and does not follow those genre expectations.

It contains explicit depictions of sex between consenting adults, graphic violence, graphic language, dark humor, psychological coercion/manipulation, mental illness relating to childhood trauma, and unhealthy relationship dynamics. The main characters are not human. Their psychology and physiology differ from ours, sometimes in major ways.

I have both ADHD and Autism, and many characters are neurodivergent. I don't name these diagnoses in the text because these concepts do not exist in the same framework in Vaeda, and they may manifest differently. For example, Cúraniel exhibits symptoms of both ADHD and Autism with relatively low support needs, but symptoms like synesthesia are common among elves. One of the elves exhibits behavior consistent with Narcissistic Personality Disorder, but he is, in fact, unique and powerful. Rafael could potentially be diagnosed with Antisocial Personality Disorder if he were human, but he's a literal apex predator.

The elves have a culture of nonmonogamy. Sometimes it resembles polyamory, sometimes not. It's important to remember they do not view the world through the lens of compulsory monogamy or follow the sexual mores of Western society. Thus, they also do not follow a lot of the standard negotiating and rule-setting many polyamorous folks do, and sexual jealousy is highly atypical. The central relationships are fraught and not intended to depict the polyamorous community or healthy polyamorous relationships.

One of the main characters is greyromantic and demisexual, but he is not meant to represent the aro-ace community at large; no community or identity is a monolith. Some BDSM practices are depicted but they do not represent the BDSM community or lifestyle, and many depicted practices are definitely unsafe for those without immortal bodies.

Please note: sign language uses different grammar. It is not a mistake or a typo when you encounter it.

Instead of only Cúraniel's POV, there are also chapters from Celebel's POV in this book. They are labeled as such.

Sexual

Explicit sexual contact (consenting adults only), dub-con, rope bondage, impact play, toy/object insertion, fellatio, cunnilingus, dominance/submission, anal sex, pegging, sadism/masochism, teratophilia (monster fucking to the uninitiated), cum worship (I really hate that spelling), knife play, blood play including consumption of menstrual blood, ethical sexual interactions outside the established relationships, vore

Social/Violence

Physical violence, general gore, murder, character death, war and battle, evisceration, dismemberment, eye injury, discussion of childhood physical and sexual abuse (off-page past events), rape mention, xenophobia, prejudice, misogyny, sexual jealousy, slut-shaming, blood consumption (from people), consumption of sentient beings, necrophagia, medical descriptions of injuries, mention of fertility & pregnancy, emesis, ableism/internalized ableism, child endangerment, child death (off-page, implied), killing pregnant sentient beings (not people), murder of sentient beings in stasis, animal death (enemy creatures/monsters), male anger directed at intimate partner (yelling), verbal abuse, intimate partner violence, dream of implied sexual assault, body horror, envenomation, big fucking spiders, even bigger fucking centipedes

Psychological

Complex and single event Post-Traumatic Stress Disorder (both PTSD & C-PTSD), Antisocial Personality Disorder (ASPD), Narcissistic Personality Disorder (NPD), Attention-Deficit Hyperactivity Disorder (ADHD), Autism

Spectrum Disorder (ASD), Major Depression, suicide mention, suicidal ideation, alcohol use, hallucinations, loss of autonomy, demons/demon possession, psychotic episodes, self-harm that draws blood, retaliatory self-harm, retaliatory violence to others, self-destructive behavior, psychological manipulation, emotional manipulation, gaslighting, intimidation, graphic language (they say fuck a lot)

Pronunciation Guide

Notes on Elvish:

"C" sounds are hard in elvish words, as in "cat"

Accent marks indicate a rising inflection.

"Ë" is pronounced like the "e" in words like "extra" and "error," and if it follows a consonant, then pronounce the letter as a full syllable.

"Ä" indicates that the letter should be pronounced separately, and sounds like the "a" in "father"

"Î" is held slightly longer, and sounds like the "i" in "slick"

"Þ"(and "þ") is a soft th or dh sound, such as in "feather" and "the"

"Ea" together without a trema over either letter in elvish indicates two syllables, with the "e" being a long sound such as "bee" and the "a" such as "aim"

"Û" is a long "u" such as "vacuum"

Generally, every vowel is pronounced separately.

Elvish Names

- Cúraniel "Maeliaressë": KOO-rah-nee-ell MAY-lee-ah-rehs-she
- Celebel Elhalanros: KEL-eb-el eh-lah-LAN-ros
- Rafael: rah-fah-EL
- Nemohee: NEHM-oh-hee
- Feanim Melranos: fee-AY-nim mehl-RAH-nose
- Araglin: AIR-ah-glen
- Beredhel: BEHR-eh-thell
- Eäriel: ee-AH-ree-ell
- Nimthil Tinunith: NIM-thill tin-OO-nith
- Feledhor: FELL-eh-thor
- Liriadis: LIR-ee-a-diss
- Carafindrien: care-ah-FINN-dree-ehn
- Cael: KAY-el
- Hithinn: HIH-thinn
- Caladris: kal-AH-driss
- Eledom: ELL-eh-dom

- Lámirië: LAH-meer-ree-aye
- Laseryn: lah-SEHR-in
- Dostael: DOSS-tay-el
- Silfanië: sill-FAH-nee-aye
- Recarmial: reh-KAR-me-all
- Rhoscellen: rose-KELL-in
- Melranim: mel-RAH-nim
- Maelial: MY-lee-ahl
- Dhraxael: THRACKS-ah-el
- Dacael: DAH-cah-el
- Adacanir: ah-DAH-cah-neer
- Faeglhingril: fie-GLEHN-grill
- Tárthanë: TAHR-thah-nay
- Dûemer: DOO-ey-mer
- Galdir: GALL-deer
- Anadanë: an-ah-DAN-aye
- Mëalidh: MAY-ah-lith
- Hestalön: HESS-tahl-own
- Talaossë: tahl-AH-ow-SAY
- Arundel: AH-run-del
- Suvanal: SOO-vah-nahl
- Háramorn: HAH-rah-mourn
- Galaron: GAH-lah-ron
- Neksarim: nek-SAH-reem
- Inelaira in-ey-LAH-EE-rah
- Neksarim: nek-SAH-reem
- Pirinlach: Peer-een-lok
- Norlissuin: Nor-LEE-soo-in
- Elairon: el-AYE-rohn
- Célesor: KEH-lehs-oar

Elvish Places
Velúara: vell-OOH-ah-rah
Férioth: FEH-ree-oth
Amrún: am-RUNE

Thraeneleth: Thay-neh-leth
Leyûduin: lay-OO-doo-in
Sirelon: SEER-eh-lohn
Seregond: SEHR-eh-gond
Rimbaras: reem-BARH-as
Orfain: OR-fa-een
Faelen: FAY-len
Taloth: TAHL-ohth
Erëlen: ehr-AY-lehn
Oseralon: oh-SEHR-ah-lohn

Elvish Vocabulary

- Pîntellum: PIN-tell-oom – term for specialized armor membrane
- Þilvor: THEEL-vore – star-blessed metal ore
- Þey/Þem/Þeir: they/them/their – nonbinary pronoun
- Moranga: more-ANG-ah – demon ore
- Fallëvaethil: FAHL-eh-VAY-thil – "Rain Jewel" an important gem
- Atani: AH-tah-nee – "Fifth Kindred" humans with spirit power
- Ardhanë: ar-tha-NAY – humans without spirit power
- Tárthanë: TAHR-thah-nay – "Long-Wakers" an extinct predecessor of ancient humans
- Lonáramir: lone-AH-rah-meer – the Singing Sword, an object of power

Elvish Nations

- Talithiri: tahl-eh-THEE-ree
- Lachanaur: LAHK-ah-nawr
- Duedellen: DWAY-del-ehn
- Astolar: AHS-toh-lahr
- Siltaur: SEEL-tawr
- Maraiya: mah-RAH-ee-yah

Notes on Draconian

"Rr" is a deep, guttural, rolled "r," started at the base of the throat and led up to the mouth. No equivalent exists in English, though the uvular "r" is a similar concept

All "r" sounds are a trilled "r" as in Spanish

Other double consonants indicate an elongated consonant sound, like a pause

Draconian Names
- Marron: MEH-rr-on
- Xyxs: ZICKS-ss – closer to one syllable than two
- Boshkt: BAHSHKT, one syllable
- Abrrys: AB-rrees
- Grenyk: GREH-neek
- Bxyldurr: BEESH-ill-doo-rr
- Vaerra: VIE-eh-rrah
- Itreynith: ih-TREY-nith
- Eszrayln: ez-SRAILN
- Tathua: TAH-thoo-ah

Draconian Vocabulary
- Arratxo/k ah-RR-AHT-sho/ah-RR-AHT-shok – elf/elves, derogatory
- Viigsakh: VEEG-sakh – third gender drake, able to both sire and give birth to offsping
- Hthrakkga: hith-RAKK-gah – sun-ripened shit from a diseased creature
- Nekarazzi: neh-ka-RAHTS-ze – striped pest
- Inuriterrege: in-OO-ree-I-rreh-geh – anthill king
- Rraysth e: RR-aysth eh – "The Red" or "Red One"
- Skeffynthir: SKEFF-in-theer – a blue dragon
- Xuatae Aitzindrerrelehen – shu-AH-tie eye-tzin-DREH-rr-eh-en – Title meaning "Progenitor of the First Flame," referring to the first dragon, Dhraxael
- Indrerra: in-DREH-rr-ah – strength and courage rooted in understanding the power of lineage

Other Names
- Faraz: FAH-rahzz
- Machi: MAH-chee
- Helicos: HEL-eh-kos

- Iruwher: EE-roo-whir
- Lettai: LET-tye
- Sylvaine: sill-VAYN
- Aa'shekahn: AH-sheh-kahn

regions of VAEDA
Oseralon
Taloth
Inelmoneth
Amrun
Ferioth
Almatherin
Narinmoneth
R. Emalen
Armon
Elayan
R. Erelen
Seregond
R. Suvalen
Aurelmoneth
Rimvaras
The Broken Lands
The Great Tree
The Orfain Tree
R. Gliralen
Velvara
Alma
Aureth
Aurel
Orma

Prologue: The Story So Far

ELVISH healer, Cúraniel, led a peaceful, isolated life on her hill until a dragon fight landed a wounded and dying man at her feet. Recognizing him as a shapeshifting drake, one of the abandoned children of true dragons, he was none other than the legendary Red Dragon. Named "Rafael" by her people, meaning "God of Carnage," it took the prompting of her goddess, the Night Mother, for Cúraniel to save him.

Worse, the Red Dragon was her soulmate. Rarely, an elf may have more than one soulmate, and in exceedingly rare cases, may bond with a non-elf. Soulmates feel each other's pain, both physically and emotionally, have a vague location sense, and may speak directly, mind-to-mind. Significantly, despite there being no guarantee of romantic love, soulmates who are distant from each other will wither in body and spirit, and if one dies, the other is likely to follow.

When Rafael awoke, furious at his savior, a slow dance began. She discovered deep-rooted trauma that kept the Dragon from intimacy of any kind and grew determined to heal his soul as well as his body. Due to Cúraniel's relentless flirting, and despite Rafael's cantankerous nature, they eventually bonded.

The Dragon continued to flee his emotions, visiting Cúraniel only sporadically. When she finally confronted him about their soulbond, he reacted poorly. They exchanged harsh words, and he abandoned her.

After 84 years of Rafael's erratic behavior, another dying man appeared at Cúraniel's hill. Celebel Elhalanros, heir of a royal lineage and the Consul of the Talithiri elves, and a second soulmate to Cúraniel. Kind and trusting where Rafael was vicious and distant, the two elves quickly fell in love.

When Cúraniel revealed her existing soulbond to Celebel, he

reacted at first with disbelief, then with slow acceptance. Unfortunately, the Red Dragon sensed Celebel's presence, and returned to her hill.

Cúraniel confessed her involvement with another. Rafael had an explosive reaction and departed once more, strangling their soulbond. Celebel talked her into aiding his cause. Fearsome, monstrous creatures called Fomorians had been attacking elves, and they could use a healer of her skills. With some reluctance, she agreed to leave her hill.

They met with the other Consul, Feanim, and made their way to the walled monastic fortress of Férioth. Before they reached safety, the Fomorians ambushed them. With the elves vastly outnumbered, all hope seemed lost. Cúraniel was forced to call upon the Red Dragon for aid.

Rafael answered the call and brought other drakes with him. They rescued the elves, and Rafael finally admitted his feelings for Cúraniel. She extracted a vow from him: to keep Celebel from harm and ally with the elves to save them, in exchange for considering his proposal to claim her as his mate.

Arriving at court with an outcast and an enemy drake in tow was not a popular choice with the court. Despite that, Cúraniel furthered her sexual and emotional connection to Rafael, while also continuing her relationship with Celebel. Rafael committed himself to making Celebel's life as difficult as possible, and Celebel often sided with the court, leading to clashes between the three of them.

Feanim revealed the existence of moranga, a demon ore in his possession, to which Rafael immediately demanded access. The Red Dragon criticized the elves' weapons and armor, insisting they must be crafted of pure þilvor, a rare and valuable metal. Feanim and Celebel had already been at work designing a special living armor to incorporate the þilvor, and Cúraniel lent her knowledge of herbalism to the effort.

Though the drakes recognized no king, they followed Rafael's command primarily out of fear. Notably, clan heads Marron the green, Tyldain the blue, and Xyxs the red and black, accepted Cúraniel's presence among them. They fought alongside the elves in various engagements with the enemy. They discovered the Fomorians were not simply attacking elves, but capturing them.

Cúraniel's longtime friend, Nemohee, joined her at court. Þey had been on a covert mission to recover the Carnyx of Calling, a powerful sidhe weapon capable of summoning the Fomorians. The Consulate made a plan to mass their enemies in one area for an open battle. In a clever use of terrain, the strategy was a resounding success. Later, as Cúraniel healed the wounded, Rafael came to her acting strangely. He'd been attacked with a weapon used to inflict madness. She healed him, but the weapon's presence brought concern to Celebel and Feanim.

Everything fell apart on the return to Férioth. Enemy drakes attacked, including a giant ice drake named Itreynith. Rafael sent the elves ahead without him. Upon arrival, they discovered treachery. Araglin had abandoned them. Elves Celebel considered friends attacked him in his chambers. One stabbed him in the back with a moranga blade. Someone opened the gates to the Fomorians, and enemies poured in. In the chaos, Cúraniel discovered that unhealing, a special ability to re-open old wounds, removed a glamour cast over Fomorians. It also killed them on the spot.

Wounded in battle, Rafael made his way back to her and aided the remaining elves in their escape. Cúraniel tried her best to heal Celebel, but barely kept him alive in her state of exhaustion. An evil clung to his injury. Pouring her spirit into him to clear the tainted power, it caught her instead. She cried out to Rafael again for help, and he answered. When she regained consciousness, both of her soulmates lay insensate at her feet.

Part 1

Chapter 1

Cúraniel

NUDITY was not conducive to dragon slaying. Not that I'd ever had any such talent. I hugged my bare arms, ducking low as an unfamiliar drake crashed through the nearby trees. At such altitude, the sparse juniper and pine boughs provided meager cover. Lacking an introduction from Rafael, as well as his ferociously enforced protection, this newcomer was either an enemy or a backbiting ally seeking advantage over its fallen leader. Gods damned drakes and their endless vying for power.

With both soulmates crumpled on the unforgiving ground beside me, and my spirit utterly drained from healing, panic crawled up my spine. Shaking, I resisted the urge to draw the men closer to me. Couldn't they have waited to succumb once we reached the safety of Amrún's walls?

Star-streaked hair fallen across his face and long ears gone slack, Celebel breathed the slow, even breath of the comatose. Behind me, Rafael made no sound at all. Not even his normal rumbling. Concern for my elvish partner made way for abject terror at my Dragon's uncharacteristic loss of consciousness.

The indestructible Red Dragon shook off the most grievous wounds, with the exception of the near-fatal fight that had brought him to me. How severe was the penalty for absorbing those foul energies I'd pulled from Celebel? A nearby snort yanked me back to the present danger.

The sun lit the new drake's rust-orange scales like a forged blade waiting to be quenched. In one corded arm, the warrior hefted a meat cleaver of a sword. No need for added weaponry with such natural armament, but it carried the blade with the ease of long familiarity. Taller than any elf, taller even than the Red Dragon himself in similar form, it cast a violent shadow in its search for prey.

Fuck, I should have kept my pack close, but it rested on a cart with our other supplies. My poor proficiency with a blade would not deter the hulking offspring of the true dragons, as my own Dragon so often teased, but I wished to at least make a show of defense. Drakes responded surprisingly well to bravado, absurd as it was from a soft, scaleless elf such as myself. Rafael found it entertaining, at any rate, and the others followed his example, if reluctantly. I dared not divert my focus from the massive predator stomping toward us to assess the beloved predator at my back.

My heart quivered like a rabbit readying to bolt from danger. Or preparing to expire from fear. All too easy to imagine those dagger-teeth rending my flesh, those cruel talons lacerating my skin. A perfect killer.

Shouts and the clang of weapons distorted as the sound echoed off the nearby granite cliffs. Hopefully, the cacophony disguised my pounding heart. If Fomorians also flanked us while two of our key fighters lay unconscious, most especially Rafael, we would be well and truly fucked. If that questing drake discovered me before my Dragon awoke… Damn my lack of athleticism. And armored scales. And sharp teeth and talons.

Crushed vegetation mingled in my nose with familiar reptilian musk as the drake approached. Stronger and more pungent than Rafael's scent, it carried an undercurrent of burning pitch. I had a wild urge to sniff each drake in our company. They differentiated each other primarily by scent; could I as well?

I bit the inside of my cheek to restore my splintering attention. Without the luxury of my Dragon's fastidious flames, the long days of fight and flight amplified Celebel's scent and my own. I prayed silently to the Night Mother to keep the wind from changing direction.

Nostrils flared in the drake's blunt snout. Swinging its head back and forth on a short neck as it sniffed, its barrel chest heaved over an expansive belly. Muscle slid smoothly under scale; a second layer of armor. A finned tail whipped behind it.

"I am fucked," I mouthed to myself.

The new drake stepped perilously close to where I crouched under the brush. Moving slowly and carefully, I surreptitiously nudged the Red Dragon with my foot.

'*Gods damn it, Rafael,*' I sent, pounding the words into an unresponsive mind. '*One of your people is about to devour me. Wake up, you great, blighting drake!*'

Surely, Rafael still lived. Surely, the nigh-invulnerable prick would rouse himself and rescue us. For all his melodies of protection, he'd certainly picked an inopportune time to faint. *Surely,* he'd only lost consciousness. The soulbonds anchored within me only whispered where they once sang. But they whispered still.

I blanketed my fear with the absurdity of the situation. Who could have foretold I would be the one to stand and fight after the mighty Red Dragon himself fell? Exhaustion made drawing enough spirit to unheal wounds impossible. Nudges became toe-bruising kicks.

Pebbles scraped under my foot, and I froze. The questing drake whipped about. Dark copper eyes trained on me, then on Rafael's prone body. Slit pupils dilated with predatory arousal. With a rocking grinding sound, the strange drake laughed. Gods, what a forest of teeth.

'*Awaken, you wretched hellbeast! Your soulmate is in danger of dismemberment!*'

I touched the braid knife bound into my hair. Made of simple steel, it was useless against a drake's scales. Scales? The scale! I clasped the serrated garnet scale hanging around my neck. It did nothing to compensate for my lack of comparative strength and fighting prowess, but I couldn't die here. Crow, I couldn't let my soulmates die. Not after everything we'd fought through, everything we'd survived together.

"Dûemer, Night Mother, hear my plea!" I reached for her protection and my weakened spirit skipped over empty space. Might as well grasp smoke. "Please! Your daughter, Cúraniel, calls you!" The goddess remained as distant as the moon.

With a dry throat, I screamed in draconian, then elvish, for the drake to leave us in peace. Surely my cries would reach the ears of allies. My heart thudded in counterpoint to my voice. Internally, I begged for salvation, tugging in vain at my hushed bonds. Prodding at my aloof goddess.

A cloud passed over the sun. The drake's teeth flashed in a

lolling grin. If Rafael were going to answer the challenge, he would have by now. I tensed, raising the scale. A deep shadow fell across the path, separating us like a river of night. Desperate for any respite, I willed it into a physical barrier. With a snort, the drake charged.

Cursing, I threw myself over Celebel's unconscious body as he was far more vulnerable than the Dragon. The irony of finally choosing between my adversarial soulmates was not lost on me. Hardly daring to look, I slashed the air in warning.

The impending collision never came. Bewildered growls caught my attention. The drake thrashed, stuck in the shadow as though sunk in tar. Muscle strained against a chasm of nothing. My ears twitched. What now? Legs shaking with fatigue and fear, I rose and staggered forward.

Liquid night flowed around me, enveloping the warrior, erasing the scene. Cutting off its cry. Meteors burst across my vision. Flailing, I caught hold of velvety nothing that dissipated in my hands with a sharp blast of cold. My head rang like a bell.

All too similar to my experience with the darkness lashing out from Celebel's wound, yet none forced its way down my throat. Frissons of tingling shock rolled through my body, giving me a weirdly weightless sensation. I kicked, unable to feel the ground beneath my feet. Heartbeats slowed.

A distant voice called out. The spangled emptiness shuddered, flaring. Galaxies poured around me. My existence balanced on a single star, a single mote of sparkling dust.

"**ENOUGH.**" The voice reverberated with power, shaking through the very core of reality. Instinctively, I turned toward an immolated figure. Pure flame sliced through the shimmering darkness.

The shadow receded, returning my senses. Folding in on itself, it shrank until only a small, cat-shaped blob remained. Two yellow eyes bobbed to the surface. The voidlet.

Behind me, a familiar, foul-tempered bass growled, "Gods fucking *damn* it, Cúraniel. I cannot close my eyes for a single *fucking* moment without everything falling into shit..." Rafael trailed off into unfamiliar draconian expletives. The language brimmed with them.

As I twisted to look at him, my eyes grazed over an unfamiliar glove. No. Not a glove. Steam rose from the cleanly sheared stump of a hand. Rusty scales covered the talon-tipped fingers. No blood pooled beneath it. My breath came fast and shallow.

"What have you done?" I sat up, tremors of anticipated conflict quivering my limbs. Sipping at air beginning to thin with altitude and forcing my breathing to slow, I found the hum of the shared song and grounded myself.

My fierce soulmate clutched his black shirt closed where I'd torn it to examine the wound beneath. What a contrast to the attacker. Rafael had far fewer outward signs of his draconic nature, mostly resembling a man in his preferred form. The strongest sign of his parentage showed in his digitigrade legs and three-toed, taloned dragon feet.

Rafael's eyes burned coal-bright, the pupils a vertical slash in the blaze. Hair like liquid flame tumbled in curling waves over impossibly broad shoulders. A good sign, that he had the energy to be riled enough for his typically blood-red mane to spark—though his bronze skin was paler than usual.

He snorted, glaring down his strongly aquiline nose at the voidlet sitting nearby. "*I* did nothing. Your pampered abomination swallowed it." The chorus growl laced under his resonant voice rose more than usual, an approaching thunder.

The so-called abomination stretched, nonchalant.

"My voidlet did this?"

No birdsong nor insect call pierced the curtain of silence laid upon the thin forest. Had they fled the skirmish, or something else? The creature bumped against me, blinking luminous eyes. For the first time, I hesitated to pat its soft head.

"I warned you. It feeds on emotion. Too much and..." Rafael imitated a rapid expansion with his hands, talons splayed. He nodded at the amputated hand lying on the ground like a dead spider. "This one was an ally."

"Some ally, charging me with a raised blade!" I mimicked swinging a sword.

"My people attempt to kill me any time I show weakness." He

shrugged off my worry. "No cause to let that *thing* swallow us all."

"I was situated directly between *your people* and your deeply unconscious self, lacking even the spirit to summon protection." I frowned at his nonchalance, itching to slap some sense into him. How dare he dismiss my genuine fear, however typical of him. "Was I to sit back and let that drake kill us? I've never witnessed you go under in such a manner."

"I only turned inward for a moment to nullify that contaminated energy." He stretched, blithely ignoring my protest.

"You frightened me, you great fucking lizard! I was unaware you had any actual limits." Anger, barbed and guarded, twisted around the vulnerability of my love for my Dragon.

That unexpected battle with the traitorous drakes had surely taken a toll. Rafael had shifted into his gargantuan, full dragon form, and maintained it for days. He'd taken a wound he couldn't immediately heal. All the flight. More battle with the Fomorians—or whatever they truly were—when they'd breached the walls of Férioth. The dead Fomorian in Celebel's bedchamber haunted me, its bestial glamour bursting apart to reveal the sidhe beneath.

To distract from my growing trepidation, I crouched beside Celebel. Road dust dulled his glossy black hair, as it had mine, and cast his distinctive silver streaks in grey. At least he'd lost some of the sickly cast to his pale skin, though it was still too close to my natural pallor for comfort.

I hadn't been able to heal my Starshine. My fingernails bit into my palms. Gods, how was he to travel in this state? I'd likely need to hoist him into a wagon.

The thick, sooty fringe of Celebel's eyelashes swept over high cheekbones. Even in such a state, his beauty devastated me. I brushed a thumb over his full lips, grateful his chest rose and fell smoothly. He made a soft sound, scrunching his straight nose, brow furrowing. I smoothed his forehead with a shaking hand. The aftermath of shock had my stomach attempting to rid itself of the bile filling it. I turned my head away, pressing my lips together to barricade the nausea.

Rafael's sharp eyes drifted over Celebel's unconscious face

and back to mine. He cocked the pointed arch of one brow. Ah. He'd never even tangentially allow his perceived romantic rival an advantage. Probably still blamed Celebel for the lavender fiasco, regardless of whether the elvish Consul had acted with deliberation.

Elvish hubris, doomed to end in violence. If only we'd also discovered the larger treachery lurking beneath before it was too late.

"Hrrm, such tribute. I save her and the *nekarazzi* from the curse in his wound. I drive back the void monster before it can devour her or anyone else. Does she express her undying love and loyalty? Of course not."

The Dragon swept his arms wide, letting his tattered shirt fall open. The wound inflicted by the white drake Itreynith crept like grey lichen from his clavicle down his left side, marring his heavily muscled torso. He had the kind of muscle that would make a sane person take a step back out of self-preservation. Aggressive, like the rest of him.

"I've no strength at the moment, but I wish to attend to that." I pointed to the wound, ignoring his petty nickname for Celebel. 'Badger', indeed. "It has not improved, and I mislike the implication."

"Save your effort. It is healing underneath." He gave me an arch look. "Unless I offend your eyes?"

"Never." I stood, but my legs wobbled like a newly foaled horse. Rafael caught me before I landed on poor Celebel, pulling me easily to my feet.

"Though anyone should appreciate your ample rump on their face," he gave my ass a firm slap, "you may smother him to death."

I barked a startled laugh. "Wouldn't that benefit you?"

Sliding my arms around the Dragon's waist, I pressed myself against his unnaturally warm, unnaturally hard body. Rafael had never acknowledged my sexual relationship with Celebel outside of a jealous argument. That hint of growth loosened one of a great many knots in my chest.

"You would be miserable. Then you would make me miserable." His lip curled in a sneer.

"You're already miserable." I tugged at a lock of flaming hair, unable to resist the smile creeping across my face. Merely touching him eased my worry. "Perhaps you should nap more frequently. You are in a remarkably good mood."

A muscle feathered in Rafael's jaw as he stared at the unconscious Celebel. I braced to defend against the inevitable, devastating insult. Instead, the Dragon said, "*You* finally released that panicky stranglehold on our bond."

"I suppose you are unaccustomed to such fear. The defection struck me soul-deep. For another elf to attack their own Consul, attack *my* soulmate—" I cast a backward glance at Celebel. "Anathema to everything we have ever believed in. How could they hate us so very much?"

"Hrrm, there is more at play here than old prejudice." The Dragon stroked my long ears and ran his fingers through my hair. I'd had no time or energy to braid it as we'd fled, and it fell in a raven tangle to my ankles. "Merely a convenient ruse."

I breathed him in. A combination of his leather clothing, a hint of smoke, and something akin to dracaena resin; his natural scent soothed me. Especially in contrast to the hostile drake's more biting odor.

Rafael's seemingly limitless strength had always meant safety, allowing me to grow complacent. The very accusation I'd hurled at the inexperienced court. Those who'd attempted to murder Celebel and thrown open the gates to the enemy. What must blight the soul of an elf to risk the gods' wrath and severance from the shared song? To be forever cut off from our pooled spirit power, to have to rely solely upon the labor of one's hands to provide sustenance rather than draw from the trees? Breaking my lineage only denied me the accumulated power of my house. The song yet flowed through me, and the Night Mother's particular interest restored much of what I lacked.

I shuddered with the force of emotions boiling up. Relief for my soulmates, fear for my friends, the throbbing ache left by the traitors. For all we'd lost in Férioth. How would we survive long enough to reach Amrún, so high up in these accursed mountains? If I'd known my return to elvish society would end in ruin, I would never—

"Enough sniveling." Rafael tilted my chin up to make eye contact. A long way up, as the top of my head came to the middle of his chest.

At my height, average for an elf woman and taller than most humans, I'd yet to grow accustomed to a lover so much taller than I. "Stay here. Rest. I will assess the damage." His eyes flicked to the voidlet. "Send that thing away."

I pressed my lips to his chest in gratitude and turned to my shadowy little friend. "We appreciate your help. Could you…?" I made a brushing gesture.

The voidlet mewed silently and blinked out of existence.

Chapter 2

"WE can use the void creature to our advantage." Feanim moved his liver mare closer to me. His mossy eyes brightened with scheming, despite the sallow cast of his olive complexion.

All around us, granite peaks rose like the jaws of a great beast, ready to snap up the stars. I misliked the implication, glancing back to where Celebel slumbered in the cart. His loyal stallion would allow no other riders, so we'd hitched him to the cart. He bore the ignobility well. We'd traveled by night as often as possible for the added concealment.

Nimthil peered from behind the Duedellen elf, studying our lips. She must have lost her horse in the attacks, as she'd ridden double the entire way. I did not ask, patting my Iruwher's silky mane with gratitude. Feanim spoke on, and I shifted my attention back to him. His clipped tenor had a thin quality. Much as he acted callus, a certain puffiness around his olivine eyes sang a different melody.

"Imagine the power this creature would grant us if we could wield it in offense? Perhaps if you—"

"No." Rafael's growl from the tree cover startled the horses as he emerged. "I forbid it." Barely visible in daylight, the glow from my Dragon's fiery hair and eyes lit his face in the darkness like a vision from hell.

Just beyond him, Marron watched the exchange with an unreadable ruby gaze. Where Rafael was all sharp angles, the amiable green drake was a solid tree trunk of a man—if trees had verdant scales rather than bark. Almost as skilled a shapeshifter as Rafael, he also favored a more elflike form, albeit one framed with those visible laminae over intimidating muscle. He caught my eye, and a grimace creased his square face.

Nimthil jumped at the deep rumble, clinging tighter to Feanim. The dainty Lachanaur elf had once said she could feel the Dragon's voice in her belly, understanding his words as vibration despite her hearing loss. Freckles stood out on her tawny brown face as pain and fear chased each other through her eyes. She looked away, twisting a coil of poppy-orange hair in nervous hands. Avoiding the signs we made, she clearly wanted no part of this conversation, and just as clearly had no desire to be alone.

I didn't blame her. Ever since the attack on Férioth, I'd jumped at my own footfalls. How much worse was it for a queen who'd lost her closest advisors and friends to a betrayal so foul it beggared the imagination? My mare danced beneath me in response to my fretting, and I patted her neck again.

Feanim shook his head, tossing dark curls limp with the same coat of grime we all wore. "Imagine the potential of harnessing such a creature!" Palm out, he fanned his hands away from his face, mimicking expansion. He brought them together in a swooping motion, pointing into the darkness. "All it needs is direction. Perhaps a small offering will sate it?"

"What is a sigh to a hurricane?" Rafael countered. "This is a piece of the void itself. Nothing can satisfy its hunger."

I'd known as much, but not what it meant. Not truly. "For centuries, the voidlet has visited my hill. You seem to know the reason, and yet you have never spoken it." My ears flicked, taut with annoyance. "As usual."

Iruwher snorted, echoing my sentiment.

Rafael exhaled through his nose. "Formless when you first encountered it, yes? Now it takes shapes that please you." He crossed his arms over his broad chest.

'Is this one of your games where I keep floundering until I hit upon the right question?' I sent, piqued at his roundabout approach. *'You know very well how I hate that.'*

The Dragon merely quirked a brow, much to my irritation.

I cast a glance at the cart rumbling along behind us. My connection to Celebel had dimmed ever since Feledhor sank that poisoned blade into his back. Like a dull whisper where once it sang.

I took any opportunity to touch him, fussing over him at every stop. Trying to fill the silence.

Aloud, I said, "It began as something like a liquid shadow. Now, it usually takes on a catlike form. You insist I stop feeding it, but you've never properly explained your meaning."

"You project your emotions with force." Rafael's voice sharpened. "Like a rolling outflow of tide, the strength of your feeling attracts that creature. It has imprinted on you because it knows you will feed it."

"Of which creature do we speak?" Nimthil muttered, hands fluttering around Feanim's waist in sign.

Rafael's eyes narrowed. Marron moved closer, watching the exchange with increasing tension. The night shaded his green scales near black.

I let out a nervous breath. "Why me, though? Why not attach itself to you? Or-or…" I gestured to everyone gathered. "Why not Feanim, for example?"

Feanim leaned toward me, ears twitching. "I've had more than sufficient emotion in these past centuries to serve as an attractant." His nose wrinkled and Nimthil smoothed his hair back.

I bit my lip on the building urge to tease him about relative attractiveness. What sufficient emotion? Férioth? The loss of his brother in the previous war?

"This is the third errant piece of the void I have encountered." Rafael's eyes glittered. Something unspoken lingered there. The green drake behind him grunted with definite unease. What did he know? "Ruinous, each one. They leave little to mourn in their wake."

"Much like you, according to our histories." The Duedellen's olivine gaze sharpened. Nimthil signed agreement. "Is this matter related to where you hid yourself for the last age?"

Marron coughed, attracting attention away from my increasingly irritated Dragon. "I once encountered a void piece myself." He held up a taloned thumb and forefinger with little more than a fingerbreadth between them. "Tiny thing. Started out only an odd mote of darkness circling my youngest. We thought he'd simply manifested a new elemental affinity. When he picked a fight and won his first broken bone, that little mote spread like shadows in the night." His ruby eyes squeezed shut, as if envisioning the ordeal.

"Vaerra and I barely held it off long enough to escape. Almost lost our offspring and ourselves. We had to abandon that den. Half of the ceiling collapsed when it took out the supporting arches. Nearly brought the whole mountainside down." He shuddered. "Looked wrong, after. As though it wiped away the stone."

Nimthil's lilting soprano startled me. "How did you contain it?" Either she was an exceptional lipreader, given Marron's general lack of lips, or the depth of his gravelly voice gave her enough vibrations to interpret.

"Similar to binding a demon, but more slippery." Marron's pale talons flashed as he pressed his palms together and made a swimming motion. The horses snorted at the movement, tossing their heads in distrust.

"You've bound a demon, Lord Marron?" Feanim stretched forward like a hound scenting prey.

"Marron. No 'Lord'. And my only attempt was unsuccessful." He glanced at Rafael, whose brows pinched a fraction more than usual. The green drake dropped his gaze immediately. "The Red disposed of the void creature in the end."

Interesting. I wanted to probe, but something in the back of my mind warned me away from it.

"If the creature strikes again, I will handle it. As I did this last time." The Red Dragon's chorus growl rose. "Meanwhile, stop *fucking* feeding it."

MY FRAUGHT conversation with Celebel looped in my mind. His frustration with the role he'd inadvertently played in the defection. His questioning of his competence. The uncomfortable truth to the claim this war was merely a game to Rafael.

'If you refuse to break with him, and he refuses to change, where does that leave us?' Celebel had asked.

Fucked. It left us fucked. Each new harmony revealed discordance beneath.

The treachery at Férioth wounded far more than Celebel's body. To be so close and yet so far away drained me more than a true physical separation. My soul frayed; silk drawn over a shattered crystal.

Our "camps" consisted of little more than bedrolls made of cloaks and saddle padding shoved between boulders, dwindling trees, and horses. Some elves slept on the wagons with our supplies. Keeping warm and fed took priority over speed. Originally, Feanim had insisted we could rest in shifts to avoid the need to stop. Outcry from bedraggled nobles, unaccustomed to hardship, put an end to that. We compromised by camping as little as possible, never staying in one location for more than a single afternoon or overnight.

Drakes roamed freely among us, raising tension where they passed, but they kept Fomorians from launching stealthy attacks. They had their occasional squabbles, often growing loud enough to alarm every elf in earshot, but a single quelling glare from Rafael was enough to put an end to most conflicts.

I took to trailing behind the other noncombatants. Close enough to appease the Dragon, but with enough distance to allow my meditation. Flat stares followed me, walling me out of conversation. That harmonized well enough with my mood.

Nemohee drew Machi alongside my mare long enough to give me a silver-eyed once over. Pursing þeir lips, þey left with a knowing look and a shrug of muscular shoulders.

My mind meandered. I should have offered to even out þeir hair. *Imagine having your soulmate hauled off by the gods damned Fomorians, and your closest friend is too distracted by her own strife to neaten up your mourning cut.*

Nem's long hair had been so lovely, bringing out the pink undertones in otherwise moon-pale skin. It gladdened me that, once cropped, it had kept that same dark red to white-blonde ombre effect. Must be the fae influence. Had þey burned the shorn hair in the Lachanaur tradition? I shook out my hands with the sudden recollection of Recarmial's torn braid burning in my grasp. The vague thoughts drifted away like morning fog as Nemohee rode off.

Sounds of a drake argument intertwined with elvish voices. Feanim's annoyed tenor rose above Rafael's snarling bass. I kept my distance. Let them resolve it without me for once.

In the restful pauses, I sang to Celebel and funneled what spirit I had into him. Dipping a rag into a decoction designed to restore his vitality, I dribbled it slowly into his mouth and prayed. Eäriel and Liriadis often joined, lending their voices and strength to mine.

Iruwher remained my constant companion. I soothed myself after by plaiting and re-plaiting the mare's raven mane and tail. I curried her coppery red coat into shining perfection. She got the larger portion of any edible tubers and rhizomes I foraged to supplement the sparse grass along the rocky path. Slowed by the pace of the wagons, I couldn't promise her better fare until we reached Amrún. So I hoped, at any rate.

I longed for the days of true freedom on the hill. The thought of escaping the relentless stress captivated me. Much like the mare, the Great Tree had provided quiet companionship. Undemanding comfort far from horror and violence. Untouched by grief and loss.

Damp spring grass under my feet. The raucous cries of the scrub jays nesting. The nervous, weary smile of a human with a difficult pregnancy seeking my healing. The scent of lilies by the creek. All the entertainingly troublesome minor fae. Drinking coffee in my cozy bower, with the rain plinking on the calcite panes.

Home.

Gods damn it, no more tears. I'd wept more in the intervening years since the Red Dragon crash landed at the base of the hill than the rest of my life combined; and far more so since Celebel's subsequent introduction. How tiresome, all that emotion. No wonder the voidlet had grown.

I lit a small fire to combat the night's increasing chill, hanging a pot over it. I'd never been fond of cooking, but the task had fallen to me this round. Huddling close to the flames, I warmed my hands and rubbed them over the icy tips of my ears. Difficult to cut up vegetables with frozen hands. We had scant enough blankets to go around, but I'd rather not ask Rafael to share his heat. Not yet.

Eyes pierced my back as I sat slicing old turnips for the soup. Almost at the last of our stored food, we had to stretch them across many empty bellies. I turned to a scaly face, watching from the shadows. A blink shuttered the lantern glow of enormous yellow eyes, like watch towers signaling in the night.

"My Lord Tyldain. To what do I owe the honor?" I stood, deliberately speaking elvish since he'd intruded on my space.

The blue drake stepped forward, scales greening in the firelight. Though lacking Rafael's intimidating musculature and force of presence, Tyldain was by no means a small man. The clan head carried himself with all the same predatory confidence, and far greater height than mine.

Like most drakes.

I'd only seen his full dragon form once and had been duly impressed. His slender stature became a lithe yet enormous dragon. He was a stormcaller and a firebreather. More than enough threat for me.

An azure tabard left his ropey arms bare. A few shades darker than his scaly hide, it was trimmed with spiky gold geometric designs. Tight grey hose and a navy leather ankle wrap complimented his three-toed dragon feet. Startlingly dapper, with his long, cobalt hair slicked back from his pointed face.

What a time for me to be asocial. I gestured with the remaining turnip. "I'd offer you soup, but I doubt the fare would be much to your taste."

"Interesting." He leaned on the sibilants. "I wished to observe you in your own element, away from Jxxysdfynn's"—or something similar—"influence."

How was it possible for Rafael's draconian name to sound different each time I heard it?

"And has my appearance changed?" I asked carefully, keeping my voice and posture neutral.

Why couldn't the other drakes be more like green Marron with his steady calm? Or at least the mostly harmless braggadocio of red and black Xyxs.

Tyldain's eyes glinted. "You look more vulnerable. *He* looks more vulnerable. Why is he not here to guard his mate?" What had he quarreled with Rafael over back at Férioth? The blue drake had retreated, and I should have asked more questions.

This melody was clear enough, and discordant to my ears. "I am Rafael's soulmate, not his claimed mate. Similar words in elvish, but I assure you there are key differences." Key differences Rafael blithely ignored, but that was a different conversation.

The blue drake's jaws parted without showing his teeth; his version of a smile. "Oh indeed. Then what claim have you on the Red?"

"Why? Would you like to move on him? I am not small-hearted; you are welcome to the attempt. Perhaps you'll find more success than the last drake." I bluffed a confidence I certainly didn't feel.

Reaching through the bond for Rafael, I cast about Tyldain's aura, searching for old wounds. Countless healed wounds wove around his body, gained over millennia of fighting. Could I perform a significant enough unhealing to disable him faster than he could pull my head from my shoulders? Drakes hardly blinked at excruciating pain.

The blue drake tilted his head to give me a considering look. He truly resembled an elf, if a bit stretched; eyes enlarged and other features somewhat flattened. Even with the shorter pointed ears rather than our long, graceful ones, he might have been comely if he didn't exude such a creeping sense of unease.

"So, he does not claim you. You do not claim him. Thus, you are available to be claimed." The sibilance collected into a harsh hiss.

I gathered my power in anticipation, and the trees creaked at my call. "Careful, Lord Tyldain. Despite my curves, I am not as soft as I appear. I once slew a basilisk with nothing but my braid knife. Plunged my little blade straight through the eye into the beast's brain." Never mind I'd spellsung the young basilisk to sleep first. Luck still led to victory. Rafael loved that story, naturally.

Tyldain sneered, muscles standing out in his arms. "An up-jumped lizard with foul breath is your great blooded kill?"

So much for bravado. I braced myself.

"Bluuuuuee, what are you doing here?" an oddly high, laconic voice called in draconian, and relief flooded me.

A familiar dragonish face, framed with fins, poked through the trees. Covered in greenish-grey scales and mottled with splotches of yellow, a mossy beard dangled from his chin. He shuffled into the firelight. Apart from starkly muscled arms and legs, the new arrival was lanky and short for a drake, only a scant few fingerbreadths taller than me. The fins continued down his back. He put me in mind of a cypress swamp.

"Causing trouble?" He stared down Tyldain.

"Boshkt! Last encountered you in the Siltaur roost, yes?" I said to my friend in draconian, and his eyes lit up. One blue and the other green, with scalloped pupils like a giant gecko. I resisted the urge to hug him, missing the days we'd spent testing various herbs on him and cataloguing the effects.

His finny ears fluttered, and he cocked his head. "Healer lady!"

Tyldain growled at the other drake, showing off an impressive number of needle-pointed teeth. I braced myself for a fight. As the blue drake was a clan head, I worried for Boshkt. He had no such status and thus must be a less powerful fighter.

"Why are you here, worm?" the blue drake hissed in their language.

Boshkt tilted his head again, wit sparkling in his mismatched eyes. "Not trustworthy, Blue. If the Red finds you sniffing after his intended mate, we all suffer. You want to fight? Challenge him direct and be done." The mottled drake made a gesture I didn't recognize, but Tyldain's expression soured further.

Drake drama. Intrigue and irritation warred at being dragged into the middle of it. Tyldain bared his teeth again. Boshkt hissed, some caustic substance dripping from his long jaws and sizzling in the dirt as it fell. I took a few surreptitious steps back.

Tyldain lifted his head, nostrils flaring as I sensed Rafael approaching like a coming storm. The blue drake withdrew into the darkness, unblinking lynx eyes remaining on me far longer than comfort permitted.

"Yeah, you don't want no venom, eh heh heh," Boshkt jeered after him.

I resisted the urge to throw my turnip at the retreating drake's back and dropped it into the soup pot instead. I disliked overly large chunks of vegetable in my broth, but I'd make an exception.

"Where have you been, Boshkt?" I lifted the ladle to my lips and wrinkled my nose at the lack of spices. "I thought you did not follow from the roost."

The mottled drake bobbed his head. "Circled back to be sure we weren't followed. Quieter, I am, than most."

True. His high voice was softer than most of the other drakes I'd met.

"More of us have joined since you left the other place. Made sure we had no more traitors." He clacked his jaws together once, and more of the caustic drool spattered on the ground, withering the vegetation. "None want my venom."

"Boshkt, what the fuck are you doing?" Rafael's draconian rumble interrupted us as he stalked into view, talons flexed. "You are only to watch."

The smaller drake ducked his head, backing away. "Following the Blue. You had the right; he was plotting. Pestering your healer lady."

Pestering indeed. I was grateful for the intervention.

Rafael's burning eyes shifted to me. "Did Tyldain hurt you?" His voice dropped so low I strained my ears to catch his words. Violence brewed in that growl.

"No. He thought to claim me," I responded in draconian, and Rafael bared his teeth in a snarl. So many pointy teeth around my campfire.

"That ratfucker." The Dragon's eyes blazed red murder. "Boshkt, stay. Kill any who bother her."

Boshkt ducked his head again, swishing his tail, as the fiery drake stalked off in Tyldain's direction.

"Your camp has some entertainment tonight, yes?" I asked.

The drake's mismatched eyes widened, and he barked a laugh. "Yes. Eh heh heh, the Red will crack some skulls. Get them back in the nest. None will dare challenge after this."

A COMMOTION rippled from the drake camp, setting every elf on edge. It ended abruptly with a sharp shriek. Had Rafael killed the blue drake? Gods, we could hardly afford more upheaval.

Boshkt watched me thoughtfully. "Blue lives. The Red won't start a clan war now." He clucked. "Shame."

"You dislike Tyldain?" I asked in draconian.

"Everyone dislikes Tyldain," he said with a snort.

Rafael returned, hands bearing a smattering of blood. Boshkt promptly shuffled off with a flick of his finned tail. He blended with the trees as well as any elvish ranger's cloak. I would have preferred to keep his company longer, but I did not blame him for avoiding the Dragon's violent mood.

Rafael switched to elvish. "You are certain Tyldain did not harm you?" The red of his eyes bled into concerned yellow as he examined me. I didn't mind his fussing.

"Quite. All Tyldain did was posture and hiss. What did you do to him?" I immediately regretted my question at the vicious sneer curling Rafael's lip.

"I ripped his jaw off." He said it as casually as if discussing the weather. "He will not speak with such audacity again."

Fucking hells, that was quite a deterrent. Could the blue drake heal such a wound on his own? I certainly wouldn't be volunteering to assist. Gods, what had Rafael done with the jawbone? I shuddered. No, I didn't want to know.

"Ah." I cast about for a nonviolent direction and landed on my mossy friend. "I'm grateful Boshkt arrived when he did." How many others could spit acid, or 'venom,' as he'd called it? Draconian did not differentiate. Nor, come to think of it, did it have separate words for poison and curse. "He recalls Marron to me. Perhaps due to his calm demeanor."

"He is Marron's distant clan."

Ah, that harmonized. The earth element the green clan shared provided a literal grounding. I chewed on my bottom lip, considering.

"Why Boshkt, in particular?"

So subtle I almost missed it. A change settled over Rafael's angular features. A certain tightening of the jaw. The way his eyes flickered.

I pressed. "Why Boshkt? Why not Marron himself? You're hardly one to rely on the might of others, but Marron is certainly stronger."

Rafael's eyes flicked to the trees where Tyldain had departed and back to my face.

"Dragon." I crossed my arms. "I hear the unsung melody. What are you hiding?" Oh, how he hated it when I forced a confession. I braced for a potential outburst.

He rumbled and crouched before the fire, poking at the coals with a talon. Fire crackled and swirled across his hand, caressing his skin like an old lover. The blood under his talons burned away in wisps of acrid smoke.

"Boshkt is...how I once thought of myself."

I sat beside him, waiting for the eventual honesty. I'd never caught Rafael in a lie, but he hoarded secrets more than gold. Flames wove around his fingers, matching the flames in his eyes.

"That rules out his calm demeanor as a deciding factor." I prodded. "What do you mean?"

"Hrrm." Rafael stared intently into the fire. "A complete lack of interest in sex."

"Fucking hells." I sucked a breath in through my nose, trying to steady myself. "How very condescending. Do you truly have so little regard for my loyalty? Lack of sexual desire or interest is perfectly acceptable on its own, but you insult me acting as..." I tried to close my mouth, but fury drove the words out too quickly, "acting as those humans who set a eunuch to guard their favorite concubine."

The cookfire flared with his snarl. "Last time I left you alone, you picked up a lover—"

"Don't you dare pull Celebel into this." I flushed, stomach tightening. Celebel couldn't defend himself in his unconscious state. "You know very well a soulmate is far more than a lover taken in caprice. The way I shun their touch, the other elves think me a pariah."

I altered the melody at the burst of heat radiating from him; too close to sticking my hand directly in the fire. "Gods, I thought you'd finally shown some growth. Are you so utterly insecure as to believe I would fuck any drake who presented me the opportunity? Do you think so little of my regard? After all the prejudice I've weathered with the court for you." My hands trembled, and I clenched my fists, nails digging into my palms. I refused to weep with anger. Not this time. "I may not always understand your culture's resistance to casual physical intimacy, but I am not some lust-maddened fool determined to cuckold you."

Rafael turned his head to me, signature scowl deepening to a hateful mask in the dim firelight. "Have you already forgotten Tyldain's threat? You are unclaimed, yet all of my people know the power you hold over me."

"And I'll simply sing along with the first drake to lay claim? Do not malign my intelligence along with my character. Everyone is well aware how you would react with all your endless threats." I twisted, pulling my hair over my shoulder to expose the back of my neck, where his bite mark still marred my skin. "I suppose this means nothing to the other drakes?"

"Not enough. Not until I have properly claimed you."

I let my hair fall. "And give you the excuse to spirit me away from my people in the midst of their suffering? Absolutely fucking not."

He rose to his feet, towering over me like some dark god of wrath. "You insisted, and now the knowledge angers you?"

I stretched as tall as I could. "Must everything be a gods damned battle with you? You can simply speak with me rather than manipulate and control. Boshkt should take similar insult! He did nothing to deserve your disrespect. You've killed for less!"

The Dragon snorted. "Boshkt cannot stand against me."

"I do not care for bullies, Rafael." I planted my fists on my hips and glared up at him. "You are meant to be their leader, not their constant torment."

"I am a fucking *drake*, Cúraniel. This is our way."

"If you continue to twist my words, this conversation is finished."

I glanced at the soup. It needed stirring before it could stick to the pot and burn. If he ruined my supper and my mood...

His shoulders tensed. Smoke billowed from his nose and mouth. A weak part of my mind tugged at me, insisting I back down and soothe him instead. That I allow his traumatic past to absolve his actions. Angrily, I shoved it away.

Of all the meandering conversations I'd held with Boshkt, it had never occurred to me to discuss sexual proclivities. Observant as my Dragon was, he'd surely anticipated how our personalities would mesh. I'd no issue with Boshkt at all, only in the way his leader used him. Was the mossy drake aware of the extent? No, he must be. Rafael was far too fond of explicit threats.

My Dragon let out a sigh that ground itself into a growl. "What would you have me do? The others watch and wait, ready to spring. Until you shoved your obnoxious way into my life, I had no exploitable weaknesses."

"Do you expect me to believe you are motivated by protection rather than your jealous nature?" I yanked my earlobes.

"Cúraniel." He barked my name like a command, and I closed my mouth. "Relying on draconian charity of spirit is a grave mistake. Only the fear of my retaliation keeps you safe. Many of my people would cheerfully rip you apart to get to me. Attacking a mate, especially unclaimed, is perfectly acceptable. Likewise, is stealing a mate from a weaker drake.

"You believe yourself safe among us, forgetting we bleed for our positions. I carry the greatest reputation for ruthlessness, but you know my limits. There are those who do not restrain their brutality, and many drakes will not recognize your personhood." He stared at me, leaning hard on the meaning.

I chewed on my lower lip. "Why do you tolerate the existence of sexual predators, given—"

"I do not," he snapped, teeth clicking with his agitation. "Do you think they willfully reveal themselves, knowing they will die a slow and torturous death?"

"If the danger is so great, why did you allow me to dance with them?" Were they all only biding their time, waiting to strike the moment I drifted too far from Rafael's side? The thought froze me more than the wintry air.

His lip curled as though I'd said something deliberately obtuse. "Have you forgotten Itreynith's attack? Its appearance shifted the dynamic enough that some allies turned. Previously neutral drakes are no longer trustworthy. Why do you think Tyldain tested the winds now?"

"Is the white drake as strong as the War Crow was?" Images of Rafael's disemboweled body and War Crow's headless one flashed through my mind, making my belly clench.

Noting the look on my face, his posture relaxed. "No, Byxldurr was stronger. She was second generation."

I could hardly fathom what it meant in context. "You could have simply told me all of this." The wind sliced through me and I hugged my arms.

"To what end?" Steam puffed from his mouth as he spoke. "Would you have me announce every fear? Shall I make a chart for your approval? Perhaps you would like to read them before your beloved court."

My heart twinged, and I surrendered, embracing him. "You and your never-ending sass."

He stiffened, reminding me of the early days. Gods, I missed the hill, but not his old, standoffish ways. Then his arms wrapped around me and he crushed me to him, burying his face in my hair.

"Fear is a poor driver of decisions, my Dragon. Speaking from experience." I had so many regrets.

Rafael's breath warmed the crown of my head. "I fear not for myself, only for you."

Chapter 3

ANOTHER evening campfire, another unexpected visitor emerging from the shadows, stepping with the silence only another elf could muster. Feanim.

"What the fuck do you want?" Fatigued from travel and fretful over Celebel's continued unconsciousness, my tone escaped my control.

Days of jostling wagon rides had not awakened my poor Starshine, nor the occasional Fomorian attack. Even with my newfound ability to use unhealing to unstitch their monstrous glamour and reveal the sidhe beneath, we'd had no luck keeping any of them alive through the process. The power expenditure exhausted me to the point Rafael had forbidden me from using the unhealing entirely, leading to some heated arguments with Feanim.

Much as I wished to help, that intervention gave me some slight relief. I couldn't unheal the enemy while simultaneously pouring my spirit into my stricken soulmate. The Fomorians' secrets remained their own, and the constant tension rode in my gut as an unrelenting, low-level nausea.

"Are you here to tell me to abandon both of my soulmates or something equally useless?" My shoulders tightened. "My soul is tired and thin, son of Melranim. I prefer to be left alone."

An understatement; I'd happily scale one of those granite spires to escape the scrutiny of other elves. Especially that elf.

The fall of Férioth hadn't endeared me to the masses any more than when I'd first introduced the God of Carnage into their midst. At least Rafael no longer openly antagonized what remained of the court, but ears pricked and swiveled whenever I passed. Before leaving my hill, I thought I'd empathized with Nemohee's feelings of otherness, until I was branded an outsider myself. Entirely different, having that otherness thrust upon me rather than claiming it by choice.

Feanim raised his hands in supplication and settled down in front of me, on the far side of my fire. Dressed in a dark green gambeson over black trousers and boots, he blended into the sparse woods behind him. Unusually reasonable, he made me suspicious.

"Celebel told me of Rafael's…issues," Feanim said carefully.

My ears flattened, tips heating. No need for a fire, after all.

"That was not his to tell. And Rafael has many issues. You'll need to be more specific." I flattened my ears and stared, daring him to speak it aloud.

"You know I went through similar…challenges in my youth. I understand, at least to some extent. It is a difficult recovery, and it sounds as though the Dragon had it worse from the very beginning." His green eyes shone like sea glass in the firelight.

I relaxed, empathy taking the reins. We would never be bosom companions. Not with his unrelenting jabs and disrespect. But here he presented me with a way to harmonize.

"The people who should have protected me failed. Chose not to save me. But eventually, others stepped in and removed me," Feanim paused, grimacing, "removed *us* from the situation. Many have shown me kindness since. Rafael has had no one but you. I cannot fathom surviving such abuse only to shoulder that burden alone for countless ages."

"You have my compassion for what you've endured." I skewered slices of shelf fungus and fern rhizomes I'd foraged to set over the fire, unsure of how else to respond. Feanim's unexpected willingness to open up left me wary.

"Intimacy with understanding partners helped me. Quite a lot. Especially Nimthil, being my soulmate and such. It provides a certain stability I lacked. I suppose I can grasp why, in this instance at least, Rafael is so fixated on you. You've no fear of him, almost unnaturally so. Tell no one I said this, but I'm quite impressed at how fearlessly you back him down when he grows fiery and threatening." Feanim pantomimed puffing up with an exaggerated scowl, and I forced down a laugh. "Even the other drakes avoid his path when he's in such a mood. Is that why he's never taken up with one of his own species to mate?"

"When has Rafael ever done the expected? Have you attempted to speak with him about any of this?"

The Duedellen shook his head, tossing dark curls across his shoulders. "I do not know him well enough yet. He's so damned touchy. Far too many sore points, and I've no desire to have my face bitten off trying to help. That fucking temper of his was untenable to start with, and he's been more on edge since Férioth."

Interesting. If anything, Rafael had been more solicitous of me.

"Understandable. So, why have you come here?"

He sighed. "Please go speak with him. Rafael has been downright vicious recently, and I've no idea why."

The aftermath of our argument over Boshkt must have had spillover effects. Or perhaps my Dragon was still angry over Feanim's pushing me to use the unhealing. Or the wound he continuously denied was troubling him. Not that Rafael ever needed any reason for one of his black moods. Crow.

Feanim scrubbed a hand over his dark curls, further disheveling his hair. "I'm trying to keep the peace, but it's nowhere near as easy for me as it is for Cel. I haven't any of his persuasion spirit. Our people are exhausted and scared. On the other side, your pet Dragon is acting like a cat whose tail has been trodden upon too many times and everyone is stomping without a care. Nothing I try has any effect on his mood." He paused, eyeing me. "Perhaps I need to grow some tits."

"Ah, there it is. You were doing so well, too." I tugged my earlobes.

Unrepentant, the Duedellen grinned at me. "Am I wrong?"

I tossed my hands up in surrender. "Perhaps not."

He chuckled and got to his feet, holding out a hand. "Come, bank your fire and go talk to your useless man. Or fuck him. Or whatever it is you do. We move again in the morning."

I eyed him, then accepted the hand.

RAFAEL STOOD brooding at the edge of the camp on a rocky overlook, wearing his usual man shape. A sheer drop to the ravine floor allowed visibility along the path for more than a dragon's length. Chilling winds howled through the canyon, honed with the edge of winter. A puff of delicate snowflakes swirled past. We'd have to hurry to reach Amrún before the snows came.

He turned to me with a questioning scowl, and I stopped him with a kiss before he could say anything. His hard mouth melded to mine. I'd always loved that moment; the unveiling of his capacity for softness, hidden by the stony density of his body. And oh, the wickedly delicious things that mouth could do. His nimble tongue teased mine, and I pressed against him in my sudden need. I sucked the long tongue curled around mine. Strong hands cupped my ass, easily spanning my bountiful flesh.

A dampening field swirled around us, cutting off the wind's whistling. Removing his cloak to act as a blanket, Rafael laid me on the rock. Buttons popped off as he yanked my coat open, baring my breasts. Much as it made my clit throb, I frowned at the mending. We had enough work to go around as it was.

My fingers brushed his chest, and a bolt of ice shot up my arm. I jerked my hand away, shaking it. "Will you allow me to attend to your wound? The burning cold must pain you." I gathered the fallen buttons and stuffed them in my pockets. "Feanim claims you've been horrid as of late. What has fouled your mood?"

He rumbled and bent to suck at my nipple, gripping my other breast in his hand.

I tugged on his hair. "Answer me." Rising lust made it difficult not to pant. "Is that injury affecting you? Or was it our last conversation? Something else?"

"I am fine." He paused to glare at me.

"You are not." We'd had so little opportunity for intimacy. Pausing here came with risks, but a calm Dragon was a much safer Dragon for everyone around him.

"Keep pressing and I will shove my tongue so far up your ass, my voice will issue from your mouth," he growled low in his throat.

I shivered under him, my body responding to the heat in his

voice, almost willing to test him on it. That glorious, prehensile tongue was already the length of my ear when he fully extended it in this form. Surely it would be longer in his larger, fully-scaled forms. Exactly how much control did he maintain over his shapeshifting?

He released my nipple to look me fully in the eye. Challenging me. Cool air chilled the freed nipple into a painfully stiff peak.

"Planning to use me as your very own carnyx?" I bit my lip.

The Dragon snorted, sitting back on his knees.

I crawled up and brushed my mouth over his. "Remember the first time I kissed you, how you froze like a mouse in a viper's den? I had to put your hands on me, instruct you on how to relax enough to kiss back, how to touch me. It was sweet. Enthusiastic student that you are, you needed little instruction after that." When all else failed, I employed distraction.

"Mmm, yes."

I laughed, warmed by the sweetness of his innocence in those days. "I don't know who or what you went off and studied, but gods, you are a fast learner. When you returned, you made me climax until I begged you to stop!"

Rafael's eyes blazed. "*Books.*" He spat it like an epithet. "*I studied only books when we were apart.*" The unspoken accusation hung between us—*unlike you.*

"Oh, cease your growling. Must we sing that old song?"

The glare intensified, flames piercing my soul.

I forced the sigh from my weighty lungs, resisting the urge to tug an earlobe and let his nonsense tumble free. Instead, I brought my palms together over the center of my chest. "Am I mistaken in the belief that we had forgiven each other?"

Would he ever truly forgive me for stumbling upon an unexpected second soulmate? Or forgive Celebel for merely existing? He'd put quite an effort into making poor Cel as miserable as possible. As though any of us had a choice with these unbreakable soulmate bonds. Distance only weakened the spirit. At least academically, Rafael understood I could truly love more than one person at a time. Or so I hoped.

The Dragon exhaled through his long nose and closed his eyes.

Immediate relief; my breath came easier. "Forgiveness, hrrm." He huffed, almost a laugh. "How many novel concepts have you forced upon me?"

"Shall I name them? Forgiveness, compromise, relaxation." I took his hands and moved one to my throat. "Trust." The other, I cupped around my breast, moving his thumb across my stiffened nipple. "Desire."

A faint smile softened his harsh features. "I suppose you are forgiven. For now." He removed the hand from my throat, sliding it down to squeeze my other breast.

"You horrid creature. That is not how forgiveness works."

I tugged at the laces of his shirt and he obligingly pulled it off. Running my hands over his chest, I traced the lines of heavy muscle. Tiny scales scratched faintly under the pads of my fingers. He smoothed them away.

The scar had indeed faded. Only swirls of pale grey marred the light bronze of his skin, like the first breath of frost rimming the leaves in late autumn. As my hand lingered, it pulsed with cold. Gods, that attack must have been agonizing.

He watched my inspection with interest. "Go on. Let us discover if you have the flame to warm me."

"Breathing fire on the Red Dragon. What a strange life I lead." I pushed him onto his back, and he folded his hands behind his head. For all his black clothing and spiky armor, he was far more intimidating bare-chested. He could win any argument simply by removing his shirt.

'*As you yourself do.*' He plucked my thoughts out of my mind with an appreciative stare at my full breasts.

"Wicked creature."

I climbed over him, pressing our hearts together. Reaching from within to touch the soulbond, my moon spirit met his fire. Our power mingled, swirling together in a maelstrom of night and volcanic fury. Cold struck me, an arrow in the side. His wounded side.

I tumbled into long years of isolation. Crushing loneliness, despondence. Drowning in the frigid waters of depression, an iron weight of melancholy dragging me under. With desperate fists, I pounded the ice closing over my head.

Rafael kissed me, pulling me back to the surface.

"This is a spirit wound," I gasped, catching my breath. "Why did you not tell me?"

Crow, what foolish complacency. He'd thrown himself repeatedly against his limits on our behalf. What would happen to him, to all of us, if he finally shattered? Spectacular violence, if past behavior was any indicator. *None of you may stand against me*. The devastation he left in the wake of battle overlaid the flayed and disemboweled elf he'd strung between the Consulate thrones.

He sighed. "How you fuss over me."

"I should slap you. Or perhaps myself for allowing this." I shook off the frustration, allowing his warmth and rumbling breath to center me. "May I delve deeper?"

"Hrrm, as you wish."

I twined my tongue around his once more, breathing with him, matching his heartbeat. His heat enveloped me as I lowered my hips to his. The leather of his pants creaked, straining to contain an impressive erection as his body answered mine. Physicality to match the mental work, then. Common enough for a patient to respond sexually to this type of healing. Much thornier when that patient had enough unresolved trauma to swallow up entire nations, and the might to make it literal.

I wrapped him in a spirit cocoon of comfort and warmth. Love and safety. Rocking back and forth, I positioned myself for only a featherlight brush of my clit against his cock. In this space, my pleasure came second to his. If I could finally, safely, bring him to orgasm, he could begin to untangle all the horrors imprisoning his tortured soul. His breathing sped, and I held it in time with mine, caressing his chest and arms.

'*I love you. Are you with me?*' I sent, to avoid interrupting our deepened connection.

He rumbled assent. '*I need you. I wish to try…to fuck you.*'

I increased my rocking, stroking my sensitized clit along the length of his shaft through the leather. The Dragon's talons tore lines in the ground as his cock throbbed. He thrust hard against me and I moaned into his mouth. I'd meant to talk him through the entire process, but my climax built with such speed and pressure it stole my wits. Lust swept through me like a wildfire and his answering growl rattled my bones.

Clamping his hands like a vise onto my buttocks, he held me in place, raking the tip of his cock against my clit as I shuddered in the throes of passion. I directed that heat to the frigid wound. The more I poured myself into it, into him, the more it thawed. Slowly at first, then like a glacier calving, the core of the frigid, draining power snapped open. I threw myself against Rafael, and he responded in kind.

"Shall I attempt to bring you to climax?" I panted against the side of his neck. He'd made only tiny increments of progress—the horrors of his childhood had threatened to swallow him whole in previous attempts—but it *was* progress.

"Yes," Rafael hissed, with a bruising thrust.

If healing him meant breaking myself, so be it. I leaned up, seeking his face. Clear, blazing eyes met my query. He was still present and lucid. He proved it further by capturing my mouth with his. No hint of ice remained, boiled away to vapor in the molten core of his need. The living magma of his tongue seared me all the way down.

He gripped my ass harder, slamming me down against him. Drunk on his scent, with a cry, I soaked the leather separating my cunt from his cock. Grinding as hard as I could, I tried to force the tip inside me through the thick material. Gods, I wanted to fuck him so badly. So many years of teasing. Hard as diamond, his cock pulsed under me.

His breathing changed, disrupting my careful rhythm. A tremor ran through him, then another. Crow. I tried to gather his increasingly chaotic power, to focus it, but it slipped away. The freezing wind whipped around me as the Dragon threw me off. I slid, scraping to a painful stop on the rough granite.

With a guttural cry, his talons raked his arms. Steaming blood splashed the battered grass. He curled on his side in a tight fetal position. A massive wave of power rolled off him at the next slash, knocking me flat on the gravel. The dampening field blew apart, tendrils of wayward energy shimmering in the air.

"Rafael!" I crawled to him, brushing off the stones embedded in my skin. He clawed his arms again. Searing blood splashed me. "Rafael, stop! You're safe. Jax, my Dragon, you're safe. You are with me!" I never knew if my pleas took effect, or if he simply overcame such episodes on his own, but I always tried to call him back.

His eyes rolled back as tremors wracked his body. Those deadly talons flexed again, and I threw my arms around him, kissing his mouth. Reckless, but it had worked in the past. With all the spirit I could muster, I breathed peace into him. He froze, panting. Blood ran freely from his palms, where the talons still dug deep.

In that moment, I wished for Celebel's calming power. Perhaps I could draw on it through our bond? Rafael went limp beneath me as I reached for it.

I pulled back and tapped gently at his cheek. "Dragon? My love, are you well?" He was still as death, not even breathing. I kissed him again.

Finally, as I pried at his fist, heedless of the burns left by contact with his boiling blood, he drew a ragged breath. His hands opened, dotted with welling crimson springs.

"Forgive me, dove," he rasped. "I tried."

I kissed his arched brows, his eyelids, the hook of his long nose, the bow of his lips. "There is nothing to forgive. You did well."

I laid my hands on the shredded flesh, closing the wounds so he wouldn't have to spend the energy. He gasped and shuddered again, threatening to sink back under. I gathered him to my bosom and kissed his forehead, singing a quiet song of gentle breezes playing over warm summer meadows. Eventually, his breathing evened out.

I kissed his forehead again. The scar on his side had faded away. I touched the area carefully, determining that his normal heat had returned. A hard won victory, but we'd won, nonetheless.

I watched over the fitful, sleeping Dragon. Amazing how a man so large could curl up into such a tight ball. Chasing away his night terrors with song, I covered him with his shirt and tucked my ruined coat around him. I wished I could insulate him from the cold ground. Instead, I settled for stroking his garnet hair, resisting the ever-present urge to braid it.

Draped over him like a blanket, I awoke as he shifted me gently into his lap and sat up. Pale and haggard, his eyes were dimmed, but otherwise calm. He pulled his shirt on and wrapped my coat around me. The sun barely peeked over the horizon, and the sounds of drakes moving in the camp drifted over. We'd have to join them shortly.

"How are you feeling?" I brushed my thumb over his lips. "Forgive me. I did not intend to push you so far."

"Tired. I must feed soon." Rafael dragged a hand across his eyes, normally rich voice ringing hollow. "No more apologies. You did nothing wrong, and I am more than capable of stopping you if I so choose." His talons rapped the bloodied ground for emphasis.

"May I kiss you?"

He leaned down and took the initiative. I twined my hands into his hair, deepening the kiss, attempting to replenish some of his spent spirit with my own.

"You are kind to me," he said when we parted.

"You deserve kindness. And love." I traced the curve of his biceps, my fingers tingling with the memory of the wounds he'd inflicted. "I hate that you claw yourself. Despite your swift healing, it is upsetting to witness."

"Better than harming you in the moment." Rafael gave me a steady look.

Gods. Had it always been deliberate self-harm to protect me? I rubbed his arm, unsure if I should feel guilty, sad, or grateful. Perhaps all three.

"Every time you approach orgasm, it initiates that reaction." There had to be a better method. I wracked my mind for ideas. "What if we attempted a surrender of control in a smaller way?"

He tensed. "Such as?" I probably shouldn't have appreciated the effect that tension had on his body as much as I did.

I exhaled and took a risk. "You've claimed you would do anything for me."

He gestured at me in his lap, at the distant camp. "Have I not proven it?"

"What do you mean by 'anything'?" I kept my emotions in check so I would not need to close off our bond again.

"Anything within my capacity to provide." Wariness crept along with his words.

"Would you be willing to make peace with Celebel?" I bit my lip, bracing for rage.

Rafael's eyes sparked with his scowl, and he looked up at the grey sky. He often looked up when his rage surfaced, as if intentionally aiming it elsewhere. Like slashing his own arms.

"You *would* choose to test me now, brought low as I am." He stretched, splaying his talons. "I congratulate you on your tactical advantage and your wickedness."

"You did say '*anything*'."

"When I say I have finally known defeat, know I am speaking of you." Rafael's mouth twisted with wry humor. "Hail the mighty Cúraniel, slayer of dragons!" I opened my mouth to protest, and he stopped me with a finger on my lips. "I am too fucking tired to argue, and you know it. Very well, heartless creature. I agree to your terms. *If* your precious *nekarazzi* wakes again."

Twining my hands behind his head, I moved to kiss him in gratitude. He shoved me off his lap.

Chapter 4

CREEKS laced our path, slowing our wagons with mud and crossings; the glacier capping the intersection of the Aurelmoneth and Inelmoneth ranges announcing its presence. We did our best to keep the horses' feet clean and dry, but it was a never-ending task. Bundled in the back of the same wagon that held our experimental armor, Celebel slumbered through it all.

The frigid slush turned my toes to ice in my battered boots. Rafael, true to his finicky nature, kept to the spires rising on either side of our rocky way. Marron trudged through the mud alongside us with no complaint. Giant red and black Xyxs groused so loudly and frequently about the silt marring his "handsome scales," he nearly started a fight.

Nimthil called for an abrupt halt. She hopped from her mount, crouching beside a stream with a furrowed brow. The Lachanaur queen raised a hand for attention, and Feanim went to her side. I pricked my ears to their conversation.

"Yes, but this is only a single fouled stream," he said. "Not a major tributary. Could be as simple as a dead animal fallen into the water up the way."

With her back to me, I could not make out Nimthil's signs, but from the set of her ears, she was clearly displeased.

Feanim rose. "No, I agree, but we are too exposed here. We must press on."

I glanced about. He was right. What remained of the path funneled water beneath our feet. Small cataracts tumbled down the cliff faces rising on both sides, adding to the poor footing. The few remaining trees at this altitude were gnarled and stunted, as if shielding their faces from the wind's unrelenting bite. With old lava fields overtaking the granite, and the weathering from spring thaws, we essentially traversed a broad slot canyon.

Very exposed, but to what?

The grade steepened as we progressed. It meant stopping more frequently to allow the horses pulling the wagons to rest. Each proud destrier took their turn as beasts of burden, and we took care not to overwork any single animal. Though I refused to pass off tending Iruwher to another, I conserved the bulk of my energy for Celebel.

At every pause, I tended the stubborn wound on his back. With so little spirit to wield and no herbs at my disposal, the most I could do was to prevent it from bleeding too freely. Each treatment saw it nearly close, and each recheck uncovered a regression as though I'd never touched it.

The ground rumbled, startling horse and elf alike. All the way down our column, we froze, waiting in dreadful silence for the inevitable earthquake. With old volcanoes creating this range, the upheaval came as no surprise. If Marron had such elemental power, surely he could contain or redirect the angry earth? Fortunately, it never came.

I unhitched Helicos, sending him off to graze on the meager vegetation. Something shot past my ear, and I clapped my hand to it instinctively. Must have been an insect. Another something whipped past, embedding in the wagon's rail. I wrenched it free. It was a carved bone dart, about the length of my palm. And it stank.

As I dropped it, wiping my hands to clear away a tingling of foul spirit, a rain of such darts fell. I scrambled underneath the wagon, and a dart pierced my foot just as I tucked it in. Myriad projectiles landed in waves, punctuated by eerie, cackling groans. A putrescence of rot assaulted my nose, and I gagged. Drakes roared, and a feathered body hit the mud with a resounding *splat!*

About the size of a human child, it lay flat on its back. Perfectly round, red-ringed black eyes stared into nothing over a sizable, hooked beak. Fascinatingly ugly. Except for a crest of dingy feathers sprouting from the crown, its naked, earless head was greyish-pink down to the wattled neck. It most resembled a condor with arms. Sharp black talons sprouted from the tips of its fingers and toes, as well as from an elongated wing-thumb. Despite its compact size, the deep, muscular keel and well-developed limbs hinted at impressive strength. It radiated an eye-watering, rotten odor.

A harpy! This one had a ruff of downy white feathers like a collar, while the rest of its body was covered with flat dark feathers. It wore little adornment other than some beads strung about its fleshy neck and a couple of simple leather anklets. A glance at the sky told me most harpies had no ruffs. Some had white streaks on the underside of their broad wings, where the others were solid. Did it indicate sex or status? I knew so little of harpies.

Why did they attack us? Had we unknowingly wandered into their territory? Gods, they'd likely soil our meager supplies as well. My foot throbbed with heat. I focused my spirit to sooth the wound. The cacophony of bizarre grunts and shrieks ricocheted painfully around my skull, flattening my ears to my head.

Oh gods, Celebel! He was still in the wagon, fully exposed! I scuttled beneath the wagon to the other side, somewhat sheltered by a tree, and climbed out. By some miracle, the angle of the projectiles meant they'd harmlessly struck mostly the wagon's side and a few bundles. Celebel was unscathed. I opened as many bedrolls as I could find, trying to cover us.

Another body landed hard beside the wagon. I jumped, but it was too small an impact to be elf or drake. I pinpointed the distinctive cadence of Rafael's wings and peeked out. He wheeled high overhead, a red dot mobbed by dark bodies. Bright plumes of fire slashed through the massive flock. Sooty feathers in shades of cream, brown, and grey fell like snow and deepened the carrion stench.

Borne into the mud by a mass of harpies, a young green and black drake crashed down. To think, the unassuming harpy could fell a drake in large enough numbers! Their weird, squealing groans echoed all around me. Between the noise and the smell, a riotous headache formed at my temples. The harpies bludgeoned the hapless drake as it thrashed to break free. Green scales flew free, followed by a blood spray.

I tugged the bedroll over my head, gathering my voluminous hair tightly to my side and hardly daring to breathe. Elves cried out to the south, punctuated by equine squeals of rage. Impacts continued all around—the smaller thuds of harpy bodies, the ground-shaking slam of drakes, and the occasional light flop of an elf. The stench stung my eyes, coated my mouth, and I bit my lip to keep from audibly gagging. Beneath me, Celebel whimpered. I covered his mouth with my hand, sending what little soothing spirit I could into the contact. Staccato footsteps approached. Did harpies hop?

Familiar leathery wingbeats announced Rafael. Harpies groaned and shrieked all around us, scattering. I dared to peek as he landed at the edge of the wagon, the talons of his feet biting into the wood. Spreading his wings over the wagon in a protective canopy, they blotted out the grey skies. Darts hit with a pattering like hail, bouncing harmlessly away.

"Are you hit?" Rafael asked. "The wounds will fester."

"My foot, but I'll manage it. Celebel is unscathed. What brought on this attack?"

Deep lines creased his face, and his mouth twisted in disgust. "There is a rookery a league to the west. Too far to draw their territorial attacks. Something stirs them."

More projectiles bounced off his sheltering wings. The light filtering through painted us all in a bloody wash. It suited Rafael's vicious countenance, but on Celebel it filled me with a nebulous sadness. Despite their delicate appearance, the stretched flight membranes rebuffed every dart.

The Dragon's nose wrinkled. How much worse must it be for him with his superior sense of smell? He propped his elbows on his knees, rolling his shoulders to alleviate the awkward wing posture. I had a foolish urge to climb around behind him and examine the muscles in his back. Last time I'd seen his wings up close, certain other activities had distracted me from making a thorough study.

Feanim's voice rang out, rallying the elves and commanding them into defensive formations. Projectiles clanged on shields. The fallen drake screeched again.

"Will you not aid your comrade?" I waved toward the sound.

Rafael snorted. "Any drake who cannot fight off a gaggle of up-jumped buzzards deserves to have the marrow sucked from their bones."

"Crow, I thought they were strictly scavengers!" No wonder they had so many bones at their disposal. Did they nest in great ossuaries?

"They are not above opportunistic predation. Nor am I." His teeth flashed in a malicious grin.

"You give up your back for both our sakes, rather than taking me into your arms and leaving Celebel exposed. I never thought to greet that dawn." I held his gaze, the unspoken questions lingering between us.

Much to my surprise, Rafael looked away first. "I cannot save you if you lose him. Much as I would have it otherwise." His sigh rumbled into a growling draconic complaint about the absurdity of shepherding elves.

I had no response for that. Another rain of bone shards skittered off of Rafael's wings. An impact from the left rocked the wagon. The same drake roared next to us.

"*Eszrayln! Kereks jahl e freyth,*" Rafael snarled.

The unseen drake made an apologetic noise and moved away.

I sounded out the words, translating slowly. "'Eszrayln'–the drake's name, yes?–'you line your hoard with shit'." I laughed. "That phrase is new. I take it to mean 'you're acting foolish'?"

"Foolish and sloppy," Rafael corrected.

"Such a beautiful language, truly."

A bugling call sounded far overhead.

He stood, relaxing his wings. "The flock is retreating. I will deal with the stragglers."

With a leap that nearly launched us all from the wagon, Rafael hurled himself into the sky. Scales rippled along his body as he ascended, his form lengthening into a more draconic shape.

Enrapt, I watched as he circled a cluster of dark-feathered bodies, searing them with bright blossoms of fire. A charred body struck the edge of the wagon where the Dragon had crouched only moments before. Only a vague outline of the body remained, completely devoid of feathers. I kicked it over onto the ground.

Lámirië danced by, loosing rapid arrows from a shortbow, dark braid swirling around her wiry body like a ribbon. Hooded brown eyes flashed in her deep amber face as she found her marks. Each arrow hit with a meaty *thunk*, and another harpy fell to the ground. The last one had a pinkish tinge to its white ruff and more elaborate beads adorned its wattled neck.

"Gods blight us all, these stinking birds are never-ending." Nemohee spun to skewer another attack, and nearly stumbled as a tall, blond, lightly tan Astolar man with muscular arms and a strong chin swept past. "Cael...?" Þey shook þeir head, and a harpy took advantage of the distraction to slash þem across the face.

I cried out, but Nemohee recovered quickly, cutting down the noxious attacker.

Around us, other non-combatants took shelter beneath wagons and rocks. The warriors among us protected horse and elf alike, shielding as best they could from the rain of bone. Drakes swooped and spat fire. Rafael soared directly overhead, ensuring no harpies entered striking distance from above.

Most surprisingly, Nimthil twirled out in the open. Others gave her a wide berth. Fire swirled from her footsteps. Rising in great ribbons, it took the form of songbirds she unleashed at the sky. When the harpies dared too close, her silhouette elongated into a lean, burning sighthound, leaping and snapping. Nemohee told tales of the 'fire elf' lineages with this unique transmutational power, but I'd never witnessed it in action. I'd always taken Nimthil for a noncombatant, but perhaps she merely hid her abilities behind that delicate façade for the sake of politics. There, finally, was the true Lachanaur queen.

Evidently unable to hold the fiery canine form for long, it wavered around her. Feanim emerged from the press to back her as she returned to her elf form. He issued more commands, reforming ranks with Nimthil safely ensconced in the center.

The pain in my foot grew insistent. Focusing my spirit fully, rooting out every trace of the contamination took a bit more effort than I expected. Sweat dampened my skin by the time I cleared it from my blood. I flexed and pointed my foot experimentally. Still tender, but I should be able to walk without issue.

Finally, the cloud of harpies receded, though their odor remained. Those elves fortunate enough to have been wearing armor at the start of the fray suffered little injury. Horses, however, took most of the damage. A few had been carried off. Helicos remained unscathed, but Iruwher had an ugly gash along her ribs that already festered, just as Rafael had said.

With the notable exception of one Eszrayln, the drakes appeared mostly impervious to the harpies' weapons. I approached Eszrayln to heal him, but he shied away from me, limping badly. With scales the shining black of a fathomless lake and a belly of bright green that trailed across his limb joints, he put me in mind of the nymphs of a certain locust. Some humans referred to it as a "lubber", and the name suited his gangling stride.

At Marron's instruction, drakes piled the dead harpies into a pyre and set them ablaze. The resulting rank smoke brought tears to my eyes. Better than allowing them to continue to foul the water in the region. Two of the scaly warriors snapped at each other over a fallen mount, and I turned away.

Feanim argued with Rafael some distance away. Something about elf bodies. Had we lost elves or merely sustained injuries? Gods, not more strife over drakes consuming the dead. What a row that had been, though we could hardly convey the bodies to Amrún for proper seeded burial before decay set in. Once again, I congratulated myself on the foresight of relinquishing my title so I wouldn't be expected to make such decisions.

Liriadis proved more valuable than I, as she had far more experience with purification. Eäriel joined me, both of us observing in awe as the Siltaur healer worked. A tendril of sun-streaked chestnut hair escaped its knot, draping across Liriadis's copper cheek. She tucked the errant strand behind her moss-framed ear.

"Oh, Healing Serpent, mighty Mëalidh, lend us your rejuvenation," Liriadis murmured, passing her hands over Iruwher's side. "Let this young one shed her skin and rid herself of the poison running in her veins."

A susurrus rose around us. Iruwher stomped and blew, but

calmed at a soothing noise from the healer. The quiet *shh* of soft snake scales brushing over each other filled my ears, replacing the harsh rattle of dragonskin. Under Liriadis's palms, the putrefaction melted away, leaving new pink flesh underneath.

She moved from wound to wound, repeating her petition to the serpent. I'd once considered asking Mëalidh to be my patron deity, as I'd always felt a certain kinship with the genderless reptilian god. But, in the comfort of my youth, I'd tarried too long. How different might my life have been if the Night Mother hadn't claimed me the day I left Leyúduin? Would Mëalidh also have demanded I save Rafael? Surely, they also shared kinship of a sort.

The Astolar man approached to have a series of long lacerations on his forearm tended. Not Cael, but close enough to be a gods damned twin. My throat closed like I'd swallowed a rock. Only hazel eyes bordering on green rather than Cael's clear blue differentiated him. Even the shape and length of their ears were the same. Surely, he shared the lineage.

Nemohee spoke up before I did. "You've the look of Cael about ye."

"Caladris is my name," he said in a tenor accustomed to whispers. "Cael was my nephew." The rock in my throat dissipated. Cael had a booming voice to rival his soulmate's.

"*Is*," Nemohee spat. "Still is. Cael lives. I feel it in our soulbond." Þey thumped þeir chest, mouth drawn tight with emotion.

Ears lowering, Caladris nodded.

The cuts along Nemohee's cheek weren't deep, but they had a rawness at the edges I misliked. It recalled the blood poisoning that sometimes afflicted the humans near my hill. The wound in my foot ached in response.

Nemohee's voice pierced my thoughts. "Always surprised at the lack of sluagh in these mountains." Þey swept a hand toward the pyre. "We kept a ready ear cocked for them in Rimbaras. Especially after a battle the likes of this."

Liriadis frowned, clamping the Lauchanaur's jaw in a firm hand to keep þem from moving þeir head while she tried to clean þeir wounds.

"The Aurelmoneth range and northward have too much iron for their liking," I said, "though I hear they plague the Vormoneth around Orfain." Those bloodthirsty fae swarmed the valley around my Great Tree as well in a ravenous blight. One of the main reasons the Tree had drawn up that chiming halite ring for added protection, though iron was more effective at deterring the sluagh.

"Small blessings from the gods, then." Þey batted at Liriadis's hands. "Healers! Always making such a fuss. 'Tis just scratches!"

"Fouled scratches." I poked Nemohee in the side. "And you will regret it if you don't allow her to purify it, you great ninny."

With a dramatic sigh and a tousle of þeir short, fiery hair, Nemohee relented. Which reminded me. I took up a pair of shears and swatted Nem's hands away while I neatened þeir ragged locks. If my friend experienced the same discomfort as I did during a haircut, with the limited sensory input from the strands, þey bore it in stoic silence. I trimmed the sides shorter and evening out the rest. When I finished, I showed off my work in the reflection of a shield. Nemohee's shoulders sagged.

Þeir normally stentorian bellow dropped to an empty whisper. "I've not had a peek at m'self since Cael was taken. Been avoiding it, but I thank ye. Mirrors only haunt these days, crowded like, with all those missing souls."

"I hear you've met Caladris," Eäriel said quietly. All ears turned to her, and she flushed with the sudden attention. "He is my soulmate. I've never met Cael, but Caladris always speaks highly of him. I hope you find him soon."

"Aye, I hope the same." Nemohee's ears flattened, lips pulling back to reveal lengthening fangs. Much like Rafael's threat smile. "Woe betide them as stands in my way."

CHILLING FOG rolled through the ravine at night, snow nipping at the tips of its ears. I tucked what blankets I could find around Celebel's still form, rolling him on his side for my wound-tending. How long could any elf survive on constant stress, travel, and no sleep? But I could wait no longer to delve deep. The harpies' attack sang us an ugly melody about the risks of vulnerability out in the open. This brief pause in the aftermath, while the others recovered and took stock of our remaining supplies, would have to suffice.

I rubbed my palms together, trying to draw upon Rafael's heat. A hand landed on my shoulder, breaking my concentration and making me jump. Eäriel's kind face appeared in my periphery.

"Allow me to assist. You are done in." She positioned herself across from me, tying back her black-tipped, burgundy hair. It emphasized her long nose and angular, oaken face. "I am rested enough, what with Liriadis taking the dragon's share of the work today." Her wide, brown eyes shone with earnestness, and I took her hands.

Distant cousins we might be, but that sweet, rare sense of honest kinship almost brought on tears. For that alone, I would always count Eäriel as family.

She sang a clear, steady note. I matched her pitch and our spirit rose with our voices, weaving together in harmony. Pitiable, the two of us in our current states, compared to my usual strength alone. My cousin was surely as exhausted as I, despite her declarations, but the support bolstered my flagging resolve. With our combined power, we pulled at the wound, coaxing it to close, to become whole once more. Prodding gently at Celebel's consciousness, we encouraged him to return. Like grasping at smoke, he remained distant, sealed deep inside himself.

When his soulbond shivered, I released the spirit. The surface appearance of the wound improved, but beneath it remained largely unchanged. I hissed with frustration, sagging backward against the wagon's side.

"Is this the true, fell power of demon ore?" Eäriel frowned down at Celebel.

I mirrored her expression. "This is more than moranga. Rafael helped me pull some form of cursed spirit from him." As I said it, the note struck true. A curse on the knife! *The spearhead!* "Crow, I've been going about this sideways. I know what must be done. Thank you, cousin. I will carry on alone."

With an upright finger, Eäriel drew her hand from the center of her brow to her heart; the Lachanaur sign for understanding with honor. I cupped my hands over my heart, scooping and pushing them toward her; the Talithiri sign for joyful gratitude. She nodded and left me.

I laid myself down beside Celebel, wrapping a leg over his for stability. Slowing my breath, I matched his, kissing him gently. Our heartbeats synchronized and I delved into his mindscape.

My feet landed in cool cerulean waters, splashing my ankles. The horizon stretched flat in all directions. Stars swirled in reflection, but the sky above hung empty; a moonless, perpetual night. My ears twitched wildly, seeking sound in the somber silence. Not even the gently lapping waves made a noise.

"Celebel!" My voice snuffed out like a covered candle flame.

Disoriented, I took a few stumbling steps. Nothing illustrated how much I relied on my hearing like rendering it useless. I struggled to regain my balance, taking small, careful steps. At least the ground was solid enough. My bare feet. My bare skin. Ah, he perceived me in my preferred state of undress.

Once stabilized, I reached for the soulbond. It shimmered to life, stretching off into the distance. Grasping it like a guideline, the energy pulsed in my hand. I tugged myself along, drawing the bond back into me as I moved.

It could have been days or mere breaths as I trudged through the endless ocean of Celebel's mind. A distant blob slowly resolved into his figure, seated in the water with his back to me. Ribs arced outward where flesh and muscle should be. His ears drooped. My poor Starshine. It pained me to see his light so dimmed.

I kneeled beside him. With his arms wrapped around knees drawn to his chest, his hair fell into his face. When I moved to brush it back, he flinched. I shifted to tap his knee instead, signing comfort and safety. Specters rose around him, glowing outlines of every traitor. Recarmial, Feledhor, Silfanië, Eledom. Araglin's face loomed largest. Others backed them in a countless host. He would know every name. Celebel's mouth opened.

No sound emerged, but a shockwave knocked me backward. It forced all the water into a single great crest rising high over our heads. Instead of diving into it, I launched myself at Celebel. He covered his face as we collided. I hugged him fiercely.

The wave fell. Rather than crushing impact, it swept us into a wild vortex. I squeezed my eyes shut and held my breath, clinging to my soulmate. Expectations, disapproval, blame, desperation, fear, *pressure*.

Pressure from the court, the prestige of his lineage, the war, Rafael. From me. Identity fragmenting, lost in the deluge. How could he be good and just, meet everyone else's needs, stay true to himself, and yet achieve victory? Impossible. The blade in his back descended again and again, a different face holding it each time.

'No. We will not drown here. You are stronger than this!' I refused to allow his panic and overwhelm to feed this deadly undertow.

I thrashed in the waters of his mind, dragging us to an imagined surface. Celebel struggled weakly in my grip. Winding our soulbond around both of our waists in a literal lifeline, I kicked through the waves. The strokes of my legs disrupted the disparaging imagery.

He choked, losing breath. I sealed my mouth over his, sharing my air.

'We will swim together. We will harmonize. Trust me.'

It took a few tries to synchronize our kicks, but when we did, the current abruptly released us. Our heads broke the surface. As our lips parted, each of us sucked in air. His eyes cleared, and we landed in our bodies.

Celebel coughed, and I helped him sit up to clear his lungs. My own lungs filled with the first truly deep breath since Férioth. So much subliminal fear had crystalized my veins, the sudden thaw nearly made me swoon. The fresh swell of spirit buoyed me.

My fingers twitched with the desire to brush the tangles from Celebel's lovely hair. Like meteors streaking across the night sky. Even road-worn, exhausted, and drawn with worry, he still had the kind of beauty that ached the heart. He looked about in confusion.

"Oh, Starshine. I've feared greatly for you." I cupped his cheek.

"Are you well?"

His brow creased as he took in the surroundings, absently rubbing his back. "These trees are different. We've left Férioth behind already? How far is Amrún?" He winced. "There remains a dull ache in my back, but the skin is smooth enough. What happened?"

"Amrún is not so far now, but Feanim says the last stretch is the most difficult to traverse with horses." I gripped his hands as if he'd disappear without the contact. "The knife Feledhor struck you with inflicted some manner of curse preventing your recovery. I tried to pull the foul spirit from you, and it nearly drowned us both. Rafael intervened."

Celebel's eyes cleared at the mention of his least favored person, focusing sharply on my face. "Intervened how?" Gods, that glare bruised my aching heart. I'd hoped our bond had mended along with his flesh.

"He drew the contamination into himself to nullify it, and it knocked him out for a moment. Without his aid, it would have overwhelmed us." I held his sky-blue gaze, willing him to accept Rafael's uncharacteristic good will. Celebel's expression remained closed, shuttered like a house in a blizzard. If I kissed him, would he rebuff me? I sighed. "You slumbered through a harpy attack!"

"Harpies?" His dark brows clashed together, ears twitching.

I filled him in on the details he'd missed, passing him small bits of mushroom jerky and a waterskin. Before the harpies had spoiled everything for leagues, foraging was already sparse. The trees provided little succor, and the drakes scared away potential game. The shared song couldn't sustain us forever.

The voidlet's involvement provoked a slew of questions to which I had sparing answers. He absorbed the information with a slight crease in his brow, chewing thoughtfully on the jerky. Motes of light drifted toward him, dancing in the darkness; tiny fae drawn to his renewed starlight. Sylphs, mostly harmless, but I tensed at their presence. They did not touch him, instead swirling lazily around us. He made a sign of gentle warding, and they retreated a short distance.

I took a chance. "You were angry with me before you collapsed, do you recall?"

He reached over to clasp my hands, the motion rocking the wagon. "In truth, my memories of that time are vague. Formless grief and anger, yes, but what I most recall is overwhelm with the situation. I apologize if I lashed out."

Something deep inside me unclenched. "During your repose, I convinced Rafael to make peace with you." So I hoped.

Celebel sat up, his eyes flashing brighter blue in a stray beam cast from a sylph. "How?"

I shrugged. "Rafael had once claimed he would 'do anything' for me, so I challenged that claim." Celebel blew out an appreciative breath, and I rubbed his arm. "Timing is essential with my Dragon. Caught him when he was too done-in to argue. A rare occurrence."

His brow creased, ears twitching. "That feels manipulative."

"It is, but Rafael is not an elf." I laughed at the look on Celebel's face. "He congratulated me on the move."

"I assumed his wrath would never run dry."

"It does when he spends it all on himself." I hugged myself. Witnessing Rafael's self-harm never grew easier to bear, even with the added context. At least it hadn't been his face this time.

Celebel shuddered. "At times, I do not truly understand what I ask of you."

I patted his cheek. "You hold no fault in this, and I was never in any danger. We made no specific arrangements. I saved that discussion until I could speak with you. If you wish to proceed, that is." No more dealing with the unintended consequences of a clandestine arrangement for me.

"Thank you. That one can turn anything to his advantage." The black slashes of his brows nearly collided in a scowl. I held my breath. He gave me a significant look, peering from under the dark curtain of his lashes, and wiggled around to present his back. "Will you braid my hair?"

I finger-combed the snarls and errant leaves from his hair. "It gladdens me to know you still hear my song." The way his ears twitched conveyed a smile. Humming, I plaited the Elhalanros lineage pattern, drawing in the silver locks to highlight the loops. My fingertips grazed his sensitive ears, the smooth expanse of his lithely muscled shoulders, the graceful length of his neck. Little by little, Celebel relaxed into my hands until I held him in an embrace.

Finally, he sighed and pulled my arms tighter about him. "Of course I want peace. I hope for peace between you and me as well."

Chapter 6

"**W**E should be able to replace some of the food the harpies fouled at this outpost," Celebel said. He'd spent most of his waking hours conferring with Feanim.

They'd redirected us east to avoid further clashes with said harpies, meandering through a narrow pass. It stretched our company into a thin line, but Celebel assured me the humans who occupied the small fort ahead were reliable.

The smoke reached us first, carrying a nauseating scent of burned flesh. Over the crest of a tall hill, a ruined outpost came into view. It must have once served as a checkpoint for any soul passing through these mountains, but no longer. Blasted with fire, whatever attack had occurred here was recent. Some embers yet smoldered. Exposed beams rose like broken and charred ribs from what was left of the main building's foundation. The roof lay in a shattered mess off to the side.

Gods, what monsters did the Fomorians employ?

Distress rippled through the gathered elves. A handful volunteered for a rescue team. Nemohee led the group, guiding Machi expertly down the grade.

"It is...it was a human outpost. Spirit-wielding Atani, some of Duke Sotherly's people," Celebel explained. "They were allies, and had been limiting enemy movement through here, sending us the occasional report."

Lámirië lingered past his shoulder like a shadow. Ever since Celebel had recovered enough to walk on his own, she'd hovered as though all of his ills were her own personal failing. As his only surviving bodyguard, I couldn't fault her diligence.

"Why did they not send for help? We were just over the pass!" Feanim paced, clearly disturbed. "Within earshot! How did this happen? And where the fuck are the drakes?"

Indeed, there was a distinct lack of drake presence. Rafael remained silent through our connection, and no other drakes made themselves known.

Nemohee's distinctive crop of hair pierced the dusk like a spark in the wind as þey strode up the hill toward us. "No survivors." The stentorian voice bounced down through the valley below. *No survivors, no survivors, n-survivors, survivors.* "No bodies at all, unless some were buried too deep to reach. Took especial care in the search, we did, sifting through the wreckage with all the structural damage. Everything was unstable."

Þey made a brief report, making significant eye contact with me. A chill ran down my spine.

"The attack must have been too swift," Celebel said. "Humans could not escape something like this, not even the Atani. They were struck from above…" He trailed off, eyes narrowing at the remains of the roof. I followed the way he tracked the directionality of the destruction. From the sky.

Fuck.

Feanim immediately dismissed everyone else. He and Celebel turned expectant eyes on me.

"We know not culprit," I signed, though the absurdity made my hands shake. Surely not. Surely it was an enemy drake.

"No?" Celebel's slashing gesture was full of sarcasm.

"You speak to Rafael. No one else," Feanim signed.

In other circumstances, the command would have rankled, but now I obeyed without question. My ears swiveled until I caught the deep rumble of draconian voices to the north.

Following the sound a short distance up the road—just on the far side of the ruined fort—I found the Dragon in conversation with Marron, Boshkt, and a brown drake whose name I didn't know. They stood under an overhang, perfectly comfortable in the deepening shadows.

Given the fencing leading up to it and a nearby water trough, this area had once been a shelter for whatever small flocks the humans kept. Used to keep. Where were those flocks now?

Rather than finer facial expressions, the drakes used head

sweeps, talon clicking, and the occasional stomp or scale rattle for emphasis. Given how scaly the others were, Rafael's expressions came across muted in comparison.

The conversation paused at my approach. Four sets of luminous, reptilian eyes landed on me. A dead tree twisted through a fissure in the rocks behind Rafael, a skeletal hand stretching skyward.

Squaring my shoulders, I strode into their midst and tugged at the Dragon's arm. "I need to speak with you." I said it in elvish, though enough of those drakes spoke the language for it to make no difference. "Now."

Rafael turned to face me fully, annoyed at the interruption.

I stood my ground. "*Now!* This is of great import."

Marron's scaly brows rose at my brazenness. My Dragon rumbled quick instructions at the others, faster than my comprehension allowed. Boshkt and the brown drake dipped their heads and backed away. The green drake watched us for a moment longer, calculating, then he too departed.

I led Rafael to a vantage of the ruined outpost. Smoke still rose lazily into the air along with that awful charred-flesh smell. My stomach turned, and I fought down bile.

"Is this your doing?"

He stared, impassive. "They were human. What do you care?"

"They were *allies!* You hid your deeds, knowing how we could react." I should have been prepared for this. Once again, I'd been a fool.

"What use are humans as allies? They are blind and deaf to the world around them." Dismissive, as always.

I'd always loved the little human village near my hill, and I'd argued bitterly with Rafael against their extermination for simply existing. "If our allies cannot trust us with their lives, is it any wonder the court turned?"

He snorted, rumbling a word in draconian that sounded suspiciously like "soft."

"You wretched blighter. As soon as we chose this path, you as well as anyone knew we naturally would have encountered these people! What if the rest of ours turn against us for this? We meant to resupply there! When they discover you have *devoured* those poor souls—" I shuddered, turning away from the image of those jagged teeth shearing into flesh.

"I have merely cleared the road. Now you need waste no time seeking *human* approval."

"So you admit your guilt."

Rafael coughed. "Guilt? No. You will draw no contrition from me."

Impotent rage choked me. Nothing I did would bring those people back to life, and well did he know it. "Gods fucking *damn* you, Rafael! Come, we must speak with the Consulate."

"Interesting how often you issue these orders and expect me to obey." We stared each other down. He smiled, throwing me off guard. "Ah, my little dragonslayer. How lovely you are in your righteous anger." He reached to touch my cheek, and I flinched away.

My fury drained as if he'd slashed open the reservoir. I tried to cling to it, but it slipped through my grasp, leaving only fatigue in its wake. "You are the worst person I know."

Heading back to Feanim and Celebel, the Dragon followed me at a leisurely pace. The Consulate mirrored each other in their individually stiff, square-shouldered, cross-armed postures.

Noting the casual expression on Rafael's face, Feanim exhaled in a harsh huff. "So, it was you. What the fuck, Raf. Why?"

Rafael rounded on him. "If these ants were strategically precious, why was I not informed?" Sharp teeth flashed in warning.

I sidled between them, shielding the Consuls.

"What wretched madness possessed you to destroy an entire outpost?" Celebel's ears flattened.

"Hunger." Rafael's eyes blistered red, the growl overtaking his voice. "You fucking flower-eating—"

"Stop!" I put a restraining palm on the Dragon's chest. I might as well have been a mote of dust for all the attention he paid me.

"You *ate* them?" Celebel's voice tightened, high and thin with shock.

Beside him, Feanim's face paled; for once, he was speechless.

Even knowing the answer, my gorge rose at the casual admission.

"I am a fucking *dragon*," Rafael snarled, glaring over my head. "Did you think I subsisted on fruit? *Yes*, I ate them. Crushed their bones in my jaws." He clacked his teeth together. "Did you think me tamed by fighting at your side? That you had clipped my talons? Turned me into a fucking *vegetarian*?" His lips peeled back, and my palm grew uncomfortably warm.

"Never that," Celebel muttered, tugging his earlobe. "Is this why you never sleep? Need the extra time to invent new evils?"

The heat flared, and I jerked my palm away before it blistered. I'd expected Rafael to bellow, but his voice dropped deadly low, almost below my hearing.

"Tell me your definition of 'evil', little elf. Shall I tell you mine?" Smoke curled from his lips. "Better yet, shall I show you?" He took a menacing step forward.

I grabbed ahold of my connection to each man, trying to pull back, to force them to de-escalate. Gods, so much for the mention of a truce.

"Yes, let her witness how you break your word." Celebel's flat expression chilled me against the blazing fire of the Dragon. "Show us all who you really are." The meaning rang out as 'sever the bond'.

With a mighty heave, I yanked the soulbonds to rein them in. Celebel winced, clutching his heart. I turned in time to see Rafael blink in surprise, but the smoke dissipated. The backlash made my pulse roar in my ears, vision swimming.

"Cel, leave off," Feanim said. He stabbed a finger at Rafael. "You as well, you aggressive blighter. Our forces are already fractured almost beyond repair. It was a mistake not to inform you of the significance of this outpost. We did not expect to pass by here, and I never thought… well, never mind that now. We'll need to rebuild and re-outfit this fort." He thought for a moment, then shot Rafael an irritated glare. "Why not eat livestock or wild game like the other drakes?"

The Dragon's smile was horrible. "*Preference*," he hissed. "As you will recall, I agreed not to devour elves. You should be *grateful*."

Celebel snorted. "Yes, surely all the new orphans are singing your praises."

"Such a shame no children were present." His teeth clacked again. "The young are the most succulent."

"Rafael, that is enough! Beyond enough. You knew very well how we would react." Privately, I sent, *'This sickens me. In the past, distance allowed me to put it out of my mind. I cannot bear the thought of feasting on people.'*

He made no acknowledgement.

I twisted my braid, the pull at my scalp helping to ground me, and continued aloud. "We need time to adjust to your ways, and obviously, the three of you must share *all* of your plans. With less venom. There must be a solution, a way to harmonize." The anxious knot in my belly hardened into a steel ball.

"I should think the solution is 'do not fucking *eat people*'," Celebel snapped. "Enough allies have turned against us already because of you."

I raised my brows meaningfully at Rafael for the echo of my earlier sentiment.

"Would you prefer I fight for your enemies instead?" the Dragon growled, unrepentant.

My world went silent and dark as Dûemer drew her mantle over me.

A visage floated before me. Long, bone-white hair, stripped of its color, flowed past a sallow face just as pale. Nearly transparent brows framed eyes like pits that drank light and returned nothing. With a somewhat wide nose, and a generous mouth, I beheld a sun-bleached stamp of Feanim, with pin-straight hair rather than tousled curls.

That mouth stretched into a gaping maw and swallowed me whole. I dropped into a nightmare chalice filled to the brim with twisted, screaming monstrosities. A thousand claws sank into me, pulling me under the fetid tangle of grotesque bodies. The chalice tumbled over and the creatures spilled out, bursting forth through the womb of the world tree. They flooded the lands, leaving them scummed with their putrid foulness. Flora shriveled and died in their wake.

I opened my mouth to scream and inhaled the sickness. It poured into me, choking my lungs, drowning me. I branched, reaching in desperation for the moon. More of the monstrosities crawled down my throat, chewing through my belly and settling into my womb. My trunk twisted, roiling with the creatures burrowing through me. My roots reached deeper, desperately searching for clean water. For salvation.

Around me, the other trees blackened, growing eyes where leaves once crowned them. More abominations clawed through rotted trunks, poisoning the world. The bulging plethora of branching eyes burst, one by one, like overripe pustules in the sun. Each eyeball that popped released a cloud of noxious gas into the atmosphere, eventually clogging out all light, all breath.

A tenor wove through the darkness. "How—we know—not some manipulation—"

My hearing wavered. That was…Feanim?

"—you not see—damned night deity swimming through her— serpent through water?" A bass rumble. Rafael. I strained to focus my ears.

Feanim scoffed. "Convenient timing."

An answering growl. "She cannot control these visions. I have attempted to trigger them myself with no success." A large hand cradled the back of my head, anchoring me in the tremulous sea of reality.

"That strikes me as cruel." Celebel's voice floated over from somewhere off to the side.

"Everything strikes you so, soft flower-eater," the drake snorted. "Typical caprice of useless gods, but the visions ring true."

Consciousness flooded back, and I was on the ground, coughing and clutching at the grass. Rafael hovered over me, eyes gone worry-yellow. Celebel and Feanim were somewhere beyond my field of vision, my still-buzzing ears blurring their presence.

"A vision." The Dragon's deep voice sheared through my cotton-stuffed hearing.

I nodded, the movement sending expanding rings of pain through my skull. "Did I faint?" A wave of exhaustion rolled over me.

"Dramatically. You have a knack for ending an argument." He scooped me into his arms. "I should try that on you next time you are obstinate."

"Argument?" Recent memories refused to focus. I flicked my ears to clear them, making my headache infinitely worse. The vision cleared, and I instinctively clutched my belly.

Rafael cupped my cheek, frowning. "Hrrm. Never seen one roll you this hard."

I shivered, turning to press my face against his chest. He looked down at me, brows pinched together in concern. The best I could muster was a shaky, rueful smile. What had we been arguing about? Humans? A fort. Already it seemed a thing of the past. Rafael's brutality paled in comparison to the horrors I'd just experienced.

"Are you well?" Celebel appeared at my side, ears back, and heedless of the Dragon's proximity. "Gods, it has been so long I'd almost forgotten about your visions."

"She will be fine," Rafael said. Normally, I would be annoyed with his answering for me, but fatigue stole my voice. "Simply needs rest."

I nodded again, pressing a hand to my aching forehead. Rafael carried me through a nervous camp. Hostile eyes and whispering hands followed his passage. I was too tired to care. Celebel trailed anxiously behind us. The Dragon paused at my bedroll, nestled as it was next to Celebel's, and glanced over his shoulder.

Rafael laid me down gently, tucking his cloak around me. He leaned over me and breathed a slow, heated breath on my forehead. The bands of headache faded. Not completely, but enough.

'*What do you require?*' His voice caressed my mind.

'*Only sleep, I think,*' I sent, but as soon as he moved away, a tremor of fear shook me. I clutched at his hand. "Wait! Wait, don't go." My voice was a husk. "Do not leave. I am...I'm afraid."

"Whist, dove, what have you to fear?" Like a cloudburst blowing over, all his earlier snarling softened into concern.

He curled protectively around me. Some formless emotion brought tears to the surface. Then I was clinging to him, crying into his hard shoulder. He cradled me in his arms, supporting the back of my head.

"I saw… I do not know this elf. A pale king. He will try to…to consume me. To consume everyone. T-to birth *abominations*. Oh, the *trees!*" The fear grew, stifling my breath, sitting heavily on my chest. "I know not whether he will take me specifically or, or…"

"The fuck he will," Rafael growled, arms tightening around me.

Celebel settled cautiously beside me on his bedroll. The Dragon tensed, moving over me in a defensive posture.

"I merely wish to assure her good health." Celebel held up his palms in supplication. As he reached to touch me, Rafael hissed like an angry snake.

With a sob of frustration, I pounded the expanse of chest above me. "You must *stop* this. You must stop fighting each other." Hiccoughing, I struggled to control my breathing.

Flashes of the red lion and silver tiger overlaid their faces. That first vision of the two of them locked in a deadly contest, superimposed on the more recent one, threatening to suck me in again.

Rafael relented, taking my face in his hands. "Look at me, Cúraniel. Tell me where you are."

I sputtered, unable to form the words.

"Speak." The barked command caught hold of my fluttering soul.

Unfamiliar trees. Different arrangements of stars. Night insects I did not know. Peaks rising in all directions. "In…in the mountains?"

"You sound unsure. Say it." His eyes burned into me, and I squirmed in his grip.

Celebel moved in my periphery. "Rafael, please. She has been through an ordeal. Is this forcefulness truly necessary?"

The Dragon held up a talon, never breaking eye contact with me. "Do not interfere. I have lost myself many times." A small part of my mind insisted this admission was important, but the tumult of vision-fear kept me from examining it. His voice gave my scattering thoughts an anchor. "Cúraniel, tell me where you are."

I sucked in a breath, gathering myself. "In the mountains."

"Why?"

"F-Férioth." Flashes of Feledhor stabbing Celebel, Fomorians bursting into light. "Férioth fell."

"And what is my draconian name?"

I smiled, the band of worry loosening in my chest. "Jax."

Rafael snorted in exaggerated disgust. "Terrible. Nowhere close." He released my face to tweak an ear tip, and said the correct, perplexing jumble of liquid consonants, sibilants, and guttural noises.

"I still cannot gargle rocks," I protested. Too weak to swat at him, I looked to a very concerned Celebel. "Can you?"

He frowned, ignoring my attempt to draw him in. "I do not wish to upset you again, but I need you to describe this 'pale king'."

I reached a shaky hand toward him, and he glanced cautiously at the Dragon before sidling over to accept. Rafael audibly ground his teeth, but did not growl. Nor did he interfere. The contact steadied me, clearing my lungs. Filling me once more with light. I concentrated entirely on the spirit flowing into me from each man, mingling with my own. Wishing I could hold them there forever.

Reluctantly, I brought myself back to the present. Giving Celebel the description brought the fear roaring back. "Oh, Cel, he's corrupting the birth trees." Tears threatened again. "He corrupted me as well, but oh gods. The groves!"

"Beredhel," Celebel breathed, eyes going wide. "Why did you have a vision of *Beredhel?*"

The vision fluttered at the edges of my consciousness, and my heart rated picked up again. "I do not know. I'd never heard his name before I met you."

Rafael rumbled with displeasure. "Enough. Let her rest."

I closed my eyes and lifted my chin, indicating he should kiss me. The Dragon huffed and pressed his lips to mine. I squeezed Celebel's hand as I bit Rafael's lower lip. Frissons of their combined power rippled over my skin, sinking into me. Making me whole. Making me *yearn.* I studied him as he released me. His eyes had cooled to only a few yellow streaks in the vivid blue.

Fuck it. I rolled on my side to tug Celebel closer and planted a firm kiss on his mouth. Both men froze, but Celebel recovered first. Watching Rafael like a scorpion poised to strike, my elvish soulmate slowly raised a hand and moved back. I twisted to look at Rafael.

His mouth twisted. "Why do I tolerate you?"

"Boundless love for my immense charms?" I pressed my *immense charms* together, knowing full well how my satisfaction showed on my face.

Scales rippled over his brow and cheekbones. For a moment, I feared he would shift. Instead, he heaved a dramatic, defeated sigh. He settled beside me, tucking my head under his chin.

"I suppose this means you've decided not to eat me in retaliation for her poor impulse control," Celebel said dryly.

Rafael growled, the sound rattling through his chest. "Both of you shut your fucking *arratxok* mouths…" he trailed off in a muttering of ill-tempered draconian. But he did not turn away. I'd only heard *arratxok* used for elves in a derogatory context. Probably some variation of "flower-eater".

I stroked his chest. "I love you both. So very much."

He grumbled and the tips of sharp teeth pricked my scalp. "I should have eaten you upon our first meeting."

Celebel drew in a sharp breath at the drake's casual mention of violence. Given the recent situation, perhaps I should have been perturbed. Instead, the implied threat was strangely endearing. Lulled by hope and body heat, I fell asleep with Celebel's hand firmly clutched in mine and the Dragon wrapped around me like armor.

FINGERS RUNNING through my hair woke me, little by little. The hand traveled to my shoulder. Groggy, I turned over. My ear ached where I'd pressed it into the bedding. Celebel watched me, the lines between his sooty brows smoothing as I sat up. Early morning sun caressed his face, but Rafael was conspicuously absent.

I rubbed my eyes and cast about for the missing Dragon. "Did I dream it?" My voice came out as a whispered puff. "Was he truly here with you?"

"Yes, Rafael was here, and he remained surprisingly calm. Perhaps his concern for you finally outweighed his hatred of me." Celebel's fingers danced along my arm. "He spoke to me with mere icy disdain rather than the usual venom. Nigh on cordial!"

I waited, annoyance at the mild pettiness warring with my eagerness to discover what Rafael had said. Celebel read my body language clearly, as always.

"Your Dragon told me of how he has witnessed these fainting spells during your strongest visions and advised me on assisting you when they occur." He paused, sighing. "Naturally, he also turned the tale into a jab about how poorly I know you, but otherwise kept his claws sheathed."

The first time I'd had a vision drag me fully under in Rafael's presence, the hot breath from a dragon snout had awakened me, snuffling over my face and neck. Disoriented, I'd given a wordless shriek. A massive red drake cocked his head, watching as I'd scooted backwards over the grass as fast as I could manage. I'd stopped only when my back hit the trunk of the Great Tree. The drake's leathery wings unfurled, burnished bright ruby by the sun.

"Do you fear me now?" A familiar rumble, though deeper, as if drawn from the very depths of the world.

"Rafael?" I'd seen various iterations of his scaly drake form, but never that one.

Significantly larger and bulkier than usual, though nowhere near his full dragon size, he'd sat on his haunches, and a sinuous tail wrapped his feet. More strikingly, he wore no clothing, though his scales obscured him far too well to appease my curiosity.

"Why did you shift?"

The mane of longer scales on his neck had rattled as he'd shaken his head. "Your energy spiked wild and strange." Brilliant blue flames danced in his eyes, reflecting faintly on the garnet scales. The snout shrank without warning, and his scales had receded as if folding into his body. The man stood in the half-dragon's place, clothed once more in shadow.

"Did you think me under attack?" I'd grinned in delight at the unexpectedly protective response.

"Stop flashing your teeth at me, fool elf."

The memory warmed me, though the vision it contained had given me nightmares for moons after. Faceless people, seizing into contorted shapes. They'd dotted a barren landscape like a burned-out forest. Thankfully, the Night Mother had spared me an encore of that one. So far.

I stretched, my spine creaking and popping in a satisfying way. "Indeed, Rafael is quite familiar with this process." The lines between Celebel's brows reappeared, and I smoothed them with my thumb. "Peace, Starshine. It may be startling when I swoon, but I was in no danger."

He brushed my hair away from my face. "Such a bizarre contrast, how tender your Dragon is with you versus how he reacts to everyone else. At every little sound you made in your sleep, he'd clutch you to his chest and make a rhythmic rumbling noise until you settled again. Like a great cat. It's almost as though he hides a different personality under all that muscle and spite."

Thrumming! The thought of Rafael so concerned over me he'd thrummed in front of *Celebel* filled me with poignant longing. I almost sniveled again and forced myself to harmonize.

"There is far more than a sexual connection between us. Rafael can be very sweet to me. It is the part of him I've worked so hard to nurture." I hugged my arms. "I'm quite surprised he let you witness that. When did he leave?"

"Feanim sought him out just before sunrise to set upon some band of Fomorians he'd located. Your Dragon only agreed once he was certain you had not fallen unconscious again. I assured him I would stay with you. We must finish that conversation about eating allies…" His brows knit together again in realization. "I've never claimed your relationship with him was merely sexual."

"True. There is also verbal sparring." With the occasional contusion.

"I can never tell if you're genuinely angry with each other or if it's some form of weird foreplay." Celebel propped his chin in his hands. That he could speak freely about the topic without getting frustrated lifted a weight from my chest.

"Both, but it's all in good faith. Better to breathe your fire in the moment, as Rafael would say, rather than hold it in and let it scorch your insides." The scale bit into my cleavage as I shifted. I pulled it out, turning it over in my hands.

"And on the hill? You've spoken of how often you wept over him."

"We had a few spectacular rows." To put it mildly. "Given his past, he simply wasn't equipped to deal with his emotions, and they surfaced as cruelty. I know it sounds like an excuse," I added, as Celebel pursed his lips in disapproval. "Rafael has always been complex. I'm grateful he no longer flees vulnerability. He's shown tremendous growth since that fight we had after he first learned of you." I sighed, unwilling to prod those particular memories. "He's led a lonely life, with so little happiness. His love is not always easy to bear, but it burns very, very true."

It lightened my heart to speak of the Dragon in this way with Celebel. The last time I'd felt such ease had been before they'd met.

"I often wonder how different he would be if he had been raised with even a glimmer of kindness."

Celebel looked away. "You truly love him. I sing this refrain as though I'm surprised by it, and yet… You two are as the sun and moon orbiting around each other, locked into a gravity I sometimes fear I will never be a part of."

I reached out to touch his lips. "If I am the moon, and Rafael the sun, then surely you are all the stars of the night sky. Your light may be gentler, more subtle, but it is exquisitely beautiful. And without it, the nights are far too grim. If you weren't here like my own Orelë, my guiding star in the night, the darkness would sweep me away. My visions are proof of that. You and I only need more time to grow the legend between us."

"You words are kind, my love, but as you say, the sun crowds away the stars in its eternal dance with the moon."

Stroking his silken hair, I sectioned out a silver streak to re-braid it. "And do they yield, or abandon her before night falls? These celestial bodies are patient. They will always have each other." I tugged his braid, and he leaned in to kiss me. "Much of the difference between my relationships with each of you is simply how much Rafael needs me. He has had so little safety or ease, and no love at all. You have had so many advantages, I doubt you could sing them all."

Until the betrayal, Celebel had carried no soul-deep wounds. Now, the injury floated behind his eyes, a lurking specter of fear. It surfaced in a heaving sigh, trembling along our connection.

"No longer." His voice dropped to a whisper. "Gods, how did we ever land here? Broken, abandoned, scorned. Attacked by those I have called friend my entire life. I have lost everything."

"Not everything." I gathered him into my arms, and he slid down to rest his head on my lap. "We have each other. We will always have each other." I teased his braids loose, fanning his hair out over my thighs.

"That would be far more comforting if it did not also include Rafael and his vicious delight in my failures." His hand tightened into a fist.

"You cannot yet hear the melody, but he *is* gradually accepting you. He protected you from the harpies without prompting. Cel, he thrummed in your presence. He only thrums when relaxed!"

"How lovely for him, to relax in the presence of one who has never meant him harm. I have less choice in this arrangement than he, and have already suffered greater consequences."

"None of it is equitable or just." My belly tensed, readying for yet another fight. "I regret causing you such complication."

"His recent behavior brings some relief, yet he acts out new atrocities at every turn." Celebel rolled to look up at me, blue eyes shining with unshed tears. "What could I have done differently? Confronted the court? I defended him against the murder charges. Perhaps that splintered the court. Could I have confronted him? That never ends well. I feel so very trapped."

His distress ached me.

"As I am oft-disliked, I have no solid advice. Perhaps you should learn to harmonize with being disliked as well? It is said the true test of rule is making an unpopular decision for the greater good."

"Certainly my grandfather cast his share of difficult decisions. My fathers had a blissful rule by comparison." He scrubbed at his eyes.

"Rafael seems to make only unpopular decisions. Though I do not know that I would hold him up as a shining example of leadership." Was it leadership or simply compulsion with the other drakes?

"Your soulmate rules entirely through fear. His people duck and scurry out of his path. I suspect Lord Marron carries most of the actual leadership." He sighed heavily. "I hope someday your Dragon won't take up quite so much space in our relationship. It's all well and good to see this soft underbelly, but we must deal with his destruction of the fort. He *devoured* our allies! Is there no way you can rein him in?"

"Rafael said it himself; he is not a tame dragon. He is and will always be a killer, and the best I can hope to do is redirect. I despise being held responsible for actions I have no control over. It exhausts me." I echoed Celebel's sigh. "Every note with my Dragon is new and untested. He has a deep, unrelenting hatred of humans, and targets them deliberately." Branches swayed over my head, and I winced, unwillingly visualizing eyes and rot.

Celebel sucked in a breath and flopped down beside me, also on his back. "I must ask you again. Where are your limits with his behavior? Do you have any?"

The question shivered, difficult to hold in my mind. "Eating humans is well beyond my limits, just as continuing to eat elves would be. But harmonizing my morals with his needs is difficult. We forget he must follow his nature. Stripping a region of all its livestock is only marginally kinder than devouring the inhabitants." I tugged my ear tips down, twisting enough for the pain to clear my head. "Humans cannot supplement their sustenance so directly off of their lands." In truth, had we elves been human, some would have starved, and many would have been far too weakened to travel by now.

"I blame myself in this instance. His power is vast, but not limitless, and he warned me of his hunger. I should have pressed, offered alternatives, even if he ignored them." Chewing on my lip, I considered all the paths I might have taken. They all led to the same inevitable conclusion. "He has solid reasons driving his hatred of humans."

Celebel sat up. "Humans abused him?"

Would it anger Rafael if I confirmed for the sake of peace? I chewed my lip and finally signed affirmative.

He exhaled through his nose. "Gods. I cannot claim to empathize with his reasoning either, but it makes a gruesome sense. If our other allies catch this melody on the wind, we shall have a serious problem. The rest of our remaining forces may depart in protest."

"I know, and I agree. I can only speak with him and hope for the best."

Chapter 6

I FOUND Rafael at our next rest amongst a fall of moss-covered rocks. To my surprise, Feanim was already there. I stepped through the humid buzz of dampening field, tinged green at the edges with the Duedellen's spirit. He had spread a map of the general area out on a flat-topped boulder and gestured at various marks. More human settlements and outposts. Rafael looked up at my approach. Feanim's ears twitched at the interruption, and the corners of his wide mouth turned down, but he said nothing.

I went to the Dragon's side, and he placed a comforting hand on the small of my back.

'*What little color you have is improved,*' he sent.

I leaned against him. '*Your acceptance of Celebel's presence means more than you know.*'

'*Anything for you,*' he replied, tinged with sarcasm, and turned back to Feanim's map.

"I've spread it amongst the others that an enemy drake attacked the fort. Taken down by your heroism, of course. If we can maintain the melody, it will spare us future headaches." The Duedellen grimaced.

"Interesting choice, to hide all human involvement from me." Rafael's talons clicked rhythmically on granite. "Brilliant tactics."

"Your reputation for human predation precedes you." Feanim scowled at him, and he scowled back. Their similarity in that moment struck me with humor, and I struggled to suppress an errant giggle. "How could we have anticipated the court turning on us, spurring this need to flee to Amrún?"

"How indeed?" Rafael drew out the last syllable, letting it hang on the irony.

Feanim grunted, tracing lines with his finger, identifying each group of allies. Far more humans than I'd expected. He spoke at great length and detail, recounting the family lineages of the particular Atani groups and their individual histories with the elves. Longer-lived than most humans, bolstered by their mastery of spirit, some of them had dealt with us for an age. Rafael's wall of stony silence through the entire speech did not bode well.

When the Duedellen finally took a breath, Rafael rumbled, deep in his chest, and looked down at me. "You are fortunate I rarely need to eat."

Frustration stamped Feanim's face. "With our numbers halved, these people are important to maintain any kind of advantage now!"

"How important could they possibly be?" Stubborn as ever, Rafael merely stared him down. "Humans breed like rabbits. They will renew their population in a blink."

"Their numbers are precisely why we need them."

"Why do you need them when you have me?" His grin was all arrogance and sharp teeth.

"Not one word? Did you truly not hear a single word?" Feanim tossed his hands up in consternation.

With a snarl, the drake recited the entire speech, word for word, in the exact cadence. Unsettling, to hear Feanim's clipped tones spoken in Rafael's velvety bass.

"I heard you. I simply am not convinced," the Dragon concluded. "And save your sad eyes, Cúraniel. You do not know these vermin."

Exactly as I'd feared.

"How will our other allies react if we cannot guarantee their safety from our own forces?" Feanim yanked his earlobes so hard I feared he might tear them.

"That is your problem." Rafael shrugged. "You requested my aid, and I have stipulations."

"But—"

"These complaints annoy me." His eyes drifted over both of us. "Did you think you could simply choose which aspects of me best please you?" I opened my mouth to protest, and he tapped my lips with a taloned finger, glaring at Feanim as he spoke. "You allowed one of your kind to draw steel on me in your great hall, all while begging my mercy. I am constantly expected to censor myself." His eyes flicked a dagger to me before returning to the Duedellen. The growling undertone of his voice deepened.

"You allow your court to insult *my mate*," the finger on my lips pressed down so I couldn't protest, "there was that quaint little uprising with the lavender, and now you dare *command* me to give up my chosen prey. Who do you think I am?" His face was closed, distant and unreadable, reminiscent of the Rafael I had first met.

The impending threat hung palpable around us. Feanim shifted uncomfortably under the weight of the Dragon's blazing glare.

I backed away from his hand to speak. "Might we put off this argument until the war has ended? Would you at least agree to wait until then before you attack declared allies?" Allowing the thought betrayed my morals, but perhaps I could change his opinion of humans if given enough time. He'd certainly made other major changes. "True, I cannot argue with your nature, but would a delay be so terrible? You said you do not need to feed often. Perhaps in those instances, you could go farther afield and seek different prey for the duration?"

Feanim immediately followed my lead. "I rarely dine on my favorite foods. Shit, I haven't had a bite of meat at my own table since Nimthil's arrival. She's too soft-hearted to hurt animals, so it's all fruit, grain, and vegetables. I'd have to grow my meat on a tree."

"A *meat* tree? That's the worst idea I've ever heard." The words tumbled out of my mouth before I could stop them. "What, growing lambs on a cottonwood?"

"Think of the potential," Rafael said suddenly, an evil glint in his eye. "Imagine a corpse tree."

I shuddered. "It would take something that fucking awful to cheer you."

"You flower-eaters love your woodlands. Let us have an entire wailing, bleeding forest." The Dragon leaned oddly on the sibilants, something horrid flickering in his eyes.

The bloated trees rose in my mind, and I clutched my uneasy belly. Rafael touched my shoulder in contrition, and the image dissipated. I laid my hand over his, rubbing his knuckles to steady myself. I could easily fit both of mine in one of his.

Feanim rubbed his chin. "Are you determined to continue raining hellfire on my plans?"

"Hrrm." Rafael's long nose wrinkled, as if scenting harpies again. "Very well. I shall exclude your human 'allies' from my hunting, so long as they prove useful."

Releasing his hand, I sank to the mossy ground in relief.

Feanim gave a curt nod in my direction. "And you, are you certain it was my face you saw in that supposed vision?"

Supposed vision. I wanted to kick him. "The very same, but sallow and stripped of color."

His green eyes hardened. "Beredhel was my twin. We share a countenance. This changes everything." He gathered up the maps and swept the dampening field away, departing before I could ask any of my thousand burning questions.

Stroking the damp, spongy vegetation soothed me. Beads of water rolled upward at my touch, sparkling prisms in the sun.

How must Feanim feel with this knowledge? When I'd initially broken with my lineage, I'd wrongly assumed I harbored no more emotional attachment to my blood kin. Silfanië had hated me from the very start, but I could not bring myself to return the sentiment. Had her friends turned her against me or had she led the charge after encountering my Dragon? Her betrayal ground into me like shattered glass in my gut.

Rafael watched as I petted the moss, tilting his head. "My people think me perverse for my interest in you."

I blinked. "Why tell me this?"

"Your position is not unique. If you knocked a few heads together, the elves would leave you be." He held out a hand, and I allowed him to pull me to my feet.

That the drakes considered his attraction to me unnatural was oddly hurtful. I had never truly considered that perspective before, assuming they would naturally understand the appeal. Apparently, I was more egotistical than I realized. Just like all the elves I criticized. I blushed at my ignorance.

Lovers and friends alike had always praised me for my beauty, but the children of the dragons valued strength above all else. With my plush curves, ankle-dusting hair, and nearly translucent skin, the last thing I resembled was a hardened warrior. Rafael had once described my body as "designed for lounging", which I'd taken as a compliment. Now I reconsidered his words.

The discomfort of recognizing my proximity to those whose attitudes I disdained made me determined to better myself. Attitudes like those Silfanië held. Crow, I had to turn this outward.

"Who is considered the most attractive drake? I assume it's you." I trailed a hand across the Dragon's shoulder.

Rafael coughed a harsh laugh. "Hardly. I rarely wear visible scales or more draconic features. My people take pride in their dragon blood."

Defensiveness for my beloved swelled in me. "That is a choice! You're capable of appearing just as dragonish as any."

"We are judged by the form we most often wear. I was born into this one, and best knows its constraints. In this body, I appear...soft." His pupils thinned.

Soft. A dire insult. Hard to imagine considering Rafael soft, given all the times I'd broken my hands punching him during sparring. Not even his lips yielded to pressure unless he permitted it. To me, he was hewn of living stone, harder than the bedrock beneath our feet. But to a drake?

Understanding clicked into place. "Your appearances allows them to underestimate you. Ah, indeed. But you didn't answer my first question. Who is the great beauty among your kind?"

His countenance darkened. Did he fear it would change my perspective? I stepped into him, running my hands over his arms.

"Come now, Dragon. You know who the elves consider our most beautiful—"

"Fucking *Celebel*," he grumbled.

"My sister, actually, and yes, Celebel as well, among the Talithiri. You recall the Lachanaur girl Feanim tried to throw at you, Carafindrien? She is their great beauty. Last I'd heard, the late Queen Polilcórë held that honor among the Astolar, alongside her Consort. I've lost the melody amongst the other nations. Siltaur, Duedellen, and gods, it's been ages since I've encountered any Maraiya." I hopped to kiss his cheek. "I would like to understand your people the same way, but only you make my heart soar."

Rafael looked away, mouth twisting. "Xyxs."

I kept my ear position neutral. Naturally, they would admire that most hulking, overly muscular beast of a drake. Even the enemy had targeted him in battle, mistaking red and black Xyxs for the actual Red Dragon. I'd have to tread lightly, recalling how Rafael had positioned himself to watch me heal Xyxs. Perhaps for a different reason than I'd assumed.

"Inevitable comparison." He tensed, as if readying for a fight.

I barely kept my exasperated laugh in check. "Rafael, please. There is no comparison to be had. If your wit is razor-edged, his is as dull as the ground we stand upon." I stamped the moss for emphasis.

Stubbornly, Rafael refused to back down. "You favor him."

"Gods damn it, Dragon. I harbor no secret desire to fuck Xyxs. It takes more than a deep voice, muscle, and red scales to turn my head." From the subtle flinch, I'd struck true. I cast about for a way to turn his mood. "What of the drake women?"

"Byxldurr was greatly admired until I killed her. Marron's mate, Vaerra, has taken her place."

Damn, if only I'd located Byxldurr's head after the fight. "And the third gender, the ones you call *viigsakh*?"

"The ability to both sire and birth offspring grants *viigsakh* a certain mystique. They also tend toward greater physical strength. 'Dhraxael', as you name our Progenitor, was *viigsakh*."

"I'd always heard Dhraxael referred to as male." No elvish historian had ever dared attempt conversation with the fearsome First Dragon, but this was a gross oversight on our part. I flushed with secondhand embarrassment.

Rafael waved it away. "He often styled himself male."

I took in his broad shoulders, the way his leather jerkin stretched over his powerful chest. "I still cannot fathom anyone perceiving you as soft for lack of a few visible scales. You are an unholy terror on the battlefield."

"Do you enjoy watching me fight?" His expression grew sly.

"The way you move is hypnotic. Yes, watching you fight is incredible." I ran my hands over his shoulders. "It would be even more incredible to watch you fight naked." I fluttered my eyelashes at him.

He laughed, a sharp cough of surprise. "Oh indeed. Very practical."

"Mmm hmm." I traced the contours of his heavy pectoral muscles, hardly in control of myself. "I could use a sparring lesson."

Rafael promptly knocked me off of my feet. I landed flat on my back, air rushing painfully from my lungs. Why couldn't I have chosen a nice, cushiony forest floor before opening my fool mouth? The uneven boulders would leave bruises.

"You ass! You didn't even remove your shirt," I wheezed, trying to roll away.

He lunged, pinning me to the ground. With a predatory grin, he held my wrists over my head. I caught the laces of his shirt in my teeth and pulled, so he dropped his full weight on me. Squeaking my protest, I struggled beneath him. His heat offset the frigid water seeping into my clothes. More rocks jabbed into my back, and cirrus clouds painted the sky far overhead.

"Unfair! You know I cannot break your grip!"

"Fighting is not fair. Be smarter if you cannot be stronger."

With anyone other than Rafael, I'd have flung the condensation from the moss into his face to induce a flinch, but unexpected contact with water sparked a terrifying reaction in him. Fortunately, the man could simply burn away dirt and grime instead of having to bathe. If only I could do the same.

I tried to buck and roll him off with my hips. No luck budging the heavy drake, but now I was trapped and aroused. Time to change tactics. I moaned in his ear as I writhed underneath him.

"This will not work on an enemy," Rafael said drolly.

"Works well enough on you." I bit his earlobe and moaned again.

Freeing one leg, I wrapped it around his waist, making sure he could tell exactly how wet I was. He sighed and released my hands, propping himself up on his elbows. My sternum creaked as his bulk lifted. I rubbed my sore rib cage, ensuring he saw me run my hands over my breasts.

"You should take this more seriously." He poked me in the side with a blunted talon, not quite hard enough to bruise.

"I wanted naked sparring!" I pouted my best pout, to no effect.

He caught my face, forcing me to look him in the eye. "Cúraniel." The rare use of my name sobered me. "The Fomorians are sidhe in truth. If you are captured and cannot fight them off, they will drag you underhill and rape you until they tire of it in a thousand years." His mouth pressed into a thin, grim line. "I was captured once, long ago." Talons flexed, and I held my breath. So much horror in his long life. "Unlike you, I am adept at defense. It still took nigh on a century to fight my way free. I no longer take risks with the fae."

A chill came over me at his words. "But you will protect me," I said in a small voice.

"You should not be so complacent. Anything can happen in the heat of battle, and I suspect a greater power at work." He stroked my face. "I want you prepared and able to defend yourself."

I kissed his hands. "Much as I complain about your tactics, I recognize your love in them. Forgive my silliness." Something about the fae prickled. "Glamour! You once said glamour does not work on you. Did you intentionally withhold the Fomorians' identity?"

"It is not faerie glamour, but a curse that obscures them." His eyes flickered with eerie light.

"A curse!" Gods, yet another layer to peel back. "Who could curse so many sidhe?" Even a cupful would be a great undertaking.

Instead of answering, Rafael kissed my forehead. Then he threw his body weight against me once more, at least thirty-six stone by my best estimate.

A discreet cough nearby got our attention. Rafael had me pinned again, this time from behind with his arms hooked under mine, wrapped up behind my head. As he released me, I looked over to Feanim watching us with keen interest.

"We are about to depart. Sorry for the interruption. Continue if you like…?"

Something slimy in the Duedellen's voice made me scoot away from Rafael, who gave me a discomfited look.

GIVEN THE large portion of foodstuffs the harpies had fouled, and our inability to resupply or forage much in these desolate lands, creeping hunger made me irritable. Though no elf would ever do such a thing, Rafael had cautioned us away from eating harpy meat all the same.

"As foul within as without," he'd said.

Evidently, not all of those bodies were burned. Eszrayln, the green-bellied black drake humbled by those harpies, hadn't listened, and spent three days projectile vomiting. Poor Lubber. The others callously left him behind when he could no longer keep pace.

Rafael had forced me to do the same. "The fool will either catch up or die to enemy attack. In a den, some might coddle him. Out here, he puts us all at risk."

"But we are so close!"

According to Feanim, we should reach Amrún late on the morrow, barring any more delays. The Dragon did not relent.

I couldn't help but cast pitying glances behind me as we moved on. He reminded me of the occasional groups of adolescent village boys who misidentified a mushroom known as "the Vomiter" for a choice delicacy. They'd inevitably spend an ugly few days before the alderman reached my hill to beg for help. That lesson repeated itself every few generations, despite my warnings and those of their elders.

"What are we to do for supplies once we reach Amrún?" I asked, shifting in my saddle.

In some ways, I envied Celebel's wagon ride. My ass and inner thighs ached no matter how I arranged myself. Iruwher's tail swished.

"Amrún houses a seed vault in the glacier. We sent necessities there long ago, along with a hand-selected crew to manage the restoration," Celebel said from my left. "The fortress descends far into the volcano, and they determined which levels are safe for use."

Helicos tossed his mane, evidently agreeing with his rider.

"Despite its appearance, the soil here is quite fertile. The natural vented heat makes for a long growing season. I expect to find a proper garden to get us through the settling-in process, but we'll have to rely on our treaties to secure enough fodder for everyone. *Therefore,* the humans matter." He glared daggers past me at Rafael, who ignored him.

As we traveled higher into the mountains, the landscape grew bleaker and more barren. Sharp granite gave way to rounded lava fields. The only common plant life was the slow-creeping moss blanketing the bulbous formations of pumice and obsidian. Nary a tree to be seen in any direction. A garden in this hellscape?

A distinct whistle caught my attention. Celebel leaned forward and plucked an arrow from the air. Just before it struck my beloved horse.

"Fomorian attack!" he cried.

"Thank the gods their aim is less true than an elvish archer," I muttered, and prodded the drake at my side with the toe of my boot. "Rafael, you did not react!"

The Dragon glanced at me. "You were in no danger."

"But Iruwher—"

He snorted. "I guard enough prey as of late."

Iruwher turned her head to cast a baleful glare at him. When her ears went back, I tapped her neck to dissuade her from trying to bite the arrogant drake. She'd likely only break her teeth and annoy him.

Fomorians swarmed up from the pits in the lave field. Around us, elves gathered in a small formation. They cried out in unified surprise when Rafael shoved his way past them. Throwing his shoulders back, he exhaled and blanketed the field in flames. Fomorians crisped and died on contact. Bits of burning moss floated on the updraft.

I expected him to charge at the enemy, but he stayed at my side. The others wisely arrayed themselves behind the fire-breathing drake.

More arrows whistled. Celebel caught two on a shield. Lámirië loosed her own from her perch nearby, taking down multiples with each bolt she let fly.

Nemohee thundered past on Machi, twirling þeir sword with a wild grin. I held my breath, but the blue roan hopped from high point to high point, sure-footed as a mountain goat in the treacherous terrain. The drakes ahead made space for the Lachanaur to fight, welcoming þem with a bellow of encouragement.

The cooperation warmed my heart. Nemohee moved easily among the scaly warriors, finding a rhythm to strike down the shared foes without blocking each other's paths. Compared to previous attacks, the Fomorians were thin on the ground.

Wise to their tactics, we guarded the horses well. A Fomorian snatched a sandy-haired Astolar serving youth from his mount, hauling him off over the rise behind us. His screams crushed the air from my lungs, growing fainter as the Fomorian dragged him away. Just as I thought him surely lost, a drake roared from that direction. To my surprise, Lubber reappeared. He had the boy tucked under one burly arm. If he hadn't straggled behind us, he wouldn't have been there for the rescue.

The green-bellied drake made a beeline to me and set the sheepish youth on his feet. "The Green says black-mane healer is you?" the drake asked in draconian. His long limbs added to his locust-like appearance.

"I am. How fares your belly, Lu—Eszrayln?" I gestured to the drake's midsection.

His pointed tongue lolled from long jaws, in a rueful gesture. It was as bright a green as his underside. "Never again eating plague birds. These have bad taste, but no sickness." He gestured to the Fomorians and dove back into the fray.

As swiftly as they'd come, the cursed fae scattered over the pockmarked landscape and disappeared beneath it.

My healing was shoddy work; long travel with scant rest took a toll on my abilities. The scars now creeping up the young Astolar's arms might be permanent. He clutched the healed arm, big brown eyes darting about.

Celebel guided his stallion over. "They are harrying us, trying to pick off stragglers. Amrún is close. Let him ride with you. We must make haste before we are attacked again."

I hoisted the youth into Iruwher's saddle and swung up behind him. When my arms slid around his waist, his ears flattened at the vicious glare Rafael threw his way.

The mare snorted as I guided her away. '*You've no competition from a child. Sheathe your claws.*'

'*That child cost you valuable energy with his carelessness.*' The Dragon echoed Iruwher's snort and strode along behind us. '*Your kind have some unpleasant lessons ahead if you wish to survive.*'

Ahead, the trail sloped up a steep ridge, and I conserved my *valuable energy* for keeping both the boy and myself astride.

Chapter 7

HALF-SWALLOWED by an ancient lava flow, Amrún rose like a great beast crouched and ready to spring. Black stone, polished to a shine and fitted into a geometric mosaic, contrasted the pitted surface of the lava. The fortress's smooth, angled walls ended in massive triangular spikes, providing little opportunity for aerial landing. Every feature exuded menacing strength.

Steam rose around us from vents in the ground as we made our way through the volcanic valley. Situated over an ancient caldera, an outflow of highly acidic water functioned as a perfect moat. Fed by the treacherous glacier perched to the north, a broad cascade cut off access from that direction. Further circled by impassably steep mountains, ground attack here posed little threat.

Boiling mud pits greeted us at the fortress vista. Ringed with red ochre and sometimes brilliant blue-green, they belched sulfurous steam. Despite their nose-stinging odor, at least they provided welcome color to break up the monotony of black pumice and greyish moss.

The terrain was too rough and inhospitable to allow the drakes space to camp in any numbers beyond its walls, a point of contention among the elves. Some drakes decided on their own to remain outside on patrols. A few more disappeared into nearby lava tubes at the first opportunity. Their numbers had swelled at least fourfold, but now only the original two dozen remained to enter the fortress with us.

Rafael was thrilled. The entire region may as well have been designed specifically to please a fire drake's sensibilities. A true hellscape. I hated it immediately.

"I will enter with the elvish vanguard," the Dragon said in a tone that brooked no argument.

A narrow suspension bridge led to the entrance. Strategically, the bridge was a perfect design; easy to drop in the face of threat. The

Astolar youth riding with me slipped from the saddle—notably on the far side from Rafael—and rejoined the others.

Amrún's main gate was almost large enough to accommodate a full-sized dragon. Intricate wrought iron twisted into stylized clouds of steam, shot through with jagged, high-polished lightning bolts, and hung from massive beams of dark ironwood. Against the black walls, the gate gleamed. Not an elvish design, and certainly not sidhe with all that cold iron. The deep dwellers who had supposedly built this place remained a mystery.

Feanim's crows had carried the message of our arrival ahead. For a long, tense moment, we waited, watching the swaying bridge. I gripped Iruwher with my thighs, unable to contain my anxiety. She snorted and shook her head. Nearby, Celebel patted Helicos' sooty mane. The grey stallion's nostrils flared as he danced with anticipation.

A distant caw confirmed. Then the mighty gates slowly swung open, revealing a portcullis in a repeating pattern of bats rising on the wing. The scalloped points made hostile, uneven barbs for anyone attempting to climb it. With a groan of metal, the portcullis rose.

Our horses were not in favor of the slight sway under their weight, nor the acrid smell rising from the moat far below. They protested with nervous whinnies and shudders. Wind lifted a stray glove from someone's pack, causing a young stallion to shy and nearly topple over the edge. The glove fluttered like a wounded bird, spiraling down to the waters below. Upon contact, it bubbled away to nothing. Logically, the crossing was perfectly safe. Emotionally, I sided with the horses.

"Rather than breadth, this fortress descends far underground." Celebel's conversational tone eased the knot in my belly. "Repeated eruptions have buried some levels that were once above ground. We cannot inhabit the very deepest, as the heat is too great, but the drakes may take to it."

"Would have been wiser to send said drakes in advance to clear the path," Rafael rumbled behind us. He navigated the bridge's sway with ease, taloned feet gripping the iron planks.

Celebel's ear flicked.

"These are my people, and I will greet them first," Feanim chimed in. "My crows would have reported any trouble."

As it was, a few crows circled far overhead. I had seen little of them since the harpy attacks and couldn't blame them for keeping their distance.

"Your crows do not report everything." The Dragon huffed, derisive.

The destruction of the human fort hung unspoken in the air. I could still smell the burning flesh.

I focused on my breath, trying not to rush through in my haste to escape the bridge. Rafael trailed along behind us, unhurried. At least he could fly if the bridge suddenly dropped.

The outer courtyard stretched in a ring past my line of sight. Without the lower levels Celebel had mentioned, the structure would have been too cramped to house our forces. On the right side, stables stood empty. Barracks occupied the left wall. We dismounted to lead our weary, nervous horses to the comforting confines of stalls. Some of our number opted to stay behind and care for them. The wagons arrived at our ear tips. I hitched my pack over one shoulder and followed Celebel's lead.

Near the entrance to the inner courtyard, the training field held an archery range and rings designed for sparring, along with one large enough to practice on horseback. An armory stood nearby, attached to a sizable forge.

Just past a wall latticed with arrow slits facing both directions, the inner courtyard made me gasp with delight. Though pointed battlements curved inward, casting long shadows on much of the open space, a glorious garden stretched before me. Ah, a balm to my soul. A shimmering net of spirit covered it. Great effort had been sung into this place. My skin tingled as we passed through.

At the eastern edge stood a large, well-appointed greenhouse crafted in elegant, curving lines of white steel and panes of shimmering glass. Rather than cold flagstones, soft ground cover of sorrel and clover lined pathways wandering alongside thin streams. Graceful trees bowed over those, leading off to a lotus-filled pool beyond the greenhouse. On the sunnier side, a vegetable plot dominated the space.

Fruit trees lined the walls. It was all a bit overgrown and in need of care, but the layout thrilled me. I immediately started planning where to put my herb garden.

Celebel put a warm hand on my shoulder, smiling. The first easy smile he'd worn in what felt like ages. "I'm quite pleased with the progress."

The potential! "Who crafted the beautiful greenhouse?"

"That was Nimthil's design."

Duly impressed, I nodded, and we moved on. Rafael followed like a long shadow, silent and watchful. His rumbling breath quieted, and the pads of his taloned feet made no sound. Many an elvish ear twitched toward the drake stalking among them, somehow made more intimidating by his lack of growls.

The great hall itself, located dead center of the keep, was both larger and darker than the previous affair. Multiple chandeliers cast soft firelight, refracting off faceted obsidian walls angled to illuminate the darkest corners. The scant windows were small, high up, and barred. Férioth's tapestries would be perfect to soften the harshness of all the stone if we ever retrieved them. The dais was roomy enough to accommodate the Consulate's thrones and other seating for important dignitaries. More seating in the gallery allowed space clearly meant for a central carpet.

All hard edges and angles rather than the curved, swooping lines favored by elvish artisans, it was not a terribly inviting space.

The tired throng filed in behind us, weaving around the big drake with far less trepidation than in the past. They ran the gamut from powerful lineages to humble. Soldiers, healers, artisans, musicians, serving youth, forest tenders, refugees, and more filled the hall, spilling out into the passageways. The most road-worn among us took the seating, eased into place by their comrades. For the first time since the fall of Araglin's fortified monastic city, a glimmer of hope hovered over the crowd. I hardly dared to breathe for fear of dispelling it.

The few Duedellen who'd managed the fortress gathered on the dais to greet the Consulate, making a show of presenting the keys on a gilt chatelain to Nimthil. Dignitaries all, but I ignored the proceedings in favor of observing Rafael. His eyes swept the room for potential threats, and his hand did not leave the pommel of his sword.

Gods, I'd almost forgotten about Galdir's confrontation with the Dragon in the great hall of Férioth, and the subsequent loss of the use of his arm when Rafael nearly ripped it from his body. The fool elf only escaped with his life due to the Dragon's acceptance of our intervention.

To my surprise, the retainers produced banners for the houses of Elhalanros, Melranim, and Tinunith. Above Celebel's seat, they raised a familiar crown of stars over white Orfain, the ancestor tree, on a field azure. Over Feanim's seat rose the two-headed crow of Melranim, split sable and white, on a field of green. In the seat of honor to the right, they raised Nimthil's house banner of a green torch with golden flames on a white field. No banners for my lost lineage, and if the drakes used them, we'd found no evidence of it.

We made a semi-circle, kneeling on the floor. Rafael held back, watching from the doorway. Celebel sang first, inviting in the gods of his lineage. When he got to the Maker, that great artisan, Feanim's tenor joined in. They shared that god in common. The ringing of celestial hammers on anvils filled the space, almost overwhelming before it settled into the stone. As it faded, Nimthil sang to her house gods, signing along with her uniquely lilting voice. Witchlights flared into being, coalescing in the lanterns placed for them. We were officially home.

"Lord Dragon, a boon?" Feanim called. "Mutually beneficial."

Rafael shifted his weight, crossing his arms. "Speak on, son of Melranim."

The elves nearest to him flinched.

"Though we have the hot springs, the volcano beneath us slumbers. Might you wake its fire? It will allow us to power the great forge."

They must have discussed the matter ahead of time, with as easily as Rafael agreed. What bargain had he struck? Feanim led the Dragon from the great hall into the bowels of the mountain.

WE WERE making our way to our quarters when a rumbling stopped us. A warm breeze wafted a hint of sulfur from a ramp descending out of sight. Had Rafael already awakened the volcano? Some tremors were bound to follow.

Celebel frowned. "The baths shouldn't be hot yet." At my confusion, he added, "That passage leads to a communal bath fed by hot springs. Since the volcano fell dormant, the water there has cooled. The pools hold far too great a volume to create steam so swiftly without also roasting us."

Gods, not another threat. He drew his sword, gesturing for me to stay behind.

I tapped his arm. "If Fomorians present, we need unhealing," I signed.

After a moment's consideration, he signed assent and to let him lead.

The downward sloping ramp opened into a large room with multiple entrances and a central pool taking up most of the space. As Celebel feared, steam curled from the water. Witchlights winked through the warm mist like will-o'-wisps in fog.

Smaller pools dotted hexagonal alcoves along the walls, and basalt columns rose in varying heights perfect for seating. Ages worth of calcite build-up draped the formations, softening the hard edges, and painting the entire bath in streaks of cream, rust, and yellow.

Feanim rushed in from a different entrance with his blade bared. Hadn't he gone with Rafael? Perhaps elvish constitutions were ill-suited to waking volcanos. Other soldiers flowed around him, fanning out before us. Nemohee entered from yet another tunnel, sword in hand. Most surprisingly, Carafindrien and her little cadre crept in at Nemohee's ear tips, anxious but determined, and all clutching knives. Losing one home was more than enough. I admired their courage.

"Water clear before, has silt now," Celebel signed to Feanim. "Something stirs it."

Nemohee crouched at the edge of the pool, extending one leg to tap the clouded surface. As the ripples reached the far end, bubbles erupted. We tensed as one. A slosh. More bubbles.

A giant, ill-defined white figure rose from the pool. The soldiers leveled spears, moving forward as Carafindrien screamed and her group scrambled backwards. Nemohee fell into formation with the others, advancing in silence. The creature snorted and shook out muddy wings. Clumps of silica flew, splashing into the steaming pool. Celebel readied himself to dash around the pool's edge.

Hold, something about that head shape…

"Xyxs," I cried, catching Celebel's arm before he could attack. "Hold, he's an ally!" In draconian, I demanded, "Why are you here?"

The silt-caked figure snorted again, clearing his nostrils. A swipe of the muck from his face revealed a blunt red snout tipped in black. "Shedding itches. This mud is good," came a voice so deep it registered more within my head than without. He blinked to clear his luminous yellow eyes.

"Stand down," Celebel called to the soldiers, straightening. "I know this drake."

The drake in question shook himself, sending globs of white mud flying. Disgruntled murmurs rose at my back. Fluttering hands told me certain elves considered drakes a contaminant to their pristine baths. I kept my ears still only by digging my fingernails into my palms.

Feanim gave a brisk command, and the soldiers departed.

"Ask him if he heated the bath himself," Celebel said, and I relayed the question.

Xyxs bobbed his head, enthusiastic. "Good strong flame! Soaking mud makes shiny scales, see?"

To demonstrate, he scraped the silica mud from his chest and belly and doused himself with scoops of hot water. It ran in rivulets down his body, outlining his considerable muscle. Preening, Xyxs flexed, striking various poses to show off his physique. Something else breached the surface as he moved. *Two* somethings. Two *very large* somethings.

Oh, he was certainly enjoying himself. I flushed and immediately closed off my connection to my Dragon.

The group collectively inhaled as the mood shifted. I glimpsed a certain sparkle in Feanim's eye. Oh gods. He did not know how insulting such a display would be to another drake. Crow, how would Rafael react if he knew I'd been exposed to another drake's erect cock? Er, cocks?

Privately, though, I was impressed. Very privately.

Why did it have to be the one drake he'd expressed insecurity about? Rafael had once told me my imagining of his dragon-sized cock being red was incorrect, though he'd said nothing about the accuracy of hemipenes... *No!* I shook my head hard enough to whip my ears.

A perusal of the others revealed parted lips, heated cheeks and ear tips, and quickening breath. Nemohee caught my eye and raised a fist, clapped þeir other hand to the crook of þeir elbow; an attempted measurement that fell short of the actual cocks in question. Even Celebel's brows raised in admiration. We exchanged a glance.

I stepped forward, grasping for a way to uproot the behemoth without starting a fight we would certainly lose. "Xyxs, this pool is elf-claimed." If it were my choice alone, I'd leave him to it.

The drake snorted again. "Little elves come and claim it, then. Or me. *Hrah!*" He pierced me with a stare. "I'll be like Rraysth e, giving little elves his strength." His skull-buzzing voice echoed weirdly in the chamber.

Feanim sheathed his sword. "What is he saying?"

"He likes the mud, and he's staying," Nemohee answered for me.

My ears twitched. Nem had picked up draconian swifter than I'd expected, but it harmonized with the time þey'd spent among the drakes of late.

"Also, he idolizes Rafael. You know that tune, eh, Feanim?"

The Duedellen scowled and dismissed the gathered soldiers. A couple elected to remain, transfixed by the scene.

A soft brown hand landed on my shoulder. Carafindrien. "This one is unmated, yes?" she asked. I should have expected her interest. She hadn't taken Rafael's rejection well. With a toss of her gilded burgundy twists, she added, "I'll take that monsterfucker title right along with you. No court left to shun us now." Her ears twitched with mischief, lighting up her warm, brown eyes.

I appreciated her willingness, however misplaced it might be.

"Yes, but—"

A shuffling drew my attention to where Feanim laid his sheathed blade and sword belt down on his neatly folded tunic. His boots followed. Fuck.

"Brave little elves!" Xyxs boomed a laugh, sloshing water over the sides of the pool to soak our feet.

"Xyxs, put your bloody cocks away," Nemohee called in draconian.

The drake's tail slashed, creating waves. "My cocks are not bloody! Yet."

Fuck, fuck, fuck!

"Fé, I doubt the wisdom of your actions," Celebel said, uncertainty tightening his voice. "We have no way of knowing how this will end."

For once, I agreed with him about a drake. But staring at Xyxs' twin cocks rising out of the water like garnet pylons while I summoned Rafael with mindspeech would cause a major incident. Yet, I couldn't avert my gaze.

Feanim waved Celebel away. "I know enough draconian to say 'yes', 'no', and 'cease'. What else could I need?"

"Drakes do not share our ways. This is dangerous!" My protests went unheeded as he loosened the ties of his breeches. Others followed his lead. Dresses, coats, and other articles of clothing fluttered to the ground. "The implications—"

"Oh, fuck your implications." Feanim turned a hard stare on me. "You cannot stake a claim on every drake."

Frustration fluttered through my hands. "I have no desire to claim him! You do not understand the context here." I was speaking to his back. "Feanim, please. Showing off his genitals is not an invitation to an orgy! I understand the appeal, but he is offering insult."

He snorted and tugged his breeches down. Easy enough to avert my eyes from Feanim's cock. Instead, I found myself ogling Carafindrien's sumptuous bare breasts. She cupped them and smiled at me, flicking a perfect dark nipple. Gods damn it, I was going to get myself killed without taking a single action.

The Lachanaur beauty stepped adroitly around the shorter Consul. "Lord Feanim, as you falsely foisted me upon one drake, I'll thank you to step back and let me lead here." She pinned him with a hard stare until his ears twitched and he looked away.

Turning to the drake on the other end of the pool, Carafindrien dropped her caramel silks completely, revealing all of her flawless brown skin. Xyxs grinned like a crocodile and slowly moved a great paw up and down over his topmost cock. Carafindrien waded in first, leading her friends, much to Feanim's annoyance. Crow. I had to stop this.

Celebel made a distressed sound. "Much as I hate to beg Rafael's involvement…" He sighed and gave me a beseeching look.

"Aye, best fetch Big Red," Nemohee said, sword at the ready. "We'll need serious muscle if this melody slips out of tune. Gods willing, all this muckle fool wants is a wee bit of loving."

I cleared my mind of bared flesh and opened the soulbond, following it to Rafael's location. Somewhere far below us. I could not pinpoint it.

'*Xyxs is in the baths,*' I sent, ears quivering.

'*So?*' Irritation. I must have interrupted him. What did waking a volcano entail?

'*So, he is surrounded by elves, and he greeted them with an erection. Eh, two erections.*' I tumbled the thoughts out in the hopes Rafael wouldn't take umbrage with me.

The Dragon's tone changed immediately. '*Fucking fools. Xyxs has no concept of modulating his strength. He will kill them.*' He approached with haste.

That solidified my fears.

I pecked Celebel on the cheek and dashed to the passage to meet Rafael. I didn't have to wait long. His flaming hair and eyes announced him in the dim tunnel, moving with deadly silence.

"Xyxs is in the central pool. We never would have known he was there, but for the steam from the water he's heated."

Rafael's eyes flashed, and he swept past me, ducking under the portal. Gods, Xyxs was another two or three ear-lengths taller than my Dragon, not to mention the bulk added by wings and a tail. How had that behemoth gotten into the baths undetected in the first place? I followed with a pounding heart.

The Duedellen stood waist-deep in the warm water, facing the big drake. Nemohee and Celebel moved on either side of the main pool, slowly approaching toward Xyxs. One slim young Astolar man sat near us on the lip of the pool, pouting, with his brown eyes fixed on the scene.

"I do not understand this rejection," Feanim was saying. "I have higher standing!"

"I doubt it's yer *standing* what interests him," Nemohee replied.

Xyxs himself appeared quite pleased, as well he should. Carafindrien was already draped over the top cock, and another bright-haired Lachanaur woman teased the lower one. They paused to kiss each other before returning to their tasks. A Talithiri woman with long russet curls and skin to match fondled his chest, stretching to reach, and a pale Astolar beauty caressed his wings.

I dug my fingernails into my palms to shoo away the toe-curling image of Rafael in similar straits. Gods, he'd boil the moon from the sky if he caught a strain of that melody.

"Your prick is not the mighty spear you believe it to be," my Dragon snarled at Feanim, standing far enough back to avoid the splashing water.

I snorted a laugh, quickly covered by my hand. From across the pool, Nemohee guffawed. Feanim startled, moving aside as he turned.

"Even if it were, that one has no interest in pricks," Rafael amended with a wry twist to his mouth.

The errant drake himself looked up with a groan at the Red Dragon's voice. Xyxs tried to shuffle around so he wouldn't present an overt insult to the stronger drake without also dislodging the women working his cocks in tandem.

"Xyxs, you stupid ratfucker," Rafael bellowed in draconian, sending vibrations across the water. All five of them froze, and the Talithiri shrieked. "If you harm even one of these flower-eaters, I will cut off your idiot sticks, dry them in the sun, and present them to the elves for a flute." He gestured to his crotch in an unmistakable jerking motion, attracting more than one surreptitious glance.

I snorted at the mental image. Across the way, Nemohee was in tears, doubled over with laughter. Noting Celebel's confusion, I sent him a mental translation.

He bit his lip in mirth. *'Gods, your Dragon is quite the poet.'*

Xyxs' tail whipped the water's surface with a loud *smack*, sending the Astolar attending his wings backstroking away from him. "Why care, Rraysth e? You have elves. I want these!"

The rest did not resume their ministrations, ears swiveling and eyes darting from one drake to the other with growing alarm.

Rafael made a guttural noise of frustration. "Elves snap like tree branches, you fucking fool. Break one, and you will upset my mate." Both drakes looked at me. I pulled my shoulders back, trying to project resolve. My Dragon pulled me to him by my waist, growling, "And if you upset my mate, I will end you."

Xyxs raised both paws, bobbing his head. His hemipenes also bobbed, and I decided to study the ceiling. His new lovers swam backward, uncertainty in the set of their ears.

"We are not so soft as humans," I said in draconian. "More sturdy, like…" I struggled for the word. To Rafael, I asked "Moose?"

"*Aeltzeri*," he translated, with an approving nod. At Xyxs' baffled head tilt, he added in weary draconian, "'Tall deer'. Antlers like so," and raised his hands to indicate the size.

Xyxs huffed recognition.

"Yes, *aeltzeri*." I slipped on the pronunciation a bit. "If your action hurts one of those, it will hurt us. But we are not glass. Best to ask each individual their limits. Frequently. If they say no, or it hurts, you stop immediately. Understand?"

Xyxs' eyes lit up like lanterns. "Yes, yes! This I can do. So careful with the elflings." He reached over and made a show of petting the Astolar's amber hair. Pey blanched even paler and swam out of his reach as soon as he stopped.

One less lover to worry about. At Carafindrien's fearful look, I translated the conversation into elvish. She and the remaining two signed acceptance.

To everyone's surprise, Rafael addressed her directly. "If harm befalls any of you, or if he pesters you beyond your liking, come to me first."

Celebel shot me a look of surprised pleasure, one I returned wholeheartedly.

Carafindrien rubbed the back of her head, where Rafael had once dragged her by the hair. "I appreciate your consideration, Lord Dragon."

He gave her a sharp nod. To Xyxs, in draconian, he said, "*You will clean this place when you finish.*"

Xyxs bobbed his head again.

Without looking at Feanim, Rafael said to him, "The volcano is awake. Come to the forge when you tire of this foolishness." His hooked nose wrinkled in a sneer, and he swept out of the baths.

Feanim watched the Dragon leave with a sour expression. "The only other gods damned drake who wants to fuck elves, and he doesn't like dick," he muttered under his breath, shoving his legs back into his breeches.

Chapter 8

DESPERATE for a meal, a proper bath and a fuck of my own, when Celebel took my arm to guide me to our chambers, I nearly skipped. Leaving the baths, we wound through the central building. The passages varied without warning, going from squared off, highly polished halls to rounded, rougher tunnels. Witchlight sconces added sparkle to the soft aqua glow from clusters of small mushrooms and shelf fungus.

A single rounded door set into mottled obsidian led to our new shared chambers. Much smaller than the lavish rooms at Férioth, the antechamber stood empty apart. The shorter second door opened onto a unique—and humid—sleeping arrangement. Moss coated an entire wall and raised corner, forming a springy bed. A trickling sound brought me to the hot spring funneled through a far wall. It pooled near the base of the small shower, deep enough for at least one person to submerge completely, and wound around the rest of the room. Fungus illuminated its course. The stream sank through the pumice in the opposite corner, framing the moss bed. Witchlights floated lazily through the air.

Small windows cast sunny squares on the stone. Beneath them, shelving had been carved into the wall. Opening my pack, I arranged my jars of Pîntellum there. Enough sunlight to promote growth, but not enough to roast them.

Once I was satisfied, I wadded up my filthy clothes and tossed them to the door. Sliding naked into the pool, I let out an obscene groan of relief. The water was barely warmer than my skin for now, but it was enough. Plucking a handful of fragrant moss, I set about washing away all the bad memories.

"We'll need to keep books and clothing in the antechamber to prevent mold. At least these windows open for airflow. That should help." I drew a star pattern with my finger into the condensation on the stones.

Celebel didn't reply. He was already face-down in the moss, snoring softly.

A GENTLE hand shook me and my eyes snapped open. The light had changed in the room. I'd fallen asleep in the pool without realizing it. In my repose, the water had warmed significantly.

"Sorry to wake you," Celebel said. He proffered an apple, and I accepted it gratefully. "We've been setting up the forge to prepare for the next stage of this armor creation. I'll soon be ready for you to add your spirit to your suit. I've the basic design laid out, but it needs your hand to guide it."

"Oh, that's sooner than I expected. Good! The Pîntellum can be applied whenever the actual forging is finished." I stretched, eyeing the jars.

Relieved, I climbed out of the pool and rolled on the moss to dry myself, much to Celebel's continued amusement. Our connection hummed, nearly restored to its previous health.

"You are in a far better mood. I take it the rest was restorative?" I asked. The springy vegetation tickled and soothed me. I plucked a clinging sprout from my shoulder.

"Immensely. Reaching the safety of the walls has been wondrous for my mental state. I am encouraged for the first time since the betrayal. The forge here is ancient, unlike anything seen by our kin in ages. We can make great progress with the armor here. Once we have workable prototypes, we'll have far more might and freedom of movement."

Finished prodding the moss, I turned my attention again to the Pîntellum. Opening each jar to apply a little nutrient paste, I murmured to my little experiments about how well they had done on the long trip.

"They're almost like your pets," he laughed.

"They may as well be. I'm very pleased with the progression. The next test is convincing them to adhere to a large surface."

"It is passing strange to have a piece of *him* growing in

my bedchambers. I've never truly considered it before."

Celebel's ears twitched as he glanced at the jar containing Rafael's specimen. It differed from the elvish samples, red with streaks of black where ours were silvery purplish-pink. The sample swirled languidly around its enclosure. I tapped the jar. The darker Pîntellum adhered itself to the places my fingers touched.

Celebel shivered. "It gives me a creeping sensation. Can you cover it?"

"No, it needs sunlight." I moved the offending jar behind the others. The specimens all tracked my movement, swirling lazily in their containers. Their responsiveness cheered me. Despite their prolonged fast, they still flourished.

"Cúraniel." He took my hands as I turned. "I wish, more than anything, we could return to your hill. We had precious few moments to learn each other's song before unrelenting crises dropped on us." The corners of his full lips twitched as though he considered kissing me. "Perhaps we should begin anew. In all the pressures of the court and the anguish of betrayal, I nearly lost the melody of what initially drew me to you. That fierce inner strength; ah, how true you are to yourself in the face of those who would prefer you meek and pliable. The sheer force of your love, even when I do not understand it. It is only a natural a dragon should admire you, with the way you breathe fire to protect those you care for."

I drew a hand along his high cheekbone, the angled line of his jaw. Our bond hummed to life for the first time in what felt like centuries, warming me from the inside.

"I have perhaps mistaken your kindness for weakness on occasion." My fingers drifted over his brow, and he closed his eyes, leaning into my touch. "You try so very hard to find accord in factions determined to remain at odds. Rarely do politics make for smooth personal lives."

He huffed. "You sing truth. The methods that harmonized in the peaceful glens of Velúara are weak here, in this opera of war. I regret having learned this at such a dear cost to you."

"You've been forced to make decisions I never could. Taken

positions I cannot fathom, for the sake of the greater good. I should have recognized that sooner. You do your grandfather proud, Celebel Elhalanros." I pressed my lips to his at his escaped whimper of emotion. Not a kiss, not precisely. Into his mouth, I murmured, "And you do it all while being the most beautiful of us all." I drew back and tilted his chin down to look me in the eye. "Now, remove that filthy tunic."

He laughed and dramatically dropped his clothes to the ground. His creamy skin stretched too tightly over his lithe, toned body. Pointed hip bones jutted, the ripple of ribs all too clear. I clucked my tongue in silent dismay. He'd had little enough flesh to spare.

"Too thin for you now?" He shimmied in a circle, showing off his lovely, rounded ass. An ashen smudge of darkened skin on his lower back stubbornly lingered over the healed stab wound.

"You will always shine for me. I simply cannot help my concern over your wellbeing." Tracing the edges of the mark with my fingertips, it whispered beneath them. Fucking moranga blade and its curse. If only the demon ore had remained a legend. "Like any healer, I've lost patients, but never have I encountered such a stubborn injury. It refuses to fully heal!"

Our connection trembled, and his head drooped. "I need to be close to you. Any hint of distance, and I am hollowed out. The darkness rises once more."

The echo of Rafael's common sentiment wrung the air from my lungs. I wrapped my arms around him, pressing my breasts to his back. My head rested against the nape of his neck, filling my nose with the reminder of our time spent on the road. Horse, dirt, the nervous sweat of pain. Heartache. Little remained of the chiming, telltale scent of starlight.

I smacked his buttocks and grabbed generous handfuls to squeeze. "You slept while I bathed. Come."

As he turned to face me, I took his awakening cock in my hand. Tugging ever so gently, I shuffled backward toward the trickling hot spring.

"Did you see the valve here?" He reached over my head and turned a copper sluice mostly hidden in the rock wall.

Steaming water splashed out in a miniature cataract. Brilliant!

I released him and he stepped under the spout, closing his eyes with a blissful smile. The water ran grey over his body as he scrubbed at his hair. Unable to resist, I tweaked a pale nipple, and he shivered at my touch. One eye cracked open, watching as I rested my hands on his slim waist, tracing the lines of his hips with my thumbs.

When I moved to cup his bollocks, he grabbed my elbows, swirling us around so the water rained down on my head. The heat stole my breath, and he spun me to face the wall. Pressing me against it, he kneed my legs apart. Bracing myself with one arm, I arched my back, wiggling my ass against his already impressive erection.

"I've been looking forward to this very thing," he said in my ear, kissing his way up the long helix. Each brush of his lips sent shivers down my spine, heating my vulva. "Tell me what you desire." He hesitated, breath tickling my skin. "Make me yours. Command me."

The request harmonized with his dismay around decision-making. Too many choices had led to discord, to sorrow, regardless of intent or culpability. I missed my Starshine's easy smile.

"And if I command you to punish me, to inflict pain, are you capable?"

He made a deep noise in his chest, bringing an immediate throb to my clit. "Yes."

"You must tell me if I venture too far. After the work you did with the crop, you have a good concept of my limits." The memory of said crop warming my ass made my thighs clench with need.

"You have remarkably few," he murmured against the side of my neck. "Agreed."

Licking my hand, I reached around to grasp the tip of his cock in my free hand. I stroked him, clenching my ass around his shaft. He moaned, throbbing in my palm, and pressed his hips forward eagerly.

"Bite me." I felt his hesitation and looked over my shoulder. "Go on, bite!"

Pulling my hair over one shoulder revealed the mating bite Rafael had left on the back of my neck. I tested the seal I automatically placed on the Dragon's bond when in Celebel's company, cautious of spillover emotion. The bond remained silent.

"Cover Rafael's mark with yours. Claim me." The very thought of such transgression tightened my nipples. "He wants me so badly. Enough to overcome his past, his society, his very nature. Do you?" A calculated risk, but I needed to stoke those sputtering embers.

Celebel hummed assent, starting at my shoulders with little nibbles. I squeezed his cock, and he gasped. "Harder. I want you enough to risk Rafael's rage. To risk my destruction."

I wanted pain. Fury. The desperation of lust. All the intensity we'd lacked. His teeth scraped the muscles of my back. Steam curled around us.

"Bite down, harder!"

He bit into the flesh of my shoulder, and I hissed, stroking him faster. His hips bucked, shoving me into the wall. I reached between my legs to flick my clit.

"Make me feel it. Bite! Draw blood."

Celebel pulled back. "I don't think I can bite you as he does—"

"*Bite*," I snarled, releasing his cock.

Kneeling behind me, he clamped his teeth into the meat of my buttocks and reached between my legs. Gods, yes! I leaned into him as he pushed my legs farther apart.

"Shall I continue to bite?" he asked around a mouthful of flesh.

I rocked against him, laughing and flicking the tips of his ears. "Leave marks or I'll make you begin anew."

A questing finger pressed against my cunt. I guided it to part my labia and enter me as I continued to strum my clit. With my free hand, I pinched and rolled my nipples.

Teeth sank into the delicate flesh of my inner thigh as he slid more fingers into me. The sweet pressure had me crying out and bucking against his hand, forcing it deeper. Encouraged, his jaws clamped with bruising force. Pain lit my senses on fire. Every flick of my hand increased the force building within. Every thrust of his shoved me closer to the edge.

He released his jaws, eliciting a shudder from me. "Is this what you want?" Moving behind me, he stood.

"Yes, yes," I panted, rubbing my clit as if I could set it alight. He bit my left earlobe and I screeched.

"I want you to come on my hand," Celebel said. His cock slid against my ass once more as he penetrated me with his fingers.

The orgasm hit right on cue. Just as I began to shake, he withdrew his hand. I whimpered, arching my back. He gripped my hair, forcing me to look ahead.

"Shall I fuck you in the ass?"

"Yes! Gods, yes."

The slick noises of my hand working his cock fueled my need. I stopped when the tip pressed against my anus. Relaxing into him, I swept my ample juices back with my hand to lubricate myself. He spat on his palm to increase his natural lubrication and eased a finger past the tight ring. I stretched, opening for him with all my muscle control, and the finger slid out. The slickened head of his cock replaced it, and he bit my ear again as he penetrated me.

Orgasmic tides crested. "Yes, fuck me. Fill me up!" I rocked against him, slowly working his length into my ass. I rippled the inner muscles against him, squeezing and releasing.

"Ah, I cannot last long if you continue that."

"Flood me, then. Fuck me hard."

Grabbing his hand, I forced it against my clit, rubbing with a frenzy. He hissed and his hips worked, thrusting his cock deep into my ass. He pulled completely out and thrust again, burying himself deep. I planted both hands on the wall to absorb the shock, and he hammered me, flesh slapping against flesh, to the rhythm of my panting cries. He bit my other ear, and blood trickled down my neck.

Words stolen by mindless pleasure, I howled as the orgasm broke me apart. The cock inside me pulsed once, twice. He released my ear, throwing his head back to cry out in harmony.

"Ah-ah-ah, FUCK!" His hips slapped against my buttocks as he pumped me full of seed. We shuddered together, singing our ecstasy.

As he slid from me, I turned and wrapped my arms around him. We held each other in the hot water, swaying gently.

"Are you sufficiently bitten?" he murmured into my hair. "Gods, you do like it rough!"

"I'll heal." I hugged him with all my strength. Oh, to press myself into his flesh, meld, and become one. If only I could do the same with Rafael here as well.

Sensing my mood dip, Celebel lowered me to the water. "We will find peace, my Moonflower."

"Moonflower?" My ears perked.

He tucked a lock of hair behind my ear. "Brilliant as the moon, strong enough to strangle a tree, and poisonous to certain types." Celebel shrugged, sending ripples across the water. "I'd no pet names for you, and it seemed inequitable. Do you like it?"

"I love it, and you."

Chapter 9

"**A**MRÚN stood abandoned for more than an age when Feanim rediscovered it." Celebel's musical baritone bounced down the snaking corridors ahead of us.

The rounded passages resembled lava tubes more than hallways at this level. As I'd once more eschewed wearing shoes, I quickly learned to watch for places where the floors gave way to rough pumice. The farther we descended, the warmer the floors grew.

Rafael had sent drakes flitting back and forth to Férioth since our arrival. Though they'd protested their roles as beasts of burden, they'd already recovered many necessities. According to reports, but for the occasional small band of Fomorians, the fortress was abandoned. The treasury and library had been looted, whether by the traitors or enterprising drakes, we could not ascertain. Neither Consul pursued the matter. Restored access to vital supplies such as tools, food, and materials—enough to get us through winter and siege alike—was well worth the price. I was merely grateful for the stack of warm woolens and books Rafael had deposited by the door. His scent clung faintly on the coat I wore.

"At his insistence, we built this place back up for strategic purposes. Feanim spent quite some time plotting out the levels and the lava tubes in the surrounding area. At least, those he could safely reach."

I begged for the comfort of the library. Designed for practicality over aesthetics, a broad, cylindrical room plunged many levels. A vast number of witchlights clustered in a sparkling central column to spread across the high, slightly domed ceiling. Their illumination reflected off strategically placed sections of mirror-polished obsidian. The maintenance alone staggered me.

Shelving cut into the walls allowed the books to stair-step downward, matching the gradual decline of a spiraling iron walkway.

Platforms with comfortable alcoves for reading dotted the walls on both sides at regular intervals.

My skin tingled as I stepped into the space, the scent of old tomes wafting over me. Spelled, then, to protect the contents. No damaging fungi or mold grew here, but if the original caster had passed, an object of power must hold it. If such an object resided here, the origin defied my focus.

Why had they abandoned their books? Few elvish characters adorned these tomes. Rushing thoughts stole my spoken words. Reluctant as I was to abandon my curiosity, when Celebel tugged at my braid, I followed.

As the clang of metal on metal led us to the forge, he kindly pointed out Rafael's quarters, situated across from the healer's wing in the outer battlements. The sharpness and volume of hammer strikes increased to a painful level, and I clapped my hands over my ears.

Celebel smiled in pained sympathy, handing me wax ear plugs.

Feanim's clipped tenor rose as the hammering paused, vehemently arguing with Rafael over the cuirass on his anvil. The heat of the forge fire drew immediate beads of sweat along my brow. My Dragon's eyes and hair flickered like hot coals. Displeasure carved the lines of his body.

Multiple hearths and anvils of all sizes lined the high walls, creating enough stations for many blacksmiths to work in tandem. Given the tools hanging from custom fittings, whoever had abandoned this place had left it almost as pristine as the library. Nearly. A massive, winch-operated hammer, at least twice my height, occupied the entire southwest corner. The mechanism that powered it hung in rusted ruin. Of what use was such a large hammer? Had it beaten out the shape of the main gates?

The Duedellen glanced up from his project. "Nice of you to deign to join us."

"I suppose you did not bathe and give Nimthil a tumble first, either," I shot back, and he scowled at me.

Celebel stepped adroitly between us. "Fé, show her."

The Duedellen shrugged and held up a þilvor cuirass, matching it to other pieces unwrapped from oiled rags. It gleamed, all flowing lines and beautiful craftsmanship, jointed in novel ways for extraordinary flexibility, and yet… I tugged my earlobes. The breastplate was entirely too literal. No wonder Rafael seemed agitated. Pointed cones adorned the front, tipped with carved nipples. Decidedly too small to fit me.

"Do you truly expect me to squash my breasts into those…what are they, pockets?" I hefted my ample bosom for emphasis.

Rafael snorted. "I have said as much."

I gave him a grateful look.

"This is purely decorative. You will never enter combat! It's simply a design flourish." Feanim furrowed his brow, tugging an earlobe. "Ridiculous. This entire exercise is a waste of my time and our precious resources."

"Shut your fucking mouth." Rafael's growl snapped the Duedellen's fucking mouth closed. "You will forge her armor correctly, or you will not forge at all." His talons clicked against the anvil.

Ever the peacemaker, Celebel interjected. "This is not the design we agreed upon." He took the cuirass from his fellow Consul, disconnecting the breastplate.

I couldn't help myself. "Why would I ever wear such a thing? It allows little room for chest expansion, let alone movement. Breasts are soft but not *that* malleable. Nearly half of our fighting force has them and you think it is absurd to accommodate us? Save this for Nimthil's dainty frame if you cannot craft better."

Rafael's amusement rippled along our connection. '*Wicked woman.*' I pulled my shoulders back, jutting my ample bosom forward with a smile just for him.

Celebel pretended not to notice. "The original was nothing like this. This new style of armor is challenging to craft, being so fitted to the body. With your membrane, we'll need no padding beneath the plates, and so we have far more joints to accommodate a full range of motion."

Feanim grumbled to himself and opened a journal full of drawings, scribbling furiously. After a moment, he revealed his modified design. It was an alluring image; sexy, fluid, and clinging.

"The differentiation in the center creates a weak point over her heart." The Dragon plucked the charcoal pencil from Feanim's grasp. He drew a few strokes on the page. "I will not have her outfitted in insufficient armor."

Feanim's ears flattened, but he examined the changes and nodded. It amused me greatly whenever Rafael casually snatched something out of the Duedellen's hands, as though Feanim were no more than a misbehaving child. I took care to hide my mirth for the sake of peace. At least Feanim was cooperating for once.

He sighed dramatically. "Fine, yes, but it will require a complete remake of the breastplate."

Rafael snorted. He strode to the giant hammer, bent, and lifted it. If the weight strained him, he did not show it. The ripple of muscle across his back, visible through the thick leather jerkin, warmed my libido. He gave the hammer a sharp jerk, snapping it free of the broken winch. Propping it on his hip like an oversized infant, he carried it over to the anvil where my breastplate rested. Glancing at each other, the three of us backed away from him in unison.

With a pointed glare at Feanim, Rafael breathed a directed flame over the breastplate. It glowed under the dragon fire, but retained its shape. He raised the enormous hammer and dropped it on the breastplate with a resounding *clang!* Even through the earplugs, the discordant note made me jump. The Dragon lifted the hammer again, inspected the now misshapen þilvor, adjusted it slightly, and struck another blow. This evidently satisfied him. He pulled the breastplate off the anvil and set the hammer in its place.

"I need that anvil," Feanim complained.

"Then move the hammer." The Dragon lifted his brows.

I snickered under my breath as Feanim cursed under his. No elf could hope to budge that mountain of iron. The mountain of drake standing beside it smirked.

"I'll make the changes. It is best for me to guide Cúraniel through bonding with her armor, after all." Celebel pulled a leather apron from the wall, and handed me one as well, leading me to another station with an anvil that appeared identical to my untrained eyes.

Feanim yanked at his earlobes and stalked off. Rafael narrowed his eyes, but made his exit, deliberately brushing the back of his hand across my breasts as he passed.

'*Remind me to show you my gratitude later,*' I sent.

'*I do enjoy your gratitude,*' he replied.

I watched him go, admiring the sinuous way his body moved. He glanced back over his shoulder, and I smiled a smile full of promise at him.

"Have you finished flirting, or can we begin?" Celebel teased.

"Tread lightly, sir." I swatted his arm, and he grinned.

As I turned, he took hold of my braid, letting it run through his fingers. Exposing the back of my neck. Rafael's bond twanged, bowstring-taut.

'*Turnabout is fair play, Dragon. This is only temporary, and you never gained my consent before leaving your mark. When we finish here, it is time to honor your agreement to make peace.*'

A disgruntled growl vibrated through our connection. '*Agreement, indeed. Very well. Bring the reforged breastplate, and I will examine it.*' Progress!

Celebel stoked the forge, and rolled his sleeves up, exposing forearms shaped by long use of hammer and blade. He glanced at me. "Will you draw upon the Dragon's fire? I need more heat."

Testing the bond, I pulled Rafael's flame around me, funneling it through my hands into the coals. The forge flared, momentarily blinding me. I released the fire.

Celebel grinned at me. "Perfect! Now, we may begin."

"You're aware I know nothing about this, correct?" I eyed the painfully bright coals with some apprehension.

"Worry not. I'll guide you. Despite his disposition, Feanim is a brilliant smith. He's taught me all manner of techniques over the years. It gives me joy to pass that knowledge to others." He lifted the breastplate with a pair of tongs and heated it evenly. "Stand here. I'll demonstrate how to hammer it. You needn't form the piece, only imbue it with your spirit. Þilvor is tolerant. I will rework any mis-strikes."

I positioned myself at his direction. He moved the plate to the anvil in front of me, holding it with one hand on the tongs, and handed me a hefty hammer.

"Take a moment to truly feel the hammer. Send your spirit into it, let it become one with your arm. With the hammer as your focus, this is how you will impart the metal with your power. Strike there." He indicated the general area. "Start with small blows. Try to round it out. When the metal sings, you will know you've struck true." He paused. "When the pitch improves, we can remove the earplugs."

Celebel sang a prayer to the Maker for a steady hand and proceeded to pound the offending cuirass into a rounded shape. As though striking the keys of an instrument, the metal chimed under his hammer, vibrating through me. As it lost its shape, the notes fell out of harmony, grating on my ears.

I'd only ever worked small bits of þilvor for simple jewelry. The process fascinated me. Far more malleable than it appeared, he heated and hammered the metal until a sheen of sweat glittered over his skin. Alluring, especially with the way his arms and shoulders flexed. Gods, I must spend more time in the forge. So much delicious muscle on display.

"If it is so soft, how does it function as armor?"

He paused, wiping the sweat from his brow with his forearm. "This is the true power of þilvor. It requires spirit to work, to convince it to accept another form. It sings with the stars when it has reached completion and holds its shape doggedly until reforged. That was why Rafael heated it. Striking it alone with such force will only introduce cracks without significantly changing the form. Forging temperature and process affect its properties to make it suitable for armor. Harder, stronger, and lighter than any steel. No other material would function in this design, except perhaps that accursed demon ore."

His cheerful chatter brought a smile to my face. Perhaps he could find a harmony with Rafael over their shared interest.

Once Celebel proclaimed satisfaction with his newly blank canvas, I sent my awareness into my arms and hands, concentrating my spirit there. Difficult at first to connect with the cold iron hammer. After some coaxing, it opened and accepted me. Feeling more confident, I swung.

My first strike went laughably awry, bouncing too hard off of the armor and nearly rebounding on me. Celebel chuckled and steadied my hand with his own, adjusting my grip.

"Ooh, teach me your ways, my sexy master smith." I leaned back into him, wiggling my hips.

"I know you've always desired a big hammer of your own," he teased.

Then we were both giggling, awkwardly trying to hammer out the armor in tandem.

"Think of this as a dance. Put your energy into the flow, not the force of the stroke. Lift the hammer with grace; and let its weight do the work." His spirit wrapped me, flowing down my arms to make my aim more true.

Even with the guidance, it went poorly at first. Every other strike flew sideways, showering us in sparks. I healed the ones that landed on skin. We paused frequently to reheat the breastplate.

It was slow progress, partly due to the amount of work needed, and partly because we attempted it all with shared tools and laughter. The loving, playfully sexual energy we poured into the piece felt perfectly appropriate.

Eventually, the þilvor harmonized and took on the desired shape. Celebel granted me a reprieve as we removed our earplugs. "I will finish it. It knows your song now. This piece is the heart of your suit, and the rest will harmonize more easily. Next, send your spirit into the other pieces until they resonate."

I picked up each piece, starting with the pointed sabatons. The harmony progressed much faster than the forging, almost as if the armor knew it was meant to be one cohesive unit.

"Might I add a small design to the helm? If it's possible." Unused to shyness, I peered at him from under my lashes.

Celebel smiled. "Of course. As long as it doesn't interfere with the functionality, you may make it as elaborate as you wish."

"A simple crescent moon on the brow." I picked up the helm with its high, peaked comb. The visor slid down to obscure the face, relying on a unique combination of Pîntellum and discreet, angled slits at the edges of the jaw to allow ventilation, auditory clarity, speech, and vision while closed. It hummed in my hands.

"Ah, of course! I have my own crest on my helm. Here, I'll help you." His hands were deft, the strikes precise.

"Have you always enjoyed crafting weapons and armor?"

Celebel paused, turning the helm over. "Much as I enjoy it, I prefer jewelry-making. Many of the pieces you wore at Férioth are my creations."

"Gods, Cel, what a talent you have! Those pieces are breathtaking." My eyes must have sparkled like Fallëvaethil itself with the way he smiled at me.

I relished the day spent laughing like children, flirting, and working together in harmony. Encapsulating that feeling into crystalline memory, I saved it for future use. For the dark times I knew were coming.

Chapter 10

WE met in the war room. Sparsely furnished with only a few chairs, its baren walls black, it was as neutral a territory as I could imagine. It was also one of the few spaces guaranteed to prevent eavesdropping, as Feanim's first act upon discovering it had been to weave wards throughout the walls and threshold. Sound could enter, but it could not leave, allowing for more flexibility than a dampening field. The meeting place had been Celebel's suggestion, and he followed me inside.

Standing with his back to the wall, Rafael's blazing glare could melt the obsidian around him. His fiery hair cast its own light over his black clothing. Like a flame under a jar, he burned all the air from the room.

'*Someday you may extinguish your fires doing that,*' I chided. His eyes narrowed, and I continued aloud. "You agreed to make peace, Rafael." The glower's intensity did not lessen. "Please." Crossing the room, I took his hand and pressed it to my heart. For three heartbeats, the humming tension in his body braced me for an outburst.

Instead, he gave a great, rumbling sigh. '*For you, anything.*' He looked over my head. "Let us negotiate then, *nekarazzi.*"

'*Must you begin with antagonism?*' I dropped his hand.

The Dragon gave me a sidelong glance. '*Would you prefer dachsqu?*'

Before I could ask for a translation, Celebel replied, "Let us begin, Lord Dragon." He settled into a high-backed chair as though it were a new throne. Regal, even in a simple undyed linen shirt tucked into fitted grey trousers.

I stood between my soulmates, touching neither. All the criticisms each had lobbed at the other, warranted and otherwise, rolled around in my mind. Hammers clanged distantly in the forge. Nearby, elves worked to establish a mews. A disgruntled falcon made a rasping *kack-kack-kack*, and a voice soothed it. Somewhere, a drake grunted.

"One of you must speak." A transparent effort to relieve the tension, but preferable to waiting out Rafael's stubbornness. "You must find a harmony, especially now with our forces drawn so thin. I'm sure Feanim would agree."

"She has the right of it," Celebel conceded. "Lord Dragon, how are we to reach a truce if we cannot speak with some level of civility to each other?"

"Your definition of civility or mine?" Rafael rumbled. "This is not an attack." He held up a taloned finger as I opened my mouth to protest.

"Fair enough. I have never considered this perspective." Celebel tapped a beat on the sideboard. "May we speak without insults or threats, direct or implied?"

"Do not insult me, and I will not threaten you."

"Rafael, please. No hostility." I tugged at my lobes. "I do not expect friendship, but might you at least establish a functional working relationship? Constant conflict helps no one. Surely even you do not enjoy it." Contentious blighter. Gods, the hill had been easier in so many ways, lack of emotional intimacy notwithstanding.

"Good enough," he rumbled, and Celebel nodded. I almost dared to feel hopeful. Then the Dragon grabbed me from behind. "Here, a truce. Never touch her again, and I will leave you in peace."

I struggled in his grip. "Gods damn it, no! You cannot make this a requirement!"

"Who are you to command me?" he growled in my ear.

I kicked his shins, bruising my heel.

Celebel remained calm, folding his hands in his lap. He must have expected something like this. "Lord Dragon, do you love her?"

Rafael stilled. I held my breath as his heat rose.

"Tread carefully, little princeling," he said.

Smoke curled around me. So much for maintaining civility. Gods damned blighter.

"It is a simple question. She sings of your love, but as you keep your own counsel, I would hear it directly from you." Celebel's cool blue gaze was at once mild and unrelenting.

"Hrrm." Rafael's hands tightened on my arms. Not enough to hurt, but the tips of his talons pricked my skin. As though he meant to cage the anger vibrating through me. "My love for her is the sole reason you still draw breath."

"Have you ever heard the phrase, 'One cannot sing through a clenched jaw'?" Celebel's tone was almost kind. "Such control is not loving, as it removes your lover's choice to stay by your side. It loudly proclaims you have no faith in her. A soulbond deprived of contact will shrivel the owner's spirit. In your attempt to wound me, you would also harm her."

"Rafael, were you at peace when you kept such distance from me?" I asked. "The stronger the bond grows, the more we need such contact. Fucking hells, Dragon. A truce must be beneficial to all of us."

Rafael's chorus growl nearly drowned out his words. "I have no need of you, but you surely need me. What possible benefit could you offer?"

The Consul did not flinch. "Do you suppose strength is all a soulmate needs?"

Crow, that was bold. I peeked at Rafael's hellish expression.

"When this war ends, will you lock her away from the world, make her merely another feature of your hoard? Will that make her happy?" His eyes drifted to me. "Cúraniel, is that what you wish?"

"Never, and well does he know it," I twisted to glare at Rafael. "I should slap your pointy teeth out of your head." Fucking hellbeast!

The Dragon released me. "Your fire breathing is immensely charming." Much to my fury, he ruffled my hair.

My palms itched. "You knew I would never agree to these terms!"

Rafael shrugged. Blighter! "Hrrm. Mutually beneficial. What do you offer?" He examined his talons, and I seethed in silence.

The abrupt change threw Celebel visibly off balance, but he recovered smoothly. "Peace between us for her sake, and the sake of our peoples. But firstly, I offer an apology. I deeply regret the lavender." His fingers twitched, likely resisting the urge to tap. "I meant only a petty deterrent from my bedchamber. It grew to a chord struck wildly out of tune, and not at all my intention. The court's response shames me."

"If she had not told you my secrets, it would not have been an issue." The Dragon's eyes flicked to me in a pointed glare.

"Please forgive my carelessness." My anger drained away at the advent of shame. "When I washed that oil away at your request, I let slip your aversion to lavender. I am ill-suited to subterfuge."

Rafael tilted my chin up, forcing me to look at him. "I have no desire to hear of his private conversations, proclivities, or anything else. I demand the same courtesy." A surprisingly reasonable request, but Celebel bristled.

"We hold no secrets between us!"

"*My* concerns are not yours to hold," Rafael growled. His liquid flame hair swirled about his shoulders. "Why should I allow you to violate my privacy with no repercussions? I would kill any drake with half the intimate knowledge you hold."

"Cel, his melody harmonizes. The fault is mine for not explicitly establishing that boundary earlier. Rafael, I have attempted to guess what should remain private in the past." My oversharing always tweaked my ears, but the Dragon's relative calm surprised me. "If you would but speak your desire for privacy, I will do my utmost to honor your request. The soulbonds make it difficult to guarantee, close as we are in each other's minds."

Celebel folded his arms, but he nodded agreement. "I'll agree if you stay out of my personal space, Lord Dragon. No more invading my—*our* chambers or tent, unless you are summoned."

"Summoned, indeed." Rafael huffed, but acknowledged the request.

I almost dared to hope.

"No more agreements involving me out of earshot, either." Celebel's ears didn't quite flatten, but they lowered. "That goes for both of you. No more plotting."

Rafael smiled, tight-lipped, the flames of his eyes flickering with malice. I wanted to poke him, but he was out of reach.

"Quite reasonable, I concur. I'm sure he does, as well." I glared at Rafael until he reluctantly nodded. "For my part, each of you must cease your attempts to convince me I shouldn't be with the other. I've heard all the arguments, and I'll hear no more. Go tell the mushrooms or fucking yell it into the night. I never wish to hear it again."

They both shifted uncomfortably under my gaze.

"And if I say it directly to him?" Always looking for an angle, my Dragon.

"That would defeat the purpose of having a truce."

We locked eyes in challenge. I sent him an image of me touching myself. His eyes narrowed.

'Fight to win.' I smiled as widely as I could without showing teeth.

'Dragonslayer strikes another blow.' He looked over my head to Celebel. "I met your grandfather once."

The subject change jarred me. I braced myself.

Celebel's ears drooped in shock. "What? There is no record of this meeting!"

"Nothing came of it. I was very young, and he had been forewarned. He drove me from the gates of Velúara before I could breach them. Alas, I never returned. To think I had the opportunity to stamp out your line before it produced you, and I squandered it." He shrugged, the movement rippling through his powerful body.

Celebel's stare iced over.

"Rafael, that counts as hostile." I caught myself as I reached to tug a lobe.

He smiled sweetly at me. "Merely recounting history, my dove." As skilled as the Dragon was in such a broad range of subjects, feigning innocence was not among them.

"You never 'merely' do anything." I tugged my lobes again. It had been going so well.

"So Elaris simply shooed the stray Dragon away?"

The Dragon cocked his head, studying Celebel's serene expression. "The elder Elhalanros was a great king, one of the few I have respected. A shame none of that power and wisdom passed to you."

"I am well aware." Celebel's teeth flashed in a quick grin. "Still, I thank you for the perspective. Good to know my lineage holds the power to frustrate you."

A threat smile and a thanks; deliberate goading from Celebel. Rafael's expression soured.

"Sometimes behaving like an ass has unintended consequences," I said, and the Dragon scowled at me. Out of the corner of my eye, Celebel bit his lip. "On that note, I would like to add further terms. I am wholly sick of being held responsible for your actions." I jabbed a finger at Rafael. "Each time you behave like an ass, I suffer the repercussions."

The Dragon snorted, long nose wrinkling. "I have never asked this of you. It is your choice to accept responsibility for the cowardice of others." Ire heated my face. He raised a hand. "Direct these complainants to me if it vexes you."

Flushed at his dismissal, I readied my hand to slap him. Let my bones break on his gods damned face.

"Rafael." The name from Celebel's lips stilled us both. I dropped my hand. "Every soul here knows only Cúraniel truly has your ear. Why should they risk death to be ignored, when they might approach her instead with their petitions? You place undue pressure on her. It is not loving."

I hardly dared to hold my breath, eyes darting from one man to the other.

"You speak on love as though someone else dropped her into a hostile court. Shall I allow the craven to file down my talons?" Rafael tapped them on the sideboard for emphasis. *Click-click-click.*

"Cease the constant threats." Celebel folded his arms, ears twitching. "Either kill us all or cooperate, but the relentless intimidation is counterproductive."

I stared hard at Rafael, pursing my lips to keep my tongue in check. Too involved in glaring spears at Celebel, he did not acknowledge me.

The Consul continued. "I am no match for you. None of us are. I do not expect you to behave like an elf, but I ask that you no longer view us as enemies. Those who turned traitor took that potential with them.

This is what I mean by 'civility'."

I dearly wished to kiss Celebel, but it would unravel his careful work.

Rafael exhaled slowly. "What do you know of drake customs?"

A classic redirect. I sighed internally and dropped into a chair.

Celebel blinked, leaning forward. "Only what Cúraniel has taught me."

"Of the drakes gathered here, how many would happily murder and supplant me?" He leaned on the tall back of a chair, carving patterns into the wood with his talons.

"Ah… Most, I would say." Celebel's ears twitched.

"Every single one."

I started. "Even Marron? Or Boshkt?" Hard to imagine either of them involved in an opportunistic killing for status.

"Marron stands to gain the most from my demise." Dark humor tugged at the corners of Rafael's mouth. "The goals of youth are the regrets of maturity. I fought my way to a position I did not understand. The only escape is death.".

Manipulative, to reveal this glimmer of vulnerability, but I appreciated it nonetheless.

Celebel took a deep breath and nodded slowly. "The threats are to maintain your position, and they must be legitimate to hold weight. That harmonizes. But surely you recognize elves do not function in this way?"

"You prefer your weapons concealed."

I laid a hand on arm. "Rafael, please. Celebel's request is reasonable, and it would clear much of the cacophony from my ears. We are all absurdly indebted to you, but it seems a small sacrifice to make. Will you attempt to curb the aggression, at least toward elves, for the sake of peace?"

Rafael gave me a blistering look. "I will always answer insult with force."

"I would not expect otherwise." I bit my lower lip, sliding my hand up his arm. "But perhaps save the force for actual insult?"

He looked up at the ceiling for a long moment. "Very well." Two words cast like stones to the bottom of the ocean.

I took a steadying breath. "Do we have a truce established?"

"Yes," Celebel said.

Staring hard at Rafael, I prodded his arm. "Speak it."

"Hrrm. As you wish," he grumbled.

Daring, I took his hand, tugged him forward, and made two long steps to take Celebel's. The Dragon tensed, but he did not resist. The moment my skin connected with both soulmates, light burst within me. My spirit surged, twining with theirs. So vast was the upward momentum, I had to check if I was, in fact, levitating. I tried to pull them both closer to me, but Rafael remained immovable as the mountain beneath our feet.

Lips parted, a new awareness flickered in Celebel's eyes. Silvery spirit flowed from his skin, lapping at mine. Starlight chimed, its sweet scent tickling my nose. Rafael's heat warmed me from the other side, but he kept tight control over his power.

"Are you appeased? I have matters to attend." His barbed tone scratched away my bliss.

'I love you,' I sent, releasing his hand.

'You had better.' Rafael stalked off with one last growl.

Celebel blew out the relieved breath we had both been holding. "That was suspiciously easy. I do not trust him."

Chapter II

"**THE** armor will be ready for testing once you've finished mucking about with those membranes." Feanim leaned over his bark trencher, waving a sharpened birch stick at me.

Ever pushing the boundaries of possibility, he'd been the one to suggest adding mycelium to the slime mold. He'd also volunteered his sample for experimentation. After some false starts, I found the correct mycorrhizal species and the response was almost immediate. The Pîntellum adapted, and I updated the rest. It created a nerve-like network, allowing the membrane to anticipate movement as well as react. It also added a pleasantly warm hue to the previous pallor.

With a single long, weathered table shoved into it, the war room made for a less ideal dining space than its previous purpose. A melancholic memory of Araglin and his well-appointed dining halls flitted by. His kindness and hospitality, even to an avowed enemy such as the Red Dragon, stood unmatched. I shoved it aside. There was no centralized dining area in Amrún, and few large indoor gathering places at all. The mysterious deep dwellers must have been an asocial people. I sat beside Celebel, across from Feanim and Nimthil. The four of us clustered at one end of the table at Nimthil's request. The dark walls pressed in on me.

Our fare echoed the simplicity I'd grown accustomed to on my hill—roasted foraged tubers, nuts, and mushrooms. The ice wine's vintage was newer and far sweeter than the fine ambers of Férioth, but I was grateful for any wine at all and I liked the citrusy bite. With winter's approach, no fresh fruits would supplement these meals. Straightening from my slouch, I resolved to scour the contents of the greenhouse. Evidently, it had a lower level for warmer climate plants, lit by angled mirrors.

No serving youth attended. Our numbers were too thin. We had taken our trenchers from the kitchens ourselves, which suited me. I'd never found ease with accepting service, despite having done my own requisite period. Too many reminders of a cast-off past that still clung like cobwebs.

"I propose applying nutrient paste at the most important flexion points in the armor to encourage the Pîntellum to adhere properly," I said, signing along. Celebel squeezed my hand under the table with an encouraging smile.

Feanim nodded, poking holes in a tuber's skin.

The Pîntellum specimens responded well to my chamber's warm humidity and single, sunny window. They had grown rapidly since our arrival, and I'd started more from volunteered samples. Before long, I'd need to utilize the greenhouse for more space.

I swirled my cup. I'd slept poorly under the watchful presence of volcano and glacier. Perhaps the kitchens had chrysanthemum tea stocked for ease of slumber.

Nimthil pushed her food around on her plate, her sage green sleeve dragging across the pitted wood table. She made no attempt to hide the bruise-like circles under her hazel eyes, the usual warmth of her freckled brown skin gone sallow. The defection had been hard on her. Perhaps harder than anyone else, save Celebel.

Nimthil tapped on the table with a slight cough.

"You well?" I signed. "I assist?"

Surprised, her ears twitched. "These last moons have been a trial. Rest will have to wait." Graceful sign accompanied her lilting accent. "There is no more possibility of keeping my people out of this war. I have been in negotiations with the nobility." Her palms rested on the table, fingers twitching as if readying to take flight. "As for the northern Lachanaur, they are scattered and have grown far too decentralized over the ages to rely upon. And so, it falls to my people."

"I do not imagine the Lachanaur are so easy to corral." Celebel kept his tone gentle, and relief at the recognition lit her eyes.

"Could Nemohee assist with the northern folk?" I ventured.

Nimthil's face went cold. "I shall have no more of your monstrosities involved than necessary."

I leaped to my feet, anger suffusing me. "How dare you malign þeir name! Nemohee has fought loyally for our cause. Þey lost a fucking *soulmate* in this gods damned war!"

"Indeed, and þey are half-vampiric fae. Do you truly believe leanan sidhe blood has no effect on þeir nature? Can any sidhe be trustworthy? Your harmony is disrupted by your perverse love of oddities." Nimthil's brow pinched, ears flattening with disdain.

Celebel grabbed my arm, pulling me back into my seat before I could reach across the table and slap her.

"Whether Nemohee is the best ambassador is secondary to the exemplary service þey have rendered. I've no doubt of þeir loyalty, and would remind you of the role þey played in securing and utilizing the Carnyx." He tactfully clamped a hand over mine to prevent my angrily signed insults. "But I agree we must seek the aid of all Lachanaur, not only those under your rule. Surely their power would be amplified in a place such as this?"

Nimthil nodded assent, still sneering at me. I returned it with ears flattened and my best death glare, the one I used on Rafael. The Dragon himself tugged at our connection, sensing my righteous fury. I sent calming energy his way, and Celebel patted the backs of my hands.

Feanim watched the whole exchange with a glint in his eye I misliked. "Cel, has the Maraiyan ruler responded? You have some familiarity with þem, yes?"

"Þey're considering sending a representative. No assurances yet."

The Maraiya elves! I hadn't seen one of our seafaring kindred in many a century. The most secretive of our kin, more likely to ally with selkies and other aquatic fae than any landlocked people, surely it would take a mighty effort to convince them. Amrún's volcanic atmosphere would pose a challenge to their comfort.

I ate in thoughtful silence, forcing myself to focus on how we might adapt the public baths to suit their needs. Keeping them free of surprise drakes, at the very least. A shame the others didn't find Xyxs as amusing as he undoubtedly found himself.

Nimthil spoke softly, keeping her signs small, as though she feared being overheard. "Another matter weighs heavily on my mind. How do we prevent that beast...the Red Dragon...from turning against us in madness? If that ensorcelled spear was a deliberate targeting, then surely the enemy will make another attempt. The foul murder that monster committed in our great hall weighs heavily upon my spirit."

I hated to agree, but a failsafe for Rafael's unstoppable might—and unpredictable rage—was simply practical. That failsafe could not be me alone, not with the possibility of inflicted madness.

Feanim nodded thoughtfully. "It presses on my mind too, ever since that incident with the outpost. Moranga is obviously the first choice, though Rafael wields it to far greater effect than we do. We must finish the new armor and hope it provides enough advantage."

BATHED IN diffused moonlight, Feanim, Rafael, and to my surprise, Nimthil awaited us at the training field. Celebel and I turned over the respective jars of upgraded Pîntellum.

"Rafael, will you gather a sample from Nimthil?" At the way her ears drooped, I added, "Fear not, his talons are so sharp you should hardly feel them."

Rafael's lips pulled back in a nasty smile. "My pleasure."

Nimthil grimaced and held out her forearm. Instead, he leaned over and neatly scissored a chunk out of her ear. She wailed in shock. Feanim and Celebel flattened their ears, horrified. My belly clenched. No elf would ever strike such an intimate blow.

The Dragon crouched until he was eye-to-eye with the diminutive Lachanaur queen and held up the bloody strip of flesh. "For the lavender." He spoke with a dangerous deliberation, enunciating each word to ensure she could read his lips. "You will not disrespect me, or my mate, ever again."

Eyes huge, Nimthil emphatically shook her head in agreement, slinging blood across her dress. Backing away, her freckles stood out against a face gone sickly. Feanim stepped forward, but Celebel stopped him with a subtle hand on the arm.

"Enough, Rafael. Stop scaring her." I spoke with a calm I did not possess. The Dragon gave me a look of deep satisfaction. I took the sample gingerly between fingertips and put it in a new jar with a dollop of slime mold. "Nimthil, I will deliver this as soon as it's suitable. Shall I attend your wound?"

"I will bandage it." Her tremulous voice was barely audible. The tips of her ears quivered as the shock hit.

Going after such a sensitive, taboo area like that was a particularly vicious choice. Gods, her ear must hurt. How her pride must also hurt. At least Rafael had left her earrings intact.

'*She deserves that and more,*' Rafael sent, self-satisfied.

I ignored him for the sake of peace. I did so more and more as of late. "Now, let us unveil these prototypes." It was a transparent attempt to redirect the conversation to a more productive direction, but no one complained.

With a dramatic flourish, Feanim pulled away a cover of muslin cloth and unveiled three glorious suits of armor. The suits stood upon their racks in a neat row; shining husks waiting for life. Similar in design, and yet distinctly styled to each wearer. My reworked cuirass was far more inviting. Celebel's stood the tallest, a head above mine. Feanim's barely crested my shoulder.

I'd never encountered their like. Less traditional armor and stylized metal sculptures of earless elves, the flexible plate construction followed the form like a second skin. Brilliant engineering on Feanim's part. He and Celebel, along with Rafael's occasional assistance, had worked tirelessly since their arrival, shrouding the forge in secrecy. The Dragon's proximity to the project gave me more hope for true peace between them.

Applying nutrient paste to the main joints, I added the respective Pîntellum to each set. It swelled into the space, expanding across the curving planes of þilvor. The reaction encouraged me.

I handed Rafael the jar with his own membrane, as his armor was nowhere in evidence. His sample disappeared into the shadowy folds of his cloak.

"The Pîntellum will need time and encouragement to adhere properly to such a large surface, so apply more nutrient paste every few days. It will not function at its peak capacity until it has fully settled, but we may test it now." I cast a meaningful look at Rafael. "For the best contact, you'll need to be nude while wearing the armor. Clothing will render the membrane less effective."

He arched a brow. *'Not fucking likely.'*

I tugged my lobes but surrendered. "I'll need a sample from Nemohee as well. Ask permission this time!"

"I am not going to make armor for every random—" Feanim began.

"Close your mouth unless you wish to return your Pîntellum." I yanked at my earlobe again. "Nem has been on the recipient list from the start."

The Duedellen gave me a dour look but kept his counsel.

I directed them to the suits. "Now, take hold of your armor. Concentrate on sending your spirit into it. Let it feel your essence. Help it understand what you want, similar to resonating with the þilvor."

I clutched my armor, singing a gentle refrain and suffusing it with my spirit. The Pîntellum reacted immediately, shivering with anticipation. Clouds parted, revealing the full moon above us. In its loving illumination, the armor shone like the stars themselves. Drawing on it, I focused the moonlight into the crest on the helm. The armor hummed to life, power shifting and glimmering along its surface. Around me, the other suits awoke to tenor and baritone.

We drew an audience. Wary elves and curious drakes emerged, first as a trickle, then a flood, until the outer courtyard filled.

"Excellent! We can begin the preliminary trial now and allow it to grow accustomed to the wearer." My Pîntellum pulsated in response to my voice, filling me with a sense of accomplishment.

I stripped and armored myself. After a brief embrace, Feanim and Celebel did the same. Rafael's eyes were hot on me, his discomfort a thorn in my mind.

'These are merely bodies,' I sent. *'Treat them like an academic study.'*

He huffed, but his energy settled.

I waited to don the helm so I wouldn't be smothered if recognition failed. The Pîntellum squelched around me as I clapped each piece into place, a strange and not entirely pleasant sensation. It adhered directly to my skin, minimizing the need for straps and closures. The membrane warmed quickly, melding to my form and to itself; a single cushiony fascia from neck to toe. I radiated my presence throughout it, letting it soak up and adapt to my consciousness. A mild tingling rippled over my skin.

Experimentally, I moved my arms. The armor was impossibly light, even for þilvor. The Pîntellum worked! Pride flushed my ear tips. Celebel and Feanim stood still in their suits, spirit flowing around them in gentle waves as they adapted.

Laughing, I gave Rafael a spin. "How do I look?"

"Like you have no idea how to fight in that," he grumbled.

"As though I ever have." I smacked his arm. Padded by the Pîntellum, my þilvor-coated hand did not sting on contact. For the first time ever.

His eyebrows shot up.

"Better than you expected?" Triumphant, I planted my hands on my hips with a broad grin. The þilvor chimed faintly in response.

"Hrrm. You might be able to bruise with enough effort."

I immediately threw a punch at his face. He deflected my hand. I danced around him, giggling and throwing jabs. My body was amazingly light and strong.

"This is incredible!" The armor flexed like leathers. Restrictive still, but far more comfortable than plate.

Rafael blocked every strike I aimed at him as though swatting an annoying fly. He caught me as I spun past and lifted me off my feet.

He held my forearm to his mouth. "Would you like a bite test?"

Squealing and kicking, I held up my palms in surrender, and he put me down.

Feanim watched dourly. "This is the strangest fucking foreplay I've ever witnessed. Cel, spar with me."

I looked over to see Celebel absolutely resplendent in his radiant armor. It hugged his body in delicious ways. I drank in the sight of him, and didn't need our shared connection to feel Rafael's dismay. Nimthil was staring, similarly enrapt, at Feanim. Appearance aside, it would necessitate a soulbond for anyone to find that sour troll attractive. But then, she probably thought the same of my reaction to Rafael.

Nimthil's ear still bled, dripping steadily down her neck to soak the collar of her gown and seep into the bodice. Well, that was at least one gown in her possession no longer dyed green. I resisted the urge to tell her to keep pressure on the wound. With its countless tiny vessels, a cut to the ear could gush for a long time if not properly staunched. I understood her reactions to Rafael, little as I liked them, but she deserved the humbling for her insults toward Nemohee.

"No actual sparring yet," I called. "Let it grow accustomed to you first."

"The worst part is folding your ears under," Celebel said. With a shared glance, both Consuls donned their helms.

When they displayed no signs of labored breathing, I did the same. Stifling at first, I almost panicked as the membrane covered my face, but it adjusted almost instantly, opening around my nostrils and mouth. The lengthy bulk of my hair, plaited into a single braid and coiled on the back of my head, fit nicely under the helm with its domed peak. The armor's enhanced strength made its weight negligible. Celebel was right. The worst bit was the way the helm pinned my ears together over my head.

The membrane also stretched across the eyes, transparent, to give extra protection without blocking vision. Hazing across my sight as I blinked, it settled into place and cleared with no discomfort. Perfection! I turned back to Rafael.

"How does my voice sound?" It rang much louder than usual.

The Pîntellum absorbed the moisture of my breath, redirecting it through the rest of the membrane instead of allowing a build up near my mouth and nose. That had been Feanim's suggestion, to make maintaining the necessary hydration of the membrane easier.

"Chirp chirp," Rafael said, and I laughed again. 'Little birds', indeed.

In spite of my advice, Celebel and Feanim went at each other. Fascinated, I rooted to the spot. They tumbled and rolled in flashing, liquid quicksilver, whirling and striking faster than I'd ever seen either of them move. When they parted, neither was winded. Greatly cheered, they embraced and slapped one another on the back with chiming peals of metal on metal.

"Cúraniel, my love, this is incredible! Better than we imagined," Celebel called, his voice clear and almost giddy through his helm.

"It needs more testing, but…it does work," Feanim said begrudgingly.

Nimthil clung to his arm like a lovestruck youth, then recoiled in horror at the bloody handprints she'd inadvertently left on the shining þilvor. He patted her shoulder affectionately.

"They underestimated you," Rafael murmured behind me.

I gave him a grateful look over my shoulder. "Where is your armor?"

"I will finish it soon enough. Moranga is…unique in its challenges." He must have drawn on the volcano's power to bolster his own. That the demon ore could challenge even him fed my aversion.

Celebel clapped me on the shoulder. His armor connecting with mine rang like a bell, and the hand landed with surprising force. My Pîntellum absorbed and redirected the kinetic energy with ease.

"We'll simply have to abide with the consequences. *Won't we*, Feanim?" A steely note in Celebel's voice pricked my ears.

Chapter 12

WE stood our suits next to each other in the antechamber. Though the process of removing the armor involved as much distasteful squelching as donning it, the Pîntellum left only a hint of moisture on our skin.

"There's an unsung melody between you and Feanim about that moranga ore." I arranged myself on the moss, delighting in the feather-soft vegetation on my bare body.

With a gusty sigh, Celebel sat beside me. "It is an old contention. Our access to this fortress stems from his decisions." He groaned. "Gods, I wish Nemohee had brought more whiskey along."

"That bad, eh?"

His fingers drummed on his arm. "Feanim negotiated with the spiders to obtain the moranga ore."

"The spiders? As in the great spiders?" I had no issue with garden-variety arachnids, but the great ones were another melody entirely. "The giants that live deep under the earth, the ones we battled away from the forests after the last war? Faeglhingril's children? Those spiders?" Phantom chitinous legs skittered over my skin. I shivered, brushing off my arms.

"The very ones. He offered them some sort of exchange." Celebel's expression soured, generous lips turning down, nose crinkling.

"What…what did he offer?" I braced myself for the answer.

"I've never been able to force an admission from him, and it strikes discord within me." His fingers danced across his thigh, tapping out his thoughts.

My ears drooped. "How did they come to possess moranga in the first place? Surely spiders do no forging. What would the spiders possibly desire from us?"

From the way he ground his teeth, none of this plan had been cleared with Celebel beforehand. He leaned back on his elbows, and I waited for him to reconcile the emotions warring on his face.

"As I understand it, the spiders came upon the moranga in places where the depths of their lair touches on the boundary with the demon realm. Feanim never clarified the rest. Naturally, I protested. Most vehemently." He hissed the final sibilants though clenched teeth.

I shook my head to clear it. Even at a direct crossroads, one could not enter said demon realm without the aid of a significantly powerful demon and a soul sacrifice. The demons themselves could not leave their realm except via the occasional fool's summoning. The moranga's presence in our world made little sense, imbued as it was with demonic essence. The spiders' involvement baffled me. In truth, it all baffled me. Rafael likely held some answers, as he always did, but prying them out of him was often a useless refrain.

Celebel nodded at my confusion. "Many questions remain, yes." The sparks in his eyes confirmed my opinion. "Evidently some aspect of Feanim's bargain displeased the spiders, and they nearly retook Amrún."

"That occurred *here?*" The skin crawling sensation strengthened. Shaking my hands out, I examined the floor, expecting angry spiders to crawl up through the pitted pumice at any moment.

"Feanim worked out a method to briefly divert the lava flow from the base of the caldera down through the old tubes. It flushed out the remaining spiders living beneath us. Lovely, yes? So now we have access to both Amrún and the moranga ore." He glared so hard at the ceiling the glowing fungi turned their fruiting bodies away from him.

I opened my mouth and closed it.

"If it eases your mind, those drakes that slipped off into the caves before we entered? That was strategic to ensure no arachnid ambush awaited. Which means your Dragon is well aware of this tangled mess."

"You must be overjoyed to return to this hellhole."

Any time I began to warm to Feanim, he either found a new way to offend or I learned another awful fact about him. So far, he had done nothing except solidify my biases about that particular Duedellen lineage. Perhaps more of their company would at least provide a comparison.

"I truly do not understand how you call him 'friend'." Pulling his arms around me, I rested my head on his chest.

"At times I do not understand it myself. Am I a fool for hoping my influence will improve his behavior? I had hoped he would learn compassion, that my measured ways would counterbalance his impulsivity. His…his cruelty. We did not speak after that incident except as strictly necessary. But the previous war threw us together again, and I could not put my personal distaste before our survival." Celebel paused, pinching the bridge of his nose.

I looked up at him, tugging a lock of his hair. "Though Feanim acts in ways that could end in the deaths of many elves, solely for his gain?"

His eyebrows shot up. "You hear your own words, yes?"

I clamped my mouth shut.

Celebel held my gaze for an uncomfortably long moment before continuing. "Feanim claims to have plans upon plans. Perhaps he had always meant to court Rafael's favor with the moranga." His ears pinned back. "This would seem to be a refrain for me, this turning aside from misconduct in the name of peace." I flinched, and he gestured at the armor standing like sentinels past the open door. "Am I led astray by brilliance? Despite his wrongdoing, Feanim does show care and concern for those closest. Am I a fool to allow him continued grace?"

"You love him."

Celebel startled. "What do you mean?"

"If you didn't love him, you would never allow such things. I should know." I propped myself up and gave him a meaningful glance. "Your capacity to love a flawed person reveals a generous heart."

"Perhaps like a brother. He has certainly pushed for more in the past."

"That doesn't surprise me in the slightest. Did you ever acquiesce?" I stroked his ear, and he sighed. The thought of Feanim's hands on Celebel's silky skin turned my stomach. Much larger, long-fingered, taloned hands, though… I bit off the thought before I invented trouble.

"Not as such, no. Feanim has desire to break things in order to prove his mastery. Strange combination in one who prefers a submissive role." Celebel grew thoughtful, and I didn't press.

The image of Nimthil dominating Feanim was far more than I needed. "You'll need to either entertain or seduce me to chase away the night terrors at this rate."

Celebel laughed. "Very well." He leaned in close and breathed slowly up the length of my ear. Gods, it took so little for him to warm my body. "On the topic of submission, I would like to offer you a more receptive type than the last time. Would you accept?"

"I do." I kissed his soft lips and rose, indicating he should stay with a push to the center of his chest. Stowed in a pack, I found a good length of rope. "If you will accept being bound, lie down on your back."

With open curiosity, Celebel obeyed my order. I tugged him to the edge of the moss bed until his buttocks nearly slipped off. Standing between his legs, I tied his wrists to his ankles and spread his shapely thighs wide. His flexibility pleased me. I doubled another length of rope and stood over him. Splayed and vulnerable, his chest rose in an alluring way. The accessibility of his cock warmed my greedy center. His body had fleshed out a bit with regular rest and meals, almost back to his original lean, yet fit state. The starlight returned to his skin; his hair had regained its luxurious sheen.

"I like this vantage point."

"I quite agree." He grinned. Already an improvement.

"Does it harmonize with you to take a little pain? Nothing too intense." I waited for the nod before continuing. "Your eyes are to remain uncovered. You shall witness what's coming." I smiled sweetly, briefly crouching to kiss his lips. With a teasing slap to his cheek, I moved down his body, raking my fingernails over him.

"Should I be concerned?" he asked.

I lightly smacked him in the testicles with the rope, causing him to jump. "Did I give you permission to speak? No. If my ministrations grow too intense, call my name. Otherwise, do not speak until I allow it."

His eyes glittered as he nodded again. I spun the rope once more, connecting with his left nipple. He yelped, but his cock twitched.

As I suspected. I smacked the other nipple with the rope, then worked down his sides to his thighs. Starting with light blows, I primed my target area evenly, giving him a chance to adapt before I laid in.

Red welts rose on his legs. The physical activity heated my body, heated my lust. Our breathing sped in tandem. Celebel whimpered with each strike, but his growing erection told a different story. The noises he made brought out the latent predator in me. I wanted to destroy this beautiful man. To make him forget all sense of place, of self. To make him so desperate for release it brought tears to his eyes.

I whipped the rope down his legs to the bottoms of his feet. Careful not to break skin or truly bruise, my flogging had him arching off the bed, fighting the restraints. I popped him in the bollocks again and he moaned. Dragging the rope across his cock, he shivered with anticipation. I flicked it with a fingernail, and he cried out.

A few gentle, experimental taps with the very end of the rope, and his cock pulsed in the rhythm I created. I brushed my mouth over the dew collecting at the tip, smearing it like a cosmetic over my lips. That garnered an extended moan from him, low and throaty, striking directly at my clit.

"You're doing well."

I licked the ridge of a mark on his abdomen, stopping my tongue's progress just shy of his cock. Celebel shivered, a ripple from the tips of his ears to his toes. Spread out and welted, his body was a tender feast. Was this how Rafael viewed me?

Setting my rope aside, I nuzzled the tightened skin of his bollocks. "You deserve a reward for your endurance."

His thigh muscles trembled. Delicious.

"You may speak if you wish."

Panting, Celebel gathered himself. "I have a gift for you. Meant to bestow it after the battle, but…" He shrugged, awkward in his bonds. "The drakes retrieved it in their last recovery mission. I did not send for it specifically, for reasons that shall become obvious, but it happened to be included in a parcel." He nodded toward the entrance. "Search the trunk, underneath the scroll cases. You'll find an object wrapped in silk."

Obliging him, I returned to the trunk. Neatly organized, the fitted top tray lifted to reveal the object in question. I held aloft the silken bundle. Hefty and nearly the length of my arm, surely this was a weapon of some sort. Raising my eyebrows, I looked to my bound lover.

He grinned. "Unwrap it, please."

I tugged at the neat bow of twine and the silk slipped away. It was a phallic pleasure implement, and it could certainly be wielded as a bludgeon if the need arose. Sparkling silver motes streaked through an inky black form like a swirling galaxy in the night sky. Beautiful. And double-sided, with a swelling in the center.

I gave a low whistle of appreciation as I smacked it against my palm. It had a slight give. How had he constructed this? I did not recognize the materials. The one Rafael had given me was a boiled leather. The thought gave me a pang of loss, and I saved my distracting questions of how Celebel had procured this gift for another time.

"What do you think?" he asked anxiously from the moss bed.

"Oh, this is glorious!" I approached him, rhythmically slapping the implement in my hand. "I should like to test it on you, my lovely captive."

Celebel's smile was infectious. "Yes. Yes *please!*"

"You'll need proper warming. And no more talking." Setting the implement to one side, I shoved my hands beneath him and grabbed generous handfuls of his ass. I yanked his buttocks completely over the edge of the moss bed and spread him as wide as his tethered ankles allowed. Taking up the implement, I gave one thigh a test blow. Celebel yelped and sat half-upright. The clench of muscles in his abdomen made my clit tingle.

"It has some heft," I laughed, and tapped his testicles with it. He whimpered, and I planted a hand on his chest, shoving him back flat. Looking him over, I clucked in mock dismay. "Your welts are fading."

The implement did, in fact, make an excellent bludgeon. The dull thud of impact with Celebel's legs reverberated up my arms in ways that tightened my nipples. Each smack pulled a soft noise from him, and a little more wetness slicked my cunt. I focused primarily on his thighs and calves, almost a massage with the fast, repeated blows aimed at large muscle groups. Almost. As with the rope, I kept the force just this side of bruising.

He watched me from heavy-lidded, slightly unfocused eyes, lips parted. Fully floating under my power. Perfection.

I cupped his bollocks, laying aside my weapon, and lifted them gently. Celebel sucked in a breath. Pressing my face into him, the chiming scent of starlight mixed with the light musk of arousal filled my nose. Perfectly fresh after the Pîntellum's adherence. I licked along the tight flowerbud of his anus. He moaned, relaxing against my probing.

"You open so nicely."

Pressing past that ring of resistance, I lathed his ass with my tongue. He writhed, trying to press harder against my face. I pulled back and gave his cupped testicles a teasing swipe of my tongue. He groaned, the muscles of his chest and shoulders standing out in relief as he tried to free his arms.

Releasing his bollocks, I leaned over him and flicked each peaked nipple with a fingernail. He stared, panting, eyes dark with lust. Gods, how beautiful would he be, spread like this, with Rafael at his back to hold his arms? Red, black, and silver. Fire and night. Stony muscle and supple skin. My Dragon's soulbond twanged in warning, and I clamped it tighter.

Returning my full attention to Celebel, I gave him a good show of licking the implement. Rising over him, I pushed it against his lips. He took it deep, sucking with a gusto that soaked me. Fucking hells. The sudden need to watch him deepthroat an actual cock lit me aflame. Taking it back, I flipped the implement so he could pay the same homage to the other side. With a smirk, he wrapped his lips around it again.

Once satisfied, I pulled it away. Rising to my knees from the floor gave Celebel a nice view from his supine position on the low moss bed. I aimed the implement between my legs and worked it slowly into my cunt. He bit his lower lip, eyes bright with desire. Thicker than my wrist, the implement stretched me. I moaned. He matched his murmurs to mine.

Thoroughly coated in my juices, I held it up for him to appreciate. Then, with a grunt, I plunged the other side into my cunt. Squeezing my powerful internal muscles around it, I wielded it like my own cock. Celebel's eyes followed the quavering tip.

"Do you want me inside you?"

He looked up sharply.

"Speak." I sat back and guided the tip of the implement against his hole. He gasped and I braced my hips against his, one hand on the implement, the other stroking his hard cock. "Yes? Shall I fuck you with this?"

"Yes," he sighed, and I thrust against his ass.

He arched under me. I licked one hand to coat it, pressing a single finger ever so slowly into his anus. He hummed with pleasure, his natural lubricant mixing with my saliva and easing the way. I added a second finger, moving them incrementally apart as his cock pulsed in my hand. Withdrawing my fingers, pleased at his progress, I guided the tip into him.

Celebel bucked, shoving himself farther down than I intended, and slamming the other end of the implement deep inside me. The friction lit me up with need, and I cried out. I braced myself and we found a steady rhythm. I slapped my hips against his buttocks, burying the surrogate cock inside us both, and worked his cock with both hands.

Ecstasy streaked across his face like lightning as I pounded him. He fought the ropes, trying to reach for me. Ah, there it was; tears shone in his eyes. Pressure built, my crescendo rose, and I held it back until his cock began to throb. With a final crash into him, he came hard, calling my name as his seed spurted across his chest and belly.

My climax took me, shuddering against him with a loud cry as I broke apart. Orgasmic waves torrented through me, filling me with such intense pleasure my vision went momentarily black. Gasping, I wailed and writhed, caught in the rip current.

I came to, ears ringing, draped over Celebel's knees. Moving gingerly, I withdrew the implement from both of our bodies and dropped it in the hot spring stream. The water swelled around its new island, rinsing away the evidence of our passion. I released him from the restraints. He straightened his legs with a groan and sprawled out, boneless. Crawling over him, I pushed sweaty hair back from his face.

His eyes sparkled in a way I hadn't seen in ages.

"How do you feel, Starshine?" I kissed his forehead. "Shall I clean you?"

"Mmm." He stretched, arms coming around to hold me against him. "Wash and braid my hair?"

I rolled off him, trying to shove my arms beneath his body from the side.

He sat up, ears twitching. "What are you doing?"

"Well, I was going to carry you, but I cannot get the leverage."

Laughing, Celebel swatted my hands away. "Are you mad?"

"Recall, I carried you to the very top of my hill as dead weight." I made a show of flexing my arms, not that it revealed any particularly toned muscle. "I am stronger than I appear, sir."

Chapter 13

WITH some drake assistance in gathering materials, the Consulate pushed forward on outfitting select elves with new armor. The forge rang day and night. The greenhouse provided both the light and heat needed to grow Pîntellum samples, and they progressed at a far more rapid pace than my windowsill provided. After hardly more than a fortnight, Nemohee and Lámirië showed off their shining suits, along with six others I had not officially met: Astolar and two other Lachanaur.

Ensconced in their smithing, neither Feanim nor Rafael emerged. The occasional argument between them drifted into the courtyard; Feanim's sharp tenor ricocheting off the Dragon's implacable bass. I spared a moment of sympathy for any other smiths trapped in there with those two.

Nemohee bounded over to me like an eager puppy. "The brawn and flexibility in this armor is incredible! I cannot wait to test this in the field!"

I couldn't recall the last time þey'd been so excited. The contrast of the shining þilvor with þeir fiery hair made an impactful image. "It suits you. Your eyes are glowing."

Þey performed an impromptu cartwheel. "I could never guide that in armor afore!"

"Aye, you ought to always trip over those tiny pegs you call feet," I teased.

Þey responded by propping an aforementioned tiny peg on my shoulder and stretching.

I laughed and shoved off þeir heel.

"I simply cannot believe the range of motion. I'm apt to have to relearn howfur to fight with all this freedom!"

It had never occurred to me some might have to adapt their

styles around the flexible new armor, versus the much heavier and more restrictive armor to which they were accustomed. Then again, the new armor added strength and flexibility. Nemohee watched my face.

"Aye, exactly. We'll be taking up a fair lot of training exercises in the field," þey said. "Didn't Big Red gain a fresh set, too?"

"He's been very secretive about his demon ore armor." I tugged a lobe. "It seems to be slow going. I've had no hint of it yet."

"I've had bare enough hint of you as well." Nemohee gave me a pointed stare.

I winced. "My apologies. I've been so swept up in the discordance of these men, I've lost the melody of my life." Such an understatement. Where had my independence flown off to?

Nem clapped me on the shoulder. "Remember to surface for air, aye? Big Red especially burns it all from every room he occupies." Eyebrows raised, þey waited for my tacit acknowledgment. "At the least, knowing what's hiding under these uglies attacking us gives me some note of hope. The Fomorians were unknowns, but the sidhe? Aye, I know them all too well. I'll raze Underhill and drive them to the hells if I must. This here armor will help me pound them into pulp." Þilvor chimed as þey smacked a balled-up fist into an open palm.

"How far would I go to rescue a soulmate?" I mused aloud. Hard to say, but from Nemohee's blazing silver eyes, tearing Vaeda apart from the inside out was a viable option.

Nemohee sighed and shuffled closer. "You need this." Digging in the pockets of the wool cloak þey'd discarded to try on the armor, þey produced a hip flask, carefully obscuring it from the others.

I took a swig and almost coughed. "Whiskey," I signed, incredulous.

A sharp-toothed smile split my friend's face. "Aye, I'd some downtime after we arrived, so I set up a still. Damned glacier has its uses. Cools and condenses the vapors right quick, it does, with a nice high proof. Been eating the excess grain for my morning meal." Nemohee made a show of kissing þeir biceps. "To yer question, I reckon you'd fight the gods themselves if either of your insufferable blighters were taken."

"Celebel is not insufferable." Rafael, I could not defend.

The Lachanaur pursed þeir lips. "No-o-o, surely not. No member of the peerage is ever insufferable." Þey threw a couple of punches at the air in Celebel's direction.

My ears twitched. "Oh, come now. I was once a member of the peerage."

"Mmm, that you still are." Þeir eyes narrowed.

I slumped in defeat. "Too immersed in it now. I hear myself. Nem, what has become of my free spirit?"

"Well," Nem pointed at my feet, "ye've taken to wearing shoes. First sign of domestication, that is."

Self-conscious, I shuffled my low, soft boots across flagstones.

Þey offered me another surreptitious taste of the firewater, and I accepted gratefully. "Truly, I worry. I watch ye bending, changing yerself to harmonize for others. Rafael is a foul-tempered prick betimes, aye, but he is indubitably himself. His Lordship Celebel vacillates, trying to please everyone. I know cultivated political neutrality when I hear it. He should've taken up for ye at Férioth. Loses his voice in the chorus, I think. Don't ye go losing yours trying to be like him. I'd plunge into the hells to save Cael, but if I contorted myself into someone else to do it, he'd not want me when it was all done. Nor would I."

Swishing the whiskey in my mouth, I nodded, enjoying the burn. "I've played this note, and now I must perform the entire sonata. No releasing the Dragon into the wind now."

A scrub jay called, and I spun toward the sound. No, not a scrub jay. One of Feanim's crows eyed me from its perch above the forge. Homesickness rushed in under a realization so pointed I hugged myself to quell the sudden tears.

"I can never go home again, Nem. It ceased to exist. The Great Tree stands, but I cannot return to isolation after all of this."

"I was wondering when you'd figure that out. And no, none of us can." Nemohee handed me the flask. "Tip it back."

The liquor stung my throat but I did as instructed, coughing into the back of my hand. How selfish of me; my Tree would weather it all, barring some world-shattering cataclysm. The war had left thousands displaced, their homes destroyed, loved ones and soulbonds lost, clinging to the last vestiges of ancient ways.

I wiped my face. "Enough feeling sorry for myself. How might I best support you?"

Nemohee scrubbed a hand through þeir hair, making the shorn locks stand on end. "Eh, find me for a drink here and again, and let us leave all thoughts of soulmates at the threshold."

"Done."

"I am loath to leave your side." Lámirië's voice pricked my ears. I swayed as I turned; crow, that was powerful stuff. Across the way, she spoke to Celebel. "Who will guard you in my stead now?"

Celebel gestured to me, smiling when he realized I was watching. "Cúraniel makes for a fierce enough guard, especially with a dragon at her back." He took her hands. "Worry not. Such precautions hardly matter without even a court to hold. I need you to direct this mission, my loyal friend."

We naturally gathered around him, his starlight drawing us in.

Addressing the group, Celebel said, "Lámirië will lead a small team to Taloth to meet with our Siltaur allies and discuss trade and reinforcements. Should be only six or seven days' ride at a reasonable pace. While in the area, you will also sweep that northwest corridor and report on enemy movement. The Red Dragon has selected two drakes to accompany you—"

A chorus of protests rose.

He raised his hands, waiting patiently until it died down. "I understand the reluctance, but we must learn to better coordinate our forces. We are spread far too thin to remain segregated, and this is a chance to test our cooperation." Celebel gestured toward the forge. "My Lord Dragon," he called, "would you join us?"

With a grumble and the clang of a hammer, Rafael strode into the courtyard. He barked a command into the air. Momentarily, a pair of drakes entered. Boshkt and the stocky brown *viigsakh* named Grenyk.

"These two have suitable temperaments. You have one fluent elvish speaker," Rafael said as the drakes approached. Boshkt certainly wasn't fluent, so the speaker had to be Grenyk. "They will assist in battle or drudgery as needed."

Grenyk made introductions for itself and Boshkt. The *viigsakh* had a surprisingly soothing voice. Almost high enough to be called baritone and buttery smooth, it held only a hint of the usual underlying growl. The relaxed manner of the drakes helped to calm the anxious knot of elves, and soon introductions flew all around. The set of Celebel's ears declared he was pleased with himself.

Preparations finalized with the swiftness of long experience. Lámirië mounted a palomino destrier, curried to a sun-bright sheen, and led her party through the gates. The pair of drakes chatted amiably as they departed, though the elves kept their ears swiveled. Everyone quieted crossing the suspension bridge. Pregnant grey clouds hung low over their departure.

"The lull was right pleasant while it lasted," Nemohee said, searching the skies for signs of harpies.

Chapter 14

ELEBEL woke me. The dream, a reiteration of the monstrous chalice vision, lay over the room etched in palimpsest. I squeezed handfuls of the moss beneath me, reassuring myself it was healthy and not full of rot. Chittering growls whispered in my ears.

His musical baritone cut through the internal noise. "The crows bring tidings. Come." My soulmate had already dressed, a wool coat over fine trousers.

I cast about for a pair of shoes, finally locating them beside the outer door. In my delirious state, I pulled them on before adding trousers. Cursing, I kicked them off and re-started dressing. I'd never grow accustomed to habitually wearing shoes.

"Cúraniel, please. Make haste."

Shaking my head did little to clear my senses. "Coming, coming."

I trotted along after him through the halls, buttoning my coat and finger-combing my unruly hair into a simple braid. Recognizing the path to the healer's wing woke me fully. The tingling brush of a dampening field as we entered perked my ears.

The many-vaulted ceiling, layered with witchlight chandeliers, illuminated Feanim, Nimthil, and a Duedellen scout with their backs to us. They parted to reveal a group of *children*.

Filthy, bedraggled, terrified children, ranging from babes in arms to a single slightly older boy barely into adolescence. Most were hardly past their toddling stage. Eäriel sat among them, binding one girl's arm.

The smaller children clustered like frightened goslings around an older Talithiri boy with the signature midnight-black hair and skin of New Moon lineage. Rarest of all my kin, I hadn't encountered a member of the New Moon branch since long before my departure from Leyûduin. My own Crescent Moon branch, with our pale skin and black hair, made up the majority. Silver-haired, pale Full Moons like Silfanië comprised about a third. I shivered at the thought of her. My distant cousin peered at us with huge, haunted eyes so dark I could not plumb their depths.

My ears drooped. I hadn't encountered an elvish child in thousands of years. The last infant I'd laid hands on had been human; one of the Ardhanë in the village near my hill. With no ability to tap into their spirit, they'd often called on me to assist with difficult births. That had been a full two seasons before Celebel appeared in my life.

Too many thoughts all at once. "Why are children here?" I blurted.

Feanim turned to me. "My crows found them wandering the lava fields. I sent Rhoscellen to retrieve them before they ran afoul of a patrolling drake."

Rhoscellen, the Duedellen scout, gave me a slight bow. Long curls of blue-black hair slid forward over wiry shoulders, and aspen leaf-golden eyes sparkled under thick lashes. She had a beautifully strong nose. "They claim to have fled Velúara, my lady."

The honorific surprised me almost as much as the news. "There were children left behind in Velúara?" My ears twitched with confusion. "Would someone please tell me what the fuck is happening?"

One of the little ones whimpered. Nimthil glared at me, perhaps offended at my cursing in front of impressionable children.

"Velúara was unsuitable as a military base, located too far from the epicenter of the conflict with the Fomorians." She spoke slowly, exaggerating her signs as if I were the child. "We agreed, however, that its impenetrable defenses were far more suitable as a refuge to protect the children than Férioth. Celebel and I drew forth a great chorus. We folded our spirit around each of them to form a chrysalis, holding them in a slumbering stasis beneath the gestation grove until the war ended. The trees provide them all the succor they require."

Given the trees themselves had birthed many, if not all, of these children, her melody harmonized. What were we to do with them? Here at Amrún, the older children would fare well enough, but we were woefully unprepared to house and care for infants and toddlers. Or at least I was. Gods, they'd fill every nook in the wing.

"Enough chatter." Celebel pressed past me to sit with the

children. A toddler immediately climbed onto his lap, and the rest piled around him like kittens. "Rest now, my brave little ones. You've all done so well. You are safe."

The eldest boy curled up at his side. Silvery waves radiated from my soulmate's skin, soothing the young elves. Some of the smallest fell asleep. Satisfied at their repose, Celebel hugged the children close.

"Now we may speak without upsetting them further." He shot me a glare.

I raised my palms in surrender. "I know nothing of children. Why did you desire my presence here?"

"I asked for you," Eäriel's sing-sing voice lilted over the clustered children to me. "I assumed they'd have more injuries than I could treat alone, but I believe I've tended to the worst of it. Mostly, they need rest and sustenance."

"Some small tidings, then."

No doubt they would need comfort for their mental distress, but it would not, could not, come from me. I hadn't a single maternal impulse. Children made me nervous with their unpredictably loud outbursts.

Celebel addressed the New Moon boy directly. "Let me lead your song, little one. How were you separated from the guardians we assigned to watch over you? Fear not for your focus and strength, I will find the pitch. Harmonize with me."

He sang. Low, sweet notes wove around the children. He encouraged their quavering voices, probing until he matched pitch. Continuing in a drone, he amplified and raised their song. Eäriel added a harmony of vitality, her soprano dancing around Celebel's baritone. I sang the note in my alto, joining the rest. Together, we eased the burden of memory from the children, adding their knowledge to the shared song.

Celebel's hands moved, weaving together shimmering threads experience. Images coalesced, sharpening into focus as the sound filtered in.

Hestalön, the boy was called. A shudder woke him, fissures appearing in his glowing chrysalis beneath the birth tree. Spirit leaked from the protective cocoon. With a swimming motion, he caught hold of the opening, pulling it apart into motes of light. By design, the surrounding roots creaked apart, granting him the first breath of air since stasis.

He crawled out of the ground and froze. A group of unfamiliar elves stood a short distance away, facing another tree. They hadn't noticed him, swaying together in eerie song. Something atonal in that melody. Something wrong. The tree, an elm, flailed as though it had been uprooted.

Not Fomorians breaching the walls. Elves. My stomach dropped to my feet. Glancing about the room revealed every adult ear flattened.

The group moved from tree to tree, singing their discordant song. Hestalön backed into the tunnel, pulled the roots closed over his head, and watched. Each tree that received the wretched melody shook, glowing from within. A sickly light.

Nights and days passed this way. The group appeared, performed their twisted concert, and the trees groaned. The boy worried at his fingernails until they bled, biting them to the quick. After what seemed like an age, the elves did not return.

Hestalön waited until dusk, a full day after the last appearance, to emerge. His movements were slow, uncoordinated; a fawn learning to walk. First, he checked the other chrysalises. Spirit rose from their subterranean nests in slow plumes, like morning fog from a lake.

"Talaossë! Arundel," he called softly, padding through the grove. "Suvanal?" The guards should have been there to greet him upon waking. Rounding a corner, he found Talaossë's crumpled form. Dead eyes stared at the sky.

Clapping his hand over a scream, Hestalön stumbled backward. Arms wrapped him, and he struggled.

"Calm, calm," gentle hands signed. Arundel. "Only me, no others. Make no sound." The Talithiri guard turned the boy to face him. "You unharmed? Good. We wake others."

"What happens?" Hestalön signed with hands gone rigid with

disuse. He coughed into his shoulder and swallowed hard.

"Bad things." Arundel clutched his side, jogging to the nearest tree. His hands fluttered. "Help pull." He dug at the roots, plunging his entire upper body into the dirt to tear away the filaments of spirit. With a brief struggle, he pulled back with an infant in his arms.

Hestalön approached a birch and did as the guard instructed. His efforts brought forth a toddling girl. Side-by-side, they approached each gestation tree, and more children joined them. Most were far too young to assist, and Arundel assigned the next oldest to keep the littlest safely corralled.

They'd worked through a third of the trees when a maple swayed wildly, leaves falling all at once in a cascading shush. Hestalön and Arundel watched in rapt horror as the trunk bulged outward. Limbs slumped, their tips blackening and raking across the ground.

The tree bent and groaned, splintering in vertical lines up the trunk. In a gross parody of birth, the bark and heartwood burst open, spewing out an oozing, grey bundle.

The vision! I fought down bile, hugging my arms. My breath came fast and shallow, laced with dread. Around me, the others stared at the illusory memory in rapt horror, ears twitching with distress.

"Back away. No touch," Arundel warned, signing in harsh slashes.

An elflike creature of adult size tore through its amniotic sac with pointed digits like withered branches. Slick, mottled grey skin stretched over a seemingly eyeless, earless face. A maw of needle-pointed teeth split its head, and it shrieked.

Another tree flailed, swelling, and another. Soon, the entire grove writhed. A redwood bowed and split open. More nascent monsters spewed forth, adding their eerie cries to the rest.

Hestalön covered his ears, and the smaller children screamed.

Arundel grabbed his arm, dragging him backward, out of the fell creatures' reach. "Gather others. Flee!"

The boy signed in wild swoops. "Rest trapped under grove!"

Arundel gave up on stealth with a harsh whisper. "Hestalön, go! I will rescue as many as I may and meet you at the north gate. Do not wait past the moon's zenith. If any of these abominations reach you first, you must flee. Follow the river Erëlen north to its source. If I cannot join you—" The boy's lip quivered, and Arundel clapped both hands on his shoulders. "No time for that. If I cannot join you, find the crows. They will lead you to safety. Stay silent, stay hidden." He turned and charged toward the emerging monstrosities.

With a choked sob, Hestalön herded the children toward the gate. Behind him, the chorus of grating cries grew.

The image dissipated into mist, revealing Celebel's ashen face behind it. His expression mirrored our collective dread. Smoothing poor Hestalön's midnight hair, he dropped a gentle kiss on the top of the brave child's head.

I couldn't stop shivering.

"No word from Arundel," he signed in silence. Small wonder none of the group sustained serious injuries. Those unfortunates wouldn't have survived the arduous journey. Just as when the drakes had consumed our wounded after battle; another hard lesson in false hope.

I swallowed bile.

RAFAEL AWAITED us in the war room. A creeping unease gripped my belly. I hadn't thought to shield our bond. How would he react to the children?

Nimthil skirted the room, arranging herself to watch everyone's lips. She paused warily when she realized her position put her within Rafael's reach. He sneered at her, and she sidled away.

"Velúara is compromised, yes?" The Dragon's sharp eyes landed on Celebel's face.

"Who told—" Nimthil began.

Rafael cut her off with a slash of one taloned hand. "Do not insult me. Why did they flee your grand, unbreachable city?"

"The traitors," Feanim said. At glares from Celebel and the Lachanaur queen, he added, "Our allies must know of this. The children witnessed elves corrupting the gestation groves. It must be Feledhor and his ilk, but to what end?"

Hearing it spoken so bluntly sucked all the air from the room and I swayed on my feet. Rafael's eyes flicked briefly to me and back to Feanim.

The Duedellen held his gaze. "Yes, Velúara is compromised."

"Why would Feledhor allow the children to escape? Hmm. Either their early waking interrupted his fell plan, or someone else directs this evil." Celebel planted his palms on the table's edge, leaning heavily on his hands. His hair slipped forward, partially obscuring his face.

"Is kinslaying a universal taboo among your kind?" Rafael said. "Perhaps others mean to depose you. Are those in smaller enclaves resentful of your precious cities?"

Nimthil's hands slashed the air. "Perhaps they believe us corrupted by *you*." She glared daggers at the Dragon.

"Would you like a matching notch on the other ear?"

"Rafael, do not—" Feanim and I voiced simultaneous protests.

"Rafael, now is not the time—"

Celebel slapped the table, silencing the room. "You heard the boy. They've corrupted the very trees. We cannot allow them to use our sacred groves to birth abominations. If Hestalön's memory is accurate, then the traitors are truly lost to us. As they are lost, so is Velúara. They know it far too well."

Every word he spoke drove a spike into my chest. Elves corrupting the trees. Elves abetting an enemy bent on the annihilation of our own kind.

"Worse awaits if they return to fortify and use it against us. If we had the numbers, perhaps we could yet hold it, but we do not. It would have been a strain even before our forces were halved. The defection has forced this new melody." Celebel took a shuddering breath. "We must burn Velúara."

"W-what do you mean, 'burn Velúara'?" The words rolled

clumsily in my mouth.

Burn the last and greatest Talithiri city? Celebel's ancestral seat of power? Its destruction would ring a death knell for elvish culture of all nations. Unthinkable. Thousands upon thousands of years of history resided in its hallowed halls. I was suddenly, unbearably forlorn for not having visited since my youth.

"Cel, let's not be hasty." Feanim laid a cautious hand on his fellow Consul's shoulder. "I hate to surrender another stronghold so easily. Perhaps we can simply dismantle its defenses, render it useless."

Rafael groaned, all ears fixing on him. "Much as I loathe the admission, Celebel is correct. Unveil Velúara, and I will raze it within a day."

"No. Not you." Celebel's face swung up, hard eyes meeting the Dragon's. "If my grandfather kept you from our walls, I will not dishonor his memory."

Rafael opened his mouth, but Feanim slammed a fist on the table before he could speak, and I jumped.

"Fuck, I hate this." The Duedellen rapped his knuckles along the edge. "But we cannot function with our ears swiveled for the rest of our lives, always waiting for that bolt between the shoulders. We must destroy it so utterly it cannot be used against us."

"What of the library? The coffers?" Nimthil asked, hands fluttering in nervous sign. "Likely already looted, but we must at least attempt to salvage as much as possible."

Thoughts and emotions crowded too thickly, stilling my tongue. It happened more often as of late. Celebel bowed his head. I breathed slowly as his pain washed over me.

What would it mean for the future of elvish society to cut away its great beating heart? I desperately wished to be back on my hill, to have learned nothing of this awful war. To return home. What did it speak about my character, that the idea of losing the eternal city was somehow more devastating, more real to me than the elvish lives lost?

"This is my burden to bear. I could never ask such a thing of another. I will recover what I may, but it must be done." His shoulders trembled.

"You are truly noble," I finally managed to say, and he took my hand.

All the paintings, the fine glass, the tapestries and sculpture, the rare plant cultivars, the massive collection of books and scrolls. Oh, there was so much to lose. I was crying before I realized it. Celebel let his tears fall. Nimthil sniffled, hiding her face behind a belled sleeve. Thankfully, Rafael made no comment on the emotional display.

I struggled to get my voice under control. "How may I be of aid?"

Celebel composed himself, wiping his face. "I need but a few extra sword arms and all the horses. We shall depart at dawn."

"Cel, come now. You cannot empty the stables," Feanim protested.

Celebel shot him a quelling glare. "Can't I? How else do you propose we carry out what remains?" He glanced across the table. "Ideally, that would include a drake, as we will have a troublesome time breaching the walls without dragonfire. *Not* your dragonfire," he added before Rafael could interject.

The Dragon rumbled, drawing out the sound as if nothing had ever annoyed him more. "Cúraniel, meet me by the barracks." He swept out of the room.

Celebel and I made for our chambers. The instant he crossed the threshold, Celebel rushed about, gathering supplies. I tried to help, but mostly hampered, and finally sat down out of the way.

"Caladris and Nemohee will join me," he said. "Perhaps a cupful of others."

"Caladris *and* Nemohee?" My ears twitched.

"Is there a problem?" Celebel paused, concern creasing his face.

Ah, he'd been unconscious during that exchange. "Warn Nem first. Caladris shares an almost perfect likeness with Cael."

He signed assent, turning back to his packing.

"Perhaps I should join you on the excursion," I ventured.

"It is far too dangerous." Celebel stuffed neatly rolled clothing into a rucksack. "I want you here, safe. And also available to curtail any of Rafael's devilry.

I nodded, knowing full well I had no useful skills to offer in such company. "Of course, my love. Whatever you need. Is there anything else I can do?"

"Left unchecked, I worry about the lack of compassion between him and Feanim. Perhaps you could attempt to know Feanim better? It would be to everyone's benefit. Don't flatten your ears. I know how he's treated you, and I know it's unfair."

I tried and failed to relax my ears. "If it would put your mind at ease, I'll try anything."

Chapter 18

VELÚARA pricked at my consciousness, a slow bleed of grief. The fading light painted the barracks at the outer wall in orange and purple, the smooth stone gleaming like a second sunset. At the sight of my tear-streaked face, Rafael led me to where his second slumbered under the eaves.

"I will remain here with you, and Marron will go in my place," he said.

The green drake wore his half-dragon form, wingless and almost twice his usual size. Ram's horns curled from his armored skull. Steam vented from a grate in the ground, drifting lazily around him. He drowsed, wrapped into a ball of forest scales, with the tip of his blunt snout tucked under his tail. *Like a cat, how cute!*

In draconian, Rafael said, "Wake," and kicked Marron's side with a balled-up foot.

Marron grunted. "Just ate. Need good sleep." The green drake's gravelly voice dropped even deeper in this form, like the very mountains grinding together.

My ears buzzed with the resonance, and I avoided considering his meal. Rafael kicked him again.

Marron shook himself with a grunt, scales rattling, and opened his ruby eyes. "Hrrgh. Leave off, *Jxxysysdfynn.*"

"Jyxafendian. Jyxsden?" I stretched my ears to catch the syllables of Rafael's draconian name, but they eluded me as always. "Jaxsdryfen? Fuck. I'll stay with 'Jax'."

Rafael's glare harpooned me to the spot, and my ear tips flushed. Crow, I hadn't meant to speak aloud.

"Sleep later," he snarled at Marron. "Listen to Cúraniel now." The guttural rumble made a strange shape of my name.

The somnolent drake turned lambent red eyes on me. Discomfort crept along my spine. Rafael folded his arms and stepped back.

"Speak elvish," Marron said. "I will respond thus. Lack of lip dexterity." To demonstrate, his scaled lip curled along the length of his snout, granting us a brief glimpse of his forest of teeth.

I nodded. "Sorry for disturbing your slumber."

He blinked and raised horned brows in obvious annoyance.

I continued quickly. "Celebel needs to assemble a small group to raze…an abandoned elvish city." Suddenly shaky from the enormity of the request, I forced the words out. "The task would be much simpler with dragonfire. We beg your assistance in this matter."

"Which one is Celebel? All your names sound alike." Marron stretched and yawned wide enough to show off each of the daggerlike teeth in his long jaws. Talons scraped on flagstones. He might as well have clawed directly into my spine for the effect it had.

Rafael snorted. "They may as well all be named 'Lalaliel'."

"Celebel is my other soulmate." I glared at my Dragon, but his expression was unrepentant. "The one he calls '*nekarazzi*'." Fucking '*badger*.' It would be humorous if it were not so pointed.

Marron cocked his head, suddenly fully alert, and looking at both of us with a careful eye. "Ah, the striped one." He crossed his front paws, resting his chin on them, furthering the feline comparison.

My fingers twitched with the urge to scratch behind his horns. Rafael's mental scoff raked over me.

The green drake's eyes closed as though falling asleep again. As I opened my mouth to prod him, he spoke in a deceptively lazy tone. "What is the benefit to me?" One eye cracked open. "And which city?"

"Vel-Velúara." Nothing motivated a dragon like gold, but I was leery of striking a deal. "Celebel will surely negotiate some amount of riches for you to keep if you assist." Or so I hoped.

He swirled a talon on the ground. "Riches, eh? Actual riches or elf nonsense? Trees, paintings of trees, and such."

"Gold, jewels, and weapons. Not only elf nonsense," I conceded with a laugh.

"Strange position for you, Rraysth." Marron cast a cautious look at Rafael, who scowled harder. The green drake's talons clacked rhythmically on the stone. "Turning down both the treasure and the chance to burn the place."

"You will not speak on it," Rafael growled low in his throat, hostility spiking.

Marron bowed his head in submission. I touched the Dragon's arm, mindful of the heat radiating from him.

'*Do not interfere,*' he snarled in my head, and I snatched my hand away as if burned. "Make your decision," he said aloud at the green drake.

Marron tossed his head, rattling his scales again. "Very well. What was his name? Kelbo?"

"Celebel. He would be honored to by your presence, Marron." The casual manner in which we discussed the fall of my people left me hollow, almost floating above my body.

"Kel-eh-bell." He snorted. "Elves. Yes, we will pound out details. Are you claiming—" he said something that sounded like 'offering' or perhaps 'tithe,' directing the question to Rafael "—when I return?"

"Depends on your harvest." Rafael's face was unreadable.

"Mmm, very well." Marron stretched, giving me a lolling grin. The movement revealed a mud pit bubbling beneath him. "But I am too sated and drowsy to shift."

"Celebel will be fine with this form." I resisted the urge to pat his snout.

'*What is wrong with you?*' Rafael's voice rang in my head like a death knell.

'*You, of all people, should appreciate that I find dragons cute.*' That was the wrong response, given the poisonous look he shot Marron. The green drake recoiled, backing away. '*Calm yourself! I find snakes and lizards charming as well. Will you hunt them all down out of jealousy?*'

Rafael's eyes flickered red as he turned his glare on me.

'*Please, Dragon. I mean no offense. I harbor no attraction to Marron, and didn't intend to imply otherwise.*'

Marron rose to all four feet as he glanced between us, clearly discomfited by the tension. Heavy muscles quivered in anticipation of a fight. With a furious scowl, Rafael held my gaze for a moment longer. Finally, he exhaled and visibly relaxed. The green drake relaxed as well, and I let out the breath I'd been holding.

"Take as many scrolls as you can, along with your own treasures. That will be my tithe," Rafael said.

Marron bobbed his horned head. I tried to look apologetic as Rafael stormed off.

Chapter 16

RAFAEL perched on the battlements, brooding in the darkness. I'd wanted to spend the intervening time with Celebel, to bolster him for the emotionally arduous journey, but the Dragon's volatile temperament took precedence.

"Go on and pluck his scales out," Marron had said. "The Red only shows contrition after you lay into him. Not even Vaerra has much luck with that one, and she's a far more fearsome presence than I."

I climbed the long flight of stairs to reach the Dragon. He sat on a crenel in the wall, looking out over the landscape. The first wisps of a pink aurora tickled the night, mirrored in a distant glacial lake like a bright gem in a dark tapestry. Biting wind whipped around us.

"What has you in such a foul mood?" Carefully, I brushed his hair back from his face, tucking it behind the short point of his ear.

"All of this," he said bluntly.

"I should think you would be pleased to have Celebel away, and f-for…" I swallowed the knot in my throat. "For Velúara to fall."

"One more aspect of this foolish war that brings you sorrow." Rafael softened and wrapped an arm around me. "I did not expect it to affect you so, as you willingly left your cities behind."

I leaned against his thigh. "That does not mean I hold no love for them. I was simply ill-suited to live there. I am still Talithiri, and Velúara was our last bastion of civilization. As it falls, so does my nation. I cannot imagine an elf exists anywhere, traitors notwithstanding, who does not hold that city in special regard. Our dirge rises in chorus; I am not so unique among my kind."

"And yet, here you are."

"Here I am." I kissed the corner of his jaw. "Better or worse?"

He rumbled and looked at me. "You occasionally put me at ease. When you are not trying my patience."

"You enjoy a challenge," I teased.

"As do you." He almost smiled. Almost.

It was a comforting and well-worn routine, arguing over who was the more obstinate. I reached down to touch his bare feet. The scales were almost invisible, seamless with his skin unless I squinted, but the rougher texture bit pleasingly at my palm. Perhaps he needed to shed. It always made him irritable. Evidently, the baths were quite helpful in that regard, but coaxing him into the water was a different struggle.

He stared off into the distance again.

Anything was preferable to dwelling on the fall of Velúara. "I didn't mean to imply I found Marron attractive, but if I had?"

Rafael's attention snapped to me, the arch of his nose wrinkling in disgust.

"Focus your ears. I am not implying any actual attraction! This is a hypothetical. What would you have done to Marron if my answer had been different? Or to any other poor soul with no bond for protection?"

His eyes narrowed dangerously. "Why should I suffer another rival to live? Have I not endured enough humiliation?" The building growl raised the fine hairs on the back of my neck.

"Dragon, you know I love you. Hurt and humiliation have never been my intent. If you think so poorly of me, why do you stay by my side?" I touched his cheek.

Rafael closed his eyes, drawing in a ragged breath. "It is... difficult...hrrm, to know you love *him*." The register of his voice dropped so deep I could barely hear it over the vibrations in my skull. My belly tightened with the return of the cyclical argument. "You would not feel such sorrow about losing an abandoned city if he did not also mourn it. I hate the way you smile at him, the way you reached for *him* when I held you after your collapse."

The heavy muscles of his shoulders and arms rippled, hands balling into tight fists. Blood trickled where his talons pierced his palms. The wind stole the steam.

"Oh, my Dragon, why must you assume my love for Celebel means less for you?" I cupped his face with my hands, trying to smooth his furrowed brow with my thumbs. "No one could ever take your place.

Your life has granted you no assurances. I know this, but true love is not a finite resource. Until you understand it, I'll sing this refrain as many times as I must." I kissed the corners of his mouth. "I love you desperately. My body responds instinctively to your touch."

His eyes opened, flames curling around slit pupils gone wide in the night. "And if I grant your wish and fuck you as you desire, will you tire of me?"

"How could I? I would break myself to pieces against you and still beg for more." An unwanted memory superimposed my thoughts. *"We all witness the way you fall at his feet."*

"Hrrm, I prefer your begging." He pulled me onto his lap, drawing a dampening field around us like a veil. From the tint, light could enter, but it would not leave, rendering us functionally invisible and silent.

As kissing him presented a better option than slapping the calculating look off of his face, I swung a leg over, straddling him. He nipped at my lower lip and I bit him back, teeth grazing over his impenetrable flesh. I shrugged out of my coat, and he pressed his face into my breasts, drawing a line of fire with his tongue.

"Shall I beg, then?" I tugged his hair. "Please, I need your hands on me, your lips on my skin. You light a fire in me nothing could ever extinguish. Gods, I want your cock so badly it drives me wild. Please!"

Rafael stood, setting me on my feet, and yanked my trousers down with a dexterous foot. Scales rippled over his face. I blinked and a massive drake armored in bloody reptilian hide took the man's place. His wedge-shaped head lowered, bringing his pointed snout level with my face. My vision filled with jagged teeth. His head alone was the length of my torso.

I tugged at the leather jerkin, and he obliged, pulling it off. Awed by the movement of scales over muscle, I traced the pebbled plates of his chest and abdomen, lingering over the tantalizing V that dipped beneath his leather trousers. He snatched my questing hands away and bore me to the floor, pinning my wrists over my head. I kicked off my boots, struggling to free both legs from my trousers.

"So, you want to fuck a dragon." Growling in draconian, deep as the night was vast, his voice rattled my bones. My clit throbbed in response.

"More than I've ever wanted anything." I spread my legs.

He took a breast gently in his teeth, flicking his long tongue over my nipple, hardening it to a peak. I arched my back to give him better access. His tongue wrapped and squeezed each breast. His hot breath on my skin, the spiced musk of him, the sheer mass of muscle looming over me stole my senses. He'd chosen his prey well.

The tip of his tail slid over my clit, sending a spear of delicious heat up my spine. I lifted my hips. His tail swirled, expertly teasing me open, coaxing my wetness to drip onto him. Without warning, he thrust it into me. I whimpered at the sudden stretch. The keeled scales, safely smoothed, made for an intense texture. He pulled back and thrust harder, making me cry out again.

"Is this what you want?" Hissed words muffled by breast tissue.

"I want your cock, you fucking blighter!" I gasped between cries.

Rafael rumbled a laugh and thrust harder, faster.

I could hardly form the words. "Please, please fuck me! Give me your cock! Split me open."

Releasing my breast, his tongue wound up the length of my ear, pushing me toward delirium. His hips lowered, pressing a significant erection against my clit as he pounded me with his tail, punishing blows against my cervix. Just shy of my maximum pain tolerance, he knew precisely how hard to hit without folding me.

"*Gods*, you have such a big cock. Please!" I thrashed against his iron hold on my wrists. "Loose it from your trousers. Let me feel it against my skin."

Spikes folded flat against the ridge of his spine created a rippling texture that strummed me like a lyre with each motion. Caught between his tail and his cock, if he'd crushed me into the rock beneath, I would have thanked him for it. The girth of his tail stretched me wide, almost beyond what I could stand. He did so love to test my limits.

In an agonizingly slow counterpoint to the thrusting, he shifted his hips to rub his leather-clad cock slowly against my clit. Three blows with the tail for every direction change. I writhed in his grip, desperate to touch him, to moderate his thrusts. When I opened my mouth to scream, he filled it with his tongue.

I could only surrender as he brought me to a gasping climax. I screamed my pleasure and pain into the Dragon's maw. He withdrew his tongue and clamped down on my shoulder. Not enough to break the skin, but the deep ache identified blossoming bruises.

"More?"

A whimper escaped my lips, and he thrust his tail into me again, rhythmically slamming into me. Leather creaked, straining to contain the cock teasing my clit.

"I want you to drown me with your release," I pleaded. "Fuck me, use me."

He growled into my flesh, hips grinding against me. Gods, I wanted his cock inside me. I wanted to feel and hear the slap of his bollocks against me as he fucked me senseless. The moment I orgasmed again, he bit my other shoulder. Helpless, I jerked and shuddered beneath him.

As the waves subsided, a telltale slick heat trickled from between my legs. "I think I'm bleeding."

"So you are. Shall I devour you?"

His tail slid out of me, and he licked away the tooth marks on my shoulders and breasts. Moving down my body, finally, he slipped his tongue deep into my aching cunt. His eyes flashed at the taste of my blood.

The predator's jaws opened wide. Thrusting the full length of his tongue into me, with the same motion, he scooped my entire torso into his mouth. The points of his teeth pressed into my belly and buttocks, and the tip of his snout rested between my breasts. He growled into my vulva; the vibrations ripping through my senses.

Rafael lifted me into the air with only the strength of his neck, hoisting my body upright. Sunk firmly into his jaws, he tongue-fucked me. My fingernails raked over his scales as I scrabbled for purchase while he punished me with his tongue. Perhaps he truly would devour me. I hardly cared past the pounding of my heart, the searing heat of him. The tongue twisting and impaling me. Curling against all the most deliciously sensitive spots, undulating to the rhythm of his growls.

Did I beg him to tear me to pieces? To swallow me whole? Did I plead for my destruction?

I wrapped my legs around his head. The spines and scales biting into my soft inner thighs brought me to new heights of blissful pain. I swiveled as far as my back allowed, brushing my nipples across those deadly teeth, pressing my breasts into his cavernous maw.

He roared, and my body burst apart with a massive shudder. I screamed, writhing in his jaws. Clawing at his scales. Shrieking obscenities. I burned alive in his flames. I shattered under his teeth. I died every small death.

The Dragon withdrew his tongue and laid me down gently, releasing me from his bite with a final lick to my clit. With shaking hands, I stroked his muzzle. Pulling his head against my chest, I wedged his snout once more between my breasts. The spines along the edge of his lower jaw poked into my skin. He wrapped his great paws around my shoulders, talon tips resting lightly on my clavicles.

"Do you live yet?" He switched to elvish. Though he'd spoken softly, his voice rattled me.

"Barely." I laughed, the motion awakening the ache within. "Ah, you amaze me. My ears are still ringing. Do you ever have moments afterwards where you wonder if you have, in fact, gone mad? Every time I think I have reached my limits with your creative depravity, you convince me otherwise."

He chuckled, making my bones buzz, digging his spines deeper into my skin. I couldn't bring myself to arrange him into a more comfortable position.

"What do you think drakes do with each other?"

It hadn't occurred to me, another illustration of myopia. "I haven't the slightest. You've never spoken of it." Shame flushed my ears.

"What use is the ability to change your shape if you cannot be creatively depraved?" His exhale of amusement warmed my face.

I walked my fingers over the scales lining his snout. "You make me delirious with lust. Obliterate my good sense. What power is that? I'd never lost my wits over anyone until you. Are you certain you're not part incubus? The world should be grateful you haven't weaponized your sexual energy." I said it with levity, yet only partially joking. "We would all be swift to fall at your feet. I fear I'm not equipped to fight off the rivals you'd attract."

"None could ever rival you." With a shake of his scaly mane, he shrank to his usual form, leaving his shirt behind. I nestled into his arms, wrapping my legs around his waist. He curled around me.

"Do you love me?" he murmured into my hair.

"I love you better all the time, you horrible man. You do realize it's far easier when you set aside your hostility."

"Hrrm. Do you love me more than you love him?"

I struggled to sit up, but he held me captive in his arms. "Rafael, stop this."

"Answer me."

"You are entirely different people! I cannot compare you like prized studs." Fire and night. Polar opposites.

"That is no answer."

The roiling, black maelstrom of despair in my belly broke free, rising to steal the breath from my lungs. "I cannot do this." Squirming in his arms, I made eye contact. "I haven't the endless capacity to navigate your insecurities. Not now, when I am grieving the impending doom of my entire culture. Perhaps not ever. You will simply have to lick your own wounds, Dragon. I assure you, they are self-inflicted."

A muscle in his jaw twitched.

"I will not apologize for refusing to pander to your moods any more than I've already done. Release me." I pushed against his chest and he let me go. "I wished to spend this time with Celebel before he departs. Instead, I am here soothing your ego over a perceived slight so others wouldn't suffer from your gods damned temper. Once again." Bitterness dimmed my afterglow.

Rafael sat up, spilling me off of his lap. "Forgive me for the horrid sin of granting you repeated orgasms." Even at his most deliberately spiky, my eyes slid hungrily over the muscle movement in his abdomen. Damn my treacherous libido. From the glint in his eye, he knew it too.

"Oh, fuck off." Unwinding my fraying braid, I shook my hair out. Mostly to give myself somewhere else to look. "No matter how furious

I am, your seduction renders me helpless. Leave me a little dignity, please."

He tucked a thumb under my chin, lifting my face with the prick of a talon. A surprising grin pulled at the corner of his mouth. "Should I be flattered or toss you off this wall?"

Simultaneously praising and cursing the gods for his mercurial moods, I leaned into the change. "Why? How far can you toss me?" I wrapped both hands around his biceps. Long as my fingers were, they did not come close to spanning that circumference.

"Hrrm, I should test that." The dampening field dissipated.

"Don't you dare. I spoke in jest!" I scrambled backward in panic.

He bundled me, protesting, into his arms.

"Rafael!"

I sailed into the air, shrieking, grasping at wind. He leaped and caught me easily, landing with grace.

"With enough lead up, I could likely toss you to the moon." He wore an evil grin. The worst part was knowing he might truly be capable. "Send you to meet your namesake."

"You blighter." Half-laughing, half-gasping for breath. "This is exactly what I mean. You're terrible!"

"And you love me for it. Therefore, I should strive to be more terrible."

Chapter 17

SICKENED by Celebel's objective, I prayed fervently to the Night Mother for his safe return. Completing the first Dark Moon ritual I'd done in ages, I bathed in the starlight and shook my hair out loose. Unadorned, I danced the night through as an offering to her.

I would not have him go without the blessing of at least one goddess. Dûemer accepted, lifting her mantle of night into the first rays of dreadful dawn.

Celebel and I snatched a precious, fervently passionate moment together before the departure. He wept, drawing my tears all throughout our lovemaking. Sweet and simple, we merely clung together and coupled quickly, sweat and desperation slicking our skin.

We finished as one, just as the call came from the hallway. He climbed into his old armor, claiming the new suit still needed testing. I wrapped him in dappled green and brown leathers for added stealth.

The company departed with as little fanfare as possible. Seven elves gathered at bubbling mud pits marking the southern approach to Amrún, horses greeting each other with subdued whickers. I gave Celebel's stallion a slice of dried apple and kissed his soft nose.

Nemohee reigned þeir blue roan stallion over. Emotion brightened þeir silver eyes as þey looked to where Caladris sat quietly on his horse. Golden hair fell over a wide, square-jawed face, and muscular arms swelled beneath his leathers. I blinked again to ensure he was not, in fact, Cael.

"Tis easier with some preparation. It does ache my heart."

"My heart aches with yours." I patted þeir leather clad knee.

Nemohee bowed þeir head, and grief radiated through my palm. I did my best to send back love and reassurance.

When Nemohee had originally introduced me to Cael, þey'd

been blissfully happy, in a way I'd never witnessed from my companion. He was a friendly sort, and gleefully supportive of Nemohee's then-recent transition from female to non-binary. Hardly þeir first change, as Nemohee's fluid gender had expressed male when we'd first met, and shifted several times as þey saw fit over the years.

Cael had outraged his family by publicly announcing Nemohee as his soulmate. He hailed from a minor noble Astolar lineage that overly prided themselves on their supposed position. His kin did not take well to the addition of a half-sidhe Lachanaur. Naturally, I'd approved of his willingness to buck tradition for the sake of my friend. I'd only met Cael once before he was taken. It was all so unfair.

Far too soon for my heart, Celebel kissed me a deep goodbye. We sang our sorrow, voices weaving a cocoon of devotion, and held each other until we could dally no longer. He mounted Helicos, and the small company rode off as one.

A shadow passed over us, great wings cast the early light in verdant hues as Marron soared overhead

I sat in the loam and pumice, watching until the last horse's tail disappeared from view. Then I stayed until I could no longer hear the clop of hooves. My tears stained the ground, swallowed by the lichen-covered lava. Finally, as the sun rose, I slinked back to my mossy chamber.

A pawing at the door got my attention some time later.

"Come," I said, too soul-weary to rise from the bed. The pawing grew more urgent. Sighing, I dragged myself up and opened the door.

An enormous lion filled my view. Thick, deep red fur, an impressive, curling mane, and strangely viperine eyes peered at me. Rafael had rarely taken that form in my presence, and not for years. Similar in size to his half-dragon form, he gazed down on me like a god surveying his subjects.

'Perhaps this will please you?'

I flung myself into his mane, burying my face in it.

"WHY DO you insist on keeping that form?" Feanim complained.

I'd tagged along with them at Rafael's insistence. He'd refused to let me out of his sight, and I counted it as honoring Celebel's wish to better know Feanim. Better than endlessly worrying over Celebel's mission.

"You don't speak and cannot write. This is a waste of time."

Instead of the claustrophobic interior rooms, Feanim had his usual maps and charts spread over a wrought iron table he'd had carried into the courtyard. A flagon of wine and a cup rested to one side. He paced as he talked, using his hands for emphasis. Volcanic warmth greening the plants gave a false sense of spring under a sky heavy with the threat of snow.

The great lion twitched a burning tail tip in annoyance. His eyes held the usual alert yellow, and the edges of his fur glowed with interior flame.

'*You hear me perfectly.*' Rafael huffed, his voice booming in my mind.

Feanim's ear twitch said he did indeed hear perfectly. Rafael settled himself on the ground. Seated with his head raised, he was still above my eye level at standing. I distracted myself with the texture of his fur, decadently swirling my fingers in his mane.

Feanim's ears flattened. "Raf, we have important work to do. Quit fucking about."

'*Cúraniel interests me more than battle.*' The lion bumped his head against my shoulder. '*Her comfort is my priority.*'

I flushed with affection and scratched behind his ears. Feanim feigned he hadn't noticed. How to make peace with him?

Studying Feanim's earrings and the golden two-headed crow cloak pin enameled in white and black, I asked, "Have you always worn gold or is that a more recent affectation?" Most of us vastly preferred þilvor.

He flicked an ear, making his earrings jangle. "I've always favored gold. Less likely to tear out of my ear if it gets snagged in a fight. The softness works in its favor."

'*I have never understood why any of you wear jewelry into battle,*'

Rafael sent.

"You say that, and yet she's wearing a gold ring in her ear for you," Feanim pointed out.

'She is not a warrior, though you would do well not to underestimate her.'

"Oh, you're only blowing smoke to flatter her." The Duedellen waved a dismissive hand. The lion huffed again and rested his chin on his paws, closing his eyes, utterly unconcerned. "Are you taking a nap?" Feanim's brows knit together.

The tip of the lion's tail twitched again. *'The ground is warm.'* A light breeze ruffled his mane.

I laughed, and Rafael's amusement tickled my mind.

Feanim sat on a protruding rock. "Fucking annoying. Fine, perhaps you," he jabbed a finger at me, "can be of use. I need to learn draconian, and Rafael has been singularly unhelpful." He produced a small notebook and a quill, looking at me expectantly. "He goes straight for immersion and refuses to translate."

Despite appearances, Rafael's sharp attention prickled my skin.

"Hmm, the same song he sings while supposedly training me in combat. That harmonizes. The language is challenging. There are no written grammar rules and no official alphabet. But I'm sure you know that."

Feanim nodded and gestured impatiently for me to continue.

"Somewhere around half of the sounds we simply cannot produce with our vocal cords. There are a few we can approximate, like the double-r that drops into the back of the throat, but most are impossible. For example, has he told you his drake name?"

"Yes, it was some bizarre combination of sounds." He looked at the apparently slumbering lion. "Jssyfxdn? Jxsyfedinn?"

The lion coughed harshly.

I grinned. "He has the same reaction to my attempts."

"Teach me the pronunciation, then," Feanim complained, glaring at the lion.

He said it in our heads. I know he did, but I still couldn't correctly decipher all the sounds.

Feanim shook his head in exasperation. "Jassxdyfedyan. Gods, that's an awful name to say."

'*Incorrect.*' Rafael opened his eyes, raising his great head and baring teeth like spears.

The Duedellen tossed his hands up. "Fine, fine, I'll stop. How does it translate?" A chill breeze ruffled his dark curls.

I thought for a moment. "Something like 'Dark Fire'."

"Shall I simply call you Dark Fire, then?" Feanim goaded.

'*Not if you wish to keep your ears on your head.*' Rafael growled a warning, flexing his claws menacingly.

"Play nice, boys." I smiled and leaned against the lion, digging my hands into his mane and tugging. He huffed but closed his eyes again, propping his chin back on his paws, and gave his tail a sharp thrash.

Feanim watched him thoughtfully. "That form surprises me. It seems…less modest than how you usually present yourself." He eyed the lion's haunches with deliberation.

'*I have more than enough fur to stop your prying eyes, you degenerate.*' Rafael's tone was harsh, and he curled his tail more tightly around himself. What other off-putting remarks had Feanim made about his body?

"You're far less testy when she's not around." He swirled his wine.

'*I could say the same of you.*'

"Feanim, perhaps if you spent less time trying to offend or discredit me, Rafael wouldn't be so testy." I settled my back against the lion. He was a warm, furry boulder that rumbled agreement.

"So sensitive, both of you." Feanim tossed his hands up. "What else can you teach me of the language?"

"It's impossible to divorce the cultural context from the language. There are social deixis in the language depending on your status. These dictate what names you can use for others." Strange, as we rarely used formal lineage names or lingered overmuch on titles. "You'll notice drakes in lower standing use more simplified grammar and honorifics in place of more personal names."

Feanim scribbled away in his notebook, nodding encouragement.

Turning to the lion at my back, I asked, "Do those social rules apply to outsiders as well?"

'So few outsiders speak the language, we have no expectations. We make quite a few allowances for you, however,' he sent drolly.

Strangely flattering to think of the drakes indulging my accidental stomping over their grammatical hierarchies. Many of them seemed entertained by my attempts, at least.

'You speak draconian with a hills accent.' His tone warmed with amusement.

"I do? Why did you never tell me before?" I'd lived on my hill long enough for the local dialect to seep into my speech patterns without ever realizing it.

'It is charming.'

I laughed, and Feanim looked up, annoyed. He must not have heard Rafael's half of my latest mental exchange.

"Apologies. He was commenting on my accent."

"Flavored with hillspeech, I would imagine. I hear it even now in the way you lean on certain words." Feanim steepled his hands, quirking a brow.

"Ah cannae seem tae escape it, sae Ah micht as weel lean in," I said. "At least 'tis yin Ah kin pronounciate."

The lion chuffed with amusement, shifting his weight behind me.

Feanim ignored my antics. "The drakes don't have a standard greeting either, I've noticed. It's more just attention-getting, yes?"

"Yes." I grinned. "Though the most important word you need is *'hthrakkga'.*"

Rafael coughed a laugh.

"What does that mean?"

I considered a prank. But the possibility of such a prank leading to dire consequences stayed my whimsy. "Sun-ripened shit. Implied to be left by some particularly odious creature, like a troll with crotch rot."

Feanim watched my face to ensure I wasn't teasing. He finally chuckled and added it to his notebook. To date, it was the most productive conversation I'd ever held with him. Rafael observed the whole thing with a deep current of amusement and offered absolutely no help at all.

Chapter 18

Celebel

THE green drake landed among us at moonrise. Helicos snorted with alarm, but did not bolt, the fine lad. The others took their cue to leave us as Marron strode toward me, folded wings shrinking into his back. He shrugged on a sleeveless leather jerkin over his stout torso. I hardly considered it bare under that thick layer of scales.

"It harmonizes Rafael would send his bloody hand," I said. "What is the cost of your aid?"

"Gold." Marron did not miss a note. "I want none of your elf nonsense. You'll pay my weight in gold, immediately."

Straightforward enough. The role he'd played in backing Rafael's bid to challenge me reminded me to be cautious, but otherwise, I appreciated the drake's open demeanor.

"Your weight as you are now?" I looked him over. He was easily near 30 stone, perhaps more. Far outstripping any elf in sheer bulk.

"No. My weight in my full dragon form." Marron spread his arms, mimicking his impressive wingspan.

A dear price indeed, but what choice did I have?

"Does that weight remain consistent?" I asked. At his nod, I signed a formal affirmative. "Done. I appreciate simplicity."

"You're the scion of Elaris himself, yes? Your grandpappy was said to hoard treasure like the true dragons themselves." His eyes were crimson flames in the darkness. "Surely you know the city's secrets better than anyone."

"I am." I would not teach that melody freely. "Velúara may be ransacked by the time we arrive, but I will ensure you receive your payment above all else, on my honor as an Elhalanros."

A distinct twinkle lit the drake's eyes. "If only my mate were here. She would love this!"

"You're to be a father again, correct?" Perhaps we could establish a base level of rapport, as we both dealt with Rafael's troublesome and mercurial moods.

The green drake puffed his chest out. "The babe is due any day now. Hoping for a daughter. I have too many sons."

"I will pray for your wishes and her safety." The topical shift came as a relief.

Marron's booming laugh startled Helicos. "Vaerra is mighty! She needs no concern for her safety. She bore our first during a break in battle and continued the fight with him clinging to her back." His eyes shone. "She will join us after this birth."

More drakes. I restrained my defeated sigh. "Perhaps we may further assist each other with a common obstacle."

"Common obstacle, indeed." Marron scrubbed a hand through his hair, slicking the dark green strands back and tying them at the nape of his neck. "Rraysth has never been so distracted, and you play a role in this new weakness. What do you propose?"

I took a risk. "What assurances do I have that you will not turn on me or my people?" He may very well harbor true loyalty to the Red Dragon, but I detected the faintest melody otherwise. "Can I trust you?"

"No." A remarkably affable smile softened his bluntness. "But what choice do you have? I will say I do not wish to bring hell upon myself and my clan by upsetting the Red's mate." He rubbed his chin, scale rasping on scale. "Rraysth plays a long game, and I know well enough to follow his shadow. If this were purely for entertainment, he'd have stolen his mate and abandoned your cause by now."

"And if Rafael falls, will you remain and fight by our side?"

Ruby eyes searched my face. "Interesting that you believe such a possibility exists, but I will humor you. If the Red Dragon falls, you will pay my dragon-weight in gold once every century in perpetuity, and I'll honor this alliance." Bright teeth flashed in a dark green face. "I would demand it every dozen years, but I am merciful and I don't want to see you that often."

It would certainly take that long to replenish our coffers. "Do drakes have a ritual for sealing an agreement?"

"We do, but you would not survive it." He leaned in. "If you forswear yourself, you will make an enemy of me and my clan will hunt yours without remorse."

"I hear you, Green Marron, and agree to your terms. My word is my bond."

MIGHTY VELÚARA. Its honeycombed towers rose majestic before me as I strode through its streets with grim purpose. I'd tasked others with burning the rest of the city, but it rested upon me to handle the keep. Not only was it my duty to secure the relics of lineage and the greatest treasures of my birthright, it must be my hand that laid the heart of the city to rest through cleansing fire.

Steadying myself, I reached through my soulbond to share this, the darkest moment of my life, with Cúraniel. She stirred, peering through my eyes, her love and concern wrapping me like a second cloak.

Once we'd sung down the concealing veil, Marron had turned toward the walls and made a show of stretching. With a mighty breath expanding his barrel chest, the green drake had brought a fist down in an arc, slamming it into the ground.

The bedrock had responded immediately; a fissure racing toward the wall from where the green drake's fist had struck. As it met the glacial estuary guarding the entrance, the river had poured into the crevice, flinging spray into the air at the sudden disruption. The wall split open vertically at the base with a loud *crack*, creating a hole large enough for three horses to enter abreast.

Marron eventually agreed to help ferry the precious cargo out, though not without grumbling about beasts of burden. Most of what he moved comprised þilvor armaments; I handled the more sensitive items personally. Unsurprisingly, the main coffers had been looted and notable objects of power such as the Protean Staff, the Book of Keeping, and the singing sword Lonáramir were missing. We each made several trips back through the walls.

I passed the great hall and throne room, the solarium and council room. Winding through the extensive private chambers of the royal family, I emerged into the gestation grove. Or what remained of it.

The stench of decay hit me first, and I staggered. All around, the trees had blackened. Some lay burst into splinters, dead. Others wilted, rotting from within under the burden of their foul get. My plodding steps gained speed until I dashed through the ruined grove. I darted around trees, finally skidding to a halt at the shattered remains of a massive white oak.

With an anguished wail, I fell to my knees. Despite Hestalön's visions, I'd still held out hope for my birth tree. I cradled a slab of the rough bark in my arms as my heart splintered.

"Gods, hear my cry! Strike down those who would tear away the very womb of my birth! Smite those hateful wretches who would rot the core of their own kindred's continued existence." I tore at the grass, tore at my hair, and cursed the destruction of the sacred trees.

Until that moment, I'd harbored secret doubt at my resolve. But no, my grandfather would not have balked at such a task. If he was strong enough to protect this city through all those ages of strife, I was strong enough to lay it to rest with honor. I tucked a piece of the oak's heartwood into my cloak, squared my shoulders, and pooled my spirit in the pit of my belly.

"Forgive me, Grandfather Elaris." Removing an unlit torch and tinder box from my cloak, I struck the spark that ignited the end of Velúara. Starting with my own, I moved systematically, stonily, from tree to tree. I sang, fanning the flames with my grief, threading the fire through the surrounding spirit.

Some few trees still gestated monstrosities. Those writhed when lit, as the creatures within tried to claw their way free. Fury warred with disgust. I drew my sword and stabbed each pregnant tree through the putrid belly of its trunk, putting an end to the cries. My movements were languid, far away, as though performed by another. A phantom of Celebel Elhalanros, providing small mercy for whatever poor, corrupted souls those bodies contained. Those trees burned hotter than the rest.

Oily smoke crawled through the air, trailing after me as I strode into the throne room with purpose, holding the torch over my head like a beacon. I kneeled before the main dais, that beautiful floating platform overlooking one of the many waterfalls curtaining the city. Making a formal obeisance, I placed my hand over my heart, clenching my fist over the sickness building there.

I lifted my voice in song, honoring those who had come before, honoring my past. With reverence, almost tenderness, I lowered the torch to the fine purple carpet under the throne. I urged the tightly woven wool to accept the flame, to embrace it. Even so, it took an age for the first curl of smoke to rise. I bowed low.

Deep within the library, I torched the empty shelves. In the great hall, I lit the tapestries. In the armory, I set the mats aflame. Through the various gardens, I dragged the torch along the shrubs and trees, burning a wake. On and on I continued, tracking the flames so they may not surround me unawares. It wasn't until I reached a sunny room in a tower that I wept again.

Modest compared to most of the others, a small bed nestled comfortably beside tall stained-glass windows depicting a heroic history. All the furniture scaled too small for an adult.

I touched the coverlet with shaking fingers, running my hand over the spines of books and the arching backs of chairs. Wispy memories overlaid the scene. Playing with a wooden sword. Taking notes at the small desk. Sleeping sprawled over the bed. All of my blissful childhood.

With a deep sigh of regret, I held the torch to the bed curtains. They sparked to life. Backing away, I left the door open so the flames would easily continue down the hall.

As I exited the grand keep, the fire was already fanning out toward the rest of the city. Once I crossed the threshold of the gates, a trumpeting roar sounded from above. I cast my gaze to the sky. There was Marron in his full dragon form, his distinctive ram's horns curled back from his brow. He swooped low overhead, casting gouts of flame along the roofs and landing with a thunderous boom in a central plaza. He raised up the front half of his body, crackling with power. Forelegs thick as the trunks of ancestor trees landed with an echoing crash.

There came a pregnant pause, and a tremor rolled over the

ground like a blanket shaken out. A nearby house dropped out of sight as a crevice yawned open and swallowed it whole. The cracks spread rapidly, devouring walls, wells, and walkways alike, heading straight for the heart of Velúara.

Marron roared again, slamming down in a different direction. Flagstones shattered in a circle around him, spiraling outward with remarkable speed. The latticed towers swayed like white birch in a wind shear. One toppled, crashing into the next, and so on in a slow dance. He studied his handiwork, giving a satisfied nod. With a mighty leap into the air, he clapped his wings and took flight. Just in time, as the plaza vanished below the surface.

Triumphant in his destruction, Marron trumpeted again, circling over the rapidly crumbling inferno of a city. The blaze painted the sky orange, gilding the surrounding forests and mountain backdrop.

Why is the light quality always at its loveliest when the world is aflame?

Millennia of history, culture, and life gone in mere heartbeats. I sank to my knees and keened. Vaguely, I sensed the others joining me.

Even the oft-stoic Nemohee shed some tears. Þeir strong contralto sounded first, rising in a song of sorrow. Caladris' surprisingly high tenor harmonized, and the others followed. My baritone wove in beneath them, ragged with mourning.

At the signal, Marron breathed sustained fire in a sweep over the glacial dam crouched above the burning city. With a groan from the heart of Vaeda, the ice calved in a rushing flood. A wall of water struck Velúara, dousing the flames. Dousing its song from existence with a hiss like a dozen furious dragons. A fittingly grand burial for the end of my world.

As the flood passed and the water receded into the fissures, the green dragon circled the icy slush of the remains, sprinkling seeds we'd given him. Pioneer species, some would sprout in the heat of the remaining coals, and others would take root in the spring thaw. Someday, a mighty forest would stand over the greatest city's grave.

We sang through the night and following day into the eventide. Singing until the last embers faded, and only the hush remained.

Chapter 19

Cúraniel

HOOFBEATS had me running to the road to greet my soulmate, elves of all nations trailing along behind me. Instead of flying ahead, Marron circled above the horses, carrying a large, wrapped load on his broad back and more clutched in his talons.

Not waiting for the party to come to a halt, I ran to Helicos and flung myself over the dappled stallion's withers. Heaving up on the flat pommel of the saddle, I wrapped myself firmly around Celebel.

He crushed his mouth to mine, prying my jaws open as our teeth clashed, pouring himself into me with ferocious passion. Formless need yawned within me, rising to meet his. I wanted to meld our bodies together, to climb into his skin. To protect him, or perhaps myself.

Trembling, we clung to each other, hardly breathing. I caressed my Starshine's ears, his face, his hair. The armor pinched me, but I hardly registered the discomfort. Carefully, Celebel slid his far leg over the front of the saddle in order to dismount without dropping me, and we slipped to the ground. Hoisting me around his waist, he carried me past the assembled elves and directly to our chamber.

Unwilling to release him from my kiss, I fiddled with his armor as we went, discarding a pauldron here and a gauntlet there in a shining trail behind us.

Should I have ached so intensely for his touch, for his cock, here at the funeral of the Talithiri nation? The madness of grief drove me to affirm life. I knew not where my need ended and his began.

Our lips finally parted as he laid me gently on our bed, and I helped him remove the rest of his armor. His deft fingers made quick work of it. He cast the remaining pieces on the floor and pushed me down on the bed, already gloriously hard. With no preamble, he slid his cock fully into me.

I locked my legs around his waist once more, and my mouth on his, as we surged together. We rolled so I was on top. I crashed my hips down as hard as I could, instinctively fucking him like my life depended on it. My tears showered his face, mingling with his.

Spirit radiated from our glistening skin, moon and stars, rising with the shared song. The heavens within cracked open, washing us in spangled night, in our cohabited sorrow. Lineage awoke. Though I'd shunned her legacy, Maelial blessed me. She had loved Velúara well. Ancestor stars shone upon us, weeping as we wept for their fallen children, for the trees, for all we had lost.

Who were we? Rootless, bereft of home and lineage. Bereft of custom and tradition. History lost forever. Bedding the enemy. Burrowing into stone, far from our forests and plains and jungles. Did the shared song alone make an elf?

We rolled again and I landed under Celebel. I knotted my fists in his hair, and he mirrored my action. His mouth crashed into mine. Splitting lips, tearing hair. Our blood, our tears. Our spirit surged, filling the chamber.

Releasing despair rather than chasing pleasure, borne of a need to join body and soul, we cried our climaxes into each other's mouths. He released his grip on my hair, and I his. Our spirit settled over us, a blanket of slowly dissipating ancestral power. We laid there together, stroking and kissing each other. I held him inside my body as long as I could, humming the note struck in my heart. I feared breaking the physical connection as if he would dissipate into fog. He rolled me on top of him once more, caging me in his arms. Matching pitch, we healed each other. Eventually, Celebel drifted into much-needed rest. Wide awake, I held him until the crickets sang.

He stirred slowly, as though surfacing from a great depth. "Oh, my love, it's good to wake in your arms. I feel as if I've walked through nightmares, or perhaps the very hells themselves."

I brushed his tangled hair out of his face. "How are you feeling?"

"Soul-sick. Exhausted. Wrung out. Glad it's over and done. May I never again have to commit such an atrocity."

We held each other in mournful silence, hearts beating in unison.

I'd grieved for centuries when Leyûduin sank. Even now, the loss still panged from time to time. How much worse must it be to sack my own birthplace? He took a shuddering breath.

I kissed his neck. "I'm grateful to have you here. How was working with Marron?"

Celebel propped himself up on his elbows. "He's an interesting fellow. Quite blunt, but cheerful enough. Sometimes I truly cannot parse when he speaks in jest. He claimed he didn't understand why Rafael has not yet killed me. As he put it, 'Elves live a long time. She would recover eventually'."

I grimaced, but it didn't surprise me.

"I doubt he misses much," Celebel continued. "At first, those red eyes unsettled me, as every time Rafael's eyes burn red, it indicates immediate violence. Marron, however, is remarkably calm for a drake. Or perhaps I have a skewed concept of them." He blew out a breath. "He didn't challenge me on the items I wished to preserve, which was a relief. How was it here in my absence?" He sat up and stretched, and I admired the way the muscles in his back moved.

"Rafael spent most of it in his lion form." He'd returned to his customary body a few days prior, and I found I missed the great cat.

Celebel turned to me, eyes wide. "Rafael has a lion form?"

"He has several other forms you haven't encountered, and likely many I haven't either. He did it to cheer me, which I appreciated. Feanim did not." I chuckled at the memory of the Duedellen's griping. "Left me to teach your sour-faced friend how to speak draconian, to which I am uniquely unqualified."

Celebel smiled at that. A wan smile, and weary, but a smile nonetheless. "That must have been quite a thing to witness."

"I take no responsibility for whatever Feanim says to the drakes," I agreed.

He laughed softly. Tiredly. "You are, in your own way, as much a menace as your pet Dragon."

Chapter 20

"I'M telling you, I believe the Carnyx was always meant to break!" Feanim's voice traveled from the lower levels of the library.

"If you are correct, then it is more than a simple faerie summoning tool," Rafael replied.

Immediately curious, I drifted down the ramp toward the conversation. No sign of a dampening field, so they must not be discussing state secrets.

"Have you not touched it, Raf?" Sounds of movement followed.

A scoff. "No, you kept your precious magic trumpet swaddled and hidden away like your tree infants. There is indeed some other power here. Have Nemohee examine the pieces as well. What, have you another with sidhe blood hidden away as well? Þey may detect other irregularities, once þey know to search."

"Why do you get on so well with that mixed blood? Is it to please your woman?"

Fucking Feanim.

A growl rose. "Have a care, *Inuriterrege*. I am also a 'mixed blood', as you say."

Crow. I quickened my pace.

Feanim sighed loudly. "Yes, I suppose you all are. Sheathe your claws. I meant no offense."

I rounded the final bend to the Duedellen wrapping a package in linen; the pieces of the Carnyx of Calling. Rafael reclined on a padded stone bench surrounded by stacks of books. Adding to the already increased heat of the depths, an enclosed fire crackled in a hearth beside him, casting shadows on his sharp features. Someday, I'd find him sitting directly in the flames.

"Take this. I have not translated all of it, but it has relevant sections." He tossed a heavy tome at the elf.

Feanim caught it, grimacing at the handling of such a rare book. He gave me the barest nod on his way out.

Rafael methodically flipped through another tome, adding it to a neat stack of those he clearly planned to abscond with. The discards he tossed into the haphazard pile at his feet. I frowned as I gathered them up, smoothing the pages.

"Save your offense. I am simply mirroring your weapons storage method," he rumbled.

I swatted him with a closed book. "Robbing the library already, eh?" That he hoarded books as much as gold was endearing.

Rafael looked up from the current page and moved some books onto the floor so I could sit. I leaned back on the curving bench, propping my feet on his chest.

"This is a diverse collection." He idly rubbed my feet with his free hand as he flipped pages with the other.

My eyes traveled over the colorful assortment of bindings.

"You read their language?"

He glared at me. Given we'd first bonded over a translation he'd requested from me, I should have known better. He hoarded languages as well.

I raised my palms in peace. "Find anything of interest?"

"Hrrm, my father is mentioned." He handed me the book, and my ears perked. Rafael rarely mentioned his parentage.

"Your father?" A stylized drawing of a mighty red dragon sprawled across the page, illuminated with a starkly geometric script.

"Eldest of Dhraxael."

"You're a direct descendant of the first dragon?" My eyes popped wide. With such a powerful lineage, no fucking wonder Rafael was an unstoppable force! The true dragons had been gods in their own right, but particularly the first among them.

"We all are, my dove." He raised his arched brows in mockery.

Very well, I deserved that. "Yes, yes, I only meant you are very close in the lineage. But tell me of your father. I know so little." A thousand questions crowded my mouth.

"Your people called him Dacael, sometimes Adacanir."

'God of Destruction' or 'the Great Destroyer'. A shiver ran down my spine. Adacanir's legend of sowing chaos and destruction was nearly as widespread as that of his most famously hated progeny.

"He had many other offspring as well, across a host of species."

I sat up, ears twitching. "You have *siblings*?" There were *more* of Rafael's ilk?

He huffed. "Half-siblings. I am the eldest by far."

"Have you met them all? May *I* meet them?" What would they think of me? Were they all as obstinate as my Dragon, or did he achieve that temperament through circumstance alone? Did they share likeness?

Rafael smirked at the questions tumbling across my face. "Only one yet lives. She is an odd creature, with some elvish blood mixed in."

"Oh ho, was Father attracted to elves as well? Did he pass his proclivities to you?" Was his father also capable of soulbonding? I prodded his arm, and he wrapped me in a headlock, dragging me into his lap.

"The extent of his accursed presence in my life is in the scales I wear, you little trial," Rafael held me firmly as I struggled, thumping my fists against his chest and arm. "Faraz is a maternal half-sibling, not a drake."

I wanted to ask about her, but the words died in my throat as he squeezed. I tapped surrender, and he loosened his grip.

"What happened to the rest?"

He gave me a measured look and let me slide out from under his arm. Ah. The clan of red drakes he'd exterminated. His clan. His kin. How many of them had children?

"It's just as well you haven't impregnated me. Birthing a drake babe, all sharp scales and claws tearing me on the way out," I blurted before I could stop myself.

Rafael bent low, grabbed me by the ankles, and yanked me into the air in one smooth motion as he stood. "If you must know, our scales are soft until the first shed, at least a moon after birth. They do not fully harden until maturity."

He made his way up the ramp as I kicked at him, dangling me over the side. Shrieking in laughter, I writhed upside down.

"I'll behave! I swear it," I gasped through my bouts of mirth.

"Doubtful." The Dragon pulled me back and released me.

I landed on my palms, righting myself. Sliding my arms around his waist, I tugged at him. Rafael sat on the bench and drew me into his lap.

I ran my fingers through his hair, briefly tangling in the curls. "What happened to your father?"

He looked away, quiet for several heartbeats. "He…faded away, like the others." The fire of his eyes flickered oddly, as though the thought perturbed him.

"As our elders did."

"Something like that." Leagues away.

"That bothers you."

His eyes sharpened, brow creasing into his usual scowl. "I wished to kill the fucker myself," he snarled, talons flexing in response to the imagined murder.

Carefully, I reached up and brushed a hand across his clenched jaw and up over the point of his ear, hidden under his thick mane. "Easy, Dragon. I know you will not agree, but I am grateful to him for siring you."

His upper lip curled. "You are quite alone in that."

Rafael found the strand of pearls braided into my hair and twirled it in his fingers. What had his sire looked like out of dragon form? Did he favor his sire or his dam in appearance?

"I resemble him overall." He answered my thoughts. I traced the line of his aquiline nose. "Though *that* is my dam's legacy. My nose and the texture of my hair are her imprint."

"She must be lovely." I imagined that long, hooked nose softened into feminine features, with the same mane of hair. Trying to envision her, I reached through our soulbond.

His eyes narrowed, and the connection clanged shut like a dropped portcullis. "Do *not*." Something shivered, fleeting, in my mind. The Dragon exhaled, gusts of heat in the already hot air. "You favor your aunt and grandmother." Answering my unspoken question, he added, "I have seen them from a distance. Legends made of their beauty, yes?"

"Yes. My aunt especially."

"You are more lovely," he said earnestly.

I laughed and kissed the side of his neck. "You are biased, but your sense of aesthetics cannot be faulted." I preened a little. "You are sweet to say it."

"I am sincere."

"I know you are, and I love you for it, but others are also allowed to be beautiful." I thought for a moment. "My joke earlier was in bad taste, but have you ever wanted children?"

He stared at me as though I were a maggot in a peach. "Have you lost your senses?"

I stroked his cheek, trying to settle him as agitated yellow streaked into the blue of his eyes. "You've truly never considered it? A soulmate implies compatibility for offspring."

"Why would I? You know what I endured. What I am still..." The connection thinned as he grew distant and pulled away.

"Calm yourself, please. I only wished to hear your thoughts, and I have never particularly desired children for myself." Outwardly soothing, inwardly I cursed myself.

That same distance had kept us apart for almost a century prior to Celebel's arrival. Rafael reacted poorly to each new pressure in our relationship, no matter how gently I tried to introduce a concept.

"Truly, I did not intend to upset you."

He held himself still as stone. Avoidant. I stretched to kiss his lips. His mouth did not yield, did not meld to mine.

"Dragon, come back to me." I slid my arms around his neck, biting at his lips.

Like the first spring thaw, he responded little by little. I pressed myself against him, savoring his growing heat, and he came to life, kissing my ear, my jaw, my throat. He scooped me up and leaned me back across the bench's arm. I squirmed at the books now lodged beneath my thighs, and he moved over me, pinning me in place.

Reading his intent, I tugged down the front of my gown and pushed up my cleavage, exposing my breasts. He latched on to a nipple. A brief thought crossed my mind that someone could easily walk in on us like this, and another, more wicked thought hoped someone would.

Directing the flow of my spirit into him, I let him draw as much as he needed. Rafael thrummed as he sucked at my breasts, the deep vibrations penetrating my body and soothing me into an almost trancelike state. His leveraged weight, trapping me in place, woke a carnality racing through my core.

I held his head, twisting my hands into his thick hair. He massaged my thighs, and I opened my legs to him, already slick with desire. As he rubbed lazy circles over my clit with his thumb, I rocked against his hand.

Two fingers parted my labia and entered me, forcing a whimper from my throat. As I belatedly considered a dampening field, his other hand rose to cover my mouth. I pulled his hair, and he thrust another finger into me. And one into my mouth, forcing my jaws apart. The thrumming changed, harmonizing with stifled breath, with his penetration.

I yanked harder, and he rumbled, shoving another finger in my mouth in counterpoint to those pounding my cunt. He took a nipple in his teeth, tugging hard enough to bring blood to the surface, just shy of breaking the delicate skin.

"You want the pain," Rafael said against my breast. "You want to be *fucked*." With the emphasis, he shoved both hands as deep as they would go.

Delicious agony arched my back, sparking from cunt to throat. I writhed under him, the fingers in my mouth effectively gagging me, his blunted talons teasing the back of my throat. Teasing my cervix. With streaming eyes, I sucked his fingers, while he fucked me with slow, hard slaps of his hand against my mound.

Clawing at his back, I scrabbled for balance against the rising tide of orgasm. He sucked harder, fingers opening me as wide as I could tolerate. Wetness spread beneath me, and I squirmed, trying to avoid soiling the books wedged under me.

"Come," the Dragon growled against my breast.

I obeyed without thought. Pulses of searing lust wrung me out like a rag, and I wailed around the choking fingers.

"What was that?" He released my breast, tilting his head.

With a mouthful of digits, I sent, *'library! This is a libr—'* Cruel fingers stretched me, relentless, and I cried out.

"Louder."

I gagged on the digits, biting the stony appendages in futility. In response, sharp teeth sank into my other breast. The climax hit its peak, flooding me, tearing loose a scream.

"There you are," he said. "My favorite song." Echoes of my muffled cry bounced off the round walls.

Rafael withdrew his hands, licking his talons clean with his sinuous tongue. Then he bent and licked the minor wound on my breast. The heat of his breath soothed the pain away, sealing the punctures.

Shifting my weight, a hard corner dug into my buttocks. "Oh gods, the books!" I pulled two from under me. Distinct moisture spotted the topmost cover.

Rafael took it from my hand with a rumbling chuckle. "I will keep this one." He held it up to his nose and inhaled.

After a rueful examination to clear the other of sex-related damage, I set it on the pile of discards. He pulled me into his arms, and I cuddled against his chest. Despite his steely body, my softness compensated. I poured my rolling cloud bank into the peaks and valleys of his contours. We simply fit together.

"No," he said. Startled, I searched his face. No flame lit his hair, no agitation burned in his eyes. "No, I have not considered children. For…obvious reasons."

"Merely an idle curiosity, my love. I appreciate your indulgence." I caught a lock of his hair, twirling it around my finger. "How about naked sparring?"

"I will take that under advisement." He kissed the top of my head.

I drowsed briefly in his comforting heat, soothed by his great heart beating its slow, triplicate rhythm. The discomfort of resting my head against the scratchy wool of his shirt kept waking me. Annoyed, I pulled open the collar. Tracing his clavicle with my tongue, the taste of his skin woke me in a different way.

"I desperately want you to climax. I want you to have that

release. To feel safe enough. To feel you deserve it." I kissed the side of his neck as he shifted uncomfortably. "Be at ease, my Dragon. There is no shame here. I'll say it as many times as you need to hear it."

"I love you." The melancholic longing in his voice struck me straight through the heart. "You make me feel…ah, you know what you do to me. I do want you, badly. You know that." He couldn't look me in the eye. "Why I cannot seem to overcome the specters of my past…"

"Easy, beloved. This is not your fault. I feel your blatant need." I slid my thigh against the substantial erection straining his leathers. He hissed, shuddering.

Gods, I wanted him so badly. Drunk on desire, I tucked my hands under the small of his back to help me resist the urge to tear open all that gods damned leather and fuck him bloody. At times, my respect for his boundaries warred with my libido, but respect won.

"Not here," he panted. He knew my frustration well, despite my attempts to stifle it, and never criticized me. "Not tonight. But I will try again soon."

"Of course. I do not mean to pressure you."

"You do. It is a sweet pressure."

Chapter 21

ARMORED except for a helm, Feanim faced off against Rafael in the training field. I watched from the fence with an anxious Nimthil. Behind us, others in the outer courtyard stopped to observe the sparring match.

Though I'd seen Feanim's new armor many times, I appreciated the fantastical form of it. Cast as if poured over his body, and yet wildly flexible. Exquisite craftsmanship. From the fluidity of movement, he was fully bonded with the Pîntellum now.

The Dragon had completed his moranga armor, but did not wear it yet, claiming the membrane adherence was slow. The poor Pîntellum likely did not wish to touch the demon ore. If only Rafael were more like a slime mold. The soulbond tightened with irritation.

The combatants closed, whirling around each other, keen swords trading blurringly swift blows. Though it was a one-sided match, Feanim parried and dodged efficiently, buoyed by the armor's increased strength and speed. He landed no strikes on Rafael, but he took none that would truly debilitate either.

Rafael allowed Feanim to break and circle him. Either the Dragon was showing his version of clemency, or Feanim was truly skilled with the blade. Or, gods, was the armor that powerful? Perhaps some combination of the three.

Feanim held out until Rafael landed a ringing stab to the shoulder, knocking the much shorter elf to the ground. With the point of Rafael's massive greatsword at his throat, the Duedellen yielded. Still, I was impressed.

Regaining his footing, Feanim strutted across the ring as though he'd won. Rafael watched from the other side, sword sheathed and arms folded.

Feanim said, "Punch me in the stomach with all of your strength!"

The most foolish collection of words in the history of language, directed at Rafael like a command.

The Dragon dropped his hands, brows raising. "Have you gone mad?"

I shook my head in disbelief, tugging at my lobes.

Feanim gestured at him. "Come, I must test my armor's true protective strength. We've performed all the strike tests on training forms we need. It is time to determine how it works on my body. I will have perfection."

Nimthil leaned over the fence. "Fé, no!" She signed wild protests, her layers of celadon silk gauze snagging on the wood.

For once, I agreed with her.

"I know you're desperate, but there are less painful ways to be penetrated," I called.

Feanim sliced a scowl at me. The corner of Rafael's mouth twitched upward.

Undeterred, I pressed him. "Do you hear your own melody? You're asking a *dragon* larger than this entire fortress, compressed into the shape of that *still-very-large* man, to punch you with all of his might?" Surely, he couldn't be serious. He must know he would die. "Have you forgotten the aftermath of battle—"

Unable to see my lips, Nimthil spoke over me. "Why not place it on a training form and have him strike that? Why must you wear it?"

"Shut the fuck up, both of you." Feanim pushed his palms outward as though shoving us backward. Or merely striking a gleaming pose. "Cúraniel could explain it if she ever paid attention. The Pîntellum must have contact to activate. I will test this armor until it reaches peak performance. If it cannot withstand such a blow, I must redesign it."

Rafael's coughing laugh snared everyone's attention. "This is the single stupidest request I have ever heard. I accept."

He stalked toward Feanim, and Nimthil screamed. She leaped over the fence, throwing herself dramatically in front of Feanim.

"Nimthil, move," the Duedellen snapped, spinning her to face him. Rafael paused while the two of them squabbled. "Nimthil, I command it!"

As neither elf relented, Rafael simply scooped Nimthil up under one arm and deposited her like a sack of turnips on the other side of the fence. She howled with indignity as I tried very hard not to laugh. Feanim dropped into a stance, puffing his chest out. The Dragon caught my eye with a wicked gleam in his. He rolled shoulders my human villagers would have measured in axe handles and pulled back a fist.

Surely he would not—

Rafael threw the punch. The casual ease of motion and follow-through belied the terrible force behind it. Feanim was there one heartbeat and flying the next. He sailed over the field, smacking into the outer wall on the far side and landing hard. Fuck, was he dead?

He coughed and gagged, curling around his midsection. *Crow!* I hopped the fence. *Fuck, fuck, fuck!* He vomited blood—no, those were *entrails*.

Shouts rang out as I ran to the Consul retching and dying in the dirt. I plunged my hands into the crumpled remains of his abdomen and, reaching as deep as I could with my power, *pulled*. Too little spirit here.

The Night Mother heard and lent me strength. From the inner courtyard, the trees creaked, their spirit stretching toward me as the wind whipped up. Light dimmed, sound faded.

I fought the sucking death pulling the Duedellen under. Shoving his intestines down his throat, I forced them right-side out and back into his belly with sheer will. As I soothing the ruined tissues, the Pîntellum responded. It pushed out embedded þilvor shards and helped me seal the bleeding.

"Rafael, come and help me! I haven't the Great Tree to lend support," I yelled over my shoulder.

"I cannot."

I whipped around. "Stop being an asshole and lend me your spirit!"

He shrugged. "I warned him not to disrespect you."

A shriek of frustration escaped my lips.

Miraculously, Feanim's spine was still intact. Rafael had angled his punch as an uppercut instead of a straight jab. If such an organ-pulping blow had connected with Feanim's spinal column, the central trunk, I'd have no hope of saving him. His spirit would scatter and no power in the world could bring it back. I drew out that spirit, coaxing him to pull himself back together.

None of our previous enmity mattered. The rest of the world melted away. All that remained was me versus a body trying its damnedest to die.

A scared little boy hid from a familiar face. Guardians looked away when they should have intervened. An angry young man tried and failed to be strong, fading into the shadow of his brother. The adult man drowned in his rage, eating himself alive in his desire to be loved by all, sharing no part of himself.

No time for that! Focus. Focus.

When I came back to myself, the sun had shifted in the sky. Nimthil sobbed, holding Feanim's head in her lap. I blinked wearily. Ah, good. He was breathing.

"You gods damned fucking *fool*." I slapped his cheek.

Nimthil cried out, but Feanim's eyelids fluttered.

He came to, drunkenly trying to focus on my face. "Where… what?"

"If you ever do that again, you are saving yourself, you fucking pompous, bombastic, shit-eating *blighter!*" I rose, disgusted at the gobbets of Feanim-viscera plastering my clothes. "If it weren't for the Pîntellum, you would have been dead before you hit the ground. I ought to take it back from you!"

"Cúraniel—" the familiar bass rumble began.

"*YOU!*" I rounded on Rafael in a blaze of fury, stretching to my toe tips in a futile attempt to yell directly into his face. "What the *fuck* were you thinking? What if you had killed him?"

He clamped steadying hands on my shoulders, which only fueled my wrath. "I did not use all my strength." Infuriatingly calm.

Nimthil dry heaved.

"It matters not! Every elf witnessed this. Why must you make everything more difficult? Gods, I am so angry with you! Both of you! Feanim, you *fucking* fool! I am sick unto dying of healing these stupid *fucking MEN!*" My throat hurt from shouting. The exertion of healing sent nauseating tremors through my limbs.

Rafael stood impassive in the face of my wrath. "Feanim received exactly what he requested. A lesson."

"A lesson *I* had to clean up! And will continue to clean up!" I furiously tried to pry his hands away. Gods damned Dragon and his gods damned loopholes. "We've lost too much, too recently. You agreed *not* to do this anymore!"

"Cúraniel—"

"Release me! Right now!" I slapped at his hands.

"You will collapse."

"Let. Go."

He released me, and I did indeed fall flat into the dirt. Celebel, who must have arrived sometime during the commotion, sprang to my side. An ear-splitting scream stopped whatever Celebel was about to say.

"Get away from him, you *monster!*" Nimthil shrieked again, ears plastered flat to her skull.

Rafael blithely ignored her, bending over to inspect Feanim.

I shot Rafael a blistering glare, and he finally had the grace to back away. "Nimthil, have Feanim carried to the healer's wing. He needs more healing than I can provide, rest, and red meat for the blood loss. No, I care not how you feel. He needs it to heal. Rafael, go the fuck away."

To my surprise, they obeyed.

NEMOHEE HOWLED with laughter, tears of mirth pouring down þeir cheeks, and pounded the wooden table. We sat in an alcove offset from the working area of the kitchen. Ceramic pots of dried herbs and spices lining the inset stone shelves filled the space with savory scents. A stew cauldron bubbled over the large hearth at the far end of the room.

"Och, *gods*, that's the best song I've ever heard. Ta!" Þey clutched þeir belly. "What a gods damned reprobate!"

"Bloody fucking fools, the lot of them!" I knocked back a shot of whiskey. Thank all the gods for that still. "Here comes another refrain of courtly outrage. At least no one died this time."

We examined our drinks and refilled. I'd spent the four nights since the punching incident in the healer's wing, assisting Eäriel and Liriadis, and dodging curious children. Feanim, surprisingly, had already smoothed over most of the ruffled feathers, including Celebel's. Nimthil had taken to scrutinizing me as though she expected Rafael to leap from my shadow at any moment. Given how much he'd terrorized her lately, I understood.

"Any word since your return from…from aiding Celebel?" Velúara was still too fresh to address directly. "Lámirië's last report was extensive."

Nemohee's face flushed. "No news of Cael. The soulbond tethers us yet, stretching off into some weird distance. He lives, but I ken nothing else. Does he prosper? Has he found some other love? Is he afraid?" Þeir eyes were far away. I resisted taking þeir hand. Good way to garner my own punch to the gut. "Perhaps better to send yer beastly Dragon after him. Run him to ground, discover the truth."

Crow. If he weren't so needed here, I would make the request. Nemohee was on friendly enough terms with Rafael.

My friend sighed heavily, drawing it out into a dramatic groan. Þey kicked þeir heels up on the table, biting a hunk off a wedge of cheese þey'd absconded. My bond with the Dragon heralded his approach.

Nemohee sat up, peering past me. "Gods, look at ye. You're a big fucker, do ye know that?"

Rafael ducked under the doorway. Many entrances catered to shorter statures. Even I had to bend my neck at times.

His presence filled the space. "Are you still feigning anger?"

I whipped around. "I *am* angry with you, you wicked creature! You've conjured up yet another batch of unnecessary woe!"

"I did less than requested." He leaned against the doorjamb, taking up the entire exit. "I had faith in your healing."

Nemohee howled with laughter again. "He's got ye there, Moon Lady."

Rafael nodded acknowledgement.

"Oh no, you don't. You two will not be my countermelody." I looked back and forth, unsure of where to direct my glare. Totally unrepentant, the pair of them. "Rafael, gods, at least leave before you scare the kitchens free of cooks!" I knocked back the rest of my whiskey.

As I ushered him out, Nemohee raised þeir glass in a toast. "Cheers. And you, Red. Return the books ye stole."

"Books?" I glanced quizzically between them.

"Aye, Celebel made me head librarian while I'm here to keep this one from bleeding the library dry," Nemohee said.

The Dragon's nose wrinkled.

Delight lifted my mood. "You're head librarian? You?"

"Aye, 'defend them with yer life', Celebel said, and I shall!" Nemohee flexed þeir biceps and pulled a grimace, flashing þeir pointed canines.

Rafael's flat stare answered my questions.

"That's absolutely brilliant!" I wiped tears of mirth from my eyes and the Dragon utterly ignored us both.

Chapter 22

THE Dragon led me to his new quarters in the battlements. Similar in size to the previous, though arranged differently. The familiar buzz of the wards and dampening field tingled on my skin as I crossed them. He had chosen another room with only one window, directly across from the door. It illuminated a large, unused bed with a plain ironwood headboard to the right of the entry. Quite a contrast to my mossy hot spring cave. A desk piled with books and a wardrobe vied for the remaining space on the far side of the bed.

Rafael swept me off my feet and laid me on the bed in one fluid motion.

I scowled at him. "Bold, sir. I'm still angry with you."

"You are not." Shrugging off his cloak, he sat at the edge of the bed, rubbing the balls of my bare feet with his thumbs.

"Stop that, I am!" I tried to pull my feet away, but he held me fast.

"Feanim is recovering perfectly well. As are you." His hands slid up my lower legs as he leaned forward.

I trembled with need under his touch. Damn, he was right. My anger had fled. If it had been anyone other than Feanim, I wouldn't be so quick to forgive.

The heat in Rafael's eyes made me press my thighs together. Releasing me, he removed his jerkin and shirt, kicking off his boots.

I sat up, running my greedy hands over his bare chest and abdomen. "What would you like, Dragon?" A thousand, thousand years could I touch his body, and never reach satiation.

"I would like a lock of your hair." His fingers trailed through my hair and across my breasts, hefting them in his palms.

I looked at him askance. "Are you planning something awful?"

Rafael huffed as he played with my nipples through my thin linen shift. "You have no faith in me."

"You have quite the reputation for being awful." I swatted his hands away. "Recently demonstrated, as I recall. Never force me to heal Feanim again."

"Nothing awful, I promise. This time." His grin revealed sharp teeth.

"Now I truly cannot trust you!" I climbed off the bed.

He grabbed me around the waist from behind, pulling me down against him and rolling us both onto his back on the mattress. I struggled, tangling myself further in the sheets.

He rumbled with amusement, trapping my legs with his. "Break yourself free. Or give me a lock of your hair. Your choice."

"Tell me what you're planning or you can simply hold me forever."

"Not a bad trade." He tightened his arms until my bones creaked.

I writhed, trying to slip from his grasp. "Bear-hugging me to death is not romantic!"

"Is it not? I have much to learn. Alas. Perhaps I shall simply eat you and take the hair." His teeth grazed my ear.

I jerked away. "This is why everyone thinks you evil." He loosened his grip, and I twisted to face him, propping myself up on his chest. "You say the most disturbing things." I kissed him anyway, and he nipped at my bottom lip.

The memory of the charred outpost popped into my head, giving me pause. I turned from it, or it turned from me.

"Perhaps they are correct. You are the only one mad enough to want to fuck me." His eyes glittered, noting the shift in me.

"I am most certainly not the only one." I traced his lips with a finger. "I know you have not forgotten Carafindrien's ill-fated advances, the poor girl. And Feanim, obviously."

Other elves must surely be curious, but perhaps unwilling to admit their attraction to him. Xyxs was a clear stand-in for at least a few. On the road, a female silver drake had watched Rafael's every move like a woman starved. My thoughts sobered him, unmasked as they were.

I pressed the finger more firmly against his mouth. "Many of us have lost the war of common sense to our libidos. Now, tell me why you want my hair."

Rafael kissed my finger. "I want a piece of you to keep close. You have no scales to shed, hair is easy to replace, and yours is lovely."

Oh, that was surprisingly sweet. I felt a little bad for teasing him. "Is this a drake custom, trading scales?"

A smile tugged at his mouth. I kissed the corner of that smile and plaited a long lock of hair. Taking his hand, I raised a single talon and used it to slice neatly through the braid near my scalp. I handed him the shorn lock. He wrapped it around his wrist and tied it.

"I do want to fuck you. Very badly." Grabbing his hand again, I put his index finger in my mouth and sucked it, making eye contact and thinking hard about our encounter in the library. His lips parted, and I ran my tongue carefully along the pad of his finger. Wishing it were his cock instead.

His erection scraped against my thigh. "May I make another request?" Red seeped into the flames of his eyes.

"Another one today?" I took small sips of air, trying to slow my racing heart.

He rolled me onto my back, leaning over me, the chorus growl gaining intensity like a coming storm. "Make me bleed."

I sucked in a full breath. "Are you certain? Last time we tried something similar, you were spectacularly upset. You disappeared for three seasons!" One of the worst reactions I'd ever witnessed from him, and one of the few times I'd ever felt truly in danger. "I will not agree unless you can tell me exactly what went too far. You've prevented me from discussing your limits in detail in the past, but no more. No guessing."

Rafael sobered. "I am…sensitive about my throat. I should have warned you."

"Yes, you bloody well should have!" I softened, stroking his cheek. Last time, I'd made a cut along the base of his throat. He had fully lost control, launching himself at me, snarling and snapping. "I have no desire to either re-traumatize you *or* put myself in harm's way. I hate causing you pain."

He took my face in his hands and kissed me for a long time, a simple press of his lips against mine, matching breath. Soothing himself, perhaps.

"Until then, it was good," he said when our lips parted. "Pain helps. Bleeding helps."

"You would have the most unnaturally high pain tolerance of anyone I've ever met," I said. He grinned, somehow a purely draconian expression. "You've claimed killing is not sexual for you, but sometimes I wonder. I've seen the look in your eyes before battle." Some mental block often prevented me from examining just how different my Dragon truly was, and where I drew the arbitrary line of my morality.

"I like a challenge." Sharp teeth flashed. "Sorely lacking thus far."

"You are a strange creature. You find no challenge in battle, so you come to me begging for hurt instead of comfort."

His pupils dilated with something not quite lust. "You can open old wounds. Do your worst." The timbre of his voice buzzed in my ribs.

That was certainly a departure. Last time I'd wielded þilvor blades. Using my power on him in such a manner… Did it defy my principles? Unhealing for the sake of pleasure? Overall, I found the concept disturbing.

"Ah, I have upset you." He moved to rise from the bed. "I have blades—"

I took his hand and guided him back down. "Not upset, merely unprepared. I've truthfully never considered using my power in that way. It could be constructive, after a fashion. If it helps you." I chewed my lip.

Rafael brought me so much bliss while always denying himself. Letting my initial objections run through me, I shifted my perspective. I would have total control over these injuries. Perhaps I could re-heal him stronger and better. More than anything, I wished to make him feel as good as he did for me.

"Tell me which areas or wounds you wish me to avoid. Be as specific as possible. I don't want to reassemble you in a real way after this. And yes, I know the areas that are obviously off-limits. I won't make you say it. Your throat as well. Is there anything else?"

He exhaled a hot breath against my skin. "Are you able to intuit what caused the injuries?"

"Something like that. I can sense the nature of an injury, like finding a seam. It gives me a general impression of what happened, and when. Occasionally a flash of who inflicted it, but no further context."

He nodded thoughtfully. "Those you once called the Tárthanë… Those will be the oldest wounds."

I cupped my hands over my heart with a nod, letting his past wash over me so it would not linger. The Tárthanë were ancient humans, the predecessors of both the spiritless Ardhanë and the spirit-wielding Atani. All the Tárthanë were gone now, wiped out in the mass extinction event of Rafael's unrelenting wrath. In the place where his legend began, he'd hunted them into the very crevices of the world until not a single Tárthanë remained.

They had cried out to the elves for help. When we responded, the Red Dragon killed enough of us for our people to become forever embittered toward him. We'd closed our gates to all supplicants after that. Those events earned him the "God of Carnage" moniker. All due to the hideous abuse he had endured as an abandoned changeling child.

I kissed him, letting him taste my thoughts, my intentions, and most importantly, my love. "Instruct me how to begin. I will need to pull from your strength to utilize so much of my spirit for this."

"Take whatever you like." He spread his arms wide, sprawling over the bed on his back. "Hurt me."

I stood and looked him over, considering my options. Hungry intensity sparked to flame in his eyes. Our soulbond sang, almost shimmering in the space between us, where it tethered our very essence together. I touched it, and energy surged into me.

Best to start with shallow, recent wounds. Sending my spirit into Rafael's body, I searched for the edges of cuts and gashes. Similar to tugging on trailing threads from a woven cloth, once I grasped one, I could pull at the warp and weft until it opened. I kept enough distance that if his hot blood splashed, or he suddenly lashed out, I would be out of reach. Despite his assurances, doubt lingered.

There. A shallow cut over his ribs ran diagonally north to south. Nothing deep enough to be serious or bleed profusely. I tugged, and it split open, blood trickling down his side. Rafael hissed. His eyes were fierce, challenging. I pulled open a slash over his chest, and another one, forming a wide "x" shape. His lips parted, breath quickening. Did I dare admit how the blood aroused me as well?

"Deeper," he growled. "This does not hurt."

I found claw marks in his right bicep and yanked. He made an encouraging noise, and I followed more furrows across his back, ripping through the thick shoulder girdle and trapezius muscles. He rumbled, narrowed eyes bright with desire. A piercing wound in his outer thigh. A laceration all the way to the bone on his left calf. I paused, studying him.

"How does that feel?"

"All the frustration you feel, take it out on me. Fuck me up." He grinned, steaming blood soaking through the sheets. "Break my bones. Sever my limbs. Eviscerate me, if you wish. I am yours."

"Your limbs and organs function best where they are."

I opened three deep slashes over his abdomen. I had no desire to sink to my elbows in his guts again, like when we'd first met. Unprepared, I'd been badly burned trying to put him to rights. My least favorite healing experience. But to paint him with his own blood, to experience the Dragon's arousal as my own? Gods, I burned with him.

To humor him, I cracked a few ribs, and he sighed. Nothing severe enough to create troublesome fragments. Based on the basket weave of seams I sensed, he'd broken them so many times it boggled the mind. Anywhere I examined his skeleton, old fractures spiderwebbed across his bones.

Rafael's absurdly resilient body healed most of the injuries I opened as quickly as I unhealed others. Encouraging. I wasn't going too far. I littered him with old bruises in one sweeping motion.

"You are leaving my face untouched," he pointed out.

"It makes me uncomfortable to ruin your handsome face," I said.

Slowly, he raised a fist. I froze; a mouse fixated on an adder preparing to strike. He hammered that fist into the ribs I'd broken with a *crack*, making me jump. The Dragon coughed a great laugh, spitting blood from the broken ribs now piercing his lungs. He aimed a talon at his cheek, preparing to gauge it.

So I broke his clavicle to drop that arm. He laughed harder, more horribly, baring blood-streaked teeth.

"Very well, if you truly desire this." Focusing my spirit into a whip, I cracked his jaw, dislocating it. It stopped the awful laugh, but his eyes lit up.

I worked faster, slashing through muscle, snapping bones, popping joints out of their sockets. He moaned, his body correcting the damage as I went.

I smashed his fingers on both hands. That arched his back. I took a moment to appreciate how much he was enjoying himself. And sincerely question my sanity. Gods, I still wanted to fuck him while I tore open his body.

The Dragon made eye contact with me. I broke his feet for good measure. Then I re-opened the compound fracture I'd witnessed from Marron. He cried out, buffeting me with his power, and I couldn't stop myself anymore. His spirit flowed into me, mine into him. His blood was my blood. His pain, my pain. And his pleasure threatened to choke me.

I crawled over him and kissed his mouth, heedlessly slipping and burning my hands in the steaming blood. He ripped away my stained shift, crushing me to his chest. I slid down his body to grind my needy clit against his hard cock, his erection barely contained by the now-ruined leather trousers. The tip of his massive cock pressed into me through the barrier of leather.

Growling, he held me tight, slamming his hips against mine. Each blow stretched me a little more, accepting the leather-clad cock the merest hairsbreadth at a time. I bruised myself trying to accommodate him, but I would not, could not stop. Frustrating as it was, the leather protected my most vulnerable flesh from the blistering dragon blood, heightening my ecstasy.

I clawed at his chest, biting his nipples as hard as I could and licking the cooling blood from his skin. Spiced copper and his unique incense filled my mouth.

Rafael's vision superimposed over mine. My hair was wild, my expression maddened with need. My heavy breasts heaved and swayed with my panting. The desperate noises I made, the scent of my sex, the plush softness of my skin painted with his blood. Voices, so many voices, whispering languages I did not recognize. He drew out my every weakness, every doubt, every fear. Layers of me; spirit, thought, flesh, emotion, potential, power, sex. His thoughts churned faster and faster. An orchestral score all at once. The volcanic force of him rose all around me.

Oh, how he wanted me. To crack open my chest and eat my beating heart. To absorb my essence and trap me within him for all eternity. To hold me and stroke my hair. To protect me with red violence from the slightest hurt. To break his body at my feet. To die at my hands. To grant my every desire. Especially the one throbbing between his legs.

We crashed together. By the time I finished screaming his name, his injuries had all healed. My vision normalized, blood rushing in my ears. Blood, everywhere.

"I submit to your strength." Rafael's voice held a tone of ritualistic acknowledgement.

A part of mate claiming? Likely so, but I could not care. "Why are you so gods damn attractive covered in blood? You are so fucking twisted." I smoothed over the spattered burn marks on my skin. "And so am I by association. Fucking hells."

He chuckled softly. "I have something for you, my mate. My beloved."

Resting me gently on the sticky, bloody sheets, he stretched forward, reaching for a drawer in the desk. The Dragon's broad back blocked my view. Just as I was about to ask, he took my hand and dropped a familiar, heavy weight into it. My original mortar and pestle! I teared up.

"When did... Have you had this all this time?" I traced edges smoothed from all the years I'd spent directing the flow of the creek over the stones. "Oh, I've missed it so much." A piece of home. My old, peaceful life.

"I made a sweep that way not long ago and checked your bower for anything that might be useful. I took some books too," Rafael admitted with a slight smile.

"Of course you did." I laughed and hugged him, heedless of the tacky blood. "I'm so happy to have this back."

"That you left it behind surprised me."

"Everything happened so fast." I clutched my precious utensils to my chest. "I would have better prepared, but…" The sadness of the circumstances took hold.

"But I chased you away," he finished for me, kissing the top of my head.

"I only wish we could have talked." I traced the mortar's smooth lines. "All things considered, you've handled this far better than I expected. I'm grateful."

He kissed my forehead and the base of my ears.

"Now, I need a bath and you need to burn these sheets." I wiped myself as clean as I could with the aforementioned ruined sheets.

Rafael reclined on the bed, eyes closed, with his hands behind his head and his ankles crossed, perfectly content to marinate in his own blood. The force of my attraction to him in that scene made me question my sanity yet again.

Chapter 23

A DRAWN-OUT, mournful hoot, followed by a series of avian grunts, caught my ear as I made my way to my chambers. Clad only in Rafael's blood, I jogged back to the outer courtyard. Lámirië had returned, mounted on a massive eagle-owl. Celebel, trailing a cluster of elves, dashed through the gates as she slid from the raptor's back to her knees.

Celebel ran to her side. "Are you well? What has happened?"

She gathered herself, pushing her dark hair out of her bruised face. "Taloth is surrounded."

A hiss of shock rippled through the gathering.

"Where are the others? Where is your horse? The drakes?" He braced her against his arm, easing her onto her less injured side.

"The drakes were on my ear tips and will arrive shortly. The others…" Lámirië shook her head against his shoulder, squeezing her eyes shut. "The Siltaur spared me their last eagle-owl to beg for aid."

Taloth was the largest remaining Siltaur roost. Nothing like our walled metropolises of old, such as Leyûduin or Sirelon, but majestic and secure. Until now, at least. Understandable that the Siltaur hadn't wanted to abandon their ancestral trees to the Fomorians. Our woodland kin had always favored smaller, more remote settlements.

"Cúraniel, attend to her wounds." Celebel paused, frowning. "Why are you naked and bloody? No, do not answer that. I can smell *him* on you." He directed a serving youth to fetch Feanim from the forge and strode into the great hall, following by a worried knot of elves.

Lámirië's wounds were many. The poor woman was bleeding from multiple lacerations and an arrow lodged between her scapula and ribs just beneath her arm. A lucky strike, that. Angled differently, it might have killed her.

Boshkt trailed in. No sign of the *viigsakh*.

"Grenyk reports to the Red," the mossy drake said at the open question on my face.

Unusually subdued, Boshkt lifted Lámirië without being asked and carried her to the healer's wing. Though he squinted at me, nostrils flaring, he wisely did not comment on my state of undress.

"Ugly buggers outnumbered us," he said conversationally in draconian. "Those hidden faeries, you call 'em Fomorians? Swarms! I'm always good to scrap, me, but Grenyk said no. Said we need reinforcements."

"Grenyk has good sense. I would hate to lose you." I patted his lichenous shoulder, and a ripple went through the drake. He tilted his head, giving me an unreadable look.

With raised brows, Eäriel handed me a fresh shift and apron. She shooed curious children away as we nestled the Duedellen warrior in the nearest bed. The older youths brought blankets, rags, and warm water. With a murmur of gratitude, I scrubbed my face and hands clean in the basin, winding my hair into a knotted tail so it wouldn't trail over my patient.

One child tugged on the drake's tail. When he turned, fanning his fins, they all shrieked and scattered, laughing. I held my breath, but Boshkt only chuckled to himself.

"Same everywhere, children," he said.

Eäriel brewed a blood-building decoction, demonstrating the process to the children as I cleaned the patient. Focusing my spirit into my hands, I laid them over each wound, starting with the arrow. I had to work fast, staunching the fountain of blood that followed the shaft's removal. My power suffused her body, knitting the flesh together, drawing away the swelling and damage. She lapsed unconscious. All the better for recovery.

"Your skill is required in the field," Celebel's voice came from the doorway. "Make preparations when you finish here. Eäriel, we need Lámirië ready to travel as soon as possible." With a quick kiss of gratitude to his bodyguard's forehead, he left us to our work.

Chapter 24

REACHING Taloth was a challenge. Heavy snows reached that boreal forest before even the higher elevations in the mountains. There were few enough woolens and furs to go around, let alone blankets for the horses. The Pîntellum armor relieved some of those concerns, as it proved an incredible insulator from the cold.

The descending western route was far easier to traverse than the trek that brought us to Amrún. Despite the snow, we'd supposedly reach Taloth in five days of hard riding. Rafael matched his pace to Iruwher, despite her protests.

As the trees closed around us, I breathed deeper. The gentle *shush* of snow falling from cedars, the scraping of rodents under the ice, the distant bugle of a bull elk searching for a mate; it brought tears to my eyes. Gods, I'd missed the forest.

At such a grueling pace, I hadn't much time to revel. My life became the wisping breath of horses, muffled hoofbeats in the snow, and the occasional grumbling huff of a drake. We stopped only to rest our mounts and lit no fires to announce our approach.

A cacophonous boom ripped through the forest, accompanied by the splintering of many crushed trees and a rising blanket of shrieking birds. The ground shook, making the horses snort and prance. Fuck, was that a redwood? We picked up speed.

Taloth rose above the winter-blanketed canopy; an ancient and massive family circle of redwoods, joined with intricate bridges, ladders, and pulley systems. The center, originally standing empty, had been built up over the ages to house the largest population of Siltaur elves in all of Vaeda.

Now with a massive hole in its defenses—that crash was indeed from the felling of one of the foundation trees. Fomorians swarmed through the gap. Fortunately, the redwoods had protective spirit of their own as well as a natural fire resistance to combat the horde of Fomorians trying to set it ablaze. The Siltaur had drawn up their ladders. Arrows rained down in a deluge, half-lost in the buffeting snow.

After a quick study of the enemy, Celebel positioned me at the rear of the left flank cavalry. He and Rafael agreed for once, naming it the safest place for me, away from the crush of fighting at the gap in the tree wall. Celebel took his place toward the right flank, and Feanim led the center.

Much to Feanim's frustration, Rafael adamantly refused to leave my side. Nor would he allow me to accompany him to his usual position, claiming the risk was too great.

"You cannot use your dragonfire that close to the roost," the Duedellen protested.

Rafael was unmoved. "I need no fire to kill faeries. Tooth and talon will suffice."

I kept my counsel. What did I know of war? My Dragon's solid, confident presence soothed my fears, though the other elves in my company were not pleased.

The command to advance came soon enough, rippling through the ranks in a continued sign. Iruwher quivered with excitement, and I reined her in to prevent her from bolting ahead of the line. Rafael jogged easily along beside me, perfectly calm, with nary a spark in his hair.

Ahead, scores of Fomorians climbed the thick, cushiony redwood bark like monstrous ants, their bronze armor glinting. Others hacked at the trunks nearest the gap. Here and there barbed ladders rose, digging into the bark. Siltaur shot them down from their high perches. Snowy owls and ravens assisted, pecking and scratching at the eyes of enemies who ascended too far.

Rafael barked a harsh command in draconian. A deep bellow answered from somewhere above and behind us. Xyxs and the bright yellow drake Abrrys winged down from the sky, directly into the industrious, wood-chopping Fomorians. Abrrys screeched like a nightmarish bird and bit the head off her closest foe.

The Fomorians hardly turned when our front line crashed into them, trampling many. As planned, our company sang as soon as they engaged the enemy. I matched the pitch, and their spirit poured into me.

Giddy, I almost lost my seat. Rafael steadied me in the saddle with a hand on my thigh. He kept attackers away as my spirit soared. I swirled the power into a spear, focusing it in my heart-mind, and searched the nearest Fomorians. They lit up with brilliant reticulation. Expelling the spirit all at once, a score of them burst apart as my unhealing struck.

As planned, I chained the attack down the entire line of our forces, spirit jumping from one singer to the next. The strongest voice in each expelled the unhealing, and Fomorians disintegrated in bright flashes. We pressed the advantage, horses stomping and biting, elves stabbing with halberd, spear, and sword.

The Fomorians at the edges of the attack screamed, turning to me. I had the strength for perhaps three more strikes. Dead Fomorians, reduced to their underlying sidhe bodies, collapsed in heaps around me.

Rafael dealt with any who dared counterattack, killing with brutal efficiency. No bloodlust this time. He remained cool and focused, decimating Fomorians with ease. His greatsword whistled as he swung it in practiced arcs. Everywhere it slashed, enemies died.

The song rose again, and I gathered spirit for another round. We needed to take at least one alive, in its true form, to learn what drove them to capture elves.

Something whizzed past my ear, taking the elf before me in the back of the neck in a blur of fletching. He was dead before he even knew he'd been hit. Another projectile whistled through the air. The target, a young Lachanaur, dodged just in time. The arrow took a Fomorian through the eye instead.

Chaos erupted. Our cavalry, now hemmed in, raised a harried defense. At various points down the line, our companies fended off the sudden barrage from deadly precise archers in the woods.

It couldn't be.

I turned in my saddle, into the hateful faces of the elvish infantry charging our flank. *Elves.* Charging *us.* Iruwher shied, rearing and wheeling toward the oncoming crush. Surely this was some mistake, surely…

Ripples of horror spread through our ranks as horses whinnied greetings to elves they knew, ears perking. As siblings cried welcome to their kin. As lovers leaped from the saddle to embrace their presumed-lost partners. Only to be slain.

The remaining Fomorians pressed their newfound advantage. Horses screamed, trapped between fae and betrayer. Riders fell. Siltaur archers aided from above where they could, but our neat ranks splintered in the bewildering maelstrom.

It couldn't be! Tears filled my eyes faster than the membrane could absorb them. I swayed, faces blurring into the trees. To turn on us in the heat of the moment and leave the court was one thing. But to anger the gods deliberately? To defile our most sacred tenets? I clutched my belly, fighting down nausea. Celebel's anguish shivered along the soulbond, mirroring my own. Surely, Silfanië was not among our attackers. She had never been martial. Would I know her in armor?

'*Steady, Cúraniel. You have trained for this.*' Rafael's bass rumble in my mind brought me back to myself.

I cast about, but the Dragon had disappeared. Damn him. "Rafael, I need you! Where have you gone?"

An eagle's peal caught my ears. I searched the dark boughs of the surrounding forest. There! A massive, red-plumaged raptor perched nearby, watching with burning, unblinking eyes.

The eagle cocked his head. '*I cannot observe if they know of my presence. Note the size of these groups.*' He nodded toward the newcomers. I followed the direction of his hooked beak. Small clusters of elves attacked strategic points in the line. '*I suspect they target individuals. Kill them with prejudice. I will guard your flank.*'

'*I cannot kill an elf. The gods—*'

'*You can.*' He swooped from the branch and caught a spear aimed at me in his taloned feet. With a barrel roll, he flung it back at the offending attacker. The elf died clutching at her face. '*You must.*' Crimson wings beat the air as he settled once more on his perch.

I swallowed hard. '*But everyone fears you! Surely the mere sight of you would route them!'*

He pinned me with an implacable stare. *'Teach them to fear* you.'

With shaking hands, I took up my crescent blades. Another elf hurtled over a fallen log. Shrouded in a white tabard, a hawk's-head helm obscured his features. He charged directly at me. Rafael made no move to stop him. Only an instinctive flinch of my hands upward to protect my face deflected the elf's swinging sword. Iruwher squealed in rage. She whipped her head around. Sinking her teeth into his shoulder, she flung him to the ground.

My opponent rolled, avoiding the bay mare's flashing hooves, and regained his feet. He grabbed my leg, dragging me from the saddle. I kicked as hard as I could. My foot connected with his thigh as I tumbled. Landing on one hand, I sprang back into a ready stance. I'd lost a crescent blade, but one would suffice. The mare whirled to kick another assailant, and I was on my own.

"Good." Rafael emerged from the trees in his usual form.

My adversary startled. I darted forward at his lapse. Hooking my curved blade around the wrist holding his sword, I twisted as hard as I could. He shrieked. Blood sprayed. A sword fell to the ground, with a hand still grasping the hilt. Gods, the Pîntellum armor was powerful!

"Kill him." The bloodlust had arrived, burning in the Dragon's eyes.

"Rafael, I cannot!" My hands shook so badly I could barely keep hold of my blade. I couldn't seem to catch my breath, heart hammering in my ears.

Drawing a long dagger with his remaining hand, the fallen elf lunged at me. He aimed for the joint under my chin. I screamed and flailed backward. Somehow, I knocked his dagger away. With a wild swing, my blade parted the maille coif over his throat as though it were no more than a scarf. Arterial spray veiled my helm.

Equally stunned, we locked eyes. Something was wrong. I squinted. The pupil shape wobbled like a drop of water on a hot skillet. He clutched his throat, gurgling. Instinct moved me to help. Rafael caught my arm, holding me back. Pink bubbles frothed from elf's lips, and toppled over. Dead.

"First hand-to-hand kill. You are a blooded warrior now," the Dragon said. I turned a blank stare upon him. He touched my cheek, curiously gentle. "The next will be easier."

Easier? Easier to kill an elf? *I'd killed an elf.*

Would Dûemer rescind her blessing? The goddess was silent. Tremors grew until I shook like an aspen in a gale. The body at my feet stained the snow crimson in a slow-spreading aura. Who would sing him to the stars now?

Rafael turned and spat fire at the remaining traitors. Despite Feanim's assertion, the flame snaked through the trees. At the drake's thunderous roar, the Fomorians broke and tried to flee. The enemy elves were no fools; they too, fled the Dragon's wrath. Our own forces backed away from him.

"Advance to center!" he bellowed.

I swung onto Iruwher's back and followed. Rafael ripped through the opposition like claws through silk. Their tattered ranks parted before him, and he led us to consolidate our formation with the others. Distant booms shook the trees as we passed.

Enemy elves melted away like the very snow that hid them. Fomorians scattered and died. We came upon the central company. The two drakes working in tandem with our infantry had made short work of the Fomorians spilling through the gap in the tree wall. Each drake now took on multiple enemy elves while our forces staggered from the shock.

My vision went strange. The tableau blurred at the edges, wavering. My hearing dampened. I equalized the pressure in my ears and blinked rapidly to clear my eyes.

Feanim stood alone, facing a single figure sharing his height and build. The Consul wore his customary green tabard, embroidered with his house sigil, over his shining armor. An unadorned, argent tabard draped his adversary's white-enameled armor. Wings rose from the helm, adding to the ethereal effect. White on white; a winter wraith. A tendril of smoke drifted across the scene.

"The dark sun remains, though bitter be the cold." The words fell from my lips unbidden. Was that my voice?

A gust of snow obscured my senses. When it cleared, the figure was gone. The entire enemy force was gone. Had we won?

Feanim stood before me, seething. "Where *the fuck* did you hear that?"

I swayed and fell from my saddle. Rafael caught me.

"I-I didn't." My breath came fast and shallow, senses clearing. "I had a sort of lucid vision."

"Tell me," the Duedellen demanded. My description knit his brow into a furious glower. "Beredhel. You saw Beredhel again. Only he would know those words. But he died at the Breaking of the Stones!"

Rafael's deep voice garnered everyone's attention. "I saw him as well. An elf with the pallor of bleached bone, and your look about him." He stared at a fixed point in the woods, but I could not determine his target. "Drifting on the smoke."

"Fucking hells. My brother must be driving all of this."

So, this was the Pale King.

I HUDDLED beside the fire and squeezed my eyes shut, trying to make sense of it all. Rafael's presence curled around me in a dark, velvety fog. A gentle hand tilted my chin up.

Crouching on his heels in front of me, the Dragon's eyes were serene blue. "You did well, my dove."

I struggled to say something intelligent, to explain my utter lack of discipline after all of his training. All that came out was a sniffle. It broke the dam, releasing a hiccoughing flood of tears. Rafael pulled me close, and I buried my face in his shoulder. He submitted no judgment and thrummed to soothe me. I clutched at his clothes, trying to burrow under his skin.

A chorus of keening drifted through the woods around us. I was not alone in my heartbreak. The Taloth Siltaur, preparing to join us at Amrún, mourned their home. Those who had closed with other elves lamented the kinslaying and wailed to the gods for absolution.

I'd spill all of my thoughts, self-doubt, and fears to Celebel later.

Currently, all I needed was the comfort of someone stronger than me. Truth be told, I needed the sort of comfort only far bloodier hands than mine could offer.

Boots crunching on snow got our attention. Rafael released me, turning as Nemohee materialized from the dark woods with wild eyes, stomping like a human.

"I saw him," þey cried. "I heard his voice!"

Concern for my friend overcame my self-pity. "Cael?"

Nemohee sank to þeir knees before us. "Aye, 'twas him. I searched and bellowed his name. Like smoke, he was. I lost him in the crush." Furious tears lined þeir silver eyes. For Nemohee to weep, the emotion must be extreme. "He's with those fuckers what attacked us! Must be compulsion. My Cael is a gentle soul, he would *never*." Þey punched the ground in helpless anguish, sending up a puff of snow. "But we caught one!"

"A traitor?" I sat up, ears perking.

"Nay, a fecking Fomorian." Nemohee scrubbed the tears away, slowing þeir breath. "Took it alive. We thought mayhap ye could only unwind him a little instead of the whole 'exploding light' bit."

We followed Nemohee to the captured Fomorian. Bound with spirit and spidersilk ropes, the grey-skinned beast had a pig's head with watery, pink eyes. Feanim prodded it with the tip of his sword, and the creature spat unintelligible insults at him. A fire at their backs lit the scene with deceptive warmth.

Feanim looked up at our approach. "Rafael, where have you been? I still cannot decipher this language."

"It is not language. The cadence, accent, and vocabulary changes constantly. I have yet to hear a repeated word," Rafael said. "Likely a geas making nonsense of their speech." Only my Dragon would catalogue every word spoken in the pitch of battle.

I approached the fae, sending out a tendril of spirit to find its wounds. Perhaps if I only unveiled part of the body? I tugged at a superficial scar on the back of its hand.

The Fomorian shrieked, writhing in the ropes as though I'd pressed iron to its flesh. The seams lit up as before, but I held my power back to the barest trickle. Slowly, carefully, I picked open only the one wound.

Instead of exploding, the rest of the seams pulsed like a heartbeat. Gradually, the brilliance faded. In its place, a male sidhe blinked rapidly. Enormous black eyes dominated a green and white speckled face with tufted ears. Shining ebony horns rose from a nest of wild, mossy curls. He still wore the bronze armor, only now fitted to a much thinner, shorter frame. Cloven hooves took the place of booted feet.

"Can ye speak?" Nemohee asked in accented sylvaine, the common fae language. I understood it well enough, but spoke it poorly.

The sidhe shuddered violently, staring at Rafael. I laid a hand on the drake's arm. He huffed, but acknowledged the tacit dismissal and departed. He wouldn't stray from earshot.

"Understand you my words?" the sidhe asked.

He had the typical singsong, almost mocking speech pattern of the greater fae. Even at their most earnest, that accent had an edge of sarcasm to elvish ears. It had led to more than one unintended conflict in the past.

"Understand them? Aye. Trust anything a sidhe says? Feck no." Arms folded, Nemohee's ears flattened.

The fae heaved a tremulous sigh. "Please, please. No choice have we."

My skin prickled with foreboding.

The sidhe continued. "Correct is the Red Dragon. A curse from the dark ones this is, overlaid with geas to prevent us from telling of our plight. From captive nightmares I wake into bondage." Tilted green brows pinched and he struggled against the ropes.

"Who are the dark ones?" Feanim asked. "Why do they attack us through you?"

The sidhe's back arched as he wailed. "To speak of them is to summon. Our most dear they hold; our entire people threatened. Compelled are we to capture the unturned. Those we cannot capture, we must kill."

Nemohee lunged forward and grabbed the sidhe by the shoulders, shaking him until his jaws clacked together. "Where have you taken them? Where are they? Fucking tell me, or I'll be the one draining you!" Þeir eyes glowed nearly white, fangs lengthening.

Feanim caught Nemohee's shoulder. Þey whirled, punching him in the nose with a sharp jab. He fell back, clutching his face. Perhaps it would be my turn to punch him next.

I inserted myself between my friend and the captive. "Nem, please! If you kill him now, we may never find our lost kin."

"I know not," he cried. "We only deliver them to the dark ones."

"What is an 'unturned'? Who is turning them? Who are these so-called dark ones?" Feanim's voice was slightly nasal from the leaking blood he pretended to ignore. "Where are they?"

"Demons," said Rafael. First curses, then traitor—turned?— elves, and now *demons?* The sidhe cowered as the Dragon leaned over him. "There are few places where they may reach into Vaeda. You will tell us which."

The sidhe wailed, trying in vain to move away from the drake. "I dare not for the sake of my kindred!"

Rafael grabbed one of the captive's horns. With a sharp twist and a *crack*, the horn broke free of the faerie's skull. The sidhe screamed, and I blocked my ears in horror.

"That was not a request."

"Rafael, no!" I grabbed his elbow. "This poor fae has suffered enough!"

Feanim scoffed. Nemohee only gave me a cold stare. The possibility of locating Cael overtook any compassion þey might have had.

The Dragon gestured with the broken horn. "Go. I will not allow your merciful heart to endanger you."

Chapter 28

I AWOKE in the bath to Celebel staring at me, with the voidlet floating past his shoulder. Startled, I splashed him with herb-scented water; after finishing my rounds in the healer's wing, I'd barely emerged from the heated pool since our return to Amrún. Whether I was trying to scrub the horror out of my skin, or merely hiding from the world, I could not discern. My fingernails were tinged rust red, having liberally steeped in the muscle-relaxing decoction I'd dumped in the hot water. Like the blood I'd spilled. I swiped them with moss.

We'd hardly spoken throughout the ride back; I, haunted by my kill, and he wrapped in never-ending debriefings with Feanim, Nemohee, and even Rafael. The torture had evidently yielded little useful information. Phantom quavering pupils in terrified eyes lingered wherever I looked, so I kept my eyes shut as often as possible.

Taloth's population had swelled our ranks. They'd left a few guardians, just as Celebel had with Velúara before it fell, and the rest joined us. All the newly arrived elves, supplies, and troubling revelations had kept him so busy we'd hardly snatched a breath together. I knew not where they'd secreted the captured sidhe or if he'd survived Rafael's questioning. No one had mentioned the dark ones, or Feanim's brother, since, and I dared not ask.

Celebel helped me climb out of the pool. He gathered me carefully in his arms and carried me to the moss bed. With a kiss to my forehead, he laid me on a blanket that smelled faintly of jasmine. He disrobed, smiling down at me.

"I'll make no demands of your remaining energy. I've little enough myself. Might I hold you instead, skin to skin, for a while?"

"As though I would ever refuse." I held my arms up to accept him.

He slid into place and brushed silken lips over mine. His body warmed me, and his cock awakened against my thigh.

"Mm, I feel the vitality returning to my limbs. Are you certain you only wish to be held?" I twined a lock of his hair in my fingers.

Celebel's breath evened out, and he lay still. He must have fallen asleep. I admired his ability to nod off at a moment's notice. He jerked in my arms, coming to with a gasp.

"Cel?" I pulled back, examining his face.

His eyes were oddly blank. I touched his cheek. He did not react, not even to blink. Alert now, I reached for our connection. It shivered, and a tingle ran up my spine. My skin prickled with power, fine hairs rising. Gods, was this what had happened to the 'turned' elves?

He blinked rapidly. Those sky-blue eyes focused, locking in on me with a singular intensity. The pupils remained steady, and our soulbond trembled, thinning.

"Starshine?" Dread tightened my belly. "Celebel?"

He drew a ragged, growling breath, and sat up. The motion was strange, somehow tense. His ears twitched rapidly, and he looked down at his hands, turning them over one at a time. Brow drawn into a scowl, his half-lidded eyes burned. My breath hitched. Something about his expression and the way he rolled his shoulders, loosening his spine.

His unblinking gaze traveled down his body, almost as if seeing it for the first time, and flicked to my face. What had transpired to make him so guarded? I let him take me in his arms, unsure of how to react. As I slid my hands down his back toward his ass, he stiffened and caught them, dragging them back to his shoulders. The strange reaction ratcheted up my unease.

He pressed his mouth to mine. His hard, unyielding mouth.

Crow.

I reared back and slapping him with all the might of my sudden rage. "Rafael! *Get the fuck out of him!*" Gathering my spirit into a flail, I slammed against the growing presence, trying to expel the Dragon from Celebel's mind.

Predictably, Rafael pushed back. Grabbing my arms, he used Celebel's body to press me back into the bed, looming over me. A familiar scowl contorted that lovely face.

"Get the *fuck* out of him now! *What the fuck is wrong with you?*"

I hardly knew what I screamed. Angry tears streamed down my face. Betrayal shocked the air from my lungs, choking off my howl of rage.

His lips brushed the side of my neck, unnaturally hot breath on my skin. Grabbing a fistful of lustrous hair, I jerked his head away from me. He grunted, baring flat-edged teeth.

Why? Fucking hells, why would Rafael do such a thing? All the progress we'd made, destroyed. Gods, was Celebel present in his own body? My heart clenched so hard, I thought it had stopped.

I reached about in panic, seeking the anchor of the soulbond in myself. There! Celebel's bond remained intact, if smothered beneath Rafael's cresting influence.

"*I CAST YOU OUT!*" I lashed out as hard as I could with my power, wielding it with blunt force.

Witchlights winked out and fungus dimmed, air sucking out of the room. Rafael's presence recoiled. I gave another great psychic shove. The Night Mother answered my desperation, drawing her cloak around me, lending me her strength.

The blue of his eyes flickered, and I shoved again.

As abruptly as it had begun, Rafael's presence departed. Celebel collapsed on top of me. The impact with my chest knocked the meager wind from my lungs.

Wheezing through my tears, I rolled him off of me as gently as I could. Healing the mark my angry blow at Rafael had left on Celebel's cheek, I kissed his face over and over, whispering for him to come back to me.

His eyelids fluttered open, unfocused gaze darting wildly around the room. I kissed him again, thoroughly. He steadied at my touch, returning fully to himself. I burst into tears again.

"What…what happened? Are you well?" Celebel asked, bewildered at my sobbing relief. At a loss, he awkwardly patted my shoulders. "Am…am *I* well?"

"Fucking *Rafael* happened. I never thought him capable of such a thing," I snarled when I was finally calm enough to speak.

Celebel's brows shot up. "It's as though I lost consciousness for a moment, trapped in darkness, and awakened to you, crying and furious." He hugged his arms.

"H-he tried to-to possess you," I choked out, scrubbing my eyes. "He succeeded, I mean to say. He possessed you. Briefly, but it was enough. Too much." I took a deep breath, trying to steady myself.

Celebel's ears went flat as he sat bolt upright, color draining from his face. "What do you mean, 'possess'?" His voice dropped dangerously low.

"Exactly as it sounds. He breached your mind and briefly controlled your body."

"Cúraniel, what the *fuck?*" Shock nearly stole his voice. "What the fuck? How does he have such an ability?"

I nodded miserably. "He tried it on me once, not so long ago. Probably to test it. I thought I'd made it clear such a thing it was beyond unacceptable, but apparently not."

Celebel's lips pressed into a thin line, eyes frosting with rage. "*How*, Cúraniel? Answer me. What else is he, other than dragon?"

"For the dragon blood, his sire was the eldest of Dhraxael's offspring."

"First generation." He blew out a breath. "That explains his might. And the rest?"

My mind writhed away from the topic and I panted, wrestling to focus. The words stuck in my craw.

"Cúraniel. Tell me." A barked command.

I sank my spirit into the moss, into the fungus. Centering myself. The veil over my thoughts lifted just enough to force the words out.

"The other half is fire elemental." It sounded so innocuous.

"A salamander?" Celebel blinked in bafflement.

"No. I initially thought the same. His dam is... They call themselves..." I scraped for the name, my body going rigid as I shoved it through uncooperative lips. "'Aa'shekahn'."

I shivered. He stared, waiting. The words thrashed, fighting me. Fighting to remain unsaid. With a push from the Night Mother herself, I forced the speech.

"We know them as... Háramorn." I finished in a small voice, dropping my eyes in the face of Celebel's sudden, incandescent fury.

"Rafael is a bloody *fire demon?* And not any fire demon, but one of the *lords* of the fucking *hells?* You have been coupling with a gods damned *demon* all this time?" His eyes flashed. "Cúraniel, what the fuck is wrong with you?"

"Why are you angry with me, as though I'm the one who violated you? As though I've ever had a choice in any of this!" I slid off the bed. Snatching up a robe and the scale pendant, I readied to leave. Fury energized me.

"It is the very nature of demons to deceive. Rafael has been lying to you this entire time. He had no intention of honoring this supposed truce or his word to you about not harming me. Are you truly running into his arms?"

Celebel had never looked at me with such contempt, not even during our row over the dampening field. I thought I'd reached my limit for wrath in one night, but I was mistaken.

"I'm going to confront the blighter, but thank you for maligning my character. I suppose I know what you truly think of me now. Honestly, fuck *both* of you." I stormed off before he could speak further, angrily wiping tears off of my cheeks.

I located the Dragon through our connection and stomped my way to the war room. Witchlights blazed and winked out as I passed, the air itself quivering with dread. The elves I encountered skittered out of my path without a word. My hair swept out behind me in a dark cape.

I kicked the door open hard enough to bounce it off the adjoining wall. Feanim and Rafael both looked up at me; the Duedellen in surprise, Rafael in grim acknowledgment.

"Feanim, get out," I spat.

He started to protest, but Rafael held up a hand. "Go."

Feanim glowered but cooperated, closing the door behind him with a flourish. The moment he was gone, I threw the scale necklace at Rafael. He caught it in one hand and looked at me with open hurt. Yanking the pearls from my hair broke the silk in two places, pulling a few strands of hair with it. One pearl hit the floor with a *crack*. I tossed the rest on the sideboard, where they rolled and bounced.

"You can fucking keep your blood-soaked trinkets. Stay away

from me." I hiccoughed through my furious tears. "Stay *the fuck* away from Celebel!"

"Cúraniel, I—"

"No, *fuck* you, Rafael. How fucking *dare* you! How could you break your word?" I wanted to scream, but sobs overtook me. I clutched my arms to my chest, swaying.

He moved to lay his hands on my shoulders.

I did scream then, immediately backing out of his reach, ears flat. "No! Do not *fucking* touch me!"

The Dragon sighed. "Come now, enough with the theatrics. Your little toy is unharmed."

"Are you fucking mad? You honestly believe gods-thrice-damned *possession* isn't harmful? Don't you *dare* treat me like a fool!" Rage tightened its grip on me, shaking and rattling through my body. His calm dismissal only worsened it.

He scoffed. "Angering Celebel is not causing harm."

"No. Absolutely not. You cannot decide that for someone else. I may never forgive you for this." I glared as though I could pierce him through with my eyes, forcing him to see the error of his hellish ways. My chest ached like my heart would crack my sternum and crawl out onto the floor. Just as well I couldn't truly fight Rafael, but oh *gods*, was I tempted to die trying. "You disgust me."

"You are spectacular in your rage. Truly beautiful, my mate."

"Oh, no you don't. You will not fucking *flirt* your way out of this. Neither of us consented to what you've done. After tonight, I don't want to hear your voice. Stay away from us both. If you wish to take your people and leave, so be it." I whirled and stalked out of the room, slamming the door behind me. Shards of glass scraped my soul, grinding and shaving me into flecks of misery.

Rafael called my name. I quickened my pace to a jog, desperate to put some physical distance between us. He could easily catch me, but if he had any proper sense, he'd choose another option.

He remained behind.

Part 2

Chapter 26

Celebel

I VIOLENTLY heaved up the contents of my gut until only bile remained. My hands shook as I wiped my mouth and watched the spring carry away my detritus. Oh Maker, how had it come to this? Elf turned against elf, curses abounded, and demons lurked in the shadows. Demons lurked in my very soulbond!

Was my body my own? My mind? If I called forth my spirit, would I instead spew hateful flame? I stared at my hands as though they might strangle me of their own accord. My skin had blanched nearly as pale as Cúraniel's, the bluish veins standing out in a tangled map to my heart.

Shaking my head, I splashed my face in a vain attempt to rinse away the shock. To rinse away the tarnish of the fucking *demon* who'd invaded me. The soulbond hummed with Cúraniel's fury, flaring loud as the vaunted Carnyx. I craved solitude inside my head, inside my soul.

The truth carved a bleeding wound in my chest. My soulmate was corrupted by a fell power and could not be trusted. Taking a deep breath, I dunked my entire head under the water. I held it there until my limbs quivered and lungs burned. Finally, I withdrew with a gasp.

The soulbond dwindled to the merest trickle. She was on the move again. Toward the greenhouse, it seemed. The damp heat of the room stifled me. I longed for the grand windows of Férioth, for the graceful balconies of Velúara. Anything rather than this dark, dank cave of a fortress. I needed air. Not the forge; the demon often lurked there. Nor the library. The hellish blighter had made himself a fixture there as well.

I forced myself to dress with deliberation rather than giving way to impulse. Silver velvet and silk, rescued from Velúara, with all the trappings of my station. I must not forget myself, nor allow that monster to diminish me. My hair, I wore loose. Using my father's mother-of-pearl brush, I worked it to sleek, shining perfection. I placed the Rain Jewel in its slender diadem on my brow.

My feet propelled me to the great hall. Much to my surprise, Nimthil sat upon the dais steps. She looked up at my entrance. Only one witchlight chandelier cast light upon her, crafting a harsh outline. The rest had benefitted her since our arrival at Amrún, but now shadows returned to her wide, hazel eyes. More than her usual regal posture, she held herself rigid, as if she feared breaking. She'd plaited fresh braids into her autumn-leaf curls since last we'd met, coiled about her head in a flowing pattern. It suited her.

"What brings you here?" she asked, hands echoing.

I sat beside her, turning to maintain eye contact. Could I say aloud my soulmate's bonded demon had invaded my soul? No, she feared the red devil as it was. Distress rolled off of the petite Lachanaur queen in waves.

"Restlessness. You?" I steadied my shaky sign. I must not burden her with my woes. Not yet.

Nimthil clasped her hands in her lap, slumping. "Beredhel." The barest whisper, just enough air pushed out to form the name. Her eyes brightened with unshed tears.

Ah, gods. An old wound struck anew.

She took a shuddering breath. "So many trees have grown, spring come and gone again. I thought myself healed…"

I leaned forward and rubbed gentle circles on her upper back. Her ribs were still too palpable, shoulder blades jutting too sharply under her fine aquamarine wool. Perhaps she hadn't recovered as well from the loss of Férioth as I'd assumed. Perhaps, neither had I.

She straightened at my touch. "What of the soulbond?" Her hands fluttered, signing so rapidly the fingers blurred. "Will it return with him? Did I truly feel his death, or was it only Feanim's severance and reconnection of the bond to himself? Fé always claimed he acted thus to save my life. What damage must we have wreaked upon Beredhel with that action? Did we craft his silence all these years?" Nimthil made a strangled noise and covered her face.

I pulled her into my arms, and she rested her forehead on my shoulder. She did not weep, but her ears quivered. So tightly did she cling, her fingers left imprints on my plush velvet robe. With a deep breath, she steadied herself and sat upright.

She cupped my face in her soft hands. "Oh, my friend. Did I ever confide my preference for women before this cursed soulbond snared me?"

That startled a ragged laugh from me. "Instead, the gods plagued you with twin brothers! Feanim alone is plague enough when he throws his weight into it."

The outward focus buoyed me. As long as I listened to Nimthil, I could ignore the yawning chasm in my soul.

"Beredhel was no plague, in truth. He was ever distant, but kind and undemanding. In time, I learned to love him. He so was noble and high-minded, so beloved of the court. He crafted such mighty objects of power! Well do I recall all the debates you held with him over such concentrations of spirit." She sighed, deflating. "I know not if he ever returned my sentiment, as he spoke little of emotion. Then he was dead, and I was bound with Feanim." The corners of her eyes creased. "You must not say such to him, but I have never loved Feanim as I did his brother."

"Your secrets are safe." I signed fealty.

"Now Beredhel returns, ostensibly as a foe. We are truly severed; I cannot feel him in my heart. And so, I mourn anew." She crafted a butterfly of flame, releasing it to flitter up into a dark corner of the ceiling.

CÚRANIEL RETURNED to our chamber with the void creature wrapped about her shoulders like a hooded cloak, her long ears poking through holes in its spangled black form. Its glowing eyes peeped from her shoulder like a living brooch. I ceased my pacing in front of the moss bed, and the pale robe swirled about my legs.

"Where have you been?" It came out more accusatory than I intended. Sleep had avoided me entirely, much as I desired oblivion.

Her shoulders tensed. "I did exactly as I said. I confronted

Rafael, returned his *trinkets*, and told him to fuck off. Then I went to the gardens to ground myself because that was incredibly difficult." Her rich alto flattened. Even with her tight hold on our connection, anger and heartache flared.

I sighed and slumped onto the bed. "I'm primarily angry with him, but I can't help but question your judgment. You knew of Rafael's demon blood and still welcomed him into your bower, into your arms?"

"I warned you about him before we became intimate." She planted a fist on the lush curve of her hip.

Ever defiant, my lady of the moon. With her fierce beauty, she could scorn the very gods themselves, and they'd grovel for her forgiveness. I shuddered internally, recalling the red monster's parentage. Perhaps she already had.

"You told me nothing of his demonic nature!" My eyes crackled with burgeoning spirit.

Cúraniel coughed, clearing her throat. "I've spent decades questioning my judgment. Fighting the bond. Fighting my heart. As he has. Now, it's obvious I'll never appease you. I wish you'd told me such knowledge was enough to break with me before I gave up my entire life."

"Tell you of such knowledge as you withheld from me? You have grown accustomed to having the sovereignty of your thoughts disrespected by that demonic beast, if mind reading is your expectation."

A tear escaped, and she swiped angrily at her cheek. The void creature shivered, expanding. Lights dimmed.

"Cúraniel, this is what the Red Dragon meant by feeding this creature." I could not bring myself to use his elvish name. "You must stop." Raising my palms, was I appeasing the creature or my soulmate? "This is dangerous, funneling your power and emotion into it."

"All of this is dangerous. All of it. I've leaned heavily on the goodwill I've built with Rafael to protect you. To protect everyone. Will any of that matter now?" She folded in on herself, hugging her arms.

If the red monster abandoned us rather than falling in battle, Marron surely would not honor our agreement. My back tightened, aching where the cursed blade had struck me.

The voidlet shivered again, enveloping Cúraniel from ear tip to toes in an expanding cloud of night. I drew on my spirit, readying to dash forward and seize her. The darkness throbbed. My hearing and vision blurred.

"Please do not eat us." She spoke in an uncharacteristically small voice.

The voidlet popped back into the shape of a small cat, blinking at her from the crook of her arm. Cúraniel sank to the floor, her long hair pooling around her.

I lowered myself beside her, my robe billowing out in a silvery cloud over her endless night. "May I take your hand?"

"Will you continue to blame me for Rafael's behavior? For his very nature?" The infinite seas of her eyes threatened to drown me. "You yourself agreed I wasn't responsible for his every action."

Drawing a hand over my brow, I sighed. "This is no fault of yours. Never have I felt such fear, and I shouldn't inflict it on you. That someone who hates me could take possession of my very being shakes me to the roots. And yes, it pins my ears back that you've tolerated him for so long. Moreso that you withheld this knowledge. Why did you never tell me about his demon blood?"

"I question myself constantly," she said bitterly. "The fucking fool heart cannot be denied, and I love him. At times, I hate myself for it. As I do now. I did not speak on it due to…" She frowned, throat working. "I cannot… I…"

"Cúraniel?"

She shook herself, frown deepening. "This troubles me. I cannot seem to…" Swaying in place, she sucked in a breath. "Would you have left me on the hill had you known?"

My ears twitched with distress. "Rafael has given you gifts. He's claimed your soulbond. Gods, it all harmonizes. He offers you these promises so easily and immediately finds every crack in the armor upon acceptance. A fucking *Háramorn*, indeed! Might as well make deals with the sidhe." I raised an eyebrow. "Are you finally willing to admit he is evil? That he corrupts you?"

Cúraniel chewed on her lip, bald emotions warring on her face.

"He has committed many evil acts, but I know his heart. He is not evil."

With an acerbic laugh, I tossed my hands up. "You grant him such grace. No great wonder he manipulates you so easily. Your soulbond is a shackle."

"Cel, please. I do not wish to fight." She tugged at her lobes. "If Rafael could so easily play my notes, why are you still here? Why am I capable of acting against his wishes at all?"

"Have you finally reached your limit?" I stared her down, implacable. I would not surrender. Not this time.

With a sob, she forced the words out. "Y-yes. Rafael broke his vow."

I gathered her into his arms, careful not to touch the voidlet. She slipped down to rest her head in my lap.

"More than ever, we need a weapon to neutralize him." I absently ran my fingers through her raven hair, teasing out the tangles. "This so-called truce was a mere farce. He's repeatedly proven untrustworthy. I cannot keep one ear swiveled and the other forward. This is untenable." I wove new plaits into her hair as I spoke, rendering complex patterns with hardly a thought. "Yet, I am trapped. Without his might, and the continued cooperation of the other drakes, we are far too vulnerable. Every single time we make progress, he finds a new way to lash out at me." I exhaled through my nose, subsuming my temper. "How did he respond when you confronted him?"

Her voice was hollow. It was as though someone else spoke, and she listened from the other side of a mirror. "He claimed he hadn't technically harmed you—yes, I told him that is absurd. I also told him he could take his people and leave, so you and I aren't far apart there." She rubbed her temples, almost tugging the braid free from my hand. "This is wearing me down as well. I love Rafael, I truly do. But I cannot constantly remain on guard against his next act of malice. Perhaps our relationship only functioned because we were rarely together. When he simply fled at the hard notes."

The voidlet stretched along the length of her, purring hard enough to vibrate her entire body. I angled myself to avoid touching it, but she hugged it as though it were her only lifeline.

With a muted sob, she said, "You finally have your wish, but at what cost?"

Chapter 27

Cúraniel

CELEBEL found me in the greenhouse where I'd hidden for several nights and wove a dampening field around it. The loquacious garden sprite keeping me company dematerialized upon his arrival, shimmering through the field. My soulmate had dressed in his gleaming Pîntellum armor, alive with spirit. It moved like a dream with the slightest twitch of his muscles.

The memory of how we had forged my breastplate together sank to the pit of my stomach, resting there like a boulder in a stream. Celebel's face was flushed, as though he had come from the training field. With no greeting or inquiry into my wellbeing, he wore his separation from me like a second set of armor.

His voice was just as detached. "I have questioned these dynamics for some time, but ever since this…*demon* shit, I question the nature of the relationship itself. There is no simple repair for broken trust at this level. No matter how I examine it, this never would have happened without your connection to the Dragon. It's simply untenable."

Untenable. His new favorite word. Everything was untenable.

He continued, "What surety do I have that my thoughts are my own after such a breach? Is any fleeting sympathy I feel toward him of his making or mine? Can I trust I am alone in my mind? And what of you? How do you know for certain your regard for him is entirely yours? I feel as though I am swimming through murky depths and cannot find the surface."

Tap, tap, tap went his fingers, driving his words into my heart.

I sank to the ground. My legs buckled more often as of late. No matter how it pained me, his melody harmonized. The emotional fortitude to defend myself was long gone. What choice did I have? Rend this side of my soul or the other? I dug my nails into the soil, seeking a center in the storm.

"Are you listening?"

I stared at the ground. If I made eye contact, I would break apart. Melancholy whistled an icy wind through the halls of my soul. The connection to Celebel stretched thinner and thinner with each argument, and with it, my sanity. I barely dared to breathe. What I wanted was to throw my arms about him and kiss him until he reconsidered, but his energy was so cold.

At least when I'd broken Rafael's heart back on my hill, it had actually been my fault.

Celebel sighed, and a muscle in his jaw twitched. "I know not if I can continue on in this manner. I need some time to consider. There seems no way forward that doesn't end in my destruction."

I nodded, miserable. The dampening field lifted, and he left me alone among the plants. A vision struck me as he walked through the arched doors.

A great hungry beast loomed over him, whispering. Skittering in the darkness. Sharp-edged shadows surged, swallowing his form entirely. Swallowing the moon.

My stomach lurched. The vision released me as quickly as it came. I dry-heaved onto the ground cover, wiping the spittle from my mouth. Why must every vision end with retching?

ESCHEWING SLEEP, I entered the shared chambers only to tend to the Pîntellum. Celebel avoided my presence. As I had strangled my connection to Rafael, so Celebel did to me, leaving me only the barest thread of connection. Too hollow to weep over the overwhelming loss I bore on both sides, I drifted aimlessly.

'*I need solace,*' Celebel sent. He hadn't reached out to me in days, or was it moons?

'*Take whatever solace you need,*' I replied. '*I am in our chambers.*'

Hesitancy crept along with his thoughts. *'I...I need physical comfort, but I cannot...I cannot take it from you yet. I do not wish to dishonor you.'*

No jealousy gripped me. I would not deny him succor. There could be no true competition with a soulmate, but it further depressed me that he chose to find comfort elsewhere. Given my situation with Rafael, I could not judge his actions. Outside consolation was no option for me. I would not doom an innocent to death at the Dragon's hands.

'Take whatever lovers you must. Only, block me from the sensations. Please.' I could not bear to feel his pleasure so far removed from me.

'I wish you could join me. I wish...I wish everything were different.' The connection shivered and closed.

I only wished to feel something other than exhausted, morose, and alone. Useless.

The healer's wing didn't need me. They were more than equipped to handle daily ills on their own. The gardens required only minimal tending. Though I was hardly the first choice to help with the children, the fresh influx of Siltaur refugees meant there were plenty of caretakers and playmates to go around. The Pîntellum required little attention. Losing myself in books was not an option, not without risking the library.

Should I even desire a reconciliation between the three of us anymore? I'd known so much suffering since leaving my hill. Was this truly worthwhile? Had I doomed myself to spending the rest of my days fighting one or the other of my soulmates, or both at once? How much of myself would I lose if I severed the connections and ran? Heartache alone I could handle, but risking my very soul?

I might survive the loss of Celebel's bond, as it was newer, though it would sacrifice a serious amount of my power and sanity. My belly tightened, a hollow gnawing. I missed his amiable smile, his musical laugh. The sweetness of his tears.

Perhaps he'd never known anyone who'd lost a soulmate. I'd never heard of anyone severing more than one soulmate bond, let alone surviving it. The contemplation woke a deep ache along my spine. Most who didn't die outright eventually committed suicide. Some by violence, others by slowly taking root as the melancholy overcame them.

The thought of severing Rafael's bond made me curl in on myself like a dying spider. He had truly planted himself in my soul. Gods, I still loved that fucking blighter, even in the face of his worst behavior.

Until I met the cantankerous drake, I'd thought terms like 'heartsick' a mere fancy. Oh, how he'd taught me otherwise. I loved him with a never-ending ache. A constriction in my chest that stole my breath and drew tears to hover just under the surface, waiting for the merest breeze to spill them.

If you refuse to break with him, and he refuses to change, where does that leave us?

Rafael's instability added another layer of complication. If I abandoned him, cut the bond, could I truly accept the resulting crescendo of death? He would surely slaughter his way through the remaining elves, as he'd once threatened.

Academically, finding a soulmate was no guarantee of a successful relationship, but must it be this fucking difficult? Some soulmates lived apart, stifling their connections because they despised each other. Regardless, they were inexorably drawn together from time to time. It seemed a highly unpleasant lifestyle, and not one I wished to emulate.

I was trapped. Celebel demonstrated the typical distancing elvish behavior I'd broken my lineage to avoid. The behavior I'd hoped he would be exempt from. I understood his fears, his hurt, and his need for sexual comfort with others, but not his blame.

Rafael regularly drove me to my wits' end, but at least he had passion. Why had the gods seen fit to wedge me between two warrior kings so utterly accustomed to having their way? Why couldn't I have some kind-hearted potter or weaver? For that matter, why couldn't the gods stop at one highly difficult soulmate instead of giving me two?

Days passed, and nights. I lost all sense of time. Colors dimmed, the shared song drifted off-key. Nemohee plied me with whiskey and humor. Eäriel demonstrated formula after formula. The children regaled me with tales of strange sounds, like plates breaking, in the deeper tunnels. With thinned lips and a drawn brow, Liriadis gave me wordless hugs, and I hung limp in her arms. The sprite dangled new and interesting plants before me. Even Feanim did his best to draw me out with insults, but I had nothing left to give.

Perhaps some fighting took place. Some plans were surely laid. I took no part in any of it. More alone than ever, my soul frayed.

Chapter 28

Celebel

A **BRONZE** axe whistled past my face as I twisted to avoid the blow. Following my momentum, I shoved my blade upward into the Fomorian's belly. Its watery, yellow eyes bulged at the impending death. It snorted like the boar it resembled as it toppled. I expelled a sharp breath at the stench of pierced bowels. The Pîntellum armor so enhanced my strength, I nearly cut the body in half yanking my sword free.

Frost-laden grass trampled into freezing mud provided poor purchase for the false, towering beasts. One lunged at me and slipped, its flailing legs tangling around another and taking them both to the ground. I was on them in an instant, stabbing through gaps in their enameled helmets.

Something clanged heavily off my shoulder and I spun, slashing through the forearm of the spear-thrusting Fomorian behind me. Another took that opportunity to leap at me, knocking me flat on my belly. For a heartbeat, my world was churned dirt, grunting, the weight of a glamoured sidhe on my back, and the screech of metal on metal as it tried to pry open a joint in my þilvor armor. The softer bronze blade bent, and it snarled in frustration, hammering the back of my helmet with its mailed fists. I squeezed my eyes shut.

I could simply lie here. Let them take me.

"Celebel!" a familiar voice shouted.

The Fomorian shrieked, making my ears ring, and the weight lifted. A rough hand flipped me over. Lámirië.

"Why are you out here fighting alone?" Her helm obscured her expression, but the fury carried through on key. "My lord," she added belatedly.

I took the proffered hand, and she tugged me to my feet. Others of our company gathered behind her. Lámirië pulled off her helm to give me a dark-eyed glare, and I couldn't meet it. I'd deliberately left her behind.

Instead of a lecture, the Duedellen only tugged a lobe in disgust. I'd almost denied her the birthright of her lineage; her parent had been so devoted to protection, þey'd followed þeir sworn lord into the grave. Though never the most personable elf, she'd stayed by my side when her lifelong counterpart betrayed me. I owed her more than this pathetic display.

"The route has begun."

I followed the point of her halberd to the retreating backs of Fomorians. Rats from a sinking ship. Humans gave chase—Duke Sotherly's spirit-wielding Atani soldiers, with their flapping red and yellow tabards and clanking armor. They whooped and cheered, cutting down stragglers. The more powerful spirit-wielders among them combined their power to hurl bolts of light that burned on contact, felling dozens more foes.

Fatigue dropped grain sacks on my limbs as the fervor of battle left me. I cut sharp lines in the frost, dragging my sabatons as I departed the field. Lámirië padded along behind me, determined to keep me in earshot.

I should have felt guilty. I should have felt…something.

The Duke's booming voice greeted us long before we reached him. The bearded human had no volume control. Spikes of emphasis in the rough Atani language made my already-sensitized ears throb. I nodded vaguely along, noncommittal. *Cúraniel must feel thusly during our meetings.* The soulbond tightened, and I swallowed hard. Sotherly squinted, and I smoothed my face.

Duke Adalbert Sotherly was a pompous man. Pink-faced with piercing grey eyes, he wore his dark beard oiled and styled into curling points. Equally ostentatious was his red and yellow coat bearing puffed, slashed sleeves and matching breeches with equally puffed thighs, both embroidered at the hems with thread-of-gold. Tall for a human, his voice tightened whenever he had to look up at my face.

His counselors and retainers were all notably shorter than he, and, just as notably, all male. As were his soldiers, whom he referred to as his men. The first time I'd heard that, I'd assumed he meant they were all sexual partners. Fortunately, I did not express that thought aloud before it was corrected, or I'd have caused grave offense.

It irked him further to look up at Lámirië. Any time she locked eyes with him, he scowled and turned toward me. In response, I shifted slightly so she would remain in his line of sight. We continued that petty dance until Lámirië gave me a furtive sign to cease. I'd irritated her enough as it was.

Feanim had volunteered to attend in my stead, but I'd been the one to forge the treaty—and the Duke had specifically requested my presence. Subtle as it was, I appreciated the concern for my wellbeing. It was well Nimthil had remained behind, though she would have bolstered me. The Lachanaur queen had a tactful hand for negotiation, but Sotherly's umbrage was all too easy to imagine.

In truth, I'd wished to escape the confines of Amrún, if only for a moon or so. The volcanic walls were far too similar to the demon's embrace. Our company's small size allowed a rapid southeastern descent to Sotherly's requested rendezvous location. It required enough of my focus to avoid rumination. At least for a time.

I shuddered, returning my attention to the human prattling on before me. He said five words for every one of import, but his eyes were cunning above that loose mouth. His verbosity struck me as odd, coming from a people so concerned with keeping precise time. Also surprising that he'd traveled from his palace to meet with me in person. He didn't seem the type to take on risk for himself, but perhaps he styled himself a hero. So many humans I'd met thought of themselves as such. Especially the human men of northern Almatherin.

They had called upon us for reinforcement. Fomorians hadn't targeted them directly, but they'd decimated all the humans' livestock in the forested foothills in their pursuit of Siltaur elves. That led the humans to send resource-seeking parties farther afield. They'd run afoul of harpies, just as we had. We agreed to send aid in the hopes it would reinforce our alliance. Fomorians attacked our company on the way, and the humans ended up aiding us.

Back and forth we went, sweeping the area. Fortunately, the Fomorians were relatively thin on the ground, limiting our engagements to brief bloody skirmishes. Lámirië divulged she'd been expecting Sotherly to send farmers, and had been pleasantly surprised when competent knights joined us instead. A sentiment I echoed internally.

I silently thanked the gods for Feanim's quick wit when the Duke had sent a questioning missive about the obliterated outpost. He'd always been a smooth liar and penned the melody of rebellious drakes as though it were a ballad of legend.

Memories of the destruction tightened my lower back. That monster had been *inside* me, moving me like a helpless construct. A rabbit in the jaws of a predator, waiting for my neck to snap. No sight, no sound, no senses, no shared song. Only the oppressive heat and sickening menace of the beast. I tucked my shaking hands under my arms.

Finished with his recounting of troop movements and plans to part ways, the Duke dismissed me with an arrogant flick of his hand. Retainers rushed to place planks under his feet so he would not muddy his shining black boots. I heaved a sigh. One last push before we returned to Amrún.

I dismissed Lámirië. She cast me a baleful glance that said she'd station herself right back outside my tent momentarily. We'd camped several days' ride from the nearest human settlement to avoid drawing the Fomorians any closer. I'd initially resisted singing to the trees for our tent poles, but the added luxury came as a relief.

Galaron caught my attention as I approached my tent. I waved the sandy-haired Astolar away. He'd been gentle and compassionate, as always, but his touch brought none of the comfort I'd craved. Not even true physical release—given the lackluster orgasm he'd coaxed from me—but the fault did not lie with him. How could I criticize Cúraniel's attachment to a void creature when its twin had taken up residence in my chest?

I winced at the membrane's suction as I pulled my pauldrons free. A dark purple bruise bloomed on my right shoulder. It joined the constellation dotting my body. Without the enhanced armor, I would have died a dozen times over.

What was wrong with me? At least one more skirmish on the horizon, and here I was lying down before the first wave. We had only to clear the area and restore the human settlements to rights. Hardly a gargantuan task.

Might as well take root and be done with it. Perhaps Orfain would grant its descendent a boon and make my sapling beautiful.

I gripped my injured shoulder, digging my fingers in. White hot pain brought me back to my body. My people needed me. My soulmate…well… The bond stretched thin and wan over the distance. Like a bow string. Or a garrote. Harrowing where once it sustained.

I dreaded the return to Amrún. Demons lurked outside the walls and within. An icy chill clawed down my spine.

What if the demon who'd wrested control of my body was the very one driving the Fomorian attacks?

Chapter 29

Cúraniel

MARRON wandered nervously through the greenhouse. His eyes darted about as if he expected an attack at any moment. Sprites flitted out of his path, streaking colorful sparkles.

"What has happened?" I approached him.

The green drake shook his head. "Whatever is happening between you and Jxxyssdrfynn"—which I *still* couldn't properly perceive—"mend it. *Stop* him. He is losing what tenuous grip he had on sanity, and everyone suffers for it. I risk using his name, but you must know. There will be no drakes left if you let him continue this way."

Fucking hells, not another petition for me to control Rafael. "Feanim told me he was moping about again. When did this start?" I gestured at a gracefully arched marble bench. Marron sat carefully, testing the strength of the seat before trusting his full weight to it. I settled on a tree root across from the burly green drake. "Why do any of you tolerate Rafael's turbulent moods?"

"The alternative is death," he said flatly. "It began two days ago. Typical cycle. He'll isolate for a time after some upset. Inevitably, something will spark his temper, and he'll lash out with full force. Some fool kin of mine crossed him, and now he will not stop." Marron expelled a deep sigh. "It is one thing to fight, it is another to…what is your word? To fight to the end. We say *hyrkka*."

"What do you mean, 'fight to the end'?" But I knew.

Same as the fight that brought him to me initially. He was trying to die in the only way he knew how. A sinking sensation gripped me, as though I had so little substance I fell through the world. And yet, once again, I was held responsible for Rafael's behavior simply because no one else dared confront him. No one else could.

"It is to take all challengers until you fall." Marron confirmed my suspicion as I struggled to maintain my composure. "Your people have other ways of ending your lives, I think? Becoming trees or somesuch? This is our way, but he will destroy us all before he ever stumbles."

"He respects you. Can't you speak to him?" If Rafael possessed a single friend in all of Vaeda, surely it was Marron.

The green drake's rasping laugh startled me. "I have known the Red a very long time, Moon Lady. If I step before him now, he will kill me without hesitation. I have no illusions about my position. As of speaking with you, he's killed three of mine, two of Tyldain's, one of Grenyk's, and a clanless loner. This will not end until either we attack in tandem, or he falls. And he will not fall. We have all tried to bring him down. The War Crow came the closest, and you know how that ended."

"You have attacked Rafael in concert?" Gods.

"The result is always the same. We take heavy casualties, and he disappears for a time, only to return stronger and more determined to make all our lives miserable until he either tires of it or gets distracted." He rolled his broad shoulders, grimacing. "Moon Lady, you do not understand. He is the only remaining first generation drake. Eldest born of the mightiest parentage we have ever known. There is a vast gulf between the Red and the rest of us."

The warrior's frank admission surprised me, but then, I was only hearing of this as an outsider. Marron knew it would have no effect on his standing.

"Rafael's horrid behavior made me cut off his song, and here is more of it." I must remain firm to prevent absolving the Dragon of with his transgressions yet again. Despite my melancholy, his hold over me hadn't weakened.

Marron's ruby eyes narrowed. "Uncut then. Unsever. Whatever it is you people do. Your mate is out of control, and you are the only one who may step before him."

"He is not my mate," I said stubbornly.

The drake snorted. "Whatever you call it. You have power over him. Use it. I would not make this request if I had any other option." He gave me a meaningful look.

Gods, it must hurt his pride to beg a soft elf to protect him, protect his people.

I chewed on my lower lip. "Do you know of his demonic ability to possess others against their will?"

Marron's lips parted, showing the tips of his teeth in displeasure. "Yes. That ability is in large part why he remains unvanquished. Is this why you have broken with him?"

I nodded, pressing my mouth into a grim line. He frowned, tapping the talons of one hand on his other arm, clicking on the heavy scales. If he'd worn a tail, he'd surely be swishing it. Clouds passing over the sun blended him into the greenery around us.

"This I understand," he said finally. "Difficult. Ah, everything about the Red is difficult. It is my responsibility to prevent another, what would you call it, Great Coming or Terrible Arrival?" He'd emphasized the terms. "Like *hyrkka*, on a grand scale. We call it the *Kyr Praetha.* When the Red first appeared among us, he slaughtered so many we could barely maintain a stable population. The more he killed, the more his damnable strength grew. We are a bloodthirsty people, yes, but none had ever witnessed that level of…kinslaying is your term for it, yes? We have never truly recovered.

"He meant to have his *hyrkka* and instead ran out of worthy opponents. Many years later, I faced him for the first time. When he let me live, it was on the condition I never allow *Kyr Praetha* to happen again. So here I am, trying to stop him." He shrugged as if he didn't expect it to make a difference. "The Red is a selfish, clanless creature, but he can be reasoned with occasionally. You are the only one who can break through to him now."

Clanless. Rafael himself had said as much. That confirmed my suspicions about who truly led the drakes. I considered my options, rapping my heels on the ground.

"I'm in a bad position, Marron. If I bend to him, I put my people at risk. If I do nothing, your people suffer. Do you harmonize?"

"Yes, I believe so."

I held his red gaze. No. I could not let his people die for my mistakes. "Lead me to him, please."

Marron rose, and I followed, rushing to keep pace with his longer stride. He paused at the greenhouse door. "You have strange taste, lady. The Red does too, to be sure, but I believe yours is stranger."

"Sounds like he's as much of a plague to you as he is to us."

The green drake barked a laugh. "He would agree."

Unmistakable sounds of fighting reached me well before we came upon the actual combat. Guards stationed at the battlements nervously perked their ears as we emerged into the outer courtyard.

When they'd first entered Amrún, most of the drakes had disappeared into the intense heat of the lower levels. The rest arranged themselves haphazardly around the edges of the outer wall. Breaking into their smaller clan groups, as more newcomers joined them, those groups naturally blended. Coming and going through the gates, the lava tunnels, and the sky itself, it was difficult to keep track of how many shapeshifting children of dragons lived amongst us.

A wall of spiky backs blocked my view of the training field. Marron bellowed something and the crowd immediately parted, revealing Rafael in his scaly drake form. He had the shoulder of a mottled greyish-green drake clamped in his jaws. Boshkt clawed weakly at the red drake's powerful chest, raking off pebbled scales. Steaming blood pooled under his webbed feet. Some splashed the mangled, motionless body of another drake at the edge of the circle. Green and brown striped, from what little unmarred hide remained.

Rafael paused his killing bite when he saw me. Bloodlust had chased away any hint of sanity in his blistering red eyes.

The other drakes watched us with rapt interest. In my periphery, more elves moved in the battlements. He'd amassed quite an audience for this pointless slaughter.

I opened our soulbond and bellowed with all the force I could muster, *'Rafael, release him this instant!'* Fury heated my face and my ears flattened. Drawing in my power, I let it fill me and darken the sky. The wind picked up, whipping my hair into a dark cloud. *'How dare you brutalize your own people in a fit of pique!'*

The Red Dragon growled, and the ground buzzed under my feet. Poor Boshkt shuddered with the force of it. As one, the other drakes held still as stone, their harsh, grumbling breaths punctuating the silence.

My skin crackled with tension, like an impending lightning strike.

'What cause have I to remain with a man who throws a violent tantrum every time he's frustrated? You fucking blighter. You should protect these people, lead them! Instead, I find you murdering them. What the fuck is wrong with you? How am I ever to have any faith in you at all?'

Rafael's burning eyes speared me, but he slowly opened his jaws and let the smaller drake slip free. Boshkt scrambled backwards out of reach as soon as his webbed feet hit the ground, leaving a bright smear of blood in his wake. The others parted, letting him through.

The Dragon opened his maw to speak, and I cut him off with a slash of my hand.

'I do not fucking care what your customs are. This mindless killing stops here, or I'll sever our soulbond and be done with you forever. If I drop dead, so be it.'

Every instinct screamed to run to him, to forgive, to soothe. To press my face into his chest and pretend none of this ever happened. To heal the already-closing wounds on his body. Fucking hells. I thrashed against the soulbond like a fish on a line. No, I could not give in! Not again.

'I cannot bear another vile act from you. These drakes are my allies, as surely as any elf, and I will not be yoked to a monster! Do you understand?'

The Red Dragon dipped his head a fraction. For a heartbeat, only he and I existed in all the world, enveloped by the screaming darkness of his soul. With a deep breath, I took the risk of breaking eye contact to search for Boshkt among the crowd. Surely, he needed healing.

"Better leave it," Marron murmured beside me, catching the direction of my gaze.

I pinned him with a glare equal to the one I'd leveled at Rafael.

His eyes widened. "Fierce little thing, you are."

"I am old, Marron. Older than all of you, save for my hateful troublemaker of a soulmate. I have no patience for bullies. He may kill me where I stand, but I will never fear him."

'Cúraniel—' Rafael tried to claw his way back into my mind.

I strangled the connection again, turning on a heel to march back to the peace of the greenhouse. The Red Dragon roared behind me, pummeling my ears. The fortress shook, and the stone beneath my feet crazed from the force. I continued on, buoyed by an almost physical push from all the eyes on my back.

BOSHKT STUCK his head into the greenhouse the next morning. He seemed well enough despite a jagged ring of puncture wounds around his shoulder and the side of his neck.

"You live yet?" I gave the common greeting in draconian as he trod carefully through the ferns.

His fins waved slowly, and he combed a clinging nightshade vine from his mossy beard. "Clan Green said tell you it worked. Mostly." His head bobbed. "The Red is stilled for now."

The tension in my shoulders released all at once, and I staggered. Gathering myself, I maintained a false show of strength for the swampy drake.

"Good, good! You look whole." I'd been desperate for glad tidings.

Breathing eased, I resisted the urge to ask about Rafael. Instead, I tugged an errant sprig of mint out of a pot. Absently, I wrapped the mint in a damp cloth for later transfer to a place where it couldn't menace the other plants. I never would have named myself peacemaker before I had soulmates.

"I am unhurt now. More fool me. Tried to stop the Red's eating a clanmate, and he turned on me. Eh heh, you showed just soon enough." His mouth dropped open in a dragon smile.

"This is good."

"What language is that?" asked a small voice in sylvaine. Its form resolved into a diminutive bronze person with hair like mimosa puffs, wings buzzing too rapidly to perceive; one of the greenhouse sprites. "Sounds like grunts and gargling." The tiny fae dodged an exploratory snap from Boshkt, spinning in circles around his finned head and giggling like wind chimes.

"Draconian. Boshkt is a drake," I explained.

"I know what drakes are, silly. I saw that big green one earlier. Tell him in lizardspeak I'll hex his tail off if he breaks my plants."

Boshkt turned his blue eye to the sprite flitting around his head as I haltingly translated.

He wheezed a laugh. "Tell the little bright one I will keep my tail. Plants are safe." Must be a universal draconian trait, those strange, coughing laughs.

"Are you safe?" I stumbled to match his simplified dialect.

He cocked his head to one side in that quizzical way dogs had.

I gesticulated with frustration. "No, ah, no strike back for yesterday?"

Understanding, he bobbed his head again. "Yes, I am safe in that way. Others are very curious about you now. Never knew elves had such *indrerra*. You stared only, and the Red backed down!" He flexed impressive biceps. Gods, even the lankier drakes had incredible muscularity.

"What is '*indrerra*'?"

"Eh heh heh, *indrerra* is strength and courage together, from knowing power with, hmm, background?" Boshkt slapped his abdomen with a flat palm. "Fire in the belly carried from the progenitors."

"Good word." I filed it away with other useful vocabulary.

Bobbing his head a final time, Boshkt turned to leave. He paused, looking back at me over his craggy shoulder.

"Something else?" I asked.

He blinked slowly, one eye at a time. Disconcerting, that. "Why did you help? I said no to the Green. 'She is an elf,' said I, but he insisted." Curiosity brightened his gaze. "Elves never help. Why?"

"Drakes are allies. Maybe friends someday? Elves must help. Too many mistakes from the past." Mind fogged, I tripped my way through all of it, but Boshkt wheezed a laugh.

"Too bad the Red got you first. We should have claimed you for Green, little elf-dragon."

Chapter 30

I WENT to the bedchamber in the early morning to check the latest batch of Pîntellum. Resting on the windowsill was a small package wrapped in brown leather and tied with a rose atop it. I almost tossed it into the stream, but something stayed my hand. Weakness, perhaps, but I had so little strength left to muster resistance.

Sighing, I sat on the moss bed and unwrapped the package. A bundle of unfamiliar dried herbs, tied with twine that hummed with power, certainly topped the list of surprises. Composed of many serrated, dark green leaves veined in red with a silvery underside, they gave off a sharp, somewhat pungent fragrance, similar to dragon musk. I'd never seen so much as a drawing of this plant in all my years of herbal study. With a growing sense of apprehension, I unrolled the note included with the package.

> *My Dove,*
>
> *I offer you this dragonsbane to demonstrate the depths of my sincerity. I place my very life in your hands. Here is more than enough to craft a lethal dose for any dragon-kin. It is exceedingly rare, growing only in certain dragon-blighted lands after a century cycle. I will show you how to prepare it. Do with it what you wish. I wait for you at the gates.*
>
> *Without you, I am lost.*

Gods *damn* him. Rafael hadn't signed it, but he didn't need to. I'd know that elegant, spiky hand anywhere. Frustrated tears splashed on the paper. I carefully re-bundled the herbs and tucked them in my coat pocket as I went to face him. Three moons had passed since the possession attempt. Three moons of hellish isolation.

'*I must show you something important,*' I sent to Celebel.

He responded slowly, as if sifting his thoughts. '*The Red Dragon told me of his intentions.'*

My ears went flat in shock. '*He…what?'*

Irony and no small amount of disbelief tinged Celebel's tone. '*Never have I witnessed such humility from him. Not a single snarl or insult, he was so downcast.'*

'*No apologies, I suppose.'* Hard enough to reconcile this with my understanding of Rafael as a person.

'*In a roundabout manner. He recognized he had hurt you and acknowledged I had no reason to grant him any favors. What truly garnered my attention was his claim that this gift would provide you with the means of his destruction. We need that assurance now more than ever.'* Celebel paused for so long I thought he'd cut me off again. '*I almost have sympathy for that demonic blighter. Imagine feeling sorry for him after all he's done.'*

Something more hung unsaid there, but I let it go. '*Did you open the package?'* Would I, were I in Celebel's position? Probably. Curiosity so often got the better of me.

'*No! Likely rigged to poison me.'*

I chuckled, but Celebel's grim tone deflated my mirth.

'*I take it your Dragon was sincere about this gift.'*

'*He was. I haven't sorted my feelings.'* That the legendary Red Dragon, with all his strength and fury, willingly placed his life utterly in my hands, was almost too much to bear.

'*You're going to him now?'* Celebel cut off the connection before I could respond.

Naught but cobwebs pasted me together.

RAFAEL WAITED at the outer gates, dressed in his finally complete moranga armor. As Celebel had noted, he kept his eyes down. Unusually submissive. He wore no helm—as was his way—and the light of early morning limned his flaming hair in gold.

If his old armor was intimidating, this was hellish. It radiated a sense of dread, and he appeared every bit a demon. The black moranga drank the rest of the light, strangely flattening his imposing silhouette.

A spray of spines jutted outward from the pauldrons covering his broad shoulders, similar to the design of his previous suit, but denser and more aggressive. All the better to protect his head and neck without the helm. The armor hugged the hard lines of his powerful body. It would have been attractive in any other material. Or if I wasn't so overwrought.

The gauntlets were cleverly designed around the use of his talons—not quite fingerless gloves, but similar. Moranga likewise covered his dragon feet, and the curved talons extended through the toe tips.

Armored for what purpose? Confrontation? His sword hung at his hip as well.

"Must you be so dramatic?" I crossed my arms, wishing I'd also worn armor.

Rafael met my gaze. The fires of his eyes had banked almost to the grey of an untended hearth. It took me aback.

"I would die for you." Stark truth. More than a willingness to sacrifice himself, there lay the open desire for death.

Had we circled all the way back to the very beginning? Why hadn't he simply used the dragonsbane then, instead of battling the War Crow? No, I couldn't afford the distracting thought now.

"Why would I want your death?" My hands raised of their own accord, buzzing with my frustration. "Is living in peace such an impossibility you would die to elude it? What I desire is an end to your aggressive bullying. Why bother agreeing to a truce if your sworn vows ring discordant?"

As always, my instincts shrieked at me to fall into his arms, to bend, to soothe him. To forgive. His pain lit the soulbond aflame, twisting like a barbed spear, lacerating my belly, my chest, scorching my lungs, boiling my mind. I fought to distance it, close it off. Drawing on the apprehension from the armor to keep me present, I pulled out the package of herbs.

"Why did you give me this?"

"Good faith." He nodded at the fortress. "All the little birds squawk their fear of my madness."

"Very well. Sing your melody." Maintaining my veneer of haughty disdain in the face of his fathomless melancholy proved more difficult than I'd anticipated. I hugged my arms tighter to guard myself.

"Forgive me, please. I have no desire for a life without you. Never have I felt so empty." A muscle in his jaw ticked. "Better to be slain by your hand than severed from you. The pain I felt on the hill is nothing compared to this."

I sighed. "And what of acting with reason and compassion? You hadn't made a single attempt to mend the rift with Celebel before you went off killing your people in a fit of pique. No one deserves to die from your temper tantrums. Especially not those stemming from the consequences of your own fucking actions. If you simply must punch someone in the face, you could at least target the enemy." His eyes narrowed, and I shifted to anticipate his next move. "And do not retaliate against Marron, either. He merely followed your command to prevent another, what was it called, *Kyr Praetha*?"

Rafael snorted, turning his face from me, but that posture belied his intent listening.

"Do you understand my distress?" I wanted to hear him say it.

His mouth pressed into a thin line, shoulders tensing.

"Rafael. Answer me." It took all my willpower to resist his draw as his presence wrapped me tighter than my skin. Enveloping me in his scent, the slow beat of his heart, and the strength of his body. My very soul quivered in response.

He rumbled low in his throat. "You believe I have somehow harmed Celebel. I admit it was not my gentlest possession, but I made certain he would remain intact."

Somehow harmed? I swallowed my rising anger. "No. I want no false apologies."

"What do you wish me to say?" he snapped, brows furrowing. So, he wasn't too forlorn to be irritable. Some refrains never changed.

"Do you truly not recognize how you committed a major violation of Celebel's consent? You, of all people, should follow this melody." It was a low blow, and he winced, but I felt no guilt over it.

"I disagree."

I exhaled through my nose in a vain attempt to calm myself. "Ah, so it matters only when you are the victim? Shall I predict what would happen if Celebel used that kind of power on you? You would lose your fucking wits and probably burn the entire fortress to the ground. Likely the rest of Vaeda with it."

He dropped his eyes once more. "Will you forgive me?" My point had finally struck home.

"Are you worthy of forgiveness?" Saying it hurt. When my eyes brimmed, the tears surprised me. I thought I'd reached my limit with weeping. At the very least, prolonged dehydration should have prevented it. "Why did you do it?"

He punched the wall, the *crack* of knuckles on obsidian ringing across the courtyard. Fractures spiderwebbed around his fist, shearing through the rock. One raced to the very top of the crenel.

Should I ask Marron if his earthshaking skills extended to stonemasonry? I shook it off. Heat rose around the Dragon in a shimmering aura. Gods, was he about to have another show of temper?

"Rafael—"

"Not here." A harsh rasp.

We walked in tense silence. Rafael moved as a spring coiled too tightly, ready to explode at the slightest touch. Sure to leave wreckage in his wake, such as the hole in the wall. The hole in Feanim's belly. The hole in my heart, in my life.

A pair of Siltaur sentries glanced up at our approach and swiftly busied themselves at the opposite end of the courtyard. Rafael paid them no heed. I followed him through the suddenly too-tight hallways. He paused in the door to his quarters, one hand bracing his weight, and hung his head. Before I could ask, he sighed and entered.

Moving a stack of books from the chair to the overburdened desk, I sat. He watched me, and I waited. With another gusty sigh, he stretched and laid his hands flat on the ceiling. An echo of a gesture he'd made in a happier time.

Almost against my will, I appreciated the breadth and power of his chest and shoulders, the taper of his trim waist. Vile the armor may be, but it hugged his body with undeniable sensuality.

He raked his talons across the stone, producing an ear-splitting shriek.

I ducked, covering my poor ears. "Gods damn it, Rafael. I hate that you're suffering, but this is another self-inflicted wound, and you are acting ridiculous."

His head whipped up, eyes blazing. "You are my *mate*. No," he snarled as I opened my mouth to protest, "you claimed me first. On the hill, you fought me and won."

Always fighting and war. "You were dying!"

"Yes, I was dying! *I finally had the opportunity, and you would not allow it.*" His head swayed with agitation, flaming curls swirling with the movement. "Did you ever stop to wonder why Byxldurr could inflict such damage?"

I sat up. Gods, I'd merely assumed the War Crow had also been supremely strong. But Marron was his second and Rafael could easily kill him.

"She had a cursed talisman, designed specifically to exorcise demons." He gave me a meaningful look.

"But you are not a full-blooded demon," I said slowly. Even in his emotional state, he refused to sing the entire melody for me, the impossible creature.

A sharp nod. "I cannot be properly exorcised. Instead, the curse tore me apart from the inside, unseating all the tatters of my soul. It should have granted me true death. But you overpowered me, dragged me back against my will. Why do you think I ran from you for so long?"

No, I mustn't fall prey to his hypnosis. I pinched the soft flesh between my thumb and forefinger, digging in with my fingernails to send a jolt of awareness up my arm. It sharpened my senses. "While I appreciate the added context, why you are telling me this now?"

He continued as if I hadn't spoken. "I could not kill you. No matter how I wished to free myself from your claim." Broken-glass teeth flashed. "Every time I approached with intent, you looked at me with those big, guileless blue eyes. And fucking *flirted* like the gods damned moon-touched madwoman you are." He heaved another sigh that built into a growl. "And I love you for it. I never needed to claim you; you had already claimed me. I kept the knowledge close out of fear for your safety."

Heart fluttering in my chest like a wounded bird, I listened and waited.

"I gave you the mark. Then I submitted, and you accepted it. You are *mine*."

Almost unconsciously, I rubbed the raised scars on the back of my neck. "Submitted…?" Oh. Oh *fuck*. During the unhealing. Gods, I was a fool to assume it was merely sexual play.

He tilted his head, raptorlike. "Yes. You formalized the claim, and we sparred together."

My eyebrows climbed and ears lowered. Fucking hells. Drake bonding. I wanted to protest, but the words dried in my throat.

"You made your first blooded kill." Rafael huffed, nodding. "And instead of returning to my bed, you remained in *his*. You spurned me again." His voice dropped to a hoarse whisper. "I know I am broken, but I had hoped…" Flaming eyes closed like shuttering a lantern. "I wished to know you in that way. Surely, *he* would not miss a few stolen moments."

I sat on my hands to keep from reaching for him. "But we would have invited you into our bed without issue—"

A furious hiss cut me off. "It was…a lapse in judgment. One I bitterly regret." He tugged off his gauntlets, tossing them on the foot of the bed. The talons of one hand scored the back of the other, drawing steaming lines in red. "When a rescued scorpion stings, do you blame it for its irredeemable nature?"

I stood, taking his hands. The touch alone nourished my starving spirit. "You are not irredeemable. I hear your melody and understand how you've followed it, however discordant. Had you but spoken with me, we might have avoided this strife. Now you tell me you've deceived me into accepting the mate claim. The mate claim I did not wish to consider until this war ended." Anger spiked my gut. "You desire forgiveness, but where is the penance?"

Exhaling through gritted teeth, wreathing me in heat, he growled a barely audible, "I apologize."

I almost relented. "Words must be accompanied by deeds. Do you swear to remain and fight for my people until our enemies are defeated? Will you continue to prevent harm to Celebel and our other allies? Will you make true peace with him? Do you swear never to commit such evil again?"

A rumbling hiss escaped his lips. "I am broken enough, Cúraniel. Must I prostrate myself as well?"

No, I must stay firm! "Rafael. Swear it. On pain of the severance of our bond."

He sank onto a knee, like a knight accepting his queen's blessing. "I swear it. I will fight for you and prevent harm to Celebel and allies." His eyes flicked to my face. "You must teach me how to make peace."

He lifted my knuckles to his lips. Red desire ringed the dancing flames of his eyes. Was it dragon or demon lighting those fires? "I vow to consult with you on the relative evil of my actions. Your morality is beyond my understanding." Hands over his heart, then offered to me.

I kissed the backs of his hands. "I accept your vows."

When I relaxed my chokehold on our connection, he heaved a sigh. Instantly, my breath eased. His emotions flooded me, and I reveled in his warmth.

"If I remove the armor, will you kiss me?" he asked softly, as if fearing rejection.

"May I watch you remove it?" I bit my lower lip and fluttered my eyelashes. I couldn't help myself. Gods, I had been so lonely, somehow worse than it had ever been on my hill.

Like a bolt of lightning from a clear sky, realization struck me. He'd deliberately worn the armor in the event I hadn't either forgiven him or chosen to strike him down with the dragonsbane. Prepared, if I allowed him to live without reestablishing our bond… All of Celebel's fears came roaring back. My hands tingled with dread. I shook them out, forcibly changing the melody.

"What is it about this distance that has you so melancholic now, when you used to disappear for years at a time with no issue?" Better not to acknowledge his unspoken threat.

"I always felt you there and knew I could reach you whenever the need arose." He stood, clasping my shoulders. I shivered at the contact of his talons. "I did not consider your needs. Another regret of mine." He paused, searching my face. "Of all the sins for which I am told I should atone, only those affecting you hold weight."

Rafael pressed a chaste kiss to my brow and maneuvered me over to the bed. Slowly, maintaining eye contact, he removed the spiny pauldrons, couters, vambraces, and rerebraces, pulling each piece away from his skin with a wet pop as the internal membrane released. Reminiscent of a viper leisurely shedding his scales before striking his victim. He stacked it neatly with the gauntlets, ensuring no piece touched me. Their proximity alone filled me with dread. The plackart and cuirass followed, baring his torso.

"You are still armored." I aimed a weighted stare at his legs.

He leaned over me, pushing me back into the bed. My lips parted in anticipation. Instead of kissing me, he snagged the blanket at my back and straightened, wrapping it around his waist.

I groaned, and he smirked, lifting a foot to remove the specialized sabatons. The greaves and all the rest followed, which he sadly managed without giving me a view beneath the obscuring blanket.

The crumpled pair of leather trousers he deposited next to his armor almost made me laugh. "You are meant to wear the Pîntellum over bare skin."

"Hush, woman."

Still, as he set the codpiece aside with a blistering look, I appreciated that he'd never willingly been so unclothed in my presence.

With painstaking slowness, Rafael gathered the armor and arranged it inside the wardrobe. The play of muscle across his back entranced me. Once he closed the wardrobe door, the menacing internal hum lessened significantly.

Staring up at his physique made me want to abandon my morals completely. A small part of me squeaked I should move slowly, resist his draw. He could have dressed me in that wretched armor without a complaint from me, as long as it meant having his hands on my body.

With a low growl, he shoved my knees apart and moved between them. My traitorous clit gave a mighty throb. I whimpered, lifting my hips. His gaze scorched my skin.

In a smooth motion, he wrapped me in his arms to pull me upright, pressing his face into my breasts. Squeezing the breath from my lungs.

I batted at him until he relented. "I missed you too, asshole. Feanim said you were useless." To be in his arms again, for our connection to hum, fed my soul, but I wasn't ready to grant him complete freedom.

"I was." My bosom muffled his voice. How many conversations had we held through my cleavage? "I have no care at all for life without you."

"Oh, by the Night Mother, you are the most dramatic…" I sighed with fond exasperation. "I do love you, you big awful hellbeast." I kissed the top of his head and he rumbled. Running my hands over his shoulders, I shivered with the tingling of his vast power. "So, you will garner my approval before you give in to the urge to be horrible, yes?"

"Mmm." Rafael nuzzled my breast, nipping through the wool at my tender flesh.

"Did you miss me or just my bosom?" I teased.

"Mmmhmm." He seized a button in his teeth, preparing to shear it off my coat.

I tugged at his hair. "No, you don't! I haven't an endless supply of coats!"

Rafael popped the button off anyway and spat it on the floor. "Fuck the coat. I will bring you more coats than you can ever wear." Need sparked in his eyes.

I slipped down to wind my arms around his neck, wrapping my legs about his waist to press my needy cunt against him. He kissed me hungrily, forcing his tongue into my mouth, both hands gripping my hair. He tasted faintly of smoke, and his dracaena resin scent veiled me in desire. I crushed my mouth against his, trembling with need and the leading edge of the despair threatening to swallow me whole.

If I must be swallowed, I would happily let the Red Dragon devour me. No, no, I must slow down…

He laid me flat on the bed, and climbed over me, still locked in the kiss. I blinked away the intoxication of lust. As he moved to slice open the rest of my coat, I stopped his hand.

Withdrawing from the kiss, he gave me a disgruntled scowl. "Cúraniel, stop making me sad. I hate it. Useless emotion." He threatened the rest of my buttons with a talon. "Take that fucking coat off."

"Not yet." I swatted at his hand. Though it pained me, especially with only a sheet to guard him.

He lowered himself on top of me, propped on his elbows. Thankfully, the bed had enough give for my lungs not to protest too greatly.

"Why?" He had me thoroughly pinned, physically and with his eyes.

"You sound like a petulant child. Because I want assurances you'll actually behave differently before I cave to your demands. I'm still not pleased with you."

Rafael traced my cheek with a blunted talon. "Beneath your strong words, you are rife with despair. You have neither slept nor eaten. I see the circles under your eyes, I feel the gauntness of your ribs, the hollowness of your soul. Why do you deny our bond?" Those eyes burned into me, through me. Helpless tears leaked down my face. The Dragon curled around me, pulling me into his protective embrace. "I am truly sorry for hurting you. Perhaps…if I can give myself to you…"

"Oh, my Dragon, you never need to bargain for my love with your body. I shouldn't have teased you about removing the armor; I simply need to reconnect slowly. After these moons of separation from both of you, I have nothing left to give."

I kissed him, savoring the feel of his lips on mine, the slow triplicate beat of his heart. Our breathing synchronized without conscious effort, and he held me that way for a long time. Perhaps for days. Such a relief to be in his arms again instead of angry and hurt. I squirmed out of my coat and trousers after all, following my instinctive need to press my body against his. Skin-to-skin contact, nothing more. His heat sent frissons down my spine.

When our lips parted, he frowned at me. "You need something

other than flowers to eat. You are far too thin. What can I bring?" He ran a hand over my once-plush hip.

Touched, I stroked his face. Rafael generally ignored such banal needs.

"Would you ask the kitchens for some venison? With yams or some other hearty root? Try not to frighten anyone."

He kissed my forehead. "I will find food with blood in it. Before I go, may I return something?"

"How unlike you to ask permission."

Rafael left me on the bed, cold without him, to open a small chest I'd overlooked on his desk. With a guarded expression, he held up the scale talisman and pearls I had flung at him in my rage. He'd restrung the pearls.

I swallowed the sudden lump in my throat and nodded. I hadn't expected to see either piece again. He fastened the scale around my neck with exaggerated care, and plaited a surprisingly tight braid for the pearls, given all his previous protests. Until that moment, I'd never known how much the simple act of wearing jewelry could feel like home.

Chapter 31

Celebel

"**W**E must secure more of the moranga." I paced about the war room, fed by Feanim's frenetic energy. Surely, whatever "means of destruction" the demon had provided Cúraniel constituted some new form of entrapment.

Passing clouds cast bars of shadow on the far wall, a prison cell of my making. Draped across two chairs, Feanim pulled the moranga dagger from his belt, inspecting the light-sucking edge.

One boot bounced as he pondered. "My brother not only lives, he's turned our kin against us, Cel! The Dragon fights for our cause. Moranga is no longer our primary concern."

"Moranga may be the only protection we have against that fucking demon, and the spiders provide the only access to it," I said. "We must secure your pact with haste."

"Are Cúraniel's intercessions with Rafael no longer sufficient?" My fellow Consul's keen eyes tracked me across the floor.

I stilled, righteous fury tightening my lower back. "He possessed me, Feanim. *Possessed!* Ripped my consciousness away and overtook my body. Of course a gods damned demon would recognize demonic involvement with the accursed Fomorians. I can hardly believe I missed the signs. Why is the song ever clear in memory?"

"How did it feel?" His question was undoubtedly lascivious.

The dark presence shoving my consciousness aside. The crackling flames. How my hands had tremored as I'd clawed in vain from the inside, completely insensate. The ultimate betrayal, my body offering itself up to that…that *aberration*.

I didn't realize I'd hugged my arms so hard my fingers bruised my biceps until Feanim pried them loose.

Rare concern stamped his features as he peered up into my eyes.

"We'll need more of the moranga then, to design restraints if nothing else. Correctly warded, it should at least temporarily hold Rafael."

I shook the lingering dread from my hands. The stiff attempt at comfort brought a small ease. At least someone guarded my back.

My fears bubbled up and out of my throat before I could stop them. "What if the red demon is the same as those who drive the Fomorians to capture and kill us?"

Feanim rubbed his forehead. "You lash out at phantoms. If Raf wished to kill us all, he would need no elaborate charade to give him an excuse." The familiarity flattened my ears. Oblivious, he continued, "Nor would he need to press these beleaguered sidhe into service to accomplish such a feat. No, my brother plucks these strings. In truth, the certainty of his involvement in this war is why we must approach the spiders once more. The ore is incidental." Pleased with his cryptic hint, dark curls tumbled over his shoulders at the twitch of his ears.

My questions sang clearly in the set of mine.

Feanim rattled out a sigh. "I have long wondered if this day may come, Cel. Call it instinct, call it a twin's bond. In the end, I could never trust my dear brother to show me any true kindness, including fucking *dying*."

"And the spiders?"

"The spiders will be our solution. Regardless of whether the Dragon can be trusted, we would be wise to not to be completely beholden to him." He nodded almost entirely to himself.

Relying on the spiders further tightened my back. "You would trust the ancient spiders to ally against Beredhel?"

"They are hungry. The promise of slaking their appetite on powerful spirit is all that matters." He caught and held my gaze. "Why settle for a sapling when you could have a century oak?"

I followed the melody and yet... "What is the nature of your pact with the spiders, Feanim?"

"Trust me, Cel. You will have your moranga, and I will end this war. Let us finish this."

I PREFERRED to approach in armor, but Feanim insisted we appear as heads of state only, for the dignity befitting the Consulate. We rode together with only Lámirië for a retinue. Best to forestall any hint of conflict.

For once, Feanim adorned himself in a velvet robe in his lineage colors of dark green and gold, rather than his far more casual doublet and trousers. I wore cobalt blue, spangled with thread-of-silver stars. Less than ideal should conflict arise, but we belted our swords about our waists nonetheless.

The soulbond twinged as I rode away without speaking first to Cúraniel, but her morose mood only fed mine. That distance, the diminishing spirit, weighed upon me as heavily as the black stone of Amrún itself. A mere half-day's ride from the fortress, but eternity spanned that divide.

Of her pet demon, I'd heard little. Talk traveled around the fortress of the monster's conflict with the other drakes. War be damned, I hoped they rose against him in concert and cast him back into the hells where he belonged. If the notes of the green drake's song struck true, we'd no lasting need of the red monster. Somehow, the ghostly tingling in my hands was the worst callback to his violation.

Late afternoon sun gilded the dark ground as we wound through the lava field toward a series of pyroducts breaching the surface. Feanim marked the largest chasm as our destination. The ceiling had caved in, creating a steep bank of scree and boulders. We dismounted where boulders sheltered the horses from the wintry winds sweeping over the lava plain. I was loath to leave the horses and Lámirië behind. She signed a sharp rebuttal, and I sent her away with a kiss on the cheek. Helicos stamped and snorted at me. He also received a kiss on his soft nose.

I picked my way down the treacherous slope at Feanim's ear tips. Cold radiated from the darkness, enveloping us as we descended. The pyroduct flattened into a small area blocked on all sides by rockfall and columnar basalt. A druzy coating of ice crystals like a lamprey's toothy maw latched around the collapsed entrance.

Feanim held up his hand, gesturing for my patience. He expelled a slow, forceful hiss at the wall. What I'd taken for a columnar structure at the mouth of the lava tube splintered into a mass of individual spiders, like icy rocks chittering across the walls and ceiling. The smallest arachnid's shiny back reached ankle high, and the largest to my knees. Their movement revealed an opening in the rock.

A spider the size of a bobcat stood in the cave mouth. Without vocal cords or spirit to create speech, box lungs and mandibles limited communication to hisses, clicks, and leggy gestures.

Feanim bowed and addressed the gathering. His audience was unimpressed. The lead spider hissed and waved its pedipalps.

"Deeper, we go." Feanim clasped my arm as he led the way ahead.

We descended into the darkness. Feanim drew up witchlights as we reached areas where no sunlight had ever penetrated. Down, down we walked, surrounded by the clicking of chitinous feet. The steady drip of water provided a counterpoint, and the air grew warmer and more humid. As the tunnel narrowed, I half-crouched to avoid scraping my ears. For once, I envied Feanim's shorter stature.

Finally, the tunnel opened into a larger space. The witchlights illuminated a high ceiling reticulated with white spidersilk threads, recalling the openwork honeycomb patterns of the great domes of Velúara. The memory hung with oppressive weight in the stillness of the tomb-like cavern. At the far end of the room, a void rebuffed the witchlights' glow. A watchful darkness, it whispered with the foreboding horror of the deep earth.

"Halt," Feanim signed with an emphatic push of his breath.

Our accompanying spiders scattered. Settling along the walls and ceiling, their eyes trained on us like sickly stars. Several chittered ahead, disappearing into the looming dark.

Faint pops and pings emanated from somewhere in the distance, with the occasional shattering noise like a dropped ceramic vase.

I glanced back at the narrow opening whence we came and the many dozens of thick-bodied arachnids surrounding us. Elvish steel cut through spider carapaces easily enough, but their sheer numbers were enough to plug the exit.

"Be calm, brother," Feanim whispered. "We pass as envoys. The ancients respect the old ways."

I restrained my survey to swiveling ears and forced an ease I did not feel.

A rhythmic susurrus drifted from the darkness, almost the quality of a laugh. Spindly legs like stalagmites emerged into the illumination of the witchlights, carrying the body of an enormous spider with them. A diadem of twelve shining, obsidian eyes stared at us from a massive body almost brushing the ceiling of the cavern. Where the other spiders were polished jet, the ancient wore a pelt of fine grey hair like that of a wolf spider. Rather than chittering clicks, this one moved with predatory silence.

My hand instinctually slid to the hilt of my weapon.

"Keep you blade sheathed," Feanim signed furiously.

"What brings you here, tender-bodies?" The spider spoke jarringly atonal Elvish. Her voice was a bitter wind; skin-crawling with the bite of death. "Where is the promised royal blood?" One pair of claws tapped on the pumice floor.

Royal blood? I held my ears still but studied my fellow Consul's face sharply from the corner of my eye. He did not flinch.

"Greetings, oh exalted one," Feanim intoned formally. "We, the Consulate of the Talithiri and Duedellen elves bring tidings of the strongest, most succulent blood power."

Succulent? Suspicion grew more legs than the surrounding spiders as it crept along my back.

"Tidings? The last agreement is yet unfulfilled." Her pedipalps lifted, exposing fangs as long as my arm.

I suppressed my automatic shiver and signed a question to Feanim.

"Steady," he signed back. Aloud, he said, "I offer payment far in excess of our agreement, oh Great One, a power more vast than we imagined possible. Long hidden, this power is now there for the taking! We come as envoys to secure this offer and receive what is owed."

The ancient spider took a step towards us. She lowered her massive thorax to the ground and spread her mouth parts wide. Her body bucked forward. Just as I was sure she meant to attack, she coughed up a large black stone. It crashed to the floor between us with the metallic clangor like a dropped anvil. I winced at the shock of the sound. The boulder glistened with the chyme of the spider's gut, exuding a foul reek. Witchlights flickered, dimming as the ore absorbed their light. My stomach turned.

"Moranga." The great spider spit the word like a curse.

"Our thanks, your greatness." Feanim bowed from the waist. "We require as much moranga as your children can carry and soldiers to seed under enemy camps. Then I shall deliver unto you mine own brother, the high king of the Duedellen!"

Damn Feanim and his schemes. How were we to offer up a brother we'd yet to encounter directly? My friend had always been selfish and audacious, but this? I strained to keep my face and ears neutral.

"*Promises!*" The spider gave a whole-body hiss, the fetid blast whipping my hair back.

Straightening, Feanim said, "Grant us one moon and you will have payment."

From the calculating glint in the spider's crown of eyes, she was well aware of his deception. "We know of the pale king. Brothers, indeed! Both would have my children fight and die in their petty family squabbles for *promises*."

Feanim's ears twitched at the revelation. He dropped his hand low, signing to me with slashing hands: "Ready retreat." His other hand slide quietly to the hilt of the moranga dagger. "Oh Great One, hear our—"

"No more promises, tender-body. We will have satisfaction now!" One pillar of a leg struck the ground between us. "You are both royal, yes? Which shall feed us? Or shall we take our fill of the interlopers above?"

Gods, she meant the population of Amrún. Feanim drew his moranga dagger.

The spider reared back, waving her front set of legs and pedipalps, fangs extended in an unmistakable threat display. "Bitter blood. You and the pale king are tainted prizes. But this one…" She turned her manifold gaze on me.

"Run!" Feanim leaped forward.

The ancient knocked him aside with a flick of her front leg. His dagger flew from his hand. In a grey blur, she grabbed me in her pedipalps and threw me down. I reached for my sword. The monster spun and shot silk from her spinnerets. Taught threads wrapped my body, pinning my arm to my torso. One leg pinned my back with immense and precise force. The stone floor was cold on my face, and the moranga taunted me with its cold malice.

"Surface-dwellers and your surface knowledge of the deep workings beneath your feet," the great one scoffed.

A wave of smaller spiders washed over Feanim, pushing him back to the exit.

"We accept this blood and consider the terms of our agreement complete. That one may leave unimpeded, so long as it does no harm." The ancient spun and fell upon me.

Fangs like spears pierced my shoulders. Lightning scorched through vein and artery, deadening my limbs and stealing the air from my lungs. My eyes burned, blurring the scene.

Winding silk around my ankles, the ancient hoisted me into the air. My sword, loose in the scabbard, fell to the ground with a feeble clang. She moved toward the darkness of the deeper tunnels. I dangled, helpless, in her grasp.

Feanim screamed my name.

Light and sound faded. My soulbond pulled taut, vibrating in my chest with a physical hum, overtaking all else as the venom nullified my senses.

Forgive me, Cúraniel.

Chapter 32

Cúraniel

A **SCREAMING** wave of panic jolted me upright. Crow, I hadn't realized I'd fallen asleep. Given the room's darkness, I must have slumbered through the entire day. My heart raced. I cast about wildly—there! It came from Celebel.

The soulbond wrenched, and I gave an involuntary wail. Whatever horror transpired was rapidly worsening. From the stretched quality of the bond, Celebel had left the safety of Amrún.

Operating on pure instinct, I leaped from the bed and ran through the courtyard. Helicos pranced and whinnied, greeting me before I reached the stable. Why was Celebel's horse here without him? And his dappled coat darkened near-black with sweat? I barely had time to swing up onto the stallion's back as he charged forth.

We flashed through the fortress gate to a chorus of surprised shouts. Helicos galloped like the wind, heading due north around the moat toward that pulsing dread.

Rafael tentatively reached for me.

'Celebel is in danger. Something horrid occurs.'

'Fucking hells, Cúraniel. Did you even think to don your fucking armor?' He must have found my discarded clothes. *'Yes, and the* dragonsbane *in your coat pocket.'*

Crow. *'No time. Follow me, please! I must find Cel.'*

Bulbous rock formations whipped past us, the stallion's long strides eating the ground at an incredible pace. It would have been exhilarating if not for the sickening fear goading me. So intent on locating Celebel, I hardly noticed when we passed Feanim riding in the opposite direction.

"Cúraniel!" He wheeled his liver mare.

Helicos reluctantly slowed at my signal.

Feanim's eyes were wild through the veil of dark hair whipping around his face. "You feel it then? The spiders have him! Wait here. I am going back for reinforcements." Lettai struggled to catch the other destrier's longer stride.

"What do you mean, the fucking *spiders* have him? What have you done?" I glared over my shoulder at the Duedellen.

"What the fuck are *you* going to do charging into the tunnels naked, other than die?" he countered with a sneer.

"Go muster help then, coward. I will not abandon my soulmate." Confirming through the bond, I added, "Rafael is aware, and he follows on the wing."

I urged Helicos forward. He bunched his hindquarters, leaping ahead. Feanim gave chase with a curse, but the mare fell behind. No time to think. I had to reach Celebel. His tenuous presence was dwindling, and I couldn't risk losing it completely.

Rockfalls and the treachery of unseen pits under the moss forced us to slow. Eventually, I slipped from the stallion's back to better guide him. After an eon, or perhaps a mere heartbeat, we arrived at the crumbling entrance of an old lava tube.

Celebel was down there. My soulbond screamed at me as his horse screamed in fury, hooves sliding on the loose scree that blanketed the steep entrance. I stopped him before he risked a broken leg. Kissing his soft nose, I begged him to wait for us. Helicos tossed his majestic head in acknowledgement. Then I was half-running, half-sliding down the dark lava shaft, leaping over boulders as I went.

Only twenty paces into the cave, the spiders alerted to my presence. From the porous ancient lava, they spilled forth. Resembling massive widow spiders, their chitinous bodies gleamed obsidian in the thin shaft of moonlight from the entrance. Pedipalps waving in threat, fangs extended, they swarmed. The clicking of their feet on pumice filled my ears.

I called with all my heart on the Night Mother to protect me. The cold light of the Moon bloomed around me in a halo as the goddess responded. It knocked the angry, skittering creatures away, burning them like frost when they came in contact with the light.

Some distant part of me felt regret. I liked spiders. Even during the wars of old, the great ones never attacked unprovoked. Like the harpies. Like the Fomorians.

I ran into the dark, trusting to the Moon to clear my path and my connection to Celebel to steer my feet. Curled bodies littered the ground where I passed. The floor of the tube leveled out. I splashed through bracingly frigid water, ankle-deep in some places, as I instinctively wove through the branching tunnels, homed in on Celebel's weakening presence.

Webbing laced over the walls of the tunnels, some of it cocooning the remains of old meals the spiders had garnered. The deeper I plunged into the heart of their nest, the thicker the webbing grew. The Moon's light helped to keep me from tangling in the sticky ropes draped from the ceiling.

Rough tunnel floors scoured my feet raw, leaving a trail of blood behind me. Furious hissing filled my ears. Clawed feet echoed off the walls in the thousands. My limbs shook and lungs burned with the effort of sustained sprinting while maintaining a spirit defense. In my diminished state, after all the strain, lack of food, and insomnia, my limits approached faster than the waves of spiders. The dank, stifling air of the caves did nothing to alleviate the sensation of walls closing in around me.

Only Celebel mattered. I plunged deeper into the oppressive darkness, descending into what must be the very heart of Vaeda itself. Perhaps the demons locked in hell heard my footfalls overhead. Certainly, their fires warmed my battered feet.

The Moon's light slowly, steadily dimmed.

Dûemer, please stay with me!

The tunnels widened into a series of conjoined larger rooms. I dashed across them, leaping over webbing more than once to avoid being caught in it. Egg cases littered the walls and floor. A few broke open as I made contact in passing, spilling countless baby spiders into the world. Some communal sense of rage took hold of the pale, soft infants. They, too, turned their fangs toward me. Kicking them away as I dashed through, I sensed Celebel nearby.

Almost there!

Around a bend, a spider the size of a small pony came into view. It held a suspiciously large silk cocoon in its forelegs. *Celebel!* The only weapon I had on my person was the scale. Gods, not again. I pulled it free.

Leaping onto the startled spider's back and shrieking like a beansidhe, I plunged the serrated point into the joint between its head and thorax. It emitted a high-pitched shriek as the light of the Moon connected with its hard exoskeleton. The scale slid home. With a heave, it bucked me off and dropped its burden.

I rolled to my feet, brandishing the scale. Rafael hadn't trained me to fight spiders, but he'd surely find some flaw in my technique. My pursuers paused, blocked by the Moon's halo as the giant spider leaped at my face. I ducked under its fangs and stabbed blindly upward. Something gave way, and ichor splashed me. The spider landed heavily and skidded to a stop against the tunnel wall.

Leaving the Moon halo in place, I fell on the cocoon that held Celebel, cutting his face free as swiftly as I could. Sawing through the thick, impossibly sticky silk with the scale proved no simple task, but my wild desperation eventually triumphed. I nicked my palms and fingers as I worked, leaving crimson handprints; an echo of the scale.

Pulling the final strands free of his face revealed an unconscious but still-breathing Celebel. His skin had a sickly tinge, the vessels beneath far too visible. I worked my way down his body, ripping him out of his velvet robe. Paired puncture wounds dotted his body.

A spider punched through the light barrier. I drew in the Moon, decreasing its circumference and reinforcing it with my spirit. The invader hissed and died as the force pushed its body out of my shield.

Rising on shaking legs, I stood over my soulmate, brandishing my little blade and the bubble of Moon light. The spiders surrounded me, hissing and testing the boundaries. Smaller spiders sacrificed themselves, throwing their bodies against the light. Dark body after dark body hit the barrier and fizzled into a lifeless knot at my feet.

Terror choked me as the light flickered and dimmed once more. I slapped and kicked the arachnids away as they broke through.

Crouching low to protect Celebel's limp form, I drew in what feeble strength remained and released it in a psychic scream.

It echoed through the minds of every living creature in the tunnels, ripping through the smaller, weaker ones, and repelling the larger. It would only stall the inevitable, but I needed as much time as possible. The wave of spiders fell back for a few heartbeats.

Distant sounds of combat echoed through the labyrinth of tunnels. Swords clanged and spiders shrieking their strange, thin shrieks. Elvish voices cried out in pain and rage.

An arachnid the size of a boarhound dropped onto my back from above. I staggered, falling to my knees. Flailing, I tried in vain to fling it off before it could sink its fangs into me. Hacking and stabbing into the softer joints of its legs, I pried it loose.

Another spider landed on me. Then another. Fangs pierced my upper arm, my hip and belly, my ankles, everywhere. Pain seized my limbs, turning my muscles to stone. The scale burned my hand as I screamed for Rafael. His heat swept me like a brushfire. I expelled it outward, burning spiders in a crisp ring around me.

As I covered Celebel with my body, exhaustion and venom overtook me. I collapsed under a wave of shiny black bodies.

Chapter 33

ACIDIC agony scarred vein and artery alike. Dissolving flesh. Necrotizing organs. I melted into nothingness wrapping me tighter than skin, tighter than breath. Sucking me under, smothering me, shattering me.

Moonless, my mind fractured and splintered, spinning in all directions. I screamed a wordless, mouthless scream, unable to thrash against the bonds that held me. Heart hammering out a staccato rhythm, it unwittingly pumped the caustic, noxious venom. Steadily killing me.

A darker presence took hold. Gripping me from within, it anchored in my very soul and pressed out against the destroying wave of toxin. Blistering through me with wild abandon, the presence fought back, reestablishing the edges of me, forging me with fire into a shape I recognized. The heat of a thousand suns burned through my blood vessels, forcefully shoving out the venom coursing through my body. White hot pain took its place.

With dreamlike slowness, the damage ground to a halt. The dark presence anchored within me dimmed its furious blaze to a gentle warmth. Soothing my vessels, organs, and tissues. Back where they belonged. Back to functioning. My breath eased as the pain dissipated like mist in the morning sun.

I peeled open my eyelids. Rafael stared down at me. His long, hooked nose nearly touched mine, reptilian eyes flickering worry-yellow. Soft light illuminated his fiery curls from behind, the fall of which obscured my peripheral vision on both sides. Like awakening inside a lava pool.

Spiders! Gods, surely there were more. Disoriented, I cast about for my scale, only to discover he held me firmly in place. A bed. I was in a bed. Or a cot? Something tangled around my legs like spider silk. I shuddered. Where was Celebel?

"Be calm, you mad creature. You are safe and so is he." Rafael released his hold on me. "You are in the healer's wing. *Celebel* is in the next bed." He leaned on the name, as if it pained him to use it properly.

The Dragon shifted slightly to reveal the outline of Celebel lying in a nearby bed. Swaddled in bandages, blankets hid him from the shoulders down. When my panic dwindled enough for me to focus, his presence hummed strongly along our connection, despite the stain of illness from his envenomation.

I looked down at the white blankets drawn over me. Filmy curtains separated our beds from the rest of the room. Blankets and curtains, not webs. I blinked rapidly. The vaulted ceiling, with its gently lit witchlight lanterns, appeared correct for the healer's wing, as did the trays of implements. It was otherwise quiet.

"Where are the children?" My voice came out in a croak.

"Elsewhere."

Rafael was not armored. I breathed a sigh of relief, taking his hand in mine and pressing it against my cheek. I couldn't bear the presence of moranga in this state.

Eäriel poked her head through the curtains at the other side of the bed, sizing me up, and entered. She wore her burgundy hair tied in a knot at the base of her neck. Black legs reached around her head.

I gasped and grabbed Rafael's arm. He gave me a sidelong look. No, no more spiders. It was only the darker tips of Eäriel's hair escaping confinement.

She smoothed her unruly hair, kindly ignoring my fearful reaction, and proffered a cup of honeyed decoction. I accepted it with grateful, if shaking, hands. Rafael helped me sit up to drink, casually winding his fingers into my own tangled black mass of hair.

Eäriel laid a careful hand on my forehead, fixing her eyes on the Dragon at his protective warning rumble.

The decoction soothed my throat, loosening my voice. "What happened?"

"*You* happened, you fucking madwoman," Rafael said. "What were you thinking, charging into spider-filled caves, alone, unarmed, and stark fucking naked?" He gave me a disapproving look and a tug on the length of my ear.

"I couldn't—I couldn't wait." Fuzzed outlines of shapes, muffled sounds. The fear though. I remembered the fear quite well. "I knew something was wrong and if I didn't find Celebel *immediately,* he would die." Tears sprang to my eyes, and my empty cup fell from trembling hands.

Rafael collected me into his arms with a heavy sigh. Eäriel moved judiciously out of his way.

"It was certainly a bold choice. I might have been impressed if it were not so ill-conceived." He grumbled a word in draconian I didn't catch, but no doubt translated to some variation of 'fool'. "Hrrm. When you said you desired naked sparring, I did not expect you to choose the fucking spiders as sparring partners." He thumped my forehead.

I clung to his neck, sniffling, and looked over at Eäriel.

"Is Cel, is he…?"

"Lord Celebel is recovering, have no fear." Her gentle smile soothed me. "It seems the spiders meant to paralyze him rather than kill. The venom is stubborn, but he's much improved since his arrival. Liriadis attends him as well. You truly reached him just in time. If he'd taken any more bites, I doubt we could have helped him."

"*I need to help him—*" I struggled to rise.

Rafael pushed me firmly back into the bed. "What you need is to settle the fuck down and eat." He gestured to a covered tray on a table beside the bed. I hadn't registered it in my disorientation. "Do you know how annoying it is to find deer in a lava field?" He poked my belly with a blunted talon. "Almost as annoying as pulling unconscious elves out of a cave full of angry spiders."

Despite his acerbic tone, I was touched. I hadn't expected him to actually hunt for me. Eäriel moved the tray to my lap and removed the cover. Steam rose, and the scent made my stomach audibly grumble. She laughed as I tore into the food. I couldn't recall when I'd last eaten. Newfound energy poured into me.

Sharp cheek propped on the heel of his hand, Rafael watched me with a sparkle of amusement in his eyes. "I have never known an elf to be so utterly fearless, nor so utterly feral."

I wiped my mouth with the back of my hand. How undignified I must look, shoving the last bite of bread into my face. No great wonder I got on so well with the drakes. Eäriel giggled and took my tray.

I studied the set of her ears. "You're not afraid of him."

She signed negative. "When he came flapping over the courtyard in that giant dragon form, carrying you all so carefully in his paws, it was the most bizarrely romantic thing I've ever seen. He caused quite a commotion, setting you, the Lords Celebel and Feanim, and two horses down amid everyone." She grinned at Rafael. "I did not know dragons could grow so large, nor shapeshift so quickly."

He'd rescued all of us?

"How else was I to retrieve you? Also, spiders are flammable," the Dragon said with a toothy grin.

I shuddered at the sensation of their hooked feet scrabbling for purchase on my skin. "Were you bitten?"

"Only the most ancient spiders have fangs strong enough to pierce dragon scales." The grin vanished as Rafael tucked an errant lock of hair behind my ear. "You were bitten hundreds of times. Together, this one and the Siltaur healer work almost as fast as you." He nodded at Eäriel, and she bowed her head in acknowledgment. Rare praise indeed. "I also…intervened." His eyes flickered strangely.

I'd save those questions until we were alone. "You saved Celebel."

"I have not forgotten my vow."

I took his hand, running my thumb over his knuckles. Eäriel took the cue, admonishing me on her way out not to expend any spirit on healing.

"How you save me?" I signed.

He hesitated. "Demon shit," he signed back, long fingers flashing. Somehow, his talons made it more elegant.

Wariness tightened the corners of his eyes. He signed with a tight precision that conveyed he was unaccustomed to signing in casual communication. Or perhaps he worried about my potential reaction?

"No time for consent. Save you, reason. Venom too much, death otherwise. Forgiveness?" To mimic the drooping ear position of contrition, he gave me a tenuous smile and indicated the motion with his hands—which I found absurdly charming. It had always struck me as odd that the shorter ears of most non-elves lacked our expressive mobility, even as sharply pointed as Rafael's were.

I nodded, signing, "Understanding. Forgiveness unnecessary."

The Háramorn part of him which had caused so much recent strife, and still he had used it to save my life. Overcome, I took his hand and kissed it, then grabbed the neck of his shirt and pulled him close to press my cheek against his. He relaxed into me with a sigh.

'*I have never used my power thus,*' he sent. '*The way you writhed...*' His arms tightened around me.

'*It was quite painful, yes, but such is the nature of that type of venom. You are clever beyond my imagination, enacting such a swift intervention.*' I kissed the corner of his jaw, and he rumbled with contentment. '*Are you certain you lack innate healing talent?*'

He snorted and flicked my ear, sitting up. '*In other circumstances, it would have been pleasurable to explore you from the inside.*' A wicked smile played over his lips.

Oh. I'd never considered those possibilities. The vague stirring of lust fatigued me.

Aloud, I said, "Will you help me out of bed? I need to touch Celebel to ensure he's stable."

Rafael huffed at my obvious tactic. "He is fine, and Eäriel told you to do nothing. Must I sit on you?" He arched a brow.

I laughed weakly. "I'd rather you lie down with me."

"These are made for your fragile bird bones." He shook my slim bed.

"Rafael." Emotion welled up, threatening more tears. "Vows or no, I can never repay you for this."

Our recent strife paled in comparison to such a gesture. Rather than dying for me, he'd granted life to the three of us.

He answered me with a gentle kiss, the heat of his lips comforting on mine. "Sleep, my dove."

I AWOKE to Nemohee waving whiskey under my nose. Coughing, I sat up, noticeably stronger already. A spark of pain arced down my left arm. Ah, that was where that first sizeable spider had bitten me. Likely some nerve damage to go along with the venom. They had impressive fangs. I shook my arm out, wincing. My pool of spirit was dry as desert sand.

Rafael lounged at my side, watching Nemohee's antics. Somewhere past the filmy curtain, a censor burned with a purifying incense. The aromatic smoke wafted over us—some combination of juniper, sage, and mullein.

"Aye, there she is! Did ye pure go on after the spider queen, naked and unarmed?" Nemohee wore a long wool robe in green picked with white geometric patterns at the neck rather than the usual leathers. Þey'd even slicked þeir blaze of hair back into something resembling formality. Þey grinned, flashing pointed canines in that pale face, but concern flickered behind the smile.

"Aye, I know it's usually your role to be the crazed one." I accepted the proffered whiskey. "I had no time to prepare."

Nemohee turned on Rafael. "Is it not it your role to watch after her?"

He held up his hands. "You stop her next time. Devious creature sent me out hunting so she could make her escape."

Þey rolled their silver eyes.

One problem at a time. "How exactly did Celebel land underground, wrapped in spidersilk? Feanim had a hand plucking these strings, I feel sure of it."

"Ask your other one. I'm sure he'll tell all when he wakes. More pliable than this one by leagues." Nemohee feigned elbowing Rafael.

Under other circumstances, the banter would have charmed me. "Would one of you *please* help me check Celebel? I promise I won't attempt any healing; I solely wish to lay a hand on him."

Nemohee scowled at the Dragon and offered me þeir arm. "Red's not done so already for ye? Nay, he wouldn't. Have a care now. You made raw meat of your soles when ye foremost landed here." Þey hoisted me out of the bed.

Even with the warning, the tenderness in my feet shocked me

when they touched the stone floor. I hissed, gingerly putting my weight down. Rafael only moved enough to prevent me from tripping over his long legs. His indignant frown pressed into my back as I staggered past. Nemohee eased me to the next cot.

Pale and drawn, dark circles ringed Celebel's sunken eyes and his skin still held that sickly tinge. Most distressingly, the starlight that clung to him was diminished, almost completely gone yet again. Noting a few new silver streaks in his black hair, I placed a hand on his forehead. The clamminess and heat confirmed my suspicion.

"He has a fever." Rare for an elf, and dangerous. I kissed him gently on the lips, reaching for his spirit—

Rough hands closed around my waist, lifting me into the air. I squeaked as Rafael sat me back on my bed. Before I could argue with him, he clamped a large hand over my mouth, bearing me down flat.

"You are to *rest*," he growled.

I glared at him and he glared right back.

"You two are adorable," Nemohee said, and we both glared at the Lachanaur. Þey grinned broadly. "I'll leave ye to it, then. Don't ye break her." Þey bowed out of the hall.

"Must I hold you down through your entire convalescence to prevent any more stupidity?" Rafael's eyes crackled with flame.

"I'll behave," I mumbled through his hand, and he released me. "But I wouldn't mind being held down."

He thumped my forehead with the back of a talon. "Why do I tolerate you?"

"Must be my lovely blue eyes. Like the sapphires of that collar, you said once." I fluttered my eyelashes, and he snorted. "I'd wager it has more to do with my generous bosom, however." I pressed my breasts together.

Accepting my offering, he cupped each breast and kissed the tops, just below my clavicle.

A soft noise at the doorway got our attention. Rafael's answering bass growl rattled my cot. The source of Celebel's comfort during our estrangement stood there; a slim, sandy-haired Astolar named Galaron. Earnest hazel eyes emphasized his rounded nose and light brown skin with its smattering of freckles. Cute, in an unassuming way.

Galaron plucked at the hem of his simple linen tunic. I laid a restraining hand on my Dragon's arm. The muscle twitched beneath my palm; always ready for violence.

"Why are you here?" Gods, I hoped it wasn't something absurd, like a grand confession of love for my soulmate. I had no energy to spare.

The Astolar visibly steadied himself, looking everywhere except at the looking drake. "I wished to speak with you, if I may."

"Privy, I suppose? Very well. Rafael, will you excuse us for a moment?"

"No," the Dragon said bluntly.

I tapped his arm. "Please, love. You needn't go far. We have some matters to work out between us, and it will be much more productive if he's able to speak freely." Tapping turned into tugging his sleeve. *'Come now, you know he's no threat.'*

Rafael reluctantly tore his burning gaze away from Galaron as he stood. *'I will be listening.'*

'I would expect no less.'

Galaron sidled out of the drake's way. Of a height with me, he glanced at the Dragon's face. Rafael pinned him with a blistering glare.

"If you upset her, I will crack your spine like a bullwhip," he snarled, baring his teeth.

Poor Galaron blanched and staggered backward until his hips collided with the tray of herbs at the foot of Celebel's cot. He scrambled to catch it as the tray tipped over.

"No need for threats, Rafael," I called. "He's suitably afraid of you."

Galaron nodded slightly, unable to take his eyes off the Dragon. Rafael grumbled and slammed the tall double doors behind him. Galaron sighed, slumping a bit.

"I'm forever apologizing for him. Let me apologize again. Come, sit, let us talk." I gestured at the now-vacant seat beside my cot.

The Astolar pushed his wavy hair out of his eyes and collected himself before approaching. He paused at Celebel's side first, started to reach out, and reconsidered. Wise choice.

Instead, he perched beside me with a sigh. "I am not entirely sure how to approach this. If it were only you and Cel, it would be simple. With him…" He nodded toward the door.

"Rafael is not angry with you. No, I know how it appears, but he's merely protective of me. He assumes jealousy where there is none." I shifted in the bed and rubbing my aching arm. "Were you able to bring Celebel some comfort?"

Galaron signed assent. "I believe so. He was fairly distraught when he came to me. I did not initially intend to take him into my bed, given the Red Dragon's proximity and Cel's poor mental state, but he crumbled in my arms. One note led to a chorus, as it does. I wish you to know I did my best to remind him of the importance of soulmates. I have no intention of deepening the divide between you, and I've never witnessed him so unsure of himself. Cel has faced nothing like this amount of hardship in an intimate relationship. I doubt anyone has, considering his opponent."

I took Galaron's hand, and he startled. "You are a good friend, and Celebel is lucky to have you. I'm grateful you could provide succor. You are also brave to come here, despite Rafael's presence. Few elves would risk catching his attention. I apologize again for his antagonism, but please know I value your presence and your words."

Smoothing his tunic again, Galaron's ears relaxed. "I should have known you would respond thusly, based on how your compatriots speak of you. But the red specter of your more *unreasonable* lover has me jumping at shadows."

"An understandable response. And that 'red specter' is also my soulmate. I would not have him devalued due to elvish sensibilities." I held his gaze until he nodded. "One favor I beg of you, should you ever find yourself in a similar position."

"Please, ask away." He leaned forward, steepling his fingers.

Like Araglin, I thought with a pang. A student of his?

"Do not involve yourself so directly again without my foreknowledge. Rafael is quick to take offense on my behalf, regardless of my wishes. He rarely understands our ways, especially in matters of intimacy. I cannot guarantee anyone's continued safety in the presence of volatile emotions."

His ears perked. "Quite a reasonable request. I confess, I am not pleased by his presence here, but that will be no surprise to you, given the general sentiment. I truly did not intend to entangle myself, except I have never witnessed Celebel so lost." He glanced back at Celebel's still form. "He loves you. That was never in question."

Tears threatened again, and I took a few deep breaths to still myself. "You are kind, Galaron. Thank you."

The Astolar stood and favored me with a formal bow. I placed a hand over my heart, and he departed. Rafael's thunderous growl rattled through the doorway as Galaron passed him.

"Come back, Dragon. I need you." I didn't, but wanted to forestall any potential for mayhem.

Rafael was at my side in a flash.

I took his hand. "Firstly, remember what you said about staying out of Celebel's personal matters. There is no conflict. Understood?"

He snorted. "Sounded like blatant disrespect to me. How can you tolerate an unfaithful lover?"

I bit my lip but couldn't stop myself from lobbing, "The same way you can."

Rafael bristled.

I raised a placating hand. "I am not trying to provoke you. Please think through your response. I am not you, and our ways are not yours. Love divided is not diminished. You should know by now that elves do not regard sex as you do. To me, this is not infidelity; this is finding solace where I could not provide it. Galaron was not attempting to replace or devalue me, nor was Celebel. At most, it merely saddens me that Celebel did not seek comfort with me, but I understand his reasons."

"I cannot imagine turning my back on you for the elvish equivalent of sentient gruel."

"You are horrid." I stifled the urge to laugh. Sentient gruel, indeed. Galaron did not deserve that. "That singular focus on me is flattering, but can stifle as well. I think you'll eventually find it unreasonable to expect one person to meet all of your needs for all time—"

"You underestimate me," Rafael growled, bristling again.

"I'm trying to help you understand. You shook Celebel to the core with the possession, and he's had difficulty coping. I don't begrudge him a harmless distraction."

His lips twisted in a sneer. "Soft."

"*You* created this discord. I want none of your self-righteousness." I crossed my arms. "Leave Galaron alone. The poor man is only trying to help."

Rafael flashed his teeth but settled beside the cot. It was as much acknowledgement as I would receive. The oppressive heat rolling off his body spoke to his general ire. He continually positioned himself between the beds when there was much more space on the far side of my cot. Contrary, as always.

"Now, I'm feeling much improved, but my hair is not. It's full of knots and spidersilk and debris. Will you help me wash it?" A transparent ploy to shift his mood.

His mouth twisted ruefully. "I suppose I owe you that." A note of complaint lingered in his voice. He hated water.

"At least I'm not covered in blood and guts like you always are!" If there was a smell worse than old, rotting blood, I had yet to discover it.

"I can burn it away," Rafael protested. "You always insisted on unnecessarily washing my hair."

"And why did you never choose to burn it off *before* coming to me, reeking to the heavens?" The scent memory rolled over me so strongly I almost gagged.

He looked past me, pensive. "At first, I was merely battle-fatigued and needed a secluded place to rest."

I had to know. "Your nose is far more sensitive than mine. How do you not perceive how awful that smells?"

"It masks my scent." A peaked brow raised.

Gods, I was foolish. How many times had I commented on his natural scent, which I found so intoxicating? Dracaena resin and the leather he wore, with a lingering hint of smoke. An obvious problem with enemies who tracked by scent.

It rankled, that tendency to withhold information until I asked a precise question in exactly the correct manner. Probably due to the Háramorn in him. They were famous for their love of riddles and obfuscation.

"So, visiting whilst caked in gore was protection for me?" I picked at the tangles in my hair.

"Initially, using your hill for recovery gave me an advantage. I rested more fully with you remaining alert. My enemies know the locations of most of my strongholds, but none knew of you. I wished to keep it that way."

I appreciated the frankness. "Fair enough. Perhaps one day, I'll actually explore one of these strongholds."

Rafael smiled indulgently. "Perhaps."

Chapter 34

THE Dragon carried me to the public baths, skirting the central pool. It quickly emptied of elves. Springs trickled into the numerous side pools, and temperatures varied from near-boiling to glacial. It gave the larger pool a slow-moving current and kept it clean of buildup, such as detritus from a certain rockhead of a drake. Witchlights floated lazily over its surface, and the turquoise glow of fungus lit the alcoves. The ceiling curved upward into darkness.

We came to a smaller pool somewhat secluded from the rest, in an alcove lined with mottled obsidian pillars. I longed for a touch of elvish artistry, as those pillars cried out for carving. Clouds of steam flowed around us.

"Will this suffice?" Rafael asked.

When I agreed, he lowered me gently into the pool. The heated water, lightly scented with sage and myrrh, was a balm to my soul. He settled on his knees at the edge. I resisted the urge to splash him, as his retaliation would be swift and terrible. I submerged myself, letting my body float weightless, dissolving the muscle tension. When I broke the surface, the Dragon watched me uneasily.

"I will never understand how you enjoy that." His memories of forced drowning rang through our connection, and I took his hand.

"I'm sorry you've had such awful things done to you." I ran my thumb over his knuckles.

"Why? You were not responsible for any of them."

I kissed his hand, resting my head on his knees. My legs drifted behind me. "I feel sorrow for your suffering."

"I never would have told you any of it, but you pried out the information with your intrusive healing methods." Rafael gave me a wry look. "Your sorrow is your own fault."

I snorted and turned so he could wash my hair. He obligingly combed his fingers through it, unbraiding my old plaits and teasing out the tangles. Plucking out debris, he was surprisingly tender in his ministrations. I'd always loved the precise, sensitive way he used his hands.

"You have an unreasonable amount of hair." He fanned it out; a growing black shadow cast on the water.

"I know."

"I am not braiding this mess." A hot huff of indignation on my ear.

"You'd better not. What if you discover the one area where you have no skill?" Granted, he'd had far longer than most to perfect his collection of skills, but I had the occasional twinge of envy at his seemingly limitless talents. At least we shared a certain deficit in harmonizing with others, if in wildly varying melodies.

Rafael traced the edges of my ears, tugging lightly at the gold ring. I shivered with sudden need. His lips brushed my right ear and my breathing quickened.

"I still find your ear sensitivity strange." He caressed the length of the helix and kissed the tip.

"You continue that song, and I'll pull you in here with me." I stretched my arms back to wrap around his neck.

His hands slid over my ribs to cup my breasts, plucking my nipples. The warmth of the water mingled with the warmth of his hands. I flushed as he nipped at my ears. The points of his teeth grazed hard enough to make me gasp. The deep rumble of his breath shivered down the helix and into my spine. Straight to my clit.

"Gods, I need to fuck you as I need to breathe." I turned. "I regret squandering the opportunity to have only a sheet separating me from your cock."

Taking my face in his hands, he turned my head forward once more. "Much less invested in keeping me at a distance now, yes?"

His tongue curled down my neck and snaked around my breast, squeezing. The need to have it buried in my cunt threatened to burn me alive. My toes involuntarily splayed and curled, as though trying to find purchase on the slick cliff of carnality.

I twisted my hands into his hair. My breath sped up as his hands crawled over me. "You did save my life."

"Again." Abruptly, he withdrew his hands.

I twisted in time to see him rolling up his sleeves. There was something impossibly seductive in that simple gesture. He had me trained to respond to the slightest hint of bared skin. I chuckled to myself. The wanton hedonism of my youth would never have comprehended such a thing.

Rafael turned me back toward the central pool. He plunged a hand under the water, parting my thighs. I blossomed at his touch, clutching his hair as he worked his fingers into me. Each flick of his thumb against my clit dragged a whimper from me. He kissed the side of my throat, his long tongue trailing fire down my chest. The tip circled and teased my nipple as he worked the other with his free hand. Biting my lip to keep from crying out, I arched my back to give him better access to my body.

"What about a—*mmph*—a dampening field?" I struggled to force coherent words out. My shivers of bliss sent rippling waves across the pool to splash repeatedly on the far side.

"*Fuck* a dampening field," he growled, withdrawing his tongue. "Never ask again. You are *mine*, and those fucking elves will know it."

His jaws closed on my left shoulder. Stars exploded across my vision, shoving me off the cliff into climax. I clawed at him, wild with the pulses of ecstasy. Each peak stabbed through me, crushing me into motes of light. Was it water or lava I bathed in? The bond surged, wrapping me in flame, in yawning need, in unity. Mending the part of my ragged soul owned entirely by the Red Dragon.

It might have been the steam, the blood trickling from my wounded shoulder, or the heat of his desire making me light-headed. I yanked on his hair. Rafael licked away the blood welling from the punctures, closing them.

"*Mine*," he growled again, long and low, in a voice so heavy with lust it prickled my skin.

He gave me no time to float back down from the first high. Withdrawing his hand from my cunt, he tapped hard and fast on my clit, bringing me right back to the brink. He paused as my whimpers increased.

"Sing for me," Rafael rumbled in my ear, taking my lobe in his teeth and tugging as he slid two fingers inside me and flicked my clit with his thumb again.

I ran my hands over his corded arms and up his powerful thighs, enjoying the press of his hard cock between my shoulder blades. Methodically, he brought me to orgasm over and over until my thrashing legs went limp in the water. I called out for all the world to hear. I hoped it terrified any lurking guards.

He smiled against my ear. "Oh, how I have missed your song. Who knew doves had such powerful lungs?"

"F-fuck you," I gasped. "Fuck you for making me suffer alone!" My protests stumbled into helpless gasps as he laughed and curled his fingers inside me.

Finally, he turned my head toward him so he could kiss my mouth to stifle my increasingly desperate cries. I cut my lips on his teeth, and he drank the blood. I dragged my nails over his thighs, and he shivered. Each action of mine, he answered with new undulations, stretching and pounding, varying the rhythm of the flicks on my aching clitoris.

Rafael pulled his hand from my cunt so abruptly I yelped at the loss. He spun my body toward him. With one hand, he caught my face and lifted me high enough out of the water for my weight to make it hard to breathe. I tried to brace against the side of the pool, but he lifted me higher.

"Who do you belong to?"

I squirmed in his grip, kicking in the water to relieve the pressure. "Myself!"

"Incorrect." The grip tightened, grinding into my mandible joint, stretching my neck. His eyes blistered into me. Pure predator, and I his willing prey. And we both knew it.

"You," I whispered. "I belong to you."

He dropped me. The resulting splash soaked his clothes, instantly steaming dry. I collapsed on his thighs, catching my breath. He let me rest for a moment, then tilted my chin up, clapping a hand firmly against my cheek.

"You are mine." Rafael drew a talon over his lower lip, splitting it open. "And I am yours." He pressed the steaming, bloody talon sideways into my mouth, slicing my lip as well. I sucked the digit clean, the heady spice of his blood casting auras into my vision.

He gathered me in his arms, pressing bloody, scorching lips to mine.

A burning moon hung low in the sky. Flame dripped from it like candle wax, spattering on the dark landscape below. The moon blinked, a slash of vertical pupil appearing. The Dragon's jaws parted, and he swallowed the world. His great wings spread across the stars. All around him, the void raged. Hateful voices screamed, hurling invectives. He heeded them not as he flew. I caressed him from the inside, closer than blood, closer than life. The voices grew louder, clawing at him, peeling his scales away.

He exhaled fire, exhaled me. The voices retreated, unbroken but deterred. The Dragon fell before me, transformed into the man. Chains of smoke and flame erupted from volcanic fissures, wrapping his arms and legs. No matter how he fought, how his muscles strained, they dragged him inexorably down into the hellish fires below. I screamed his name, unable to reach him across the molten ground. He looked up and saw me. Smiling, he took hold of the chains and yanked upward with all his considerable might. Horns broke the surface.

I collapsed, utterly exhausted. "Rafael, the vision—"

"You pronounced my draconian name correctly!"

I blinked, glaring up at him. "Is that truly all you gathered?"

He smiled his mysterious feline smile and lifted my spent body from the pool. Snagging a towel from a peg, he wrapped me in it. Cradled in his arms, I breathed him in, scraping my teeth over his leather clad chest.

"Keep your secrets then."

"My Aa'shekahn parent is hardly a secret now." The demonic name crept along my spine. He caught my recoil. "Surely you do not fear me?"

"Not you. The rest of them." I tried to burrow into his chest.

Gods, even the lesser demons were extraordinarily dangerous, making discordant notes in history whenever one breached the gates of their hellish prison. A single háramorn could blight the entire world.

"Whist, dove. I love you." He kissed the damp top of my head. "Your pleasure heals me."

"If you don't actually fuck me soon, I will truly descend into madness. Fighting spiders naked is nothing. Gods, I've missed you and your bitey ways." I rubbed my shoulder where the teeth marks had already faded almost completely away. As had the nerve pain.

He rumbled in amusement and carried me back to my cot in the healer's wing.

When he set me down, I tugged at his jerkin. "Now, as far as ownership is concerned, I would remind you I also belong to Celebel, and he to me. Your claim does not erase my bond with him."

"Obnoxious elf. I am well aware." Rafael cast a sneer at the neighboring bed. "No need to speak it for his edification."

"Oh, it was for yours, my wretched hellbeast." I smiled at his scowl.

Chapter 38

WITH proper food and rest, Eäriel lifted her ban on my helping Celebel. With both of us stabilized, the children filtered back in. Rafael's reaction to the sudden influx of little ones became the subject of much stifled laughter between Eäriel and myself.

At first, the children hid from him. Some wept silent tears. He treaded warily around them; a cat in strange environs, glancing about as if he expected an attack at any moment.

I sat conversing with him when I caught the small footsteps of a Siltaur girl barely out of her toddling phase. With curling waves of black hair and skin like a silver oak, she wore a grey wool frock mottled to look like bark in the manner of her people. Certain Siltaur had a more fae appearance than elvish, and this girl was among them. When she developed the lichenous growths around her ears at her majority, the effect would be complete.

The girl approached with hands held behind her back, stealing glances at the pair of us and Celebel's cot. Rafael stiffened.

I turned to her. "Greetings, little one. What is your name?"

"Inelaira," she said shyly.

'Night Eyes', indeed. Her eyes were the darkest midnight blue I'd ever encountered. She shuffled her feet.

"I made a flower crown for the Consul because a ruler should have a crown. Then, I thought his consort should have one too, so I made you one. But I didn't want Lord Dragon to feel left out, so I made another for him."

My heart swelled as she proffered the crowns. Woven of lily, moonflower, and tea rose, she'd included moss and ivy to brace them, and tiny white mountain asters to fill in the gaps.

I cupped my hands over my overflowing heart. "My, these are fine! Did you make them all yourself?"

Her ear tips flushed. "Eäriel helped a little. Well, she did most of the weaving since I kept breaking the stems by accident. At least it wasn't plates! My friends broke lots while they argued over which one sounded the most like the noises in the deep. Then we all took the blame when the adults found us. They were cross and said the ugly old plates were relics from the folk who built this place. But I broke no plates, I vow it!"

"I believe you." Children and their rambling tales.

A noise near the door caught my attention. Eäriel peered in, eyes sparkling. She ducked around the corner when Inelaira turned her head.

"How did you know our favorite flowers?" I glanced at Rafael with a smile.

He held himself perfectly still in the chair beside my cot.

"Well, Eäriel might have also helped with that," Inelaira admitted, pursing her lips. "May I put Lord Celebel's crown on him?"

"What a coronation! Yes, of course." I led her to Celebel's side.

He slumbered deeply, as he had ever since his salvation from the spiders. I brushed an errant lock of star-shot hair from his face, and his brow creased. With a deep breath and the gravest formality, Inelaira bowed low. She placed the lily crown on his head. I helped her position it so it would not fall in his eyes if he moved.

"He's as beautiful as they say. Will he recover?" She clutched the other two crowns to her chest.

I hugged her, utterly charmed. "I'm sure he'll be much improved now."

She beamed and held the moonflower crown out to me. I took a knee, bending low so she could set it on my head. My ears twitched at her gentle touch.

"You are beautiful, too," she said.

I kissed her brow and seated myself on my cot. "Not half so lovely as this crown, nor its maker."

Inelaira turned to Rafael. "Lord Dragon, sir?" She held out the rose crown.

I held my breath. Lord Dragon himself gave me a pointed look, but his hair remained garnet.

'*Bow your head and accept that brave girl's gift, you old curmudgeon,*' I sent with an energetic prod. '*She even picked red roses for you! I may have no child-rearing instincts, but only the worst kind of monster refuses a child. And what is a king without a crown?*'

'*I am no king,*' he sent irritably, but he gave a gusty sigh and lowered his head.

Inelaira hopped to place the rose crown on him. I thought my heart would burst. She scrambled backwards, as if suddenly realizing who she'd touched. The Dragon snorted and propped his chin on his hand, watching her.

She gathered herself, puffing out her chest. "You have pretty hair."

Rafael's eyes widened.

"And you aren't as scary as the others say." The girl nodded to herself, youthfully short ears twitching. "My mam says, 'the most sorrowful hide beneath a hard exterior'." She intoned it with the formality of a memorized quote. "I hope the crown cheers you."

My ears drooped in shock.

Rafael blinked, brows raising. "You are indeed a brave child."

She beamed at him. "I saw you at Taloth. You helped save our roost! And, well, if you're here, you must be on our side."

Much to my surprise, he coughed a laugh. "Yes."

Her eyes rounded, ears twitching. "Do you truly breathe fire? Can you fly? Oh, of course you can fly. How big is your dragon form? Must you eat a lot? Oh, do you eat in this form or your dragon form?"

Rafael cast a droll expression at me. "This one must be related to you."

Eäriel entered and bustled Inelaira away.

"Can you hear properly with such short ears? Oh, do you hear that pinging noise in the deep right now?" The girl continued to lob rapid questions at the Dragon until she was out of earshot.

To my dismay, Rafael immediately removed the flower crown. I counted it a victory when he set it on the table with a defeated sigh rather than burning it.

After that, the children regularly made flower crowns, songs, and drawings for Celebel. I received gifts as well, and Inelaira mustered a courageous few to leave offerings for Rafael. I caught him palming a little clay dragon figurine.

AS I hadn't yet recovered my spirit, and Eäriel conserved hers for the increasing stream of refugees, we worked primarily with herbs. We made a tincture with feverfew, lobelia, violet, and honeyed licorice root to draw out the venom lingering in Celebel's body. I administered it in slow drips under his tongue.

For a topical poultice to address the puncture wounds, we added ground centipede, with proper reverence and thanks. With my needle set, I punctured the heat-clearing points on his hands and the tips of his ear to release the fever pushed to the surface by the herbs. Using the tools from my hill tangibly reconnected me to my purpose. Bit by bit, Celebel's color improved.

Amongst the steady stream of visitors, Rafael only dropped in occasionally, mostly to ensure I didn't overspend my newfound energy on my patient. Such a reversal would have made me laugh if I hadn't been so concerned.

We were alone when Celebel's eyes finally opened. My first instinct was to smother him with kisses, but I held back. We'd been estranged for so long, I had no idea how he might react. I hated how frail he was, a shadow of his usual self, especially without the ever-present starlight.

I settled on a simplistic approach. "Welcome back, my love. I've been so worried for you."

He frowned and tried to rub his eyes, but his hands shook so much he settled for blinking rapidly. I wiped his eyes with a damp cloth.

"You're safe in the healer's wing at Amrún. I don't know how much you recall, but the spiders took you. You've been heavily envenomated. The recovery is slow, but you should have full function back soon enough."

He didn't need to know about the demonic assistance I'd had with recovering from my own envenomation. Not yet. Perhaps not ever.

Celebel tried to speak, and a weak rasp came out. I held a cup of honeyed water to his lips, tilting his head up, and he drank deeply. He closed his eyes.

Just as I thought he'd fallen asleep again, he said, "I should not be here. I recall…I recall Feanim angering the spider queen. I recall the swarm. How came I here? No! The spiders will attack!"

I took a deep breath, steadying myself. "I went after you. Our bond shrieked something was amiss—"

"*You* did?" His ears flattened in shock.

"Do you truly think I would leave you to die? As I said, I could feel the horror. Granted, I acted on instinct, but ah…" I paused, reluctant.

His eyes hardened. "What is it?"

"Rafael saved us both. We would have been lost if he hadn't followed me into the tunnels. He saved Feanim and the horses as well."

Celebel struggled to sit up, ears flattening again. I moved to help him, but he weakly pushed me away. My heart clenched.

"Rafael put his *hands* on me?" Storm clouds rolled over his face.

"He *saved your life*, Celebel. And mine. He carried us out when the spiders overcame my defenses, and none too soon." I'd known he wouldn't be grateful, but I hadn't expected whatever this reaction was. "You've been through an awful ordeal, and you have the right to be upset. I'm simply grateful to have you back and safe, regardless of whether you're happy to hear my song."

Observing the set of his ears, I took his hand. Would he flinch away or allow the contact? His lips thinned, but he didn't pull back.

"I should not be here." His voice was thin and reedy. "The queen would not hear Feanim's proposed plan, and took me instead. It was the only way to avoid a slaughter." He squeezed his eyes shut, ears drooping. "Now, we are doomed."

Words failed me, my heart stuttering over the enormity of this confession. Finally, I forced out, "I refuse to believe sacrificing yourself was the only option."

"I was serving the greater good—" His voice broke.

"Why did you not speak to me before meeting the spiders?" Anger masked my heartbreak, as Inelaira's mam had said. I fought it, reining in the furious disbelief to hear the despair in his words. Was he truly so willing to throw his life away, and mine with it? "How could we be doomed when the single strongest force in all the world awaits my call?"

"There was no time for a measured response. The spiders would have attacked Amrún." His voice unraveled, and he sipped at the air. "You should have left me down there. Now we'll have all the spiders at our throats. At least my death could have meant something."

I softened. If only I could take him in my arms.

"Let us speak on this later when you're more recovered. Are you hungry?" I tucked the blankets in around him, unable to stop myself from fussing.

After a moment, he nodded. He would need something easy to digest in his weakened state.

"I love you, and I'm grateful you're safe." I left before he worsened the ache in my soul.

Chapter 36

Celebel

AWAKING nightmare settled beside my bed. What a fool I'd been to assume the flaming hair was a draconic trait. That slight hint of smoke lingering about the demon. Was it his true form? I cursed the weakness trapping me abed.

The Red Dragon's eyes glowed with hellish light. "Saving your life is more than adequate repayment for my debt. Our conflict is settled." He said it with an air of imperious finality. Perhaps his voice had such depth because he drew it directly from the evil realm that spawned him.

"How came you to that conclusion?" Bitterness stained my voice. I pressed as far to the opposite edge of my cot as possible without tipping it over. "You'll find no absolution here for your foul deeds."

"A Háramorn ability saved your life." He shrugged. "Balance."

Jolted upright, I coughed with the sudden pain in my chest. "Did you possess the spiders as well? Are you venomous now, as well as fire-breathing?" My skin crawled with phantom arachnids, and I suppressed the rising panic. *I must not show fear.*

"I cannot hold multiples at once." His masklike scowl never wavered. "No, I used the infernal flame."

"What fell power is this?" Curiosity got the better of me.

"It destroys the body, banishing the soul to a hell of my choosing. Each soul in the lineage follows, allowing me to reduce numbers rapidly." The monster spoke as casually as if commenting on the weather.

That skin-crawling sensation grew. "Is there any aspect of you not entirely doused in evil? What assurances have I that you will not simply seize control of me whenever the mood strikes? To use me as your flesh puppet and discard me once broken?" I trembled with the exertion of wrath. "Did Cúraniel know and encourage this, or were you planning to assault her with my body?"

The demon closed his eyes with a low rumble. I tensed in anticipation of his attack.

"Cúraniel is blameless." He looked at me askance. "I should not have done that."

"No, you bloody well shouldn't have!" The winding tension stole my breath, and I struggled to catch it once more. "Why not simply leave me to die? Cúraniel could not have held it against you." Though, she surely would have. Some small glimmer of hope for her intact morals.

The Red Dragon exhaled slowly through his hooked nose. "Your death would hurt her. She has already suffered far too much."

To think I'd once considered the possibility of finding him attractive. Only hate carved such harsh lines into the face of an immortal.

"Oh, fuck off. How generous of you to realize this now, after all the irreparable harm you've caused." The ancient spider had almost freed me from this turmoil. From the bitter reality that no matter how hard I worked, I faced only grief and failure.

"Irreparable harm such as saving your life and securing the moranga you so poorly bargained for?"

Moranga. Surely that was his true reason for delving into the caves. Ill-advised as provocation might be, my tongue refused to remain sheathed. "How do we know you are not the same demonic force driving the Fomorians?"

He blinked. "Why would I need an elaborate charade to kill you?" An echo of Feanim's logic.

I couldn't stop myself. "Convenient way to rid yourself of Cúraniel's attachments without shouldering the blame."

"Fear has made you delusional. Have not the Fomorians attacked elves long before you dragged her, and thus me, into your so-called war?" His eyes scorched through to my quavering soul.

I refused to concede another defeat. No matter how loudly his argument rang true.

Reaching under his cloak, the demon produced a bright circle of þilvor and tossed it at the foot of the bed. My sword, bent tip to hilt—a succinct demonstration of his awful strength.

"It was weak." *You are weak.* "Foolish, carrying an ornamental sword into an obvious trap."

"That sword came from Velúara," I forced out between clenched teeth. It had been in my family for an age, only to meet its end at the hands of a sneering monster. The cabochon sapphire set in the stopper pommel had a significant chip. A lineage treasure; it would have to be recut. Even the hilt was mangled. "Fuck you for destroying yet another artefact." Perhaps he'd strike me down and be done with it. It might not be too late to toss my body back to the spiders. Oblivion sang sweetly.

The Red Dragon stood, towering over me like a fell beacon. I held his hellfire gaze, partially from the fear if I looked away, he would seize control again. His mouth twisted, and he spat blood upon the floor.

CÚRANIEL BROUGHT me a restorative stew. Licorice root barely masked the bitter herbs she'd included, likely the same as the ones she'd used on the hill. "Blood builders," she'd called them. Grains and cooked-down root vegetables made up the bulk of it. Hearty, it bolstered me.

She held the steaming, cloth-wrapped pot in her lap, and served me from it. Humiliating as it was to be spoon-fed like a child, I'd spent my meager strength on the strange confrontation with her pet demon.

"From the set of your ears, something vexing occurred while I was away." She smoothed my tangled blankets.

I told her, pausing only to take mouthfuls of stew.

The mention of infernal flame took her aback. "'Brings the Dark Fire, End of Days'. Rafael's draconian name." Her words gave me an involuntary shudder. "It must reference that ability. I've never witnessed it. There was that snaking, directed flame he used to rescue us at Seregond pass, one to melt stone at Férioth, the forge fires, a more typical flame for hearth fires and such, and the gentle heat of healing he claims is due to my influence. Drakes have names for all of them; perhaps more words for fire than we have for music," she mused aloud, in her meandering way.

What other foul secrets hid within the Red Dragon's labyrinthine mind?

As the sustenance restored my energy, I managed to take the spoon and feed myself. Slowly. My arms weighed thrice what they should.

Cúraniel's curiosity could only stand so much. "Did Rafael finally apologize? Twice now he's spoken to you without my presence, and it hasn't ended in violence. I am cautiously optimistic."

I snorted, nearly sucking broth into my lungs. "A generous interpretation would be he hinted at regretting where his choices led."

"How very like him. And how do you feel?" She leaned forward, the shine in her eyes prompting me toward an acceptance I did not desire.

I swished the stew around in my mouth as I considered. Swallowing, I said, "I do not know how to feel. I still hate the blighter, but he's never offered any peace without prompting from you." I chewed on my lower lip, and she dabbed at it with a cloth. "Now he has the advantage, and I'm merely waiting for him to exploit it."

My ears twitched as she visibly bit back her instinctive urge to defend the monster.

Finally, she sighed. "Did he say anything else?"

I huffed. "It was a brief conversation, and he left once he'd sung his tune. I assume spitting blood on the ground is a derogatory gesture?"

She nodded, eyebrows creeping upward. "Very offensive. It signifies you will never be strong enough to taste his blood otherwise. What prompted that? Seems you had a productive conversation otherwise."

"I told him to fuck off. That I didn't ask him to save me."

Her eyes widened with a deep inhale. "Ah."

"Fuck him," I snapped.

"Have I gone mad? How is Rafael suddenly the reasonable one, and *you're* picking fights? Have you no consideration for what your death would mean for me? Perhaps you do not care. Or have you simply forgotten what it means to lose a soulmate?" Her ears lowered.

"Do you desire my death as well as your own?"

I'd never meant harm towards anyone, least of all her. "Of course not."

Sickened, I studied the linen curtain on the far side of the bed. How many hands had beaten, spun, and woven these fibers? How far had it traveled from simple flax growing in its boggy habitat? An uncomfortable, itching silence stretched between us.

Cúraniel sighed as if expelling a weight from her lungs. "Galaron came in while you were asleep."

It was my turn for caution. My old lover's gentle embrace had offered some meager comfort in the darkness, but in some ways only reminded me of what I had lost. What I had abandoned.

"We had a good conversation," she said. "I also told Rafael to leave him the fuck alone in no uncertain terms."

I sank back into the bed with relief. I'd feared another absurd reaction from her demon and yet another fraught conversation. How unnatural, to live in constant turmoil over the insecurity of a man I had never fucked. Nay, a monster I *would* never fuck.

"Do you wish to take visitors?" She'd made an obvious ploy to redirect my thoughts, but I allowed it.

"Not Feanim. Others are welcome." My ears flattened, and her eyebrows crept upward. "I must rest now." Enough conversation for one day.

"May I kiss you? A healing kiss?" She held her breath as I considered the request.

"I consent to a healing kiss," I said slowly.

She beamed, and a pang of guilt struck me. She did so earnestly wish to help, but often it was a help with no lasting benefit. I settled into a comfortable position. The lush softness of her full lips soothed me as she suffused me with her power. Her kiss chased away the lingering pain and loosened the tightness in my chest and back.

The buzzing of deadened tissues reawakening remained in her stead.

Chapter 37

Cúraniel

LOATH as I was to leave Celebel again, I carried the remaining stew to the kitchens. The scant time I'd spent away from his side affected his recovery. Even if my Dragon was well-intentioned, my Starshine needed rest more than conflict resolution. Every setback cost him strength, and the melancholy pooling in his eyes worried me.

On my return to the healer's wing, I passed Feanim in the hall. His hair was more tousled than usual, with purple, bruise-like circles under his eyes. Much as I wished to hold on to my anger, compassion snaked through my resolve. Though he'd healed the fastest according to Eäriel, he'd also survived a terrible ordeal.

"Are you still unwell?" I asked.

He sneered, but a flicker of doubt crossed his face. "Quite a lot of strain, as my two most important figures are *yet again* embroiled in their drama over you."

"Rafael is perfectly fit for murder." I flicked an ear.

"He's been utterly unreasonable. He believes it's somehow my fault you chased after Celebel in the nude like a madwoman." Indignant fury carved deep lines in his face.

"He has the right of it. If your decisions hadn't led to Celebel being captured, I wouldn't have acted as I did. Since you were so content to let Celebel die." I said it with deadly calm, letting him sputter.

"How is it my fault you wouldn't pause long enough to make a gods damned plan? How could I have predicted your madness? Elves died due to your rash behavior!" Feanim tossed his hands up.

That took me aback. Other elves had joined us? "*You* could have prevented the entire situation by not being a selfish, hubristic ass." I yanked at my earlobes to clear his nonsense from my hearing. "You'll simply have to take responsibility for your own actions. Celebel doesn't want you near him. At all."

Stunned for a breath, Feanim quickly composed himself. "He'll recover. He always does."

"Many assumptions there. You know how cold and distant he grows with upset. This melancholy is worse than any I've experienced from him." I hated all of this.

"I know him far better than you do." Feanim's snide tone made me itch to slap him.

"Very well. Don't you dare ask me to intervene with Rafael again. I will not be held accountable for his actions." If only I still had the pot in my arms, so I could have bounced it off the Duedellen's stubborn, selfish skull.

He scoffed. "You would truly sacrifice the good of our people for your ridiculous pride?"

"My pride?" I stopped cold. "*My* fucking pride?"

Quick as a striking snake, I slapped him after all. Purely out of reflex. He recoiled in shock. Gods, that was satisfying. Had no one else had ever popped him in the mouth to stopper the nastiness? Well, no. That gut blow from Rafael counted. And Nemohee had punched him in the nose. Perhaps each person in the fortress should take a shot at him.

"Shut your fucking mouth, Feanim! I nearly lost a soulmate because of you." I swept past him and he grabbed my arm.

"Good thing you have a spare," he hissed.

I sucked in my power and *pushed* outward, flattening him against the wall. Concentrating, I found an old slash wound crossing the backs of both hands. A nasty one, nearly severing the tendons. Without treatment, it would have rendered his hands useless.

Pulling the healing inward, I unknit the tissue and reopened that wound. Feanim's eyes widened in fascinated horror as blood spewed forth, staining his cuffs. Pushing the healing outward once more, I tapped his hand, and the cut sealed. Simple but effective; he didn't need to know how much effort it took.

"Don't you ever fucking touch me again." I stormed off without a backward glance.

"This is not over," Feanim called.

I rounded the corner and nearly smacked into Rafael's solid chest. I'd been so focused on Feanim, I hadn't noticed the Dragon's approach. Gods, I would never grow accustomed to the way encountering him in an enclosed space emphasized how massive he truly was. I looked up into eyes gone killing red, the slit pupils venomously thin.

"What was that?" he demanded in a low growl, lips pulling back from his teeth.

"Handled. At least for now," I said. Feanim had no concept of his continued fortune. "Let it pass, please."

Rafael's brow furrowed into a crevice as he glared past me down the hall. Abruptly, his eyes trained back on me, and he inhaled through his nose. As I opened my mouth to ask, pain stabbed through my lower belly. I grunted, clutching my abdomen.

"Of all the damned things," I grumbled to myself.

"Blood." Rafael's eyes flickered to yellow as he touched my face with the back of his hand.

I kissed his knuckles, pressing my cheek into his hand. "I seem to be starting my menses. It's been, what, a dozen years?"

"Seventeen." His nostrils flared with another inhalation.

"I should have expected this. My body has never been so terribly out of balance." I'd all but forgotten the way he reacted to my menstruation. Ever since we'd grown intimate, Rafael had paid far closer attention to my cycles than I. To me, they were a minor inconvenience once every dozen years or so. To him…

A wild hunger took the place of his earlier rage. He rumbled, lifting and cradling me against his chest.

"Rafael! Put me down," I laughed. "I'm not that delicate."

"You are not returning to the healer's wing tonight." Intent darkened his voice.

"No, you don't. I need to care for Celebel, you brute!" I struggled in his arms, and he gave me an evil grin.

"Your princeling will keep." Rafael never looked more demonic than when he showed all of his teeth, eyes glowing like embers. "You are mine alone while you bleed. I will happily slay any who object." He raised his voice, ensuring Feanim would hear the echoing boom down the passages. "*Inuriterrege* will simply have to prove his own strength and wit. I am not some hound to heel, and I will not leave your side until you have recovered."

"I am hardly incapacitated by menstruation, Dragon. Surely we could better use your aid on the field of battle."

'*Consider the consequences of bleeding freely around my people.*' His lip curled.

Gods. If Rafael scented my blood, other drakes would as well. An image of his blood-soaked grin made me shiver. '*Do no drakes have a menstrual cycle? Are other menstruating elves in danger?*'

'*Drakes can protect themselves, and other menstruating elves are not my concern.*' He dragged a thumb over my ribs. '*You are still weakened. Too thin.*'

'*Careful, Dragon. You'll wreak havoc on your fearsome reputation with your fussing over me.*' I sighed, but his devotion pleased me. "Very well. Put me down. I'll follow you."

"No. Each time I leave you alone, you pick a fight you cannot win. First, the spiders. Now with Feanim. You should be grateful he was not armed, my dove." Rafael scowled, but I caught a glimmer of amusement in the set of his mouth. He moved easily through the halls toward his quarters.

"Could he run me through before I opened all of his wounds? Would you rather I pick fights with you, then?" I poked his solid chest.

Snow billowed into the hall as he opened the door to the outer courtyard, melting on contact with the warm stone floor. A few flakes settled like stars in the night of my hair. The rest steamed away before it dared land on the Dragon.

He huffed. "What did I say about picking fights you cannot win? Feanim is much faster than you. Surviving the encounter?" He shrugged. "Good solid slap, though. Nice to know you slap someone other than me on occasion."

I smiled sweetly. "Some people need slapping. You seem to need it more frequently than most."

Rafael coughed his strange laugh. "How fortunate you are at least as entertaining as you are annoying."

"I could say the same for you."

My uterus cramped insistently by the time we reached the Dragon's quarters. He kicked the door closed and laid me on his bed. I cursed myself. Normally, I had no cramping at all. With the upset and depression leading to the spider attack and envenomation that followed, my cycle reflected the trauma.

"Still having pain?" Rafael pulled my dress off.

I blew out a breath as another cramp crested, spearing through to my lower back. "It's intensifying."

He crawled over me and breathed on my belly. The heat eased the tight, aching bands. I relaxed, leaning back as he pushed my legs apart. I tried to pull his shirt up and over his head. Infuriatingly, he swatted my hands away.

Burying his face in my cunt, he inhaled deeply. "You are the most exquisite wine."

Drakes and their blood wine. Still, my face flushed with the compliment.

The first time Rafael had come upon me during my menses, his reaction had been swift and intense. His hair and eyes had gone to flame. Before I could react, he'd pushed me to the ground and pinned me. The predatory intensity in his eyes stole my wits. I'd invited him to do as he pleased, and he'd simply shoved his face between my legs and stayed there until I had nothing more to menstruate, releasing me only to tend to bodily needs. He'd thrummed the entire time.

My initial reaction, after the startlement and orgasms faded, was horrified fascination. But lapping up my blood made him so content, I grew accustomed to it. Not that I ever minded his adept tongue inside me, but the extended attention took some adjustments.

"We have such strange methods of bonding." I twined my fingers in his hair as he teased my labia apart. His tongue swirled languidly. Since that first experience, he had never missed visiting me during my menses. I'd hoped that surge of sexual aggression would translate in other ways, but alas. "Why do you enjoy my blood so much? Some cultures would call this an aberration."

He looked up, flashing bloody teeth. "I enjoy consuming you

without causing harm."

"You're vile," I teased, tugging at his hair.

Maintaining eye contact, he thrust his tongue deep inside me, and I moaned.

"Mmm," he agreed, rumbling into my vulva. "Every culture would call us an aberration. Recall what happened when you drank my blood wine?"

"Why? Are you planning to give me more and transform me into your sex slave?" I tugged on his hair, and he made a contented noise.

The blood wine had shown me the entirety of Rafael—all of his past, his childhood wounds, how he'd murdered his way into power. His loneliness. And the confirmation of his vast, untapped sexual energy. Helpless in the wine's grip, I'd unwittingly orgasmed in his arms.

"Tempting."

He sucked hard on my clit, rhythmically undulating his long tongue. Burning heat raced through me, concentrated at my cunt as he caressed me from the inside. His hands slid over my breasts, flicking and twisting my nipples. Playing my body like his preferred instrument

The climax hit hard and fast. I bucked against his mouth. As it faded, he growled, sending vibrations up my spine. His tongue pressed against that sweet spot, and I clenched. He thrust deeper, spearing me. I locked my thighs around his head, squeezing.

Rafael looked up at me, eyes as red as the blood smeared across his nose. Withdrawing his tongue, he circled it around my clit, maintaining eye contact. Pressure built and exploded across me again. A thousand points of light.

"Not much blood yet." Sweeps of that long tongue collected the blood from his chin. "Tell me your desires."

Desires indeed. "Fucking hell, Jax. You know what I want. At least let me *see* your cock."

Rafael rocked back on his knees and sat up. Licking his lips clean of my blood, he sighed.

Damn my loose tongue. "You were unclothed during that first healing, but I would much rather you show me of your own accord." I crawled upright. He'd been unconscious and a patient then, a stranger to me. Hardly the same context.

"Cúraniel, I …" His long tongue swiped the bloodstain from the arch of his nose like a lizard.

"Will you show me a promise of the future? I will not touch you unless you ask, but I wish to see you uncovered, if only for a moment. Please."

Rafael drew a shaky, rumbling breath, still unable to meet my eyes.

"I know what I'm asking," I said gently. "You claim to desire this consummation. If it is not so, then be clear about it. You may always refuse me without creating rancor, my love. I simply wish to progress, if that is also your wish. Great as my desire is, this will benefit you more than me."

He exhaled through clenched teeth, a tremor running through him. Just as worry prickled my spine, he pulled up the hem of his shirt and unlaced his trousers. He tugged the leather away, uncovering himself. His cock rose, as hard and massive as the rest of him. As I knew it would be, but I sucked in a breath at the sheer size of it. I hadn't expected him to maintain an erection, but it encouraged me.

Emerging from a nest of dark red curls, Rafael's cock was easily as long and thick as my forearm. With a textured ridge up the center, it curved gently back toward his muscular belly. Cartilaginous spines emerged, ringing the pointed head in a backward-sloping, rough star shape. They flexed with his breath. How much control did he exert over those spines?

Unable to keep the racing thoughts at bay, I cinched them tight. In all my long life, I'd encountered few cocks of such size, and only two larger. All had been terribly painful with penetration, beyond my high tolerance. Generously endowed partners tended to over-rely on their size with disappointing results. As sensitive a lover as Rafael was, I doubted I'd have any issues. Already, he carried me far beyond previous limits with ease, bringing me to heights I'd never imagined possible.

I ached to take him in my hands. To taste him, though I'd hardly be able to wrap my jaws around that intimidating girth. I might at least run my tongue along the ridges and spines. My beloved Dragon deserved the most blissful release I could grant. In that moment, he could have asked me to spend the rest of my life worshipping his body, and I would have agreed.

Gods, I wanted to fuck him with abandon. To ride him hard. Dash myself to pieces on that glorious cock. I wanted him to stretch and fill me beyond capacity with his hot seed. It would hurt. Oh gods, it would hurt in the best possible way. Fuck, he could destroy me with his cock alone, with those spines clawing along my inner walls. I clenched my thighs together to control myself.

Should I ask if I could touch myself while I gazed upon him?

Meaningfully, Rafael caught and held my eyes for a strained, shallow breath. Then he covered himself. Guilt twinged at the way his hands trembled as he rearranged his clothing. I should have prioritized his comfort over my selfish thoughts.

"What do you need, my Dragon?"

He held out his arms. I clambered onto his lap and hugged his waist. Draping myself over his thighs, I fit his erection between my breasts and rested my cheek against his cobblestone abdomen. I hoped he found it comforting. He sighed like a rusty hinge, his hands sliding across my back.

"Gods, you are beautiful. I could never tire of looking upon you." I whispered mindless praise, but his eyes were far away. "Look at me." I tapped his side. "Rafael? Come back, Dragon."

Finally, he met my eyes. I put a hand over his heart. Silently, he stroked my hair and caressed my face.

"Did I push you too far?" I asked in a small voice.

Rafael made a pained expression and laid me back on the mattress. Pulling his shirt off, he stretched out beside me.

"I have no gods nor kings, only you," the Dragon said.

Chapter 38

RAFAEL strongly suggested I practice more with my armor to learn its limits. His version of 'suggestion' included forcibly armoring me. I argued I would rarely see any actual fighting, but he remained steadfast. My suit and crescent blades made me a strange feature in the healer's wing.

Celebel's recovery picked up swiftly, but the tight worry never left his eyes. We remained locked in a frustrating discordance. I tried to respect his wishes and give him space, but I couldn't bear to go far. Leaving his side strained me, despite how much I'd also needed the rest and reconnection with Rafael.

Lingering around the doors to the healers' wing, likewise, did Feanim no favors. The Duedellen took to lurking in the forge like a gloomy shadow when Celebel steadfastly refused to cock an ear at him.

"Feanim wishes you to know our scouts have heard rumblings of dark shadows moving beneath the surface to the north and east," Nimthil said, hands flowing through the signs. She rattled off updates on supply and troop movement while steadfastly ignoring my presence. "Feanim wishes to strategize. We could use your insight."

"I can strategize perfectly well right here." Signing came slower as of late to Celebel. A fine tremor made itself evident when he held his hands aloft for too long.

"Won't you at least acknowledge him?"

"I care not."

Nimthil looked at me, pleading, and I shrugged. Even if I'd been so inclined, Celebel's stubbornness rivaled Rafael's in certain ways.

She sighed, smoothing her seafoam skirt. "I know you despair, but my people are joining us. Some have already arrived, and it will bolster our forces alongside those Siltaur who can fight."

That made Celebel sit up, and it perked my ears as well. Had

Feanim and Nimthil officially declared their intent to formalize their union? When the ceremony would be held amid all this chaos, I did not know.

"Congratulations?" I wasn't sure how she felt about it. Her eyes were guarded, but surely some kind of acknowledgement was in order.

She inclined her head.

"Is it necessary to hold the ceremony before your people join in force?" Celebel asked.

"The binding is enough for them. I will not have the wedding rushed." Nimthil's voice held a note of imperiousness.

I respected her for that; I knew all about having strangers put pressure on personal relationships.

"The new arrivals have begun training in formation with our existing companies. Feanim can tell you the particulars," she added hopefully.

Celebel's brows drew together. His ear twitch and glance at the door told me he worried over the new arrivals' reactions to Rafael's presence. Surely they'd been forewarned.

"I will need to meet with the new commanders," Celebel said. "Thank you, Nimthil. This is indeed encouraging."

I made my reluctant way to the training field. Feanim had arrived first. Also dressed in armor, he worked through a series of forms. A recent drizzle tamped down the surface of the ring, enough to solidify the ground without turning it to mud, so his footwork kicked up no dust. As he flowed from one movement to the next, my attention caught on darker lines through the joints of his armor.

That hadn't been part of the original design. They drank the þilvor's spirit sheen.

"If you're planning on adding me to your bed, I should tell you I'm about to marry," he called over his shoulder. "Nimthil may be difficult to convince."

"I'm studying your armor design, you odious gremlin." I tugged both lobes and shuddered. No doubt he would spring at the chance to bed my soulmates as well. "How long has the moranga been part of your suit?" I kept my voice controlled, grounding my emotions.

He turned to me. "Why do you care?" The helm rendered his expressions unreadable.

I pooled my spirit in my belly to keep from raising my voice. "Did you give the spiders a good show?"

Feanim removed his helm to glare at me properly, giving his damp curls a toss. "What the fuck do you know of anything? You saw the robes we wore."

"Then tell me what happened." I leaned on the fence, waiting. So much for practice today.

"You wound me and now you demand favors?" he snapped. "Spar with me. If you can avoid being knocked unconscious, I'll tell you everything."

Immediately uneasy, I considered Rafael's warning of Feanim's speed. The Duedellen was likely disinclined to pull his punches. But then, if I could conceivably dodge strikes from the Red Dragon himself while wearing my armor, surely I could manage an elf?

Ah, but how would Rafael react if he came upon us sparring? I cast about for his presence and found him deep in the forge, down in the heart where he used the magma to assist his fire. He responded to my mental touch, shifting his considerable focus to me.

"Are you certain you wish to spar?" I nodded toward the forge. "What if you land a solid hit? You know how protective Rafael is, and I have no illusions about my skill."

"I'll go easy on you," Feanim jeered, shifting his weight.

I changed tactics. "Would you be willing to teach me some swordplay? I've done far more unarmed grappling than melee practice with weapons."

Much as it grated on me to ask, the Duedellen was not immune to flattery. I didn't want his hands on me if I could avoid it. Nimthil glared enough as it was. I'd hoped perhaps saving Feanim's fool life after taking that gut shot would have warmed her toward me. Instead, she'd blamed me for the entire ordeal. No winning with that one.

"I will not use padded weapons," Feanim said.

"Come now, you've trained with the Dragon. I've only practiced with edged blades." Not that I'd likely come away with fewer contusions, regardless.

"And he never taught you the basics?" The Duedellen's brow arched.

"He taught me to regret asking. Unarmed self-defense was his idea. It was mine to train with weapons. He's annoyed I didn't practice every day in his absence. Nor did I read the two dozen fatally boring books he brought me on the topic."

As much as I hated to admit it, I needed the help. Rafael steadfastly refused to teach the basics, insisting I read instead. That I'd abandoned them in a dusty pile never ceased to irritate him. Almost as much as the haphazard pile of weapons.

Before Rafael had released me from my menstrual imprisonment, he'd stubbornly dropped more books in my lap. Copies of the same titles I'd neglected on the hill. I'd held one to my nose, hoping for a whiff of home. I sneezed instead.

He'd jabbed a talon at the stack. "You *will* read them."

Suitably chastised, I'd tried my best, but I could not force myself to focus.

Feanim's voice interrupted my memories. "Rafael was right, you should have. What an incredible luxury, to ignore the fundamentals of defense whilst also being on the losing side of a war. You do not deserve such valuable books! Draw your weapons."

Strange to have what felt like a productive conversation with Feanim after all the discordant notes. Especially considering his general, unrelenting disdain for me. And mine for him.

My crescent blades rode in crossed belts over my hips. I opened the straps holding them, and Feanim immediately criticized my stance. He held a shortsword in his left hand and a dagger in the offhand. A moranga dagger hung sheathed at his hip. I shuddered and raised my guard.

He darted forward with an underhand diagonal slash of the shortsword at my right side. I barely avoided his blade as he spun fluidly into another stab with the offhand blade at my back. I knocked it away with pure luck, jerking my elbow backward in a reflexive defense. As he circled, I realized my height could be a disadvantage. Feanim crouched low, making himself a small target.

Experimentally, I lashed out at his sword arm. He dodged it easily, using the opening to jab me in the ribs with the pommel of his dagger. My armor redistributed the force, and I brought the other crescent blade to bear. If he'd moved slower, it would have sliced through his ear. As it was, it merely whistled through the space where he had been. Then he was at my back, kicking my left leg out from under me. I hit the ground and rolled, dodging several downward stabs from his shortsword before regaining my feet.

"Lighter on your feet," a familiar voice called.

Celebel leaned on the fence, also armored and helmless. When had he armored himself? As far as I knew, this was his first venture out of the sickbed. Taking advantage of my distraction, Feanim smacked my belly with the flat of his blade, knocking me backwards.

"You're dead," he crowed. "That didn't take long."

I pushed off my back foot and charged him, whirling my blades to catch his sword and rip it from his hands. Feanim skipped backward, out of my reach. Planting his feet, he used my momentum to dive under my guard and vault me forward. With a ringing crack, he brought his elbow down on my spine. I crouched and spun, trying to sweep his legs, but he hopped out of reach as easily as a cricket.

"Fix your grip. Your hands are too far back," he sneered.

At my slight shift of focus, he shot forward and struck a ringing blow on my helmet. It didn't hurt, but my poor ears were momentarily deafened. I staggered, and he knocked me down, disarmed me, and pointed his sword at my throat.

"Dead again. This is too easy. You should use a shield."

I kicked upward with all my might, aiming squarely between his legs. He yelped and barely dodged in time.

"Not dead yet, asshole." I heard laughter from the fence.

"So, you do not fight with honor." Wind whipped his hair into a dark cloud.

"Oh, fuck your honor. I refuse to die in battle for some foolish notion of honor." I climbed back to my feet, thoroughly tired of being knocked on my ass by condescending men.

Feanim circled again, watching my face.

My helm disguised my eyes, but I was careful not to turn my head and cue him. "You haven't told me what happened yet."

"You haven't proven yourself yet."

I tried a kick. He dodged it, but ran into the blade in my opposite hand. I used it to wrench the dagger from his. He spun it into a crushing sword strike to my left thigh. From the way the armor rang, and the feel of the nasty bruise forming already, he did not limit his strikes as he'd claimed. So I punched him in the ear, gauntleted fist barely connecting as he dodged, but it was enough to rattle him.

"You're a true ratfucker." Feanim rubbed his ear as he backed away.

"'Monsterfucker' is the preferred slur." If only he could see my vicious smile.

He charged, light glinting off of his gauntlets. I barely danced away, desperately dodging the first flurry of stabs. He wasn't as fast as Rafael, but faster than me by far. Changing direction, swift as the wind, he threw my rhythm off. A few body blows connected, and my armor sang out with the impacts. I knocked his sword away with a lucky parry. Feanim dropped it and pulled the moranga dagger.

He stabbed me in the gut. I doubled over, panicked at the screech of metal on metal and clutching my belly. With an ugly smirk, he held the black blade up hilt-first.

Someone rushed past me. Celebel had vaulted the fence. His gauntleted fist connected with Feanim's jaw, snapping the shorter elf's head back. How had he the strength for such action? Was it spirit or rage alone that compelled him? Or was the Pîntellum that powerful?

"How fucking dare you strike her with moranga," Celebel roared, scattering my questions. He'd drawn his sword; it was not his usual blade. Blood streaked his left gauntlet. "How dare you endanger my fucking soulmate!"

Perhaps Rafael's unrelenting fury had simply overshadowed Celebel's. Some small part of me purred at his unexpectedly protective response.

Feanim wiped his chin, backing away and dropping into a stance with a glare. "Cel, she's unhurt! I only struck her with the pommel." Without shifting his focus from Celebel, he used the tip of his sabaton to flip his shortsword back into his hand.

The air grew staticky with tension. I scrambled away from the field, pulling off my helm. Sparring would have a deleterious effect on his recovery, but Celebel was utterly unconcerned. He squared off with Feanim, anger radiating from his body in nigh-visible waves.

Rafael appeared at the entrance to the forge across the way as if summoned. I caught his eye. With a moranga greatsword propped on his shoulder, he joined me at the fence. I took an instinctive step back from the sword's malevolent energy.

"Lover's quarrel?" He eyed the elves. "Never thought Celebel would actually champion you."

I blinked. Today was full of surprises.

"When they've finished their little duel, I will grind Feanim into dust for that gut strike." Rafael's voice was dangerously flat.

"I thought Feanim was your new favorite co-conspirator."

He snorted and untangled my hair from the knot I'd tucked up into my helm. "None who would harm you will ever be spared my wrath."

"Tempting, but I'm unharmed. It's nowhere near as bad as your beatings when we spar."

His mouth tightened. "If that blow had landed as it began, it would have pierced your armor. If you will not hear me, at least listen to your princeling. He recognized it as well."

Celebel and Feanim clashed, and I had ears for nothing else. Swords rang as they met and glanced off each other. Their bodies whirled into a blur of shining metal and singing strikes. This was quickly becoming a fight in earnest. Should I intervene?

Rafael watched with keen interest. "Your princeling has the height and reach advantage. He is stronger, but the anthill king is faster and more aggressive."

"If Feanim gets a real strike in with that moranga blade, it bodes ill. Cel has hardly recovered from the last one." Watching Celebel fight gave me a new appreciation for his sheer ability. And the way his body moved. Gods, the flexion of his thighs and ass alone, even through the armor…

"That may not be an issue." Was that a note of respect in Rafael's voice?

Celebel slowly but surely pressed an advantage. The air around the Talithiri shivered as he drew in power. Black and silver hair made a nebula about his head as his attacks grew more vicious. Feanim faltered under the onslaught.

Other elves gathered at the fence. A few captains I recognized, as well as Carafindrien and her friends. Nemohee appeared at my other side.

"They're pure going at it, eh?"

"Seems like." Tension knotted my brow and the back of my neck.

The distinctive belling peals of swords glancing off of þilvor created an almost rhythmic melody.

"Tell them all, Feanim. What was your plan?" Celebel cried, shoving the Duedellen backward and knocking him to his knees with a vicious gut strike, not unlike the one Feanim inflicted upon me. "Tell them how you baited the spiders with the promise of handing over your *brother* to assuage their thirst for royal blood. Tell them how you first tricked the moranga out of them with the body of a minor noble. But that wasn't enough, was it?"

Gasps from the crowd, including mine. To desecrate a body in such a manner was unthinkable; iniquity worthy of severance from the song. This must have been the deal Celebel mentioned. When had he learned the truth? Fucking hells. There was the spiders' provocation.

Feanim mounted an increasingly desperate defense as Celebel rained down blows. The air itself quavered around my soulmate.

"Tell them of how the spider queen called you 'bitter blood'." He struck Feanim's arm, knocking the sword from his hand and sending it flying. "Tell them of how she took me in exchange for attacking Amrún. How if she'd taken you, we would have lost us all hope of the Lachanaur's aid. Do you know how it feels like to be paralyzed by spider venom? To be wrapped in choking spidersilk, preserved for a slow, agonizing death?" Another strike whipped the offhand dagger away.

Celebel bore down on the hapless Duedellen with all the fury of his lineage, flattening his opponent to the ground. He brought the tip of his sword to bear on Feanim's throat. Ears flattened, Celebel's eyes blazed with cold fury. The audience held a collective breath.

"My soulmate risked all to save me. Now, you've heaped upon me yet another debt owed to the fucking Red Dragon." Celebel's normally smooth baritone hitched with strain, and his chest heaved.

Rafael huffed. "We have settled our respective debts." The timbre of his voice caught everyone's attention.

Without releasing Feanim, Celebel whipped his head toward the Dragon. "I will have *silence* from you, demon."

I tensed, but Rafael only coughed with startled amusement. The fence creaked under his weight as he propped his elbows on it. I shifted forward with him.

Celebel held the point of his blade perfectly steady. "The spiders will attack us now. There will be no more negotiations. *You* caused this. *You* brought this ruin on us with your selfishness!"

Tension crackled. Gods, surely he would not run Feanim through? Straightening, Celebel tossed his weapon away in disgust. He stalked off of the training field. Feanim lay on his back, panting, but made no move to rise. His armor was sullied, and a cut on his cheek bled freely. The very future of the Consulate might be drawn into question, but I would not involve myself directly with matters of state. I had enough complications.

Rafael's talons clicked on the fence. "Hrrm. I did not think he had it in him."

"I doubt he'd ever felt truly helpless afore the spiders got him. It'll change ye," Nemohee said.

Þey shared a knowing look with Rafael. Nemohee's silver eyes landed on the moranga greatsword and questions welled up. I excused myself from the conversation.

Despite Feanim's terrible choices, I hated witnessing Celebel push away his closest friend. Especially right after pushing me away. Melancholy killed elves. If he surrendered to the crushing sorrow and took root, nothing could stop the transformation and his consciousness would be forever lost. Not even our great ancestor trees could reach him then.

Chapter 39

WITH a heart of lead, I wandered into the gardens. Though frigid, a clear sky promised no snow for now. Settling on a silver birch root, I dipped the tips of my sabatons into a pool to wash away the training field dirt. Stars reflected on the water and my armor. Like swiping the grime from my suit, I healed the bruises from my earlier scuffle and relaxed into the music of night insects.

As I braided my hair, Celebel's feet rang on the paving stones.

"Hello, Starshine. How are you faring?" I did not look up, fearing his expression.

If I demanded he grovel over the unfairness of his actions, I'd likely seal permanent damage in our relationship. Or I could actively work to repair our connection. To repair our very souls.

"Cúraniel." His voice was tight with emotion.

Celebel stood without a helm, his lovely meteor-streaked hair disheveled. Grief threatened to shatter his carefully maintained mask of calm. I slid off the root and went to him. He grabbed me, crushing me to him as best he could. Odd, to embrace in the armor, but I was grateful. This was the first open expression of affection he'd given me in an age.

He took a shuddering breath. "Gods, I am a fool. Forgive me, please. I miss you terribly."

"For what am I forgiving you? For having complex emotions after a traumatic series of events? Sorrow is natural; it's the melancholy and self-destruction I fear. I hate the distance and I've been terribly sad, but not particularly upset with you. At times, I forget how much younger you are." I cupped his face in my hands. "You are here now, and it is enough. I would be a source of comfort rather than strife."

Emotion brightened his eyes. "How are you still so patient after everything?" Tears spilled over. "Forgive me, please, for being horrible to you out of fear and strain. You cared for me when I nearly surrendered our lives. Forgive me for not being the partner you need, the partner you deserve. I have transformed into someone I do not care for, someone I barely recognize. In my fear of losing myself, I've almost lost us both. We each have our flaws, but I love you. I do love you, and I've failed to prove it to you."

There was my Starshine; the man I'd fallen in love with. Earnest, emotional, sweet.

He swallowed hard. "When I thought Feanim had stabbed you, my body moved of its own volition. I am not a wrathful sort, but never have I felt such searing rage as I did witnessing your fall. Before I had a conscious thought, I was at your side. Where I belong."

"Welcome home, love," I said simply.

He kissed me fervently, worshipfully. The starlight sang around us and our entwined spirit filled my senses. Filled the void in my soul. A thousand nights passed before our lips parted again. I clawed at his armor, desperate to taste his skin, and he pulled me to the ground.

"I want—" I started.

He covered my mouth with his and tugged at the codpiece of my armor. My body surged with desire. I shimmied out of my codpiece and frantically ripped his away. The moment his cock sprang free, I wrapped my legs around him and guided it home. No foreplay necessary; my cunt was already slick with need. That most visceral connection lit my skin aflame. Surely my armor glowed red hot.

We fucked harder than ever, armor clanging, echoing off the fortress walls. The Pîntellum absorbed and redirected the impacts, rippling the force through us in a way that heightened our frantic lovemaking. Physical gratification receded in the animalistic need to couple. If only I fucked him hard enough, melded our bodies strongly enough, he could not leave me again.

The layers of metal and membrane meant he couldn't sheathe himself to the hilt, but it mattered not. An orgasm struck me like a bolt of lightning. Sharp, fast, and brutal. Celebel cried out as I clenched around his cock. He spilled himself into me, jerking and shuddering. It gave me a malicious delight to think of alerting the entirety of Amrún to our activities.

"Remove that gods damned armor. I need to feel your skin." I tried to pry apart the joint between his breastplate and pauldrons.

He merely stood, clapped his codpiece back into place, and scooped me into his arms. I laughed as he handed me my codpiece and covered myself as he hauled me through the gardens toward our chambers. How would the Pîntellum handle the seed leaking from my cunt?

I twined my arms around his neck. "How have you found such energy?"

Surely he'd overextended himself.

"Anger and lust are powerful motivators." He gave me a wolfish grin.

"If I'd known beating Feanim into the ground would prove so therapeutic for you, I'd have suggested it long before now."

Celebel snorted. "He never should have involved anyone else in his scheming with the spiders. Speaking with Nimthil helped me understand how we've all made excuses for him over the years. I've demanded you force accountability on Rafael, which I did not expect of Feanim. And I haven't a soulbond to feed my enabling. Fé may not make such overtly violent gestures, but the self-serving and callous nature is all too similar. Nimthil told me of certain actions… As you've said, he does not respect his own soulmate."

He climbed the stairs as though completely unencumbered. Rafael often slung me around like I weighed no more than a feather, but Celebel surprised me. His slim build belied long years of intense conditioning. He had the muscle definition to show for it, if not a drake's bulk.

Kicking open the door to our chambers, he marched in and tossed me onto the moss bed. He pounced after me, landing hard enough I worried he'd chip the stone beneath. I moved to take off my armor.

He stopped me. "May I? It's been far too long since I've undressed you."

"Please." I laid on my back, arms spread in surrender.

Like dawn breaking after a long night, Celebel's eyes were

brilliant. He started at a gauntlet. Slowly pulling it free, he kissed my fingertips, my palms, and as he freed them, my forearms and shoulders. He moved to my legs, removing the sabatons and lingering to both kiss and massage my feet. Greaves, poleyn, and cuisses followed shortly as his lips traveled up my lower legs to my thighs. The slight sucking sensation of the Pîntellum pulling free from my skin enhanced my sensitivity.

The languid, deliberate undressing fanned the flames building in me. Celebel smiled against my inner thigh as a small moan escaped my lips. He took extra time in removing my plackart and breastplate, gently lifting me to pull the backplate from under me. Instead of fondling my breasts as I assumed he would, he merely breathed over my exposed nipples, the sudden gust of air tightening them to hard peaks.

Watching my face, he tapped a rhythm on my codpiece, having loosened it from the rest but leaving it in place. When I tried to sit up and reach for him, he playfully pushed me back down.

"Perhaps I should tease you more, as you respond so well to it." His voice grew husky with desire, and he tapped his own codpiece.

I groaned, tugging an earlobe. "Don't you dare. I receive more than my share of teasing!"

He laughed and removed only his codpiece, showing off his beautiful cock. It gleamed almost as much as his armor in the moonlight spilling through the windows. I reached for him again, and again he pushed me back, leaning over me. Pulling my codpiece free, he rubbed his tip against my clit. Gritting my teeth at the denial, I wrapped my legs around his waist to force him into me.

Grabbing my thighs, he pushed me back onto the bed. "Let us discover just how well-made this armor is, eh?" He drew a gauntleted hand across my breasts. "The finest craft will not snag silk. Stay here."

I held my breath as he trotted over to the pool and snagged a bottle of oil.

He held up the bottle and his armored hand, fingers coned. "Shall we test your fortitude as well?"

Gods. Was this some competition with Rafael to discover who could challenge my physical limits in the most extreme manner? I'd thought it ended at a taloned foot, however…

"Slowly, if you please." I exhaled, chewing on my lip.

The mischief in his eyes healed another tatter of my soul. This was the Celebel I'd fallen in love with. Flirtatious, clever, and whimsical all in one. Gods, how I'd missed him.

He doused his gauntlet in oil, uncovering one hand in order to work the lubrication into every joint. I spread my legs.

Whispering conspiratorially, he teased my entrance with oiled þilvor fingers. "I must admit, I very much enjoy when you come to me stretched wide from your other amorous activities. How unfortunate that it fades so quickly."

His words stampeded through me, ringing all the bells of lust. I moaned, lifting my hips.

"You have such a vast need, I can hardly work alone." Celebel brushed his lips over my thighs as he parted my labia. "I find your sexual appetite incredibly arousing." A single finger pushed into me, ever so slowly. The þilvor was warm. "How is this?"

"G-good, it is good. Ah!" I arched my back as he curled the finger. "You steal my senses."

As a second finger joined the first, working gently, his un-gauntleted index finger swishing over my clit. Ripples amassed into a tidal wave. The orgasm caught me by surprise. I clawed at the moss as it rolled me. Stretched and pounded, just as I needed. My world shrank to his fingers and my cunt.

"Interesting. The þilvor allows for some sensation transfer. I can tell you're clenching around my fingers. Shall I add another, or are you sated?"

"More," I gasped. The orgasm lingered, waiting to sweep me away again at the slightest provocation.

A third finger, and he added more oil. I raised my hips in encouragement, and he worked in the smallest. Getting past the knuckles was always the challenge. The stretching, the pressure. Gods. I pinched my nipples, hardly aware of my actions. Shallow breathing. Slow progression, a hairsbreadth at a time. I opened for him, accepting his entire hand. More oil.

With the gentlest of motions, those fingers undulated inside me, brushing around my cervix. I rose and rose. Had I lifted off the bed?

"Such a sight. I should paint you this way." Celebel leaned in to drop a kiss on my clit.

I shattered at the contact. Ecstasy exploded through me, ripping away memory, time, gravity, my name. A single clear note escaped my lips. The gauntlet in my cunt thumped into me, following the rhythm of my breath. A plush mouth sucked at my clit. Rise and crash; orgasms crested one after another. Whimpering, I came back to myself.

Satisfied, Celebel gently removed his hand the same way he'd entered me; one finger at a time. Once free, he held up the gauntlet. My juices laced the glistening þilvor.

"I'm enjoying the way you've painted my armor as well. Perhaps I should keep it thus."

Breathless, I smiled.

He brushed my errant hair out of my face. "Are you entirely spent? Too sore?"

"N-never. I want your c…your cock."

"Insatiable!" With a laugh, Celebel sat back on his heels, pulling us both upright.

He tugged my legs up around his waist, holding me tightly and poised so I couldn't quite drop my hips down. He licked my ear, and I sighed, pressing my breasts against the þilvor. Not as warm as the gauntlet, but not cool enough to be unpleasant. Maddening in his leisure, he lowered me onto his hard cock, nibbling at my ear.

He raised and lowered my hips with excruciating slowness. After the fisting, I needed more stimulation than a gentle fucking could provide. As he'd said, the stretching gave me more space to work with. I rocked against him, forcing him deeper.

Shifting, he gripped my buttocks and let me drop hard on his cock, hissing in my ear. I gasped and his cock throbbed inside me. Picking up speed, he raised and dropped me, pounding me hard, and my orgasm built along with his own. I bit his ear.

Crying out, he hammered me.

The pulsing of his cock, slamming against my cervix with

delicious pain, brought me to the peak. I yanked his hair as I screamed. The bond swelled, twining our songs, twining our souls, our spirit. Bringing us home.

"This armor wants a thorough cleaning," I said once I could speak again.

We both laughed as he extricated himself. I helped him remove the rest of his armor. We tangled our limbs together, enjoying the skin-on-skin contact.

"I believe we're both in need of a thorough cleaning." Celebel eyed me.

"And food. You need to put some weight back on." I poked at his hollowed cheekbone.

"You as well, my dear. There is noticeably less of you to grab!" His gaze was drowsy, yet soft with concern. "We'll convalesce together."

Absently, he rubbed the center of his chest. I nodded, mostly to myself. The painful distance had struck me in the same place. One emotional fuck wouldn't heal all the damage, but already my body was more solid, my spirit properly moored.

Celebel was asleep before I climbed out of the bed, mouth lolling open in that particularly undignified, charming way. Starlight glimmered once more on his brow.

Chapter 40

Celebel

"**Y**OU *will* harmonize." Nimthil's glare slid from Feanim to me. She'd almost dragged her soulmate into the forge by his ears. "The Consulate is in shambles. Our people are lost, frightened. They cannot have their leadership in such discord."

Feanim snorted, resting his elbows on the anvil in my preferred work area. I'd taken up a position against the far wall. All the better to observe one another. The Lachanaur queen stood with her back to the entrance. She'd always cultivated an airily delicate mien, misdirecting opponents into believing her weak. Now, illuminated by forge fire before and sunlight behind, wearing a gown of varying yellows and oranges, she took on an almost otherworldly appearance; a phoenix readying for flight.

I'd hidden away here for the last three days, hammering my rage and despair into the sword Cúraniel's pet demon had destroyed. Blighter that he was, his point about ornament harmonized. I'd begun with removing all the gems from their settings and prying the blade loose from the hilt. This new sword would embody streamlined practicality.

Cúraniel visited with food, words of encouragement, and sweet kisses. Her sultry alto, the quirk of her full, violet lips as if she knew a secret, the sway of her hips; it all soothed me. Gods, I'd missed her wit and laughter.

Mending our frayed soulbond lifted a crushing weight from my lungs, but the melancholy ran deeper than the struggles between us. I hadn't spoken to Feanim since the fight three days ago. Nor had he sought me out.

My hands itched to take up the hammer again, but Nimthil's imperious stare quelled the urge. I wiped them on my leather apron instead.

"Very well. Feanim, explain precisely how you planned to deliver your brother, whom none of us have encountered in person since he supposedly died at the Breaking, to the spiders as you vowed." I folded my arms to keep myself from drumming my fingers in agitation. "How do we know he is more than a mere phantom plaguing Cúraniel?"

Feanim's mouth worked, and he set down the hoof pick he'd been examining. "Her visions are not the only proof, merely the most distressing. My crows reported signs and a possible location before we met the spiders. If they are correct, he's dug himself into an abandoned fortress up in the tundra." He refused to meet my eyes. "I did not expect the spiders to demand payment immediately. I thought we'd be able to investigate first. Last time—"

"When you fed them the corpse of a fallen noble?" I seethed.

If Nimthil hadn't told me out of guilt for my ordeal, would I have ever learned the truth? It had shaken her to the core as well, but not enough for her to denounce Feanim. Perhaps she had more commonality with Cúraniel than either of them realized.

The Duedellen waved it away as though it were of no consequence. "The spiders previously allowed a grace period to arrange these things. I do not know what changed, and they gave me no chance to negotiate."

"Because you betrayed them. On a bargain you had no right to strike in the first place." I pinned him with my gaze and he squirmed. "You fed an *elf* to the giant spiders."

Feanim's head snapped up. "He was already dead! Natural causes! Royal blood was their requirement for surrendering the moranga, and they would not budge on those terms. So many of us have fallen in battle, subsumed by the earth or eaten by beasts or drakes. What difference does one more body make for the funeral rites?" Catching a hint of advantage with Nimthil, he pressed on. "You hate the drakes. Moranga is the only hope we'll ever have of defending against Rafael should he turn on us. Doubly important now that we know his true nature. Only moranga can bind or exorcise a demon."

"He is an *abomination*," she spat. "And that woman—"

"'That woman' is my soulmate," I said sharply, just as Feanim said, "Leave Cúraniel out of this."

Nimthil glanced back and forth, attempting in vain to read both of our mouths at once. I signed each statement as I exchanged a bemused glance with Feanim. Her lips thinned, but she held her peace. I gestured for Feanim to continue.

He straightened. "Cúraniel is the reason we all yet live. Even if you disregard all the aid Rafael has previously lent our cause, without her, Cel and I would have been lost to the spiders. He had no cause to rescue us, but he did it for her sake. Cúraniel may be mad as a rabid fox, but could any of us bring the fucking Red Dragon to heel like she does? You do her a grave disservice to discount her so."

If only he praised Cúraniel within her earshot as well. It irked me to find myself nodding along with him.

Impassioned by his own argument, Feanim paced and gestured. "I know how heavily the court's betrayal presses on you, my heart. I would beg you to sing this melody with a new voice. We are reforged as a people in this fire." With that squinting expression he always wore when his enthusiasm crescendoed, he took up the blade I'd been working on and brandished it like a standard. "No nations. No courtly machinations and petty squabbling. We are all fashioned into one whole, with one purpose. The slag has burned away, leaving only the shining strength of the core."

"And what of the damage wrought upon Celebel?" Nimthil asked.

I tensed, hands tingling.

Feanim set my blade down with reverence, giving it a look that meant he'd have suggestions later. "Hasn't Rafael made overtures of peace toward you?" At my reluctant assent, he scrubbed the back of his head with one hand, nodding. "Good. We all need to fucking move forward. He's a prickly fucking blighter, but he's also a permanent fixture. Learn how to harmonize or be left exposed when Beredhel attacks again."

Nimthil started, ears pinning back.

Feanim took her hands, looking deep into her hazel eyes. "My heart, I am not asking you to bed him. But this prejudice has to end. Not only with Rafael, but all the drakes, and also the mixed elves among us. We are all one now. One people, one purpose. One core."

She exhaled through her nose, closing her eyes. Feanim shared a look with me. We waited. An ember popped in the fire. Finally, her ears relaxed and her eyes fluttered open.

Nimthil pulled her hands away. "I hear you and harmonize. I too will make peace as I may." She cast an arch look at me.

I raised placating palms. "I will speak to the others as well. They should hear of our accord from me."

"You two are not to leave this forge until you've truly made peace." In a flounce of bright silks, she marched out.

Ears twitching, Feanim approached me and gestured to the unfinished blade. "Interesting."

"That demon bent it into an armband, so it needed reworking." I couldn't keep the bitterness from my voice. "May as well convert it to a two-handed design, as the Pîntellum almost completely negates the necessity of shields."

Tentatively, the Duedellen laid a hand on my shoulder. "Cel, what would be worse? Losing it completely, or regaining it in a form that can still be worked?"

What a metaphor for my life.

I stepped back, ear tips heating. "Is this an attempt to keep me focused on Rafael so you will not have to atone for your own wrongdoing?"

He took a deep breath. "I deeply misjudged the situation with the spiders. I thought I had it all well in hand, but I did not, and I should have sung you the entire melody before I involved you. Everything went tits up, and I very much regret it. We almost lost you, Cel. *I* almost lost you. No amount of moranga is worth that price."

It was as close to a sincere apology as he would ever make. I ground my teeth. Oh Maker, I was so weary of conflict.

I stared at him long enough to make him squirm, then opened my arms and embraced my old friend. He squeezed me tightly, pressing his face into my shoulder. I hadn't meant to weep again, but his sniffle started mine.

"I suppose I forgive you, you horrid little shit," I hissed in his ear.

Feanim snorted a laugh, then we were both laughing, bent double with the mirthful release.

Wiping his eyes, he said, "You know I allowed you to win that fight, right?"

I punched him in the shoulder.

Part 3

Chapter 41

OMORIANS massed lower in the valley like a carpet of ants, visible from Amrún's tallest battlements. Scouts reported enemy drakes with larger creatures like stone giants in their midst. No sign of treacherous elves, but siege engines rose among the ranks. Unsurprising, as attempting to tunnel under these deep-set walls was perilous at best in the volcanic terrain.

Nothing created unity like an exterior threat. Even Feanim had somehow made up with Celebel. I didn't press Celebel for the details, as it was still a sore subject. Regardless, our people rallied behind their Consulate once more; or perhaps that was Celebel's spirit influence.

Bored with inactivity, our allied drakes sprang eagerly into action at Rafael's behest. Preventing their infighting was far more of an issue than their readiness to face the enemy.

Celebel was still recovering from his ordeal, worsened by his public fight and ensuing reunion with me. From a safe distance, he helped direct our attempts to throw off the enemy forces before they could turn their attacks into a full-blown siege. He'd bargained hard with Eäriel and then with me, to be allowed that much. It vexed him. His hand kept twitching over to the sword at his hip as his fellow Consul readied himself for battle.

"This is a fool's errand." Feanim swept a hand over the encroaching Fomorians. "They'll never take Amrún."

"They will not have to if they starve us out," Celebel countered.

The drakes surely would not allow that, but they'd grumbled mightily at the recovery missions.

Feanim shrugged and donned his helm.

I stood with Celebel, Nimthil, and a cupful of the remaining gentry on the battlements. A chill wind sliced through the cloudless day. We'd raised a thick hide awning, reinforced with steel plates overhead to stymy attacks from above. It provided us with a vantage point of the action without risk of involvement, though we all wore armor as a precaution. Large shields rested nearby, should harpies target us. My proximity allowed for emergency healing if needed.

Archers in the walls provided cover as our ranks crossed the perilous bridge. Rafael waited on the other side with the rest of the drakes. As the last elf rode across, the bridge fell.

"Is this not a risk?" I asked.

"All will be lost if the enemy breaches the gates." Celebel gestured in a broad half-circle. He wore his hair in a single, thick braid over one shoulder, and I itched to adorn it. "Your Dragon volunteered to assist our people in their return if the need arose."

Shock stole my response. I merely blinked.

Most of the drakes took to the wing, gaining size with altitude. Dragon met dragon in the air with a cacophony of roars. Searching the skies, I found no sign of the monstrous white Itreynith and breathed easier.

Small, fast groups of elves mounted on surefooted horses harried the Fomorians at every break in their formation. Which was frequent, as the Fomorians had grown more ragged and less organized with each engagement. Were their numbers finally dwindling?

Dragon fire decimated the siege engines, though surprise ballista bolts caught more than one defender. The young black and green drake I thought of as Lubber fell with a bolt through the chest. My belly clenched as I searched for him beneath the crush of bodies in the field. He did not rise again. Blue Tyldain descended on the offending ballista, lifting it from the ground and flinging it across the valley. His jaw had healed nicely.

Nemohee led a sortie on the east side, closest to us. I knew not how þey coordinated with the others, scattered as groups were, but they all moved almost in tandem. Precision strikes split larger mobs of Fomorians apart. Even from where I watched, Nemohee fought with a new ferocity.

My knowledge of tactics might have been sorely lacking, but as the sun crept across the sky, we appeared to be winning. The enemy lines halted in their advance and were beginning to buckle and disperse. Celebel seemed pleased, at least.

Until a behemoth erupted from the loamy ground. Scattering both debris and bodies, it was a nightmare of shadow and death.

"*Neksarim*," Celebel hissed.

"A demon of the dance?" Descriptors failed me. The monster was difficult to look at directly. I perceived a twisting, towering, screaming mass of shrouded atrocity in a state of constant flux. The more I tried to focus on it, the more it hurt my mind. "Gods, are you certain it's a demon?"

"My grandfather wrote of their columnar movement. Beneath the exterior, they are an abominable mass of limbs and heads. They force any caught in their influence to 'join the dance'. The victims become part of the body."

"Did he note how to banish them?" I could barely gather my thoughts through the sudden upheaval. Who had summoned a fucking *demon* to the battlefield? And how?

"According to the histories, a gargantuan Neksarim led a few dozen smaller demons in an attack on the city. He banished the great one with the collective spirit-song of all of Velúara. The smaller Neksarim dispersed with it, unable to maintain their toehold in our realm."

"*All* of Velúara?" Thousands of elves working in concert to banish a single demon?

Celebel gave me a grim nod. "They are greater demons. Immensely powerful."

The Neksarim's immediate effect was utter chaos. Elves and Fomorians alike panicked. The demon cut a swath of indiscriminate carnage. It headed steadily toward the gates, the apex of its column aligning with the tallest parapets. A nauseating sense of impending doom squeezed my lungs. Our people were as helpless as wheat in a wildfire.

Parting the fleeing ranks like a cleaver through flesh, hurling soldiers aside, a familiar figure in black burst forth from our lines.

Charging straight at the Neksarim.

"Rafael!" I screamed, though he couldn't possibly hear me over the din of battle. I sent a desperate, *'What are you doing?'*

His loping stride hastened to a full sprint, covering the distance with astonishing speed. The Red Dragon roared a challenge and leaped at the Neksarim. Stunned silence fell around me.

Though Rafael's terrific strength was the melody of legends, he was also widely considered more than a little mad. What combination of strength and madness sent him racing toward certain death, even for such as he?

And yet…and yet the Dragon was not broken and tossed aside like the others. Did his Háramorn blood negate the Neksarim's power, or was it a matter of raw strength?

The churning shadow obscured Rafael's moranga armor and fiery hair, and the monster's forward momentum came to an abrupt halt. Fire burst around it, flowing upward. The fight resembled nothing so much as a roiling column of fire. The only sounds were the shrieking gasps of intense heat.

Reaching as far as I dared, I searched for Rafael's soul to shield him from the worst of the demon's assault. To my shocked dismay, the energies tangling within were not so distinct. I pulled back quickly, lest I touch the wrong mind and lose myself.

Celebel laid a concerned hand on my arm. I collected myself and reached out again, seeking the familiar draconic signature. Mentally scrabbling for purchase, following the bond, I finally located him.

Horrifying images flooded into my mind, nearly unseating me. The demon sought to use Rafael's past against him, to drown him in trauma. To drive him truly mad. I held firm, shielding his mind from the unthinkable attacks, and wept freely for the child no one had protected.

A deep boom shuddered through the valley. The force threw those nearest the scene to their knees, and it knocked me away from Rafael's consciousness. Celebel caught me as I fell. Another echoing *crack*, and the ground yawned opened beneath the demon. No, not merely the ground. Black-edged flames licked from the crevice. A gate to hell.

"Rafael!" I cried, desperately seeking our soulbond.

Wild, disorienting power buffeted me. I could only hold my

breath and hope as the smoke cleared.

A lone figure remained, and I sagged with relief. My Dragon yet lived, though he swayed on his feet. The ground around him was blackened and charred, but no sign of the gate remained.

Why the few remaining Fomorians did not attack him, weakened as he was, I did not know, but he left the battleground unmolested. Our ranks parted respectfully—or perhaps fearfully—to let him pass.

I grabbed Celebel's sleeve. "Have them raise the bridge!"

"It may not be safe—"

Nimthil tapped on the wall, getting our attention. "I've given the order."

I signed deep appreciation as I dashed to the stairs. The buzz of conversation registered vaguely as I focused on reaching Rafael. For him to stagger so, his injuries must be terrible. The sickening nature of the Neksarim's attacks meant the worst of those would be to his mind.

I reached the outer gate as Rafael trudged across the restored bridge. With strange energies whipping around him in a foreboding aura, he made a furtive, dismissing motion at my offer of support. Naturally, he would not want his people to witness how weakened he truly was.

As we passed under the portcullis, he stumbled, catching himself against the wall. I slid under his arm, and he leaned heavily on me. Contact with the moranga cleaved my stomach to my spine. I fought down a wave of nausea, grateful for the buffer of my þilvor plate.

Rafael did not speak, nor even glance at me. From the state of our bond, he was not fully conscious. Probably hadn't been since the fight ended. His body demonstrated that incredible defense mechanism of functioning completely on instinct to remove him to a safe resting place. Would the moranga be a help or hindrance in that regard? The Pîntellum membrane was designed with that sort of aid in mind, but I had no idea how it interacted with the demon ore.

I struggled to get Rafael out of his armor before he collapsed. Prying at the edges, I removed my gauntlets for better purchase while trying not to cut my hands and accidentally feed the infernal stuff. Waves of nausea wracked me at the direct contact. Eventually, his Pîntellum recognized me and relented, and I peeled off the armor piece by piece while trying not to vomit.

He still wore those damnable leather trousers underneath. I laughed in pure, frustrated admiration at his stubbornness.

The big drake buckled in my arms as I lowered him onto the bed, nearly taking us both to the floor. Only the reinforced strength of my armor kept us upright. I wrangled his broad shoulders onto the mattress and heaved the rest of him after, wrenching my back in the process.

The moment Rafael was prone, his eyes rolled back in his head, insensate. I pulled the single blanket over him. That would not do. I yelled down the hall for a serving youth to fetch me furs and heated bricks from the kitchens. The others would simply have to deal with my rude volume.

Moments later, a small Lachanaur boy, unable to enter due to the wards, anxiously piled the requested items by the door. I unwrapped the hot bricks, carefully packing them along Rafael's right side and around his feet. With that accomplished, I peeled off my armor for better skin-to-skin contact and settled on his left, beneath a small mountain of furs, to begin the real work.

I synchronized my breath, kissing his lips to initiate the healing, and felt…nothing.

Crow. Delving too deeply into the Dragon's mind was fraught, but there was no help for it. I kissed him more intensely, matching his slower heartbeat, and strived to reach farther into his mind than ever before.

Strain weakened his defenses, allowing me to slip through.

Volcanos spewed rivers of glowing lava under a starless, whirling night. Some puffed billowing black smoke into the air, others erupted endlessly. The constant tectonic rumbling reminded me of his breath, and the barest hint of his scent wove through the choking atmosphere. Even in the astral form I wore, I kept my feet from touching the shifting, steaming ground beneath me.

Every intimacy I had shared with my Dragon over the years carried the tinge of this mental landscape, yet the lack of his active presence made it eerily hollow. There was no sharp observation here, no layer of dark humor, nor the usual simmering potential for violence. No lust, no rage—nothing.

I cast my thoughts in all directions, seeking traces of his scattered soul. I had to double back a few times before I finally caught a thread. Trying to get a better sense of it, I gathered myself and flew toward the source.

It led me over a craggy peak and down deep into the belly of a live volcano. Though impervious to the heat in my incorporeal state, its tremendous force gave me pause.

As I cast about and found nothing but rock and magma, confusion sprouted like knotweed. The thread was there, teasing me, but I could not grasp it. I'd almost surrendered when I spied a reddish gleam, like a splash of arterial blood, behind a ridge on the volcano's inner wall. I floated over, and it resolved into a single dislodged dragon scale.

The moment I picked up the scale, the scenery changed. Before me lay a mountainous addition to the landscape. Black bands of cooled lava held the Red Dragon fast, even in his full-sized form. He appeared to slumber in his bondage, but experience told me how deceptive that could be.

I approached with caution. What to free first? Not the head. I wanted no gouts of flame aimed at me if he awoke feeling cantankerous. My attempt to clear his long tail from a distance without the danger of being swatted was a failure. The stone refused to budge.

Fuck. Trust Rafael to test me. I had to put myself at risk in order to save him, to hope his predatory nature would not overtake his senses.

I built a protective, glowing blue shell around my astral body and set to work. As I made myself vulnerable, the black rock softened to pliancy under my hands. As soon as I freed it, his tail lashed the ground, creating a tremor that threw the rock from the trapped wings. If I hadn't floated, I would have been thrown as well.

The massive paws were more challenging, buried as they were, and required me to change the ground itself. I persevered. Toe by toe, the dragon pulled each limb free. It took me nearly twelve dozen full breaths to trot from his left hind leg around to his entrapped muzzle.

His eyes opened, focusing on me with keen interest. I struck *away the last of the bonds holding him prisoner. With a leap and a thunderous clap of his wings, the dragon disappeared into the dark sky. The backdraft tossed me halfway across the mindscape.*

Sighing, I picked myself up and cast my probes again, searching for a new thread. Instead, I found an odd, twisted door set into the side of the nearest volcano. It swung open at my touch, and a mighty wind sucked through to the other side.

The door deposited me in the midst of a red sand desert. Here, the magma had cooled to obsidian, the volcanic glass stabbing upward from the ground in jagged knives. Combined with an angry orange sky, it put me very much in mind of the hells the demons called home. I increased my shields. His Háramorn aspect was more dangerous and unpredictable than the dragon.

A distant, familiar voice called to me. I ignored it, trying to force my way deeper. The call grew more insistent, prodding me. Any distraction while confronting the demon could spell disaster; best to heed the summons. Like swimming upward from depth, I slowly rose to consciousness.

Chapter 42

THE sheets beneath me had soaked through with my sweat. Rafael's intense body heat combined with the still-hot bricks made me gasp for air. I tossed off the furs.

'*Cúraniel!*' The voice in my head took on a panicky edge.

'*Celebel, my love. I am here.*' I stroked Rafael's garnet hair. Not even in this unconscious slumber did his troubled brow relax.

Urgency struck, and I scrambled off of the bed. As far as I knew, Rafael shifted forms and departed to take care of those necessities. He'd never given me the chance to compare our relative body functions, squeamish as he was about such things. As he consumed food and drink with less frequency than an elf, I did not worry about that aspect of his care.

Biting my lip, I hurried out to the compost pile. My Dragon would be perfectly safe; no one could pierce those wards uninvited.

'*I was so concerned,*' Celebel sent, with an edge of panic. '*I've heard nothing since yesterday and I'm quite sure you've neither eaten nor slept. Damn these wards! I can sense nothing through them!*'

'*A night has passed already?*' How had I lost so much time? I dug a hole in the freezing ground and relieved myself, shivering in the wind.

'*I'm sending a meal to you. As I won't be much welcome, I'll also send Nemohee to force sleep upon you if I must.*'

I managed a weak chuckle.

'*I'm quite serious. I'll have þem clout you over the head if it's the only way to ensure you rest.*' He was indignant. '*My Moonflower, what am I to do with you? How is it such an accomplished healer can take complete and utter leave of her own health?*'

I smiled at his concern for me. '*Caring for others rarely translates to caring for the self, but in this case, it was entirely unintentional.*'

'*I miss you. I'd visit, but I don't want to exacerbate anything.*'

'Rafael is still unconscious, but rage is a powerful motivator. Perhaps you should visit.'

Celebel's tone turned apprehensive. *'How is he?'*

I was touched. After everything my Dragon had put him through, Celebel chose to grant him grace. A more cynical part of me insisted Celebel's only concern was for the potential loss of our greatest weapon. I clung to hope.

'I've made some progress, but that demon wreaked havoc on his psyche.' I jogged back to Rafael's quarters, rubbing my bare arms—and my bare ass—to warm them. The temperature differential made my bones ache.

'So there's a chance he may be more *erratic when he awakens?'* Celebel sounded incredulous.

I sighed heavily. *'Your concern for an avowed enemy moves me.'* I'd almost said "rival" but held back at the last moment. "Rival" indicated there could only be one victor, and I a mere prize to be won. The last thing I wanted was to feed that narrative.

'It isn't charity, my dear. I know your welfare is inextricably tied to that...to the Dragon. I also know you'll expend every mote of your strength to save him. This is difficult to admit, but I must admire anyone with enough courage, or madness, to single-handedly take on a gods-thrice-damned Neksarim *and actually win.'*

Someone banged on the door hard enough to rattle it on the hinges. I jumped, accidentally interrupting the connection. Nemohee called my name, and I rose on shaky legs to open the door.

Þey proffered a steaming tray loaded down with food. "Eat!"

"Wait, I—"

Nemohee shoved the tray into my hands. *"Eat!"*

I surrendered and laid into the thick, honeyed porridge. Only after I'd swabbed the last morsel from the bowl, downed a flagon of water, and a mug of blessedly strong black coffee, would Nemohee allow conversation. A faint, Celebel-flavored sense of satisfaction tickled the back of my head.

From the door, Nemohee looked over my slumbering patient. Rafael's chest rose and fell so slightly under the mound of furs, only a weak rumble indicated he still drew breath at all.

"Helooksterrible. PeacefullikeI'veneverseenhim, though, 'tisapity. Braveman." Þeireyeswidened. "Feckin' pure *strong* man," þeyamended.

"'Tis a terrible thing, this type of fixing." I fell easily into hillspeech.

"Ye speak the truth, and I don't envy it." Nem pointed imperiously at the bed. "Sleep!"

"I have work—" My protest met a wall of Lachanaur muscle.

"*SLEEP!* I have orders to dunt ye on the head if ye've a mind to argue! D'ye suppose these wards will keep a rock from flying through? If I find ye stirring around in that head of his, I'll dunt ye regardless!" Þey made a threatening fist.

I laughed. "Quit your fuss. I'll sleep, I'll sleep!"

WHEN I awoke later in the evening, another steaming mug of coffee awaited me in the doorway. There was a touching note beside it from Celebel. His scent lingered on the parchment. I drank it in, along with the coffee and his words of encouragement.

I took Rafael's hand in both of mine, stroking his palm. Limp as it was, I could still feel the strength in the long fingers.

"I'm doing all I can. I can only hope it's enough."

Breathing deeply and shielding myself again, I dove back into his mind.

Homing in on a presence, I floated over the red sand, weaving in and out of the jagged obsidian spires. A hissing sibilant pressure built... There! A little boy. I moved closer. Here was a painfully gaunt, filthy child with hollow blue cat eyes too large for his face, nearly lost under a tangled fall of blood red hair almost as long as mine. He darted behind a spire.

'Rafael, come back. You know me!' *I followed as quickly as I dared, catching only flashes of the trailing ends of his hair.*

As I rounded the corner, the child backed into a dead end. He opened his mouth wide, showing a multitude of sharp teeth, and screamed.

A seething, fiery mass engulfed me, like a cloud, but somehow wrong, unnatural. The hissing grew to an ear-splitting force, coming from all angles, even from inside me. It stripped my shields away, laying my soul bare to the Háramorn. A thousand teeth grazed my skin, a thousand tongues lapped my blood. Flames scorched me from the inside.

I shrieked, 'Rafael, no, please! It's me, it's Cúraniel!'

Panic and pain overwhelmed me, my ears full of the awful hissing, my eyes blinded. Something deep inside me tore. He was devouring me! Devouring my soul.

Gathering up the last of my reserves, I called out with all my might. 'JAX!'

As suddenly as it started, I was dropped unceremoniously on my ass in the red sand. The cloud coalesced into a multitude of familiar eyes, all focused on me. His eyes, in all the variations I'd ever seen; perfect calm blue, anxious yellow, lustful yellow streaked with red, murderous burning crimson, living flame. Pupils slit venomously thin or dilated near-round. The eyes blinked eerily in unison, and all narrowed with irritation.

*'**YOU SHOULD NOT BE HERE**,' a thousand voices hissed in chorus.*

Slamming back into my body, I woke with my heart pounding. Beside me, Rafael coughed, stirring. One eye slit open and focused on me. A reminder of the cloud of eyes. I shuddered, pressing a hand to my chest, feeling for wounds in my spirit, and found none.

"Cúraniel, what the fuck?" His voice was hoarse, more growl than words.

I burst into tears and threw my arms around his neck. "I'm so thankful you're awake! You're alive. Oh, by all the gods, you glorious lunatic!"

Rafael propped himself on his elbows and pushed me back, eyes sparking to flame. "What were you *thinking?* You know it is far too dangerous to probe that deeply without my expressed consent."

"But the Neksarim—"

"Is banished from this realm. Not my first." He looked up at the ceiling. "All I need is sleep."

"But you were in an awful state leaving the field!"

"*Sleep*. Same as the last time I absorbed and banished demonic energy." He glared until I nodded. "Stay out of my head, foolish elf. I almost devoured you!" He paused and gave me a small, knowingly evil smile. "Your soul is quite delicious. Do not tempt me again."

"You rotten beast. I worked diligently to heal you, and you scared me witless with that fucking demon shit." A grimace crept across my face.

Rafael sank back into the bed with a defeated sigh, crossing his forearms over his eyes. "Let me sleep, you pest."

The solace of his lucidity won over my frustration. The way his annoyed arm motion brought the serratus muscles wrapping his ribs into sharp relief certainly helped. Gods, how did such an obstinate creature manage to be so attractive?

I tucked a curl behind his ear. "As you say, you don't always need healing, but I'll stay with you. And don't you dare wake after this demanding human flesh!"

He smiled thinly and closed his eyes, pulling me close, and sank into slumber once more.

A hesitant rapping at the door kept me from nodding off with him. Celebel's presence eked through the wards. Rafael's breath was slow and even. Carefully, with some struggle, I removed his heavy arm from around my waist and padded to the door.

"Oh gods, Cúraniel. I was so worried! It felt like you were being pulled to pieces," Celebel whispered urgently, eyes huge with concern. I stepped through the wards and closed the door behind me. "Please tell me you're unhurt."

"I'm only a little shaken." I kissed him, and he held me close for a long moment.

"What *was* that?" he asked when we parted.

"My poking around where I shouldn't have. That ingrate tossed me out of his head, woke up fully to chide me for being there, then dared to tell me all he requires is a pleasant sleep after facing off against a fucking *Neksarim!* Unbelievable!" I yanked my lobes in frustration.

"You'll rip those lobes free some day." Celebel caught my hands, laughing. "Your Dragon is a legend for a reason, I suppose."

"He's so frustrating!" I tossed my hands in the air. "I make a great effort to heal him, and all he says is '*I just need a nap*'." I mimicked Rafael's deep voice.

Celebel laughed harder. Something banged off the door, and we both jumped.

"Shut the fuck up or go somewhere else," Rafael growled from the other side.

In sign, I promised to find Celebel when I could. I opened the door to a disgruntled drake glaring at me from the bed.

"Sorry, sorry, I didn't mean to disturb you." I slid back into my place beside him.

"Chirping birds," Rafael grumbled.

Chapter 43

FEANIM lurked in the doorway, kept out by the wards, and clearly frustrated by it. Rafael sat between me and the exit as I handed him the pieces of his armor. He'd added a dampening field to keep external sound out as well.

Petty perhaps, but also highly entertaining.

Celebel had brought me comfortable shift of fine linen when he fetched my armor. Rafael had donned his usual black wool shirt and leather trousers, foregoing the leather jerkin. His mane of curls retained its true blood red. If Feanim hadn't been glaring at us, the Dragon's eyes would likely be the piercing blue I so loved, rather than the hearth fire crackling around his slit pupils.

Gingerly, using the sheet as a buffer, I grasped each piece of his armor and held it away from my body. The metal's light-drinking property disguised intricate engravings all along its surface. Sharp as my eyes were, I wouldn't have noticed without feeling the delicate dips and ridges through the sheet. If I stared at any single design for too long, my vision swam and nausea rose. Demon armor, indeed.

We deliberately turned away from Feanim's increasingly dramatic posturing. I made a show of examining Rafael's unusual sabatons, flexing and straightening the jointed toes customized to his dragon feet. Slots for his talons marked the toe tips. The fine craftsmanship fascinated me.

The Dragon watched with an amused smirk. "Similar to gauntlets." His voice had regained its usual resonance. "Your innovation with the Pîntellum and the moranga's malleability allow me to utilize my dew claws." He curled the small, medial toes.

"They don't seem useful for kicking," I said.

"I do not use them to kick." He swung a leg over and snatched the sabaton out of my hands, using the surprisingly flexible dew claw like a thumb. Similar to raptors locking their talons into their prey, but the spurs on his heels reminded me more of a rooster.

"You and your chicken feet." It slipped out before I could stop myself.

Rafael's brows shot up. "Chicken feet? *Chicken feet?*" He grabbed my shoulder with one of those feet and tossed me off the bed. "Audacious flower-eater. I should remind you what else my *chicken feet* are capable of." With a significant glare at my crotch, he made a cone of his toes.

I barked a laugh, covering myself and scuttling back out of reach. *'I should fuck you like this on their little thrones,'* he'd said, stretching me past my limits with his foot.

Rafael snorted and slid his feet into the sabatons, pressing his talons through and spreading his toes. The armor hooked around his spurs and molded into place. He clapped the greaves over them and continued to armor himself, blithely ignoring Feanim's desperate gesturing.

I knew better than to tease the Dragon about the codpiece, but my treacherous ears twitched wildly when I handed it over. He pinned me with a sharp look and I feigned innocence. Why must his armor have tassets? Impracticality be damned. Surely everyone appreciated muscular thighs.

With a lazy sweep of his hand, Rafael lowered the dampening field.

"—stop *fucking* ignoring me!" Feanim pounded on the door frame. Realizing we could hear him, he gathered himself. "Rafael. Not that you apparently care, as you've been blissfully napping in your lover's arms for two days, but we took significant casualties after that fucking demon appeared."

Guilt crept down my spine. The healer's wing was full, but I dared not leave Rafael's side again until I was certain his mind was no longer fractured.

The Dragon cocked his head. "The Fomorians retreated, yes?"

"Yes, but—"

Rafael shrugged. He'd never cared about casualties, elvish or otherwise.

The Duedellen's hands fluttered above his head like wounded birds. "How the fuck did you kill a gods damned Neksarim in single combat?"

"Punched it until it could not be punched anymore." Rafael gave me a conspiratorial look as he accepted the spiny pauldrons from my hands. Even those were far more flexible than I'd expected. At the edge of the bed, he rolled his shoulders as he fastened them in place.

"Oh, fuck off. What did you actually do?" Feanim folded his arms, stepping in front of the Dragon. With Rafael seated, they were of a similar height.

"There is no secret, *Inuriterrege*. I hit first and harder. The demon is banished."

Feanim sighed with frustration. I snickered, and the corner of Rafael's mouth twitched.

"After all the noise you fools made about my Háramorn blood, this is surprising?" His hair sparked. Trust Feanim to sour a mood.

"But how does it work?" Feanim persisted.

The Dragon exhaled at the ceiling, and I tensed. He dove forward, grabbing Feanim's face in his hands. Fortunately for the elf, Rafael hadn't yet pulled on his gauntlets. The lack of moranga would be little consolation for that viselike grip and the thumb talons punching bloody holes into Feanim's cheeks.

"*Like so*," Rafael hissed. Staring directly into the elf's eyes, his own burned red.

Feanim struggled briefly, then fell slack. As I moved to intervene, Rafael released him, dropping the elf in a boneless pile on the floor.

"What did you do to him?" I kneeled beside the unconscious Feanim.

"Calm yourself. He will wake shortly."

Feanim stirred, eyes snapping open. He swatted me away, straightening his gambeson and rising to his feet. He'd blanched under his normal olive complexion. Matching lines of blood trickled from the punctures on his face.

"Are you hurt?" I asked.

He focused instead on Rafael. "What *the fuck* was that?" Feanim swiped at the blood with the back of his sleeve and successfully smeared it across his face. Frowning, he pulled a kerchief from the pocket of his gambeson and dabbed at his cheeks.

"You were not prepared to resist. I could have shredded your mind as easily as your body, but I am feeling generous." The way Rafael said 'generous' made it the vilest curse. He bared his teeth, ever so slightly. "I only poked a hole. Or two." He jabbed a talon, and Feanim took a reflexive step back.

Rafael snatched up his gauntlets and stalked out of the room.

The Duedellen watched him go with an odd expression, touching a tentative hand to his temple. "He is fucking *dangerous*."

"Rafael has punched your guts out through your mouth, murdered his way through walls of enemies, felled a fucking *Neksarim* on his own, and you're only now realizing this?" I couldn't keep the condescension out of my voice. Unbelievable.

Feanim shook his head with a jingle of earrings, dark curls bouncing. "How has this never been documented, this ability to invade the minds of others? No wonder Celebel panicked so badly."

"Likely very few have survived to sing the melody."

He looked at me then, his face returning to its usual shrewd, calculating expression. "How do you handle him when he's in these moods?"

"What do you mean, 'when'?" A laugh escaped my lips despite the darkening glower.

I had enough self-control not to point out Feanim should have been thrilled, as this was as close as he'd ever come to kissing Rafael. My Dragon sent a disgruntled growl along our connection.

'Oh, come now. Surely you've noticed his attraction to you,' I replied, teasing.

'He is not subtle,' Rafael shot back sourly.

'Has he propositioned you?' I couldn't keep the wicked glee at bay. *'What did you do? Did you know he's propositioned Celebel as well?'*

'Fuck off, Cúraniel.'

"What are you giggling over?" Feanim demanded, and I blushed with guilt. "I know you're speaking with him. You wear a particular faraway expression when you use mindspeech."

"I cannot help teasing him."

He pursed his lips. "You needn't tell Rafael I want him to fuck me. I've told him so myself."

The candor surprised me. "And you live still? I admit, I'm impressed." I looked him over. "So, you're a backbiting submissive. That harmonizes."

Feanim laughed, and I followed him outside. The sun told me it was early afternoon. I adjusted my internal temporal sense. I'd spent too much time indoors as of late. The breeze blew stronger today, ruffling Feanim's hair and whipping my thin skirts and heavy braids around my legs.

"He had no idea how to respond. It was almost cute," Feanim said.

"Did he go stiff as a statue?" I mimicked the posture.

Feanim laughed again. "Yes, exactly. You know how he has that sort of half-lidded, almost languid look?" His fingers fluttered near his face. "I believe that was the widest his eyes have ever opened."

I blew out a breath, Rafael's talons raking across his arms in the back of my mind. Feanim must have presented the flirtation in a non-threatening, roundabout way.

"Truly, you're fortunate he froze instead of lashing out. Took twenty years for him to *begin* to accept that sort of attention from me."

"Rafael is a strange creature, to be sure. You don't seem bothered." He cast a sidelong glance at me.

"Why would I be? Unless you offend or re-traumatize him, I think it's good for him to know he's desirable to someone other than me. He hides his self-loathing well under all that charisma." A different thought occurred to me. "What does Nimthil think of your fixation?"

"It matters not what she thinks," he snapped. I shouldn't have been surprised, but I felt a bit sorry for Nimthil. A sly look crept across Feanim's face, making my skin prickle with unease. "And what will you do if I convince him to fuck me?"

"Nothing. Unless you can get there before I do. Then I'll murder you in your sleep," I said sweetly, and meant it. "Good luck, as you haven't a 'magic pussy'." Another mental growl from Rafael, this one with significantly more force behind it. "Ah, we're fouling his mood. Best sing a different song."

Feanim stopped me in front of the great hall and gave me another appraising look. "Again, how did you develop such a strong psychic bond with a drake?"

The blood wine, I almost said. The words turned from my lips at the last moment. "Rafael is my soulmate. Do you not have such a connection with yours? And you know very well the unconscious mind is the domain of the Talithiri. Particularly my former lineage."

"You don't have the same strength of connection with Celebel." He neatly sidestepped my question.

Celebel must have complained to him. "I've hardly known Cel a full year. Like a redwood, these things take many seasons to grow." I thought for a moment. "Was this conversation recent?"

A corner of Feanim's generous mouth turned down. "No, Celebel is…not precisely avoiding me, but not making himself available, either. Perhaps you could—"

"No." The fucking audacity. "I am no longer accepting responsibility for anyone else's actions."

THE UPPER level of the forge was deserted, the fire banked instead of blistering hot. Hammers clanged somewhere below. In the far corner, past the racks of tools, hammers, and various sizes of anvil, the top of a wrought iron spiral staircase peeked from behind the massive hammer.

Descending into the belly of the forge, the air grew significantly warmer as the hammer ringing grew more insistent. The humid heat made my linen shift cling to my skin and weighed down my hair. I emerged into a larger room to Rafael bent over a project, fiddling with something on the anvil before him. Surprisingly, the hammering wasn't coming from him, but somewhere farther off. With the torches dimmed, his hair might have gone to flame or it could simply the orange forge glow highlighting the deep red.

He didn't turn at my approach. My conversation with Feanim had obviously put his back up. Not surprising, but I hoped one day he wouldn't react with such reflexive hostility.

"What nasty little trinket are you working on?" I rose to my tiptoes to look past his broad back.

Rafael straightened and turned to me, eyes as fiery as his hair. "You are not going to leave me in peace, are you." Not a question.

"Well, you are my favorite person to bother." My winning smile bounced off him.

The scowl didn't budge. "Caltrops." Rafael scooped the project off of his anvil and held it out to me. Cupped in his palm, a tripod of spikes rested there, blacker than black.

I shuddered. The poor horses. "Forgive my ignorance, but it seems like a large expenditure of moranga that may not be recovered." I examined it as closely as I dared.

He had an air of grim satisfaction. "These will not be lost."

No, I did not want to know. "You are most uniquely wicked." Surely the poor beasts did not deserve such torment.

He vanished the caltrop into his sleeve, folding his arms and leaning against the anvil. "Why did you come here?"

"Don't be cross, please. I know so little of what occurs between you and Feanim, and I simply wanted to speak with you about it." I reached to touch his arm. He stepped back, and I dropped my hand. "Come now, must everything be a secret?"

Rafael turned his face from me, looking down at the anvil. "He asks very…probing questions. About my body, my past, the time I spend with you. Recently, these questions turned openly lascivious."

Far more than a harmless flirtation, then. The tips of my ears heated with protective wrath, but I set it aside to be present for my soulmate. "How did you respond?"

"I ignored it." He was quiet for a few heartbeats, shoulders tensing again. "Until he asked me outright to fuck him."

Gods. Mentally, I kicked myself for assuming Feanim hadn't been so foolishly blunt. "I'm surprised he lives. Why do you tolerate his behavior if it so vexes you?"

"His past is similar to mine." That ever-present specter haunted the Dragon's eyes.

My heart ached for him. I dared to touch his arm. When he didn't immediately shrug me off, I moved closer.

"No need for shame. Do you find Feanim attractive?"

Rafael's head snapped up. "No." The building growl echoed in the small space.

"I'm not jealous if you do—"

"I do not. At all." His expression grew stormy, and I backed away. "Is this licentiousness standard for elves? Drakes do not behave in this manner."

My poor Dragon had only wanted a friend. Feanim muddied the water with his lewd lack of boundaries.

"Come now. Nemohee considers you, if not precisely a friend, at least a friendly acquaintance. Þey've never propositioned you, have þey? This isn't a friend or elf problem, it's a 'Feanim wishes to fuck everyone' problem. I won't tease you about it again. Please forgive me; I misjudged his actions." I dared to pull Rafael's arms around me, turning to rest the small of my back against the anvil. "Granted, I've wanted you from the moment we met, so perhaps my judgment is out of tune. What did you do when he propositioned you?"

He sighed like the forge bellows, frustration etched into his posture. "Initially, nothing. He asked again, more forcefully, so I left."

"And you haven't spoken to him about it since?"

I was suddenly thankful for the wards on Rafael's quarters, and that I'd stayed with him in his convalescence. Not out of fear of predatory behavior from Feanim, but for the strength of Rafael's reaction in that state. The Duedellen certainly dealt with his childhood trauma differently.

Rafael's silence was answer enough. I traced the line of his jaw.

"May I make a suggestion?" Rare, to offer him advice on anything other than healing, but at least he was listening. "If you are not interested, tell him 'no' clearly. Make your boundaries known. He strikes me as the type to interpret silence, or an ambiguous answer, as possibility. He'll likely continue to pester you until you clarify. If he can respect those boundaries, then the friendship can be salvaged. If not, well. Try not to cause another mass defection either way."

The Dragon's scowl deepened, teeth clicking. "You have experienced this type of pursuit." The muscles of his arms rippled, as though he imagined choking a rival.

"Resolved long before we met. Some friendships are poorly defined, and sometimes lonely people misinterpret accord as attraction. Sometimes it works out well. Sometimes the friendships end. There are those who simply wish to discover how far they can push boundaries." I poked his arm. "You yourself do it, albeit differently—always searching for the openings in our agreements. Regardless, consent matters. It's why I continually ask if you're sure you want me to keep pushing you."

"I always want you to push me, dove." His shoulders finally relaxed, and he cupped my cheek in his hand. "I appreciate your efforts."

I covered his hand with mine. "You and I differ in this regard, but it does not tweak my ears if you find someone else attractive. I could never be such a hypocrite. Only..." I grinned, unable to stop myself. "Promise you won't fuck anyone else before you *finally* fuck me?"

Rafael growled, grabbing me by the buttocks. His talons dug into my flesh with bruising strength, yet he did not pierce my skin. Lifting me with ease, he set me on the anvil, shoving my dress up around my waist and pushing my knees apart. My lips parted with desire; already my breath sped.

"I want only you." He kissed me before I could say anything else foolish.

Kneeling and propping my legs on his shoulders, he pressed his face into my cunt and inhaled. I moaned, growing wet, and grabbed fistfuls of his hair. Hammers rang out in the distance, punctuating the heartbeat now pounding between my legs.

The Dragon gripped my thighs and plunged his long tongue into me. The heat of his body mingled with the heat of the forge, slicking my skin with sweat. I arched my back, tilting my hips up for better access as his tongue writhed inside of me. Hot breath teased my clit. I twisted my hands in his hair, pulling hard, trying to force his face closer. Gods, he knew exactly how to use that tongue.

Just as the pressure reached a crescendo, Rafael withdrew his tongue.

"Continue!" I panted. "I'm almost there."

Wicked fire danced in his eyes. He stood, tearing my hands free. "This is your punishment for the annoyance."

He took a step back and favored me with a small, sinister grin. The forge light danced over the slick juices on his face as he licked them away.

"Rafael, please!" I reached for him and he took another step back.

"No."

I slid my hand over my throbbing clit. Much to my chagrin, he snatched my wrists away and pulled me to my feet. With a spin of my shoulders, he ushered me toward the stairs.

"This is a working forge. Return to your chambers if you must finish yourself off." He swatted my ass.

"You wretched *hellbeast!*"

I stomped over to the staircase and turned to glare at him one last time. Rafael bowed sarcastically. That coughing laugh followed me up the stairs.

Chapter 44

I FLUNG open the bedchamber door and whipped off my sodden shift, tossing it in a corner. Rummaging through my trunk, I found both items I needed—the red implement and the sparkling black.

Rafael laughed darkly in my mind. Bottle of oil in hand, I positioned myself over the black implement on the edge of the bed.

'If you weren't such a stubborn blighter, this could be more than a fantasy,' I sent as I impaled my cunt with the black implement. Propping the red one in front of me, I wrapped my lips around it and sucked. I sent him the clearest images I could of both my actual actions and my desired ones.

'So, now you openly antagonize me?' Anger crackled at the edges of Rafael's statement.

'You deserve it,' I whipped back. *'Consider this repayment for your own endless antagonism.'*

With a mental snarl, he cut off our connection. I worked myself into a nice rhythm. As Rafael's denial allowed my imagination free rein, I relived my greatest desires. I'd have Celebel behind me, and the Dragon splayed on the mossy bed before me, building a slow climax. The body heat, the breathing…gods, yes. The growls and moans. The scent of dracaena resin and starlight and sex. Let me serve as a conduit for pure carnal desire.

Celebel himself flung the door open, entering the bedchamber with an anxious set to his ears. Finding me engaged, he stilled.

"Ah," he said. "Not the discovery I expected, but one I quite appreciate. Your distress had me rushing out of an important meeting!"

I pulled the red phallus out of my mouth. "Come here and finish me."

He hesitated, watching with growing, obvious appreciation while I pounded my cunt with the black implement he'd given me. That appreciation tented the pleats of his long silk satin skirt. Making eye contact, he took hold of his cock through the skirt.

Lust-maddened, I slammed down harder. "Cel! *Now!*"

He scurried to obey, shedding clothes as he went. Gripping my buttocks, he gently replaced the sparkling black implement with his cock. With both hands free, I had a better hold on the red implement and rested on my elbows. The way it filled my mouth as he filled me from behind. Gods, if only Rafael were so cooperative. Celebel began a slow, rhythmic thrusting, groaning as he did.

Speculation of how the Dragon would taste had me gagging myself on the red implement. Heightened as I was, the crescendo peaked almost instantly. Celebel moaned again as I shuddered on his cock. He slapped my ass, drawing a whimper out around my mouthful. Having both cocks inside me lit a wildfire of need. Let my men skewer and use me. Make me a sacrifice to their lust. Gods, let Rafael embrace all of himself, and allow me to bring him the pleasure he deserved.

Celebel paused, rearranging himself. I cast a look over my shoulder, only to realize he was positioning the black implement to penetrate himself while he fucked me. I whimpered, and he grinned.

"Gods, you're exquisite," I breathed.

"You've already given it a liberal coating of lubricant." His eyes half-closed and he bit his lower lip as he pushed the implement into himself. "Seemed a pity to—mmph—waste it."

I bucked backward, slapping my buttocks against Celebel's lower belly. We worked into a sucking, fucking, thrusting rhythm. I lost myself in the ache of my jaws, the stretch of my cunt, the sweat slicking our bodies. He thrust harder, and his cock gave a mighty throb. Pulling out suddenly, he spilled himself over my lower back. The hot splash, and his groans shivering through my ears, brought me to another crescendo.

Following my melody, Celebel reached between my legs to flick my sensitized clit. I reached a new pitch, quivering until the waves passed.

He flopped down beside me on the moss, casting the used black implement into the stream to rinse. "What riled you so?"

"That fucking crocodile teased me to the edge of climax and left me there as punishment for annoying him. So, this is my revenge." I tossed the red implement beside the black one, irritated by the memory of the self-satisfied look on Rafael's face.

Much to my surprise, Celebel started laughing. I swatted his shoulder.

He laughed harder, clutching his belly. "Oh gods, forgive me. I probably shouldn't laugh, but that is hilarious. I'm glad he's being an ass to you instead of me for once."

"Get out of my bed, get out!" I tried to shove the traitor off the edge, but he caught my arms and rolled me under him, still laughing. Struggling in his grip, I gained enough leverage to flip us both off the bed. We landed in a tangle of limbs on the floor, splashing across the slow-moving stream. Celebel tickled my ribcage. I dissolved into helpless giggles.

"How did I manage be caught between the two most obnoxious menaces—STOP THAT—in the entire gods damned world?" I gasped through the mirth, trying desperately to smack his darting hands away.

"Oh, come now, surely I'm the current favorite! I eased your suffering!" His grin was huge.

I tackled him back to the floor. "You were the favorite until you sided against me! I'm swearing off of men. You're all awful."

He feigned offense. "Surely you're not placing me in the same bracket of 'awful' as the famously awful Bloody Drake?"

I trapped him in a headlock. "True, you did bring me to orgasm today. Your trespasses are forgiven. For now."

Celebel reached up and pinched my ear, making me squeal in pained surprise and release him. "You aren't the only one who can pull a dirty trick."

I mock-scowled at him, but couldn't force my mouth to turn down as he gathered me into his arms. He kissed away the creases on my brow and I settled against him. The soft light filtering in from the windows made the silver locks of his hair glitter, giving him an almost holy countenance.

I kissed his neck. "How many hearts have you broken, beautiful

Celebel Elhalanros, with the sweet scent of starlight ringing on your skin?"

He chuckled, stroking my hair. "I would break them all for you."

"WITH THE Neksarim gone, we broke and routed the forces massing nearby for siege." Feanim paced in the war room in front of Celebel, Rafael, and a few other leaders, including Nemohee. Marron was conspicuously absent.

Rafael positioned himself as far from the rest as he could, lurking in a corner. Stoney-faced as ever, he was either bored or irritated. Nemohee had strategically placed þemself between the Dragon and the rest.

I perceived the meeting through Celebel, as Rafael was closed off to me; still spiky after I'd taken my revenge for his teasing. Celebel had encouraged me to take a more active interest in the goings on, but there was no need for me to physically attend war council meetings.

"Your presence is soothing," he'd said, "and if I must be near the Red Dragon, there will be voices in my head that need calming."

Outside in the garden, I enjoyed the winter sun. Volcanic heat kept the grounds free of the snow piled along the peaked battlement. It allowed an unnaturally long growing season this far north. Dividing my attention in this manner took some effort. I kept my hearing keyed to Celebel's, but my vision faded in and out.

"Unfortunately, they have relocated and are now massing here." Feanim tapped a gorge to the northeast. "If we allow this to continue, we'll be right back where we started with the fear of a potential siege. Scouts have reported new supply lines emerging. There is an abandoned fortress in the area, once underwater and recently returned to the surface. The crows tell me my brother uses it as a base."

Feanim resumed his pacing. "We will need the added might of the Lachanaur before we engage the enemy again in the field, especially with the demon involvement. We took more losses than expected before Rafael neutralized that Neksarim. There will surely be more."

Every ear in the room shifted to the fire drake. He stared back, unblinking.

The Duedellen scrubbed a hand through his unruly hair in irritation at losing the group's attention. "As I was saying, we'll need the full support of the Lachanaur before we engage again. To that end, I am announcing my wedding to Nimthil, my long-time consort. The merging of our lineages will seal our alliance. It will be held at the first waxing of the new moon, sky-clad, beginning in the great hall."

At "sky-clad", Rafael snorted. The group's focus shifted immediately back to him.

"Those of you who are partnered are invited to attend," Feanim continued, pointedly ignoring the drake as he stalked from the room.

I prodded Celebel to focus on Nemohee, wanting to know þeir reaction to the slight Feanim had just offered.

'*You should discover what Rafael is doing instead. I mistrust his intentions when he departs so abruptly,*' Celebel sent.

'*He's still angry with me.*' Yet, the melody harmonized.

'*Seemed he was also angry with Feanim.*'

'*Feanim propositioned him, and now he's asking for public nudity with this wedding. Of course Rafael is displeased.*'

Celebel's shock rippled through me. '*And Feanim somehow retains his head?*'

'*I was equally surprised. Perhaps you should take Feanim aside. Tell him to retreat before he pushes too far and causes a major incident. He won't hear such things from me. I think I accidentally encouraged him, not understanding the context.*'

With the bond strangled, it took more concentration than usual to locate Rafael. Combing through the library and the forge, I discovered him in the training field. I should have guessed that first.

That dreadful moranga greatsword whirled and chopped. I leaned on the fence, entranced by Rafael's liquid movements. His attention seemed far away, though that certainly wouldn't be the case if I stepped into the ring with him.

"Too many troubles to punch in the face?" I called.

With a whistling blur, I looked up the length of the blade. The tip hovered a few fingerbreadths from the end of my nose.

"How rude." I refused to let him bait me.

The Dragon growled, lowering the sword.

"Why did you leave the council so soon?" I asked. "Did you not want all the details of Feanim's naked wedding? You're partnered, so you're invited."

Rafael crossed his hands over the pommel of the sword and stared flatly at me, also refusing to be baited. Wind swept his hair in a conflagration about his shoulders.

"Oh, come now, Dragon. Are you truly determined to remain angry with me for touching myself the way *you* told me to?" I straightened, mirroring his stubborn posture.

His lip curled. Instead of dropping into a fighting stance, he sheathed the sword and hopped the fence. In a lunge, he grabbed me around the knees and tossed me over his shoulder.

"Rafael! Not this again. You said you wouldn't!" I pounded my fists against his back.

"*You* should not have shown me such disrespect." He hauled me off to his quarters.

At least he wasn't wearing that damnable armor. Instead of fighting, I surrendered and hoped for minimal witnesses.

The moment we entered the room, he dumped me face-first onto the bed. I scrambled to my hands and knees. He planted a boot on my ass and shoved me back down. A jangle told me he'd unbuckled his sword belt. On my belly, with my legs dangling off of the bed, I waited for his vengeance. The anticipation stirred the desire always lurking beneath the surface. I didn't have to wait long.

He ripped my silk dress down the back and yanked it off my body. As I squawked in protest, he pushed my face into the mattress.

"Quiet." The rumble tickled my spine, making my treacherous cunt slick. Then he slapped my ass hard enough to make my ears ring.

"Damn! Warn me!"

He slapped the other buttock harder. "I said *quiet*."

Recalling the delicious spanking he'd inflicted on me as "punishment" for our fight on the hill, I squirmed with rising lust. Rare, as Rafael usually preferred to receive pain. In the beginning, he had been fearful of genuinely hurting me. It had taken much convincing for him to stop treating me like spun glass. We both knew from experience how easy it was to induce his bloodlust by accident. Slowly, with some false starts, he'd allowed me to teach him my limits.

This, however, was new. No plan, no negotiating, no warm-up; just straight into it. It both excited and intimidated me, but I trusted him. No one understood pain like the God of Carnage.

He slapped my ass twice in quick succession. I cried out, so he slapped harder. Each whimper brought another hit. My buttocks burned with his handprints; the heat transferred directly to my clit.

Rafael leaned over me to hiss in my ear. "The more noise you make, the harder I will strike you."

I bit my lip to keep from moaning, terrifically aroused. Moisture pooled beneath my hips, dripping down the side of the bed. Each blow was precise, landing only on my buttocks and the backs of my thighs where he wouldn't damage an internal organ or major vessel. The edges of his talons bit into my skin as his palms connected. Holding my silence shrank my world to only his hands and my ass. A whimper broke free after one particularly hard blow launched me forward.

A growl. "What did I say?"

crack-crack-CRACK! The collision of his palm on my ass echoed.

It brought tears to my eyes and drove me into the mattress. The hole in Feanim's gut flashed in my mind. What would the aftermath be if Rafael struck me with all of his strength?

The Dragon paused, massaging my aching buttocks. I dared to look over my shoulder. With a dark glower, he lifted the sword belt and slid the sheathed blade free.

"What are you—"

CRACK! The blow slammed me down, clacking my teeth together.

"Quiet. I am going to fuck you with this sword."

Crow! I twisted around again. "Not the moranga! No, Rafael."

His eyes blazed. "You wanted to play games. Here is the prize you have won." He hefted the blade.

As I opened my mouth to protest again, he grabbed my hair. Forcibly turning my head around, he crushed me into the bed with his weight. Dread released a deluge of arousal, soaking the sheets beneath me. Surely he wouldn't cut me with the demon ore. Surely, he wouldn't allow it to sap my spirit.

"Not another sound until I command it," he growled into my ear, pressing his fingers into my vulva. "Your flooding defies your protests. I will not cut you."

He was right. I relaxed in his grip, sending my submission, my consent, along our connection. Held tightly by the hair and pinned under him, all I could do was squirm as the cold flat of the blade pressed against my vulva. None of the stomach-churning discomfort arose. Perhaps he shielded me somehow?

Another growl, low in his throat, rattled through me. He worked oil into my cunt, slicking me further. Despite my protests, I sighed when he eased the blade into me. It stretched me in an uncomfortably strange manner, but he'd spoken truth. The edge did not slice. He withdrew it slowly, then thrust it forcefully to my cervix. Gods, it was as if he'd impaled my diaphragm!

I clenched my teeth to keep from crying out, arching my back against my better judgment. He slapped my ass again, lighter this time, and rhythmically worked the blade in and out. Listening intently, he sped and slowed the thrusts in time with my panting. Drunk with pain-sparked ecstasy and the floating sensation of complete surrender, I rose with the tide.

I didn't want to climax this way, not with the moranga inside me. Rafael's aggression, the deft thrusts, the weight of him on my back, his hand in my hair, his searing breath on the back of my neck…

"Sing," he commanded.

I clamped my jaws stubbornly together, trembling with the strain of resistance.

He slapped my ass again. "Sing for me!"

I bit my lip and pressed my face into the mattress. The point of the blade collided with my cervix again, threatening to knock it into my brain. Rafael growled, and the bed shifted as he straddled me, one hand still tangled in my hair.

His fingers teased my anus, coaxing out my natural lubrication and pushing inside. How was he holding the sword that still pounded away at me? I turned to look, but he yanked my head straight.

"Sing, or I will not release you." Rafael shoved three fingers hard into my ass as the blade slammed into me.

My entire body quivered as the pressure built, rolling up from my toes to explode in my chest. I gasped.

His teeth pricked my ear. "I like you filled this way."

The climax took me, forcing a moan through my teeth.

The Dragon laughed, twisting his fingers inside me. "Someday, you will moan like that around my cock."

That destroyed me. I screamed, bucking wildly under him. Wave after orgiastic wave dragged counterpoint shrieks from my throat. Too intense, almost agonizing. I convulsed in the grip of ecstasy. My heart pounded so loudly in my ears, I feared I'd lost my hearing entirely.

Rafael withdrew his fingers. He left the sword buried deep until my breathing slowed, then finally, gently pulled it out. The moment he released my hair and lifted his weight from me, I flipped over and lunged for his face.

Prepared for my reaction, he caught my wrist before my palm connected with his cheek. Probably saved me from a fractured hand, but I was too furious to care. I fought him until he simply held up the empty leather sheath wearing a new filigree of my juices.

I blinked, lacking comprehend. Rafael pointed to where the sword rested, untouched, in the far corner. I'd never had the moranga anywhere near me. As the realization dawned on my face, he gave me an infuriating smirk.

"You-you absolute, fucking gods-forsaken, *shit lizard*," I spat.

The smirk grew into an enraging grin.

"I *hate* you!"

"I would not defy your wishes. You know that."

Anger heated my abused body. I tangled my fists in his hair and yanked with all my might. Maybe one day I'd finally snatch a strand free.

He rumbled happily. "'Shit lizard', that is new. Better than 'chicken feet'."

"Shut your fucking mouth and kiss me."

Instead, Rafael lifted me by the waist and rested my thighs on his broad shoulders. As I braced myself against the ceiling, he kissed my clit well enough for me to forgive all of his horrible ways. The heat of his breath eased the ache in my cunt. Cleansing me with gentle fire. Teasing loose a final, more subtle climax.

He held me there until my legs stopped shaking, then laid me on the bed. It took a while to catch my breath. The Dragon leaned on an elbow beside me, brushing my sweaty hair back from my face.

I frowned. "How did you wield the sheath while you fingered me?"

He raised a brow, and a scaly red tail snaked around his legs and mine to jab me in the meat of one buttock. Gods, of course.

"You are inordinately pleased with yourself." I poked at the tip of his nose.

He caught my finger in his teeth, swiping his tongue across the pad, and released it. "Inordinately? This is your fault for testing me." The chorus growl curled around me like another lover.

I stroked his cheek. "Even when I test you, I think of you still. You are never far from my heart." A garnet lock fell forward across his face, and I looped it around my finger. "You've gotten more than your fair share of revenge for this round. Crow, I'm unsure if I'll be able to walk out of here."

Rafael had the nerve to lick his lips. "I tasted a bit of blood."

"Horrid creature. Absolutely incorrigible." I tugged at the lock of hair. "This was a departure for you, testing my consent, and indeed my safety, in this manner." In truth, he'd thrilled me as much as he'd angered me. I should have known.

"You push me, I push back." The warning lay plain in his molten gaze. He held up a taloned hand, examining it thoughtfully. "It is far easier to be strong than gentle."

I released his hair and slid my hand into his. Both of my fists could easily disappear into his one. "A bit of a warm-up next time would be appreciated. And quit destroying my clothes. I haven't much to wear as it is."

"You were quite warm by my estimation." He gave me another self-satisfied look.

I laughed. "Wretched beast. May I make a request?"

"I am not removing my shirt."

Chapter 46

A ROARING commotion in the outer courtyard had more than one elf clamping their ears. Huge gouts of flame streaked across the sky. In the stables, the horses kicked their stall doors in panic. Rafael hadn't warned me of any danger. Three elves ran past, holding their ears.

I came upon a ring of shouting, stamping, uproarious drakes. Backwinging over its center was Marron, in his full dragon form. The ram-horned green behemoth breathed a continuous stream of fire to the heavens. Despite the crowd, the others gave Rafael space. He turned as I looped my arm through his.

"I take it Marron's child is born?"

"A healthy girl," he confirmed.

My heart swelled. "Wonderful! He must be so proud!"

A reverberating screech from overhead drowned out whatever Rafael might have said. Another green dragon, one I'd never encountered, swooped down from the cloud cover. Comparable in size to Marron, it wheeled in elaborate spirals around his flame. This must be Vaerra.

The newcomer had a long neck and tail compared to her relatively stocky body. With a short, pointed snout and massively muscled hindquarters, a pale belly darkened to emerald scales on her back. She rolled through the sky, revealing a stripe of burgundy fur down her spine that ended in a tuft at the tip of her tail, as well as dark red mottling on her wings.

Marron rose to meet her, and she twined her neck about her mate's. Together, they breathed twin flames into the sky. The crowd of drakes roared. Rafael roared with them, though not as loudly as the others; likely to spare my ears. It warmed my heart.

"What is the best way to congratulate them?" I already fell over myself avoiding thanks.

The Dragon shrugged. "Say 'congratulations'."

The celebrants shifted into their smaller forms, landing as they did. Vaerra kept her tail, where Marron eschewed wearing one. Her enormous yellow eyes tilted up at the outer corners, and emerald scales framed a pointed face the color of new leaves. A fluffy stripe of burgundy hair trailed down her back to the tip of her tail. Her scales covered a notable bosom. Of a height with her mate, and equally muscular, Vaerra's wide hips flared from a solid waist.

Individual drakes approached, bearing weapons, heavy chains of gold, and other treasures. Each bowed low and laid the items on the ground at the couple's feet, backing away without raising their eyes.

"I take it these are tribute rather than gifts?" A large aquamarine caught my eye.

"Yes. Required of lower status clanmates or those recently defeated in combat by either parent." Rafael nodded with his chin toward the group. "If a tribute is deemed lacking, they will exact punishment." At the way my ears twitched, he added, "Note how each tribute is offered first to Marron. He is more merciful than Vaerra by far."

The drakes offering tribute were predominantly green-scaled, although a few blues made an appearance along with a whip-thin silver drake with near-elvish features, and a shiny black drake with a short, blunt snout. Almost all were unfamiliar.

I followed Rafael to the inner ring surrounding the couple. The group parted for him, eyeing me with flat stares. Marron beamed. He unwrapped a bundle, shaking out a set of clothing. On cue, Vaerra lifted one foot at a time, allowing her mate to dress her in creamy deerskin hose that fit like a second hide. Looping around her dragon feet and tail, it allowed a full range of motion. She wiggled the waistband into place, and he held up a dark green coat made of a heavier leather. Tooled with interlocking, geometric patterns, it split neatly in the back, once again allowing room for her tail.

Strangely intimate, witnessing this tender moment. I hugged Rafael's arm, and he leaned into me.

Vaerra spied me, half-hidden behind my Dragon. Her already-wide eyes opened wider. Then she was a fingerbreadth from my face, sniffing my hair. I froze. Rafael rumbled something about tributes in draconian.

She replied in a throaty rasp. "Ha! No tribute from you, never. Definitely none so sweet as this. Your mate, yes?"

"Mine," Rafael agreed with a growl.

For once, his possessiveness gave me an inward smile.

The feminine wall of muscle bent to stare directly into my eyes. Up close, her facial structure reminded me of the blue drake Tyldain, with his almost nonexistent nose and lips. A faint tinge of green ringed the slit pupils, and each movement of her wide mouth flashed an intimidating bristle of needle-pointed teeth. How could such a dainty jaw contain so many?

Atavistic instincts rang out in fear of a predator in such close proximity. I squeezed Rafael's stony arm to steady myself. Vaerra did not blink, so I returned the stare in kind.

Finally, she cackled like a gate swinging on a rusty hinge and straightened. "Tough little thing. She does not flinch." Addressing me in smooth elvish, she said, "So, you are the one what tamed our vicious Red?"

My throat worked for a moment before the words formed. "I would not say 'tamed'." I glanced at Rafael. His mouth twitched into a feline smile.

"Ha!" Vaerra circled me. "Gossip has it you are almost drake-like yourself. Hiding a tail under all that mane?" She lifted the bulk of my hair in pantomime. "No tail, but oh ho, look at that shapely rear!"

Reaching over me, she balled up a fist and punched Rafael's shoulder with a resounding *thwack!* The impact rippled down his arm. "*Jyexsdfl*"—again, those unintelligible syllables—"Proud of you!"

Rafael grunted, nose wrinkling. "I do not require your approval."

I burst into laughter, earning a glare from him. Vaerra grinned, close-mouthed, her luminous eyes sparkling with mischief. Friendship bloomed between us, melting away my tension.

Marron turned from the last tribute, joining us. "I told you my mate is strong." He clapped Vaerra on the shoulder. "Behold, the mightiest legs of any drake!"

She preened, sticking one leg out at a time, foot pointed, and flexed her impressively developed thighs.

"Proper skull crushers." I did not have to feign awe at her rippling muscles. "Surely a single kick from you would be devastating."

"Ask your own mate of our first meeting." Vaerra gave Rafael a smug grin. "He won the fight, as he wins every fight. Memorable though, yes?"

I laughed again. "He surely deserves a few kicks."

The Dragon snorted. "She shattered my knees." Crow! The force such a kick must have required. He gave her a sour look. "She also aims first for the groin in every fight."

What a woman! No wonder she held such admiration.

I cleared my throat. "My heartfelt congratulations on your new daughter! May she be as strong as her mother." If she were anything at all like Vaerra, she would surely be an interesting—and challenging—child.

The couple thumped the centers of their chests in unison. I took it for a positive sign.

"Enough tribute. We will talk now." Vaerra clamped a taloned hand on my shoulder, glaring about. "Away from these pesky men."

She spun me toward the inner gate and propelled me through the crowd. I cast a startled glance back at Rafael. He gave me a resigned nod.

Was it the red dragon blood that made Vaerra so ferocious? What a contrast to her mate. I kept a wary eye on the swishing burgundy tuft of her tail, fighting a wild urge to touch that fur and determine if it was indeed as soft as it looked.

"Your coat is lovely. Did you craft it yourself?" I asked. Rafael always diverted such questions.

She glanced back over her shoulder. "My mate did. All the clan's clothing he makes."

I tried and failed to imagine Marron lovingly sewing children's garments with his huge, paw-like hands. What an adorable family dynamic.

"He's quite talented!"

"He is clan head," she said, as though it was obvious. When she realized I wasn't following the melody, she added, "Clan head is not only the protector. Must care for all the needs of the clan."

"Ah, so the larger the clan, the stronger the clan head must be, in all ways."

Vaerra bobbed her head in approval. Moving toward the more secluded end of the inner courtyard, she cracked a bough off of a birch to make way for her passage. I did my best not to wince at the tree's silent cry. She hurled the broken limb aside.

Perhaps Rafael was the strongest simply because he didn't crash around and constantly announce his presence. Hard to ambush an enemy who heard your approach from leagues away.

"Very strong, us," Vaerra said. "I do most of the hunting. He stays near the caverns. The two oldest keep watch while we are away."

Did all drakes occupy such caverns? The shine quickly faded as I considered what other family activities they might have, such as raiding kingdoms and murdering innocents for gold. At what age were drake children brought along on killing sprees?

"When the Red gave the call to come here, we had to consolidate our clan, make sure our young were protected." Another glance over the shoulder, this time with narrowed eyes. "To move numbers quickly is difficult. Good, that our oldest are now almost as strong as we two."

Resentment or something else? I held my tongue. Vaerra sprawled over a rock at the edge of a pool and gestured for me to do the same. I perched across from her, tension once again knotting my muscles. Though her shoulders were slimmer than her mate's, they put mine to shame.

"He kept you a fine secret, the Red. None of us knew you existed until he flew in spitting flame about how his mate was stolen. Stirred us up." Her eyes were sharp.

I pulled my coat closer around my shoulders. "I knew the first part, but nothing of the rest."

Vaerra snorted. "Seen him rage many times, many, but the despair, *hrah*, that sort was new. You know how he goes mad and tears into himself, yes? At our den he arrived, all fire and death, mostly aimed at himself." She snorted again. Her tiny nose seemed ill-suited to the gesture. "Angry and useless is a bad combination."

That startled a laugh out of me. "Yes, it is."

She leaned forward, eyes narrowing with shrewd intensity. "He spoke his heart to you when he returned, yes?"

"He did." The discomfort manifested in a new way. Where did this melody lead?

She held my gaze, unblinking, for an overly long moment, and finally nodded. "Good. I roared at him over it."

"You…roared at him? About me?" My ears twitched rapidly, far beyond my control.

Vaerra rasped a laugh similar to Marron's. "I cannot abide moping. Wallows in his own misery too much, that one, but so dire? Had to be love. No one has ever before turned his head. 'Tell her your heart, you stubborn fucking thorn', roared I. 'You will lose her forever if you cannot.' He did not care for that." Her talons clacked on stone, expression turning thoughtful.

"Ha! I'm sure he did not." The image of Vaerra berating Rafael over his inability to acknowledge his feelings was almost too absurd. That Rafael had allowed it broke my mind a little. "Are you always so bold with him?"

The green and red drake snorted a third time. "Have to be. Heeds nothing less, that one. Better than the old days, but still so fucking stubborn. Always the best thinker, in his estimation, but such a child in the heart. Worse than any of my young. I kicked some sense into him first, before the roaring. Gained the truth of what burrowed under his scales."

"I wish I had witnessed that." I struggled to contain my mirth.

Vaerra hopped to her feet and kicked the discarded birch bough, bark flying, until it was mostly splinters. "Tell! Her! You! Love! Her! You! Fucking! Dolt!" She emphasized each shouted word with another kick.

Overcome, I dissolved into helpless giggles. *Did Vaerra truly kick you out of your misery?* I couldn't help but needle him. Just a little.

Fuck off. The irritation in Rafael's response confirmed it.

She watched me intently.

"Why are you telling me this?" I asked.

"My mate says you are a good egg. That you stood down the Red when he grew wild and unreasoning. That he is much more manageable in your presence. I wanted to take my own measure of you." She sat again, propping her elbows on her knees.

The tips of my ears warmed at the compliment. "It gladdens my heart to hear this. Your perspective is valuable. You've known R-Rraysth far longer than I." The draconian title tasted strange in my mouth.

Vaerra grated out a chuckle. "Cannot help but think of him as a foundling. Overgrown and furious, and like to kill us all one day if he cannot find himself. Seems he found you instead. Strange creature, the Red, but no drake has ever set him right. Might as well be a fucking elf who finally triumphs. And by saving his life, no less."

"I don't know about triumph." My ears flicked. "Are you disappointed Byxldurr failed to claim him?"

The multi-hued drake barked an echoing laugh. "That rotter? No. A pustule, Byxldurr was. Broke every mate she could sink her claws into until she tried it with him. Even tried to steal Marron from me once." Her eyes flashed venomous green. "Bloody strong, though. Rraysth intervened that time." Had Byxldurr been the second before she died? Their estimations of strength confused me. "Rraysth said that wretched crow used some fell curse on him when they fought. If she'd won that claim…" She squeezed her eyes shut.

A weight I'd never quite realized I carried lifted from me. "Before Rafael finally confessed his feelings, he'd always maintained concepts like love and friendship didn't exist among your kind."

Vaerra sucked her teeth. "Cannot listen to every word of his. Rraysth was not raised among us. My mate, I do love, as I understand your word. He loves me. I love my children, though little shits they are. Though someday they will kill and supplant us."

I ignored the part about patricide and focused my ears on the positive. "Marron most definitely loves you. He brags about you frequently."

"As well he should." Her eyes and nose crinkled with pleasure.

"Do drakes form soulbonds with each other?" Rafael had always been cagey on the topic.

Vaerra's talons clicked on her naturally armored forearms as she considered my question. "Powerful, mate-claiming is. I have heard these 'soulbond' and 'soulmate' words. Hrrm. Similar, I think, but also different. We do not leave claiming to chance."

"Obviously, none of you use the trees, but what of your mated pairs who cannot bear children?"

"Some women claim more than one mate or allow another into their mating for a time. Some *viigsakh* bear young and often do not claim mates, moving from one season to another in their clans." She tilted her head, considering me. "How to say your name? Kah-ray-nee-ahl?"

"Close! KOO-rah-nee-ell," I corrected. "I'm sorry to admit I'll never be able to pronounce yours properly."

"Not your fault you have a short neck." Vaerra rose, stretching until I thought the buttons might pop from her coat. "Come, I'll walk you back. No secret enemies should eat the Red's Koo-ree-nah-yell."

Close enough. I trotted beside her longer stride.

She peered down at me with a wicked glint in her yellow eyes. "Tell me this: do you actually fuck the trees? Seems uncomfortable."

Chapter 46

"**YOU** needn't worry about strife. Rafael will never attend a sky-clad ceremony. Nor would any other drake, given how flashing one's genitals is considered vile mockery." I adjusted the scale around my neck as Celebel wove an intricate net of braids into my hair. He'd refused the pearls, claiming they would interfere with the patterns, so I knotted them about my upper body in a makeshift harness.

Miraculously, Xyxs hadn't caused any more trouble waving his hemipenes around. As far as I knew, he continued to slip into the baths for the occasional soak and tryst. Carafindrien gave me knowing looks every time our paths crossed, which granted me an odd sort of pride.

"He doesn't seem the type to attend any elvish ceremony," Celebel said, "though I suppose the invitation was political."

Nimthil expressed some reservations about Feanim's plan for the ceremony due to the drakes' presence. The sky-clad styling had been more popular in the early days of my youth, and reserved for small, intimate occasions. A calculated move on Feanim's part to demonstrate openness, vulnerability, and unity; none of which he truly offered, but desperately needed for continued support. Regardless, there was a certain wisdom in holding a celebration. It would give our battered people a reprieve, as well as sealing the alliance with the southern Lachanaur.

Though all of Amrún buzzed with excitement, I'd avoided the preparations entirely. As Celebel's declared consort, it was bad enough I'd be expected to participate, but I refused to labor outside of my healing scope for my least favorite people. The droves of arriving Lachanaur were eager enough to help. Soon, we'd be lost in a sea of redheads.

The ceremony was to begin in the great hall and spill out as a procession onto the garden grounds, ending at the larger reflecting pool. Various green artisans had been at work coaxing the flowers and trees to arrange themselves in an aesthetically pleasing, matrimonial fashion.

Sprites emerged to play minor tricks on the poor, unsuspecting artisans.

"I must admit, that styling of the pearls is quite alluring." Celebel stepped back to admire my handiwork. "Will you wear this diadem, please?"

Fallëvaethil flashed peacock hues from the delicate þilvor setting. I perched the diadem on my brow, admiring the diamond's scintillation. It hummed to life with a comforting warmth. Celebel produced a circlet set with moonstone for himself. I separated and plaited silver strands of his hair about the piece to hold it in place.

Feanim had supplied us with watered black silk robes to wear, barefoot, to the ceremony. Celebel's draped in a way that left little to the imagination. I brought my lips to his ear and let out a slow, lustful breath. Fabric rustled as his cock stirred.

"I greatly enjoy you in silk," I purred, walking my fingers over his firm abdomen toward the growing protrusion in his robe. "Let them hold the ceremony without us."

He laughed and caught my questing hands. "Stop that. We cannot be late. And you'll ruin the braids I so artfully wove."

"You're making the fool's choice." I attempted to nibble his ear.

He dodged, and my teeth caught only air. "Fool I may be, but I vow to ravish you *immediately* when this is done, you insatiable creature." He pulled me upright and kissed me, pinching my nipples through the silk.

I gasped, arching into his hands, and gave him a look of reproach.

Celebel laughed. "Now I'm the troublemaker, yes. Trouble begets trouble with you, my Moonflower. I will have the comfort of your scent during the festivities. Now, off with you." He pushed me to exit with a smack on the ass. "I must ensure you actually attend the ceremony."

"Be honest, you wish to enjoy the view." I shimmied my hips.

"Undoubtedly."

As the sun sank below the horizon, we joined the lines of elves heading to the great hall. Attendants at the door encouraged us to produce witchlights, which we held in our palms. Celebel and I were shown to the place of honor at the edge of the dais. I caught a few sharp glares in my direction, landing in the general vicinity of the scale around my neck. An unfamiliar couple took the position across from us—likely kin or close advisors to Nimthil. When the last attendee arrived, the great doors closed. We waited, the soft glow of the witchlights the only source of illumination.

In true dramatic fashion, the moment full dark settled on Amrún, a high bell tone rang from the outer wall. On cue, we dropped our robes in a unified susurrus of silk. A harpist perched at the back of the dais struck the first lilting notes of a processional. The doors swung open with deliberate lassitude, revealing the couple of honor.

Feanim wore a long robe of dark green brocade, with gold stitching at the collar and double box-pleated sleeves. His two-headed crow adorned the back. Nimthil wore a pale green, diaphanous gown that swirled around her like fog. Fine embroidery outlined her lineage heraldry on the bodice, winking with tiny emeralds and demantoid garnets.

Both had their hair braided back and held in place; his with a crown of gold laurel leaves, and hers with a glittering þilvor tiara set with more emeralds. Mesh of gold draped Feanim's ears, and a matching mesh of þilvor draped Nimthil's. Knowing Feanim had crafted their jewelry in true Duedellen style, I was duly impressed.

Arm-in-arm, the couple made their way to the dais. The music changed, and they stepped gracefully around each other in a dance, symbolizing their entwining lineages. As the higher-ranking figure, Nimthil led first, then Feanim.

Rafael's disdain pricked the back of my mind. *'Are elvish mating ceremonies always so ridiculous?'*

I bit back a laugh, taking a furtive glance around the hall. But he was nowhere to be found. *'Well, this one is especially dramatic, but they are rarely subtle. Especially not for royalty.'*

'Why is everyone nude? Is Feanim hoping it will devolve into an orgy?'

'Stop making me laugh! I've enough trouble focusing without your help. And...yes, likely so.' I must have made a face, as Celebel surreptitiously elbowed me in the ribs.

The initial dance of the lineages ended, and the couple stood palm-to-palm, lips moving in silent vows. As they pressed their foreheads together, Celebel stepped forward, lifting his voice. His warm baritone made my heart flutter. He sang of Feanim's many exploits and victories in battle, of his swiftness, his clever hand in crafting, his genius.

When Celebel's song ended, he rejoined me. One elf in the pair across from us stepped forward—a tall, thin Duedellen woman with dark, hooded eyes over high cheekbones in a poplar-gold face. A complimentary gold circlet held back her curtain of sleek, dark hair. She sang of Nimthil in a bell-like soprano. Her melody told us of her queen's generous heart, her wisdom in ruling, and her steadfast kindness. A brief sourness flit over me, but the song was so pure, I let myself be swept away.

The singer's partner, a shorter, plump Lachanaur woman with ebony skin and a fluffy cloud of black cherry hair, swayed to the music. A finely wrought choker of rubies, spinel, and fire opal graced her throat. She smiled, bashfully dropping her gaze when our eyes met.

Witchlights flared as Feanim and Nimthil turned to face the crowd, raising entwined hands. The couple glided out of the great hall, and we gathered our robes as we followed.

Pacing slowly through the garden and releasing the witchlights to float above our heads, I joined the crowd's chant and stepped in time with the others. A delicate new dais rose over the reflecting pool, woven of silvery-white birch roots. Branches sprouted from the platform, twining together to form a latticed gazebo. Celebel and I took our place beside the steps, just below Feanim and Nimthil, with the newly arrived couple on the far side. Another bell rang out, and we slipped our robes back on.

The couple shrugged out of their clothing, easier for Feanim than Nimthil, as her elaborate bodice took some work. In a moment of what must have been pique, Feanim produced a small dagger and sliced through the laces. They fluttered to the ground like wings cruelly plucked from a butterfly.

Nimthil's ears twitched, but with her back to the crowd, her expression remained her own. The couple laid their raiment aside to stand naked under the night sky, crowned with the barest waxing sliver of moon.

'*Absurd*,' Rafael sent. Eyes flashed in the darkness near the greenhouse. Ah, so he was in attendance.

Wickedness prompted me to poke at him. '*Aren't you meant to claim your mate sexually in front of a crowd?*'

'*That is…not uncommon*,' he admitted.

'*If it means you'll fuck me, I am willing.*' I envisioned Rafael's strong hands clamped on my hips, his knee forcing my legs apart, bending me over before a roaring crowd of drakes. My ear tips flushed.

'*What a filthy mind you have.*' Was that a hint of a smile?

'*Did you see the pearls?*' I sent the memory of admiring myself in the mirror. Ah, it *was* a smile.

'*Indeed. You must wear them again for me in that manner.*' His appreciation curled around me like licking flames.

'*A true shame you didn't receive one of these robes. It would be exquisite on you.*' Something about the way silk draped and pooled on a muscular body simply unraveled me.

'*I did. I set it ablaze.*' An image of Feanim's horrified expression flashed through the bond.

I snickered and Celebel elbowed me again, a little harder this time. Crow, I was meant to be singing with the chorus. I listened until I found my place, voice hitching in the cool night air.

'*You can sing better than that,*' Celebel chided.

I glared from the corner of my eye and hit a high note held longer than anyone else. Rafael's mocking amusement in the back of my mind only fueled me to raise my volume. We sang our hopes for the future, wishing blessings and peace on the couple, warmth without argument, prosperity, fertility, and unity in all things.

Feanim and Nimthil ceremoniously wrapped a length of gold and emerald silk over and under their entwined hands, chanting in unison. Ironic gratitude that elves didn't follow the drake tradition of public claiming filled me as Feanim grabbed Nimthil and kissed her. He lifted her off of her feet, carrying her down the dais. The brief flash in her eyes said she wasn't particularly pleased about it. Normally, they would walk out hand-in-hand, but Feanim had chosen theatrics to center himself instead.

"I declare before the moon, the stars, and all the gods, that I, Feanim Melranos, have married Nimthil Tinunith, joining our hearts and our houses as one, for all ages to come," he cried, setting Nimthil on her feet. "Soulbonded we are by choice, soulmates by nature."

"I, Nimthil Tinunith, declare before the moon, stars, and all the gods, that I have married Feanim, joining our hearts and houses for all ages to come," Nimthil echoed in a softer voice. "Soulbonded we are by choice, soulmates by nature."

They raised their bound hands, and the crowd cheered, erupting into a new song of celebration. I searched again for Rafael as I clapped and sang, but the glowing eyes were gone.

Chapter 47

S EEMINGLY overnight, we were back on the road to war. Scouts confirmed what Feanim's crows had said about the hidden enemy stronghold, and Rafael pushed for more aggressive tactics. If we could seize this seat, we would discover more about their objectives and hopefully break their power.

Each mobilization went more smoothly than the last as our forces became more accustomed to the routine, and to each other. We left enough defenders behind to hold Amrún against invaders—a coterie of elvish soldiers inside the walls and a few drakes without.

Feanim surprised me by joining the departing company instead of staying behind to revel in the ongoing celebration of his marriage. Celebel explained his friend had never been one for feasts and merriment. Thus, Nimthil once again assumed responsibility for leadership in the Consulate's absence.

Both soulmates insisted on my presence for the march. Celebel cited my ability to uncloak the Fomorians and assist with healing the wounded. Rafael simply demanded I remain close. The treachery at Férioth must have put him off of leaving only Boshkt behind to guard me.

Heading for the gorge Feanim had mentioned in the council meeting, I rode behind the main company with Liriadis and the other healers. Eäriel had elected to remain at the fortress. I understood her position, but missed her gentle presence all the same.

Liriadis and I had ample time to compare our tallies of supplies as our horses picked carefully over the pockmarked lava fields. Although we were well-stocked, winter's bite was vicious, and our planning began in earnest. Together, we mapped out and marked the areas likely to have the best foraging along the way.

The two newcomers I'd spotted at the wedding were indeed Nimthil's closest companions and advisors. Surprisingly, they accompanied us on the road instead of remaining behind with their queen. The slender Duedellen singer turned out to be a skilled artisan named Pirinlach. Her specialty was imbuing objects and weapons with spirit. She introduced her soulmate, Norlissuin of the beautiful cloudlike hair, as a historian.

Said historian cleaved to my side. Steering her dun mare directly in-between Liriadis's horse and mine, Norlissuin overtook the conversation with a barrage of excited, probing questions aimed at me. Draped in swirling peacock blue and purple damask, light-catching tourmalines trimmed her robes. Though perhaps not the most practical choice, they provided a welcome contrast to the landscape's preponderance of dull greens and greys. Not that I had the right to criticize a lack of practicality. Liriadis tugged her lobes and rode on ahead of us.

"What is the exact date you first met the lord of the drakes?" Norlissuin asked with shining eyes, tossing in a "my lady," as an afterthought.

Her direct approach was refreshing after all the tedious social posturing. I also admired her ability to write legibly while astride a moving horse.

"I'm far too old to track time like a human," I laughed. "It was perhaps eight-and-five or eight-and-six years ago now, in the early autumn."

I gave her an outline of the fight that led to Rafael's fall at my hill and how I'd healed him. Norlissuin nodded thoughtfully, hair bobbing as she scribbled notes. Keeping certain details vague, I explained how we'd slowly formed a friendship, and eventually a stronger bond.

"There is no historical precedent for this! No elf has ever had a *drake* for a soulmate. It's rare enough for it to happen at all outside our people." Her eyes never drifted from her writing as she spoke. "Do we know for certain drakes *have* soulmates? Are you quite sure this is a soulbond and not merely strong emotion?" An echo of so many other voices, but Norlissuin's tone held no malice, only curiosity.

"Do you know my former lineage? I may have renounced my position, but some of the power still flows in me." I said it gently, but it garnered her full attention.

The Lachanaur stared at me for a long moment, appraising, and then nodded to herself. "Yes, yes, that harmonizes. You have the visions too?"

"Ever since I departed Leyûduin, yes." The visions that marked our lineage nearly consumed my mother. She'd drifted through life like a dream. By the time she rooted as a tree, she'd been absent from the court for centuries. As I'd been unafflicted in my youth, and subsequently broken the lineage, I wrongly assumed I'd never have them. The Night Mother had other designs.

Norlissuin chewed her lower lip as she scratched at the scroll with her quill. "I'll be observing you closely. Not only do you have a completely unique position with a drake, but you *also* have a second soulmate in Celebel Elhalanros? Multiples are quite rare...ah, as I'm sure you know." Her ears twitched with the look of mild self-reproach she gave me. "Might...might I interview your, ah..."

I let her flail for a moment before rescuing the poor thing. "You wish to speak with Rafael?"

Norlissuin's ears twitched wildly. "Yes, please. If-if it could be arranged. The events he has witnessed, or took part in directly..." She let out a dreamy sigh. The light in her deep russet eyes said she would be fully willing to risk death and dismemberment to further her academic interest.

I appreciated her fervor, however misdirected it might be. "I will ask. Rafael is ill-tempered and often contentious. If he agrees, I beg you to only speak to him in my presence. He is quick to take umbrage, and my presences helps ensure your safety."

"Ah, yes. I have heard that melody."

How much had Nimthil told her and were those tales plain or embroidered? "You don't seem intimidated."

She looked up at me, eyes sparkling in earnest. "The Red Dragon is living history; a legend made flesh. As are you, in truth. The opportunity to interview both of you at once is beyond my wildest imagining. I cannot thank you enough. Piri wished me to remain at Amrún, but I convinced her to bring me along so I may complete my volume on the drakes. You may have noticed how lacking our records are on that accord. I had begged Nimthil for an introduction before we departed, but alas, she was too busy."

I smiled in spite of myself. Nimthil would have been quite disinclined to make such an introduction. I only hoped Rafael would be cooperative.

RAFAEL WAS not cooperative. I led Norlissuin—her arms stuffed with scrolls, dangling quills, and inkpots—to the drake camp as promised. Winding through the sparse trees, we emerged onto an open field of granite rockfall. Apart from us, Rafael was the one spot of contrast in the monochromatic grey of land and sky. Hair aflame and dressed in the demon armor, with a soot-black cloak billowing about him, he painted a vision of hell.

Norlissuin gaped in awe. "Oh, Lord Dragon, you are nothing at all as I expected. I've never met a drake, but the legends did not accurately describe—"

"No," he said flatly.

"Rafael, hear her song," I protested.

"No." He turned away, cloak swirling behind him.

Norlissuin's crestfallen expression, drooping ears and all, steeled my resolve. "Would you stop being an ass for one entire breath? Norlissuin here is an historian—"

"I said no." Rafael moved toward the drakes gathered just over the hill.

The rasp of scales and rumbling voices carried, punctuated by the echoing smack of a flat palm striking flesh and Vaerra's sharp laugh. She must share my opinion on slapping.

I grasped the trailing edge of the Dragon's cloak, giving it a tug. "Wouldn't you appreciate the opportunity to correct the elvish records of your life? Were you not complaining of the inaccuracies?" I pouted my best pout. "Please?"

"You continue to be a trial," he muttered, but his posture relented.

He gestured to the wide-eyed Norlissuin to speak. She grinned broadly, flashing brilliant white teeth against her dark skin.

Rafael held up a talon. "Hide your teeth unless you mean to challenge me." A terrifying smile stretched across his face, exposing a forest of pointed, flesh-rending teeth. Effective.

With a squeal, she clapped a hand over her mouth. "Forgive my blunder, Lord Dragon. We have no accounts of your social mores."

At his sharp nod, Norlissuin set down the bulk of her scrolls and selected one. Cutting a fresh quill with a practiced hand, she inked it and spread her parchment over a tall rock. Rafael only narrowed his eyes.

She raised her quill expectantly. "Is it true you dye your hair with the blood of kings? Some tales say it's infants."

"Only virgins." Sarcasm curled his lip.

I sent him a mental prod.

"I had heard your hair only burns when you, ah, consume innocents." She raised her eyebrows, quill perched expectantly.

He snorted. "I have not recently eaten any infants. Perhaps I should inquire after the surplus at Amrún."

Norlissuin froze, eyes popping wide.

"Don't record that. He's being an ass," I said quickly. She wrote it down anyway. I sighed. "Come now, Rafael. Give her genuine answers."

"She could have asked you this nonsense." With a steaming exhale, he calmed himself enough for the flames in his hair to dim and reveal its true bloody crimson. "You are aware I am a *red* dragon, yes?" The aforementioned red scales sprouted briefly over his brow and cheekbones before he reabsorbed them into his skin.

Norlissuin took furious notes, utterly unaffected by his blistering sarcasm. "Fantastic, Lord Dragon! The scale pattern is quite interesting. Do they change shape depending on their location?" True, she could have asked that of any drake, but Rafael watched intently as her quill flew over the page in a rapid sketch.

"Form follows function." He pointed to a particular spot in the drawing. "Square plates ventrally. I am no belly-crawling serpent."

Norlissuin shook her cloud of hair, making the recommended

change. Rafael seemed mollified for the moment. I perched on a rock beside him, letting my legs dangle as I leaned against his shoulder. He played idly with a braid of mine, twining it in his fingers.

"I know of at least one cult devoted to worshiping you as a deity, but there is no record of their end. Do you know what befell those people?" Norlissuin's quill waited at the ready.

"I did." He said it casually. Aghast, I snatched my braid out of his hands. "What greater sacrament than to be devoured by your own god?" He clicked his teeth together.

Norlissuin blanched, ears drooping, but she dutifully recorded his answer. "Do you follow a deity yourself?"

He snorted in derision. "Gods are useless."

"Dûemer is far from useless," I interjected, offended on behalf of my goddess.

"Interesting that you follow a death deity." Rafael eyed me thoughtfully, side-stepping my protest.

"She is more a goddess of transition. Day and night, life and death, waking and sleep; the spaces between are her domain."

Speaking of the Night Mother summoned her graceful form to ghost over the rocky scene. With skin and hair of the blackest night and strewn with stars, the long hem of her robe shimmered with the light of dawn below the heavy curtain of hair. She strode across the twilight of my thoughts.

"I would have expected you to follow a healing deity as well, my lady," Norlissuin said.

"As would I, but she chose me first. I understand her better than most of the gods of healing and medicine, as they tend to be narrow in their focus. Being on the very edge of society as I am, I was bound to be hers."

"Ah, she is the reason you wear your hair so long." The Lachanaur gestured to where my black hair trailed on the ground as I sat.

"Yes, indeed." I slid off of the rock, twirling to cast my hair in a halo around me. The ubiquitous moss buoyed my steps.

"So *devout*." Rafael caught a braid, stopping my progress.

"*She* helped me save your ungrateful carcass," I replied pertly.

"The Night Mother was the one who insisted I rescue you. You could show the barest hint of gratitude."

"I would rather go for a swim." He pulled me close with the braid, trapping me in his arms. I laughed and struggled in his grip.

Our banter perked Norlissuin's ears. Hopefully she wasn't writing everything, but from the way her fingers twitched, I doubted it.

The historian licked her lips. "Lord Dragon, could you tell me of what happened with the Tárthanë?"

"No." Rafael released me, hair sparking to flame once more. I rubbed his arms to relieve the sudden tension.

"But you massacred—"

His deep growl cut her off. Norlissuin backed away, scooping her precious scroll into her arms and nearly tripping on the rough terrain.

I touched Rafael's jaw. *'She doesn't know your past. Be calm, please.'*

"My apologies, my lord. I did not mean to offend!" The historian bowed low, and the tips of her ears trembled. It seemed she had finally realized who she was dealing with. "My thirst for knowledge occasionally outpaces my sense of decorum." Norlissuin tapped the feathered end of the quill on her lips as she pondered. "Would you be willing to speak on how you rose to power amongst the drakes? Based on what I've gleaned, before you ascended, the drakes were too fractured to truly be called a society. Did you intentionally unify them into a more cohesive structure, and if so, how?"

From the sudden glint in Rafael's eye, the question had sparked his interest. "You wish for history. Here is ours. I am Adacanir's eldest scion, but hardly the first drake. That distinction goes to Tathua the Gilded, the only one of Dhraxael's three drake offspring to survive to majority. She created our current structure."

I hardly dared to perk my ears lest I break the spell cast by his resonant voice.

"We say our persecution was birthed alongside the first generation. To combat this, Tathua traveled to the most remote reaches of Vaeda, gathering as many discarded children of the dragons as she could. The firstborn especially suffered." A shadow passed over Rafael's face. Gods, what a grim culture of parental abandonment. "Many did not survive. Thus, Tathua established the clans for protection.

"Over the ages, the clans structured themselves around parentage, affinity, and might. Consolidating power, they had offspring of their own. The red clan grew to the most numerous, though Tathua's gold held sway.

"Those reds stirred the others, clamoring to spill the blood of their absent progenitors. Many desired those legendary hoards as well. Though she initially counseled against it, Tathua eventually led an attack against a small enclave of true dragons.

"It was a bloody, ferocious battle, lasting nearly a moon. Tathua fell, along with the rest of the known first generation. Their sacrifice allowed their offspring to emerge victorious. This reckoning began the exodus of true dragons from Vaeda."

Norlissuin hung on his every word. As did I. As did the small audience of elves clustering at the very edge of earshot.

"Fear is a powerful motivator," Rafael continued. "Toward the end of the exodus, I discovered my people, still licking their wounds. They discovered one last firstborn, much to their dismay. I had intended to cut down only my kin, but others interfered, so I retaliated. The red clan collapsed by my hand. The gold clan organized, calling for a unified front to combat the threat."

Norlissuin was enrapt, nodding as her hand flew over the scroll. "And you fought them all at once?" She did not glance up from her work.

Rafael huffed. "Of course not. I murdered the gold patriarch in his sleep and the rest scattered. Drakes are disinclined to fight shoulder-to-shoulder in a unit as elves do. It was that very individualism which allowed me to break them. Only later did I learn this action granted me status over all the rest. Death is the only abdication."

Norlissuin looked up in startlement, the motion jangling the crystal trim of her sleeves.

He gave her another glimmer of formidable dentition. "Thus appointed, I hunted down and killed the remaining gold clan to prevent future trouble."

The historian's eyes lit with fascination. She opened her mouth, and Rafael held up a hand.

"The clan heads are all here. Pester them with your questions." He waved in the general direction of the drake camp. "I have fought each of them. Some more than once." Tyldain's face flashed in my mind. Interesting.

"And they live?" Her voice was tentative.

"What good are those long fucking ears if you do not listen?"

"Rafael—"

He tapped a finger on my lips. "The green clan head and his mate argued well against wholesale extermination."

I pushed Rafael's hand away. "Marron is far friendlier than this one. Perhaps you should interview him instead."

My Dragon rumbled and kissed my forehead. Norlissuin's eyes went round as an owl's. I chuckled to myself.

'I am adding this to the long tally of favors you owe me,' Rafael sent as he stalked off. If he'd worn a tail, it would lash with irritation.

"Did I give offense?" Norlissuin asked in a small voice.

"No, Rafael is always prickly. I'm surprised he spoke as much as he did. It took him two dozen years to stop casually threatening to kill me," I said with a shrug. Her lips made a perfect 'o'. "Drakes favor the bold. You should take more care in your approach, however."

"You have my deepest thanks." The historian gave me a small bow. "How do you have no fear of him? He's, ah, quite intense."

"He is, but I met him by packing his organs back into his body cavity. The intimidation fades. Come, I'll introduce you to some others."

Swallowing hard, she gathered up her scrolls and ink pots.

I caught her eye and held it. "Never forget they are predators, and we, their prey."

FURTHERING MY surprise, Marron and Vaerra were thrilled, and invited Norlissuin to sit and ask questions to her heart's content. More astonishingly, she drew a small crowd. Xyxs, Boshkt, Abrrys, and a few others gathered. The crowd made me nervous, though I'd explained some basics of drake courtesy. Norlissuin took to covering her smiles with a hand.

Rafael was nowhere to be heard, but his proximity pinged through our connection. *'Be at ease. Their conceit will protect her for now. No one has ever written of the lesser drakes.'*

'Lesser *drakes. Now who is conceited?'*

'It is truth.' Impossible man.

If only I'd brought my journal, I would have made drawings of the scene. Norlissuin sat ringed by scaled warriors, eyes bright, as Marron translated their words for her to record. Xyxs had felled an entire gathering of stone giants on his own. Abrrys and a few of her clan had hunted down and killed the storm queen. Marron held the record for the largest city razed—he'd opened a fissure under a massive human metropolis, dropping it into the sea. Vaerra claimed she'd felled her own progenitor, though others protested she was too young.

Boshkt and Grenyk acted out a legendary fight. As Marron described the scene, their reenactment drew blood. Boshkt spoke of how his branch of the green clan had broken off and ended up far to the south. Nestled in the tropics, they'd develop a caustic venom as a hunting strategy over the use of fire in the damp environment.

The slender silver drake, she of the gleaming metallic scales, spoke long on the various differences between the clans. Her voice had a heavy, raspy sibilance that made following her words difficult. Interest piqued, I made a mental note to ask Norlissuin for her records later.

Marron admitted to the burning of one of our sacred groves himself. A centuries-old mystery. I bit my lip not to comment out of offense. Norlissuin's hand blurred over her scroll, and more than once, the green drake hushed the others to give her a chance to catch up.

I aimed my casual musings at Rafael. *'Grenyk seems formidable.'* An understatement. The brown drake was as solid as a tree stump.

'Grenyk has both sired offspring and laid fertile eggs.' Amusement colored his tone as I watched the brown drake demonstrate its strength. *'Most* viigsakh *have a heavy build. They are highly sought-after as mates, and so must fight more frequently than most.'* He'd answered

my unasked question.

The drakes took up an impromptu dance, swirling around each other in a riot of color. They stomped, rattled, and bellowed their cheer. I itched to join them, but did not want to interrupt. Norlissuin's hand raced as she tried desperately to sketch them all. I'd offer her one of my liniments for the inevitable wrist cramping she would experience if she continued at that pace.

Through the bond, I sensed Rafael's presence nearby. *'Will you dance?'* I asked.

'They will not be so relaxed if I join,' he replied.

I'd forgotten they feared him as much as they respected him. A certain sadness struck me for all the distance he had created and steadfastly maintained.

'I do not need your pity.' His tone held an edge fine enough to cut.

I winced. *'Do not mistake my compassion for pity. I only wish you could move amongst the others freely and easily.'*

'If I did not hold my current position, Byxldurr would have never fought me, and I would not have met you,' he pointed out. *'I have known most of these fools for thousands of years and have no desire for amity.'*

'Marron doesn't strike me as a fool. Nor do most of the others.'

'Thousands of years, dove.' At least he was finally relaxing. Likely, his derision of the other drakes put him in a better mindset.

'Do you think me a fool as well?' I braced for the answer.

'What would you call rescuing me from death? Wisdom?'

Chapter 48

ERIE howls floated on the wind. The horses stamped and blew; even Iruwher danced under me. Gods, we weren't halfway to our destination yet and we'd been riding for days. Shadows roiled through the darkening valley, moving with unified purpose. Figures coalesced into a band of riders astride slavering beasts nearly twice the size of our largest destriers.

Umbrawolves!

They charged into our line with a chaotic uproar of clanging weapons, horses screaming, and the strange, ululating cries. Like solidified wisps of wolfish smoke, hazy at the edges, they blinked in and out of reality as they wove through the shadows of their namesake. Those howls—a weird marriage of wolf, loon, and nightjar—faded in and out with them.

I drew my crescent moon blades as they edged closer, pairs of citrine eyes floating in the purposeful, lupine fog. Each tree and boulder in the landscape around us cast a threatening darkness. As the umbrawolves attacked, their shifting, immaterial state did not prevent them from inflicting wounds. Likewise, their riders jabbed freely with spear and sword, following their mounts through the transition from shadow to solid form.

"Call as many witchlights as you can," Feanim's tenor rang out. "Light forces umbrawolves to solidify and makes them vulnerable!"

Nemohee, who'd hung back to chat with me, was the only warrior among us. "Hear it; there are *elves* riding these beasties!"

I followed the tip of þeir sword through the glittering swarm of witchlights as an umbrawolf crashed through the line directly in front of me. Indeed, a traitor in a white tabard sat astride the beast! I blinked. No, her lower body melded into her mount rather than perching atop it. Like peering through a dense cloud, the silhouettes of elves on its far side showed through the creature's form.

Nemohee swung þeir sword in a deadly arc at the umbrawolf's neck. It passed cleanly through. Meeting no resistance and leaving no damage. We needed more light! I dragged witchlights to us, plunging my hands into the motes.

The elf wheeled her hazy mount to attack. Nemohee dropped into a defensive stance, deliberately putting me at þeir back. Calling on the Night Mother, I pulled my spirit from the pool in my lower belly and concentrated it in my hands, readying either unhealing or protection.

Flame streaked over our heads, momentarily blinding me and forcing the umbrawolf to fully materialize. It halted, shaking its head as if stung. I could no longer see through its wavering body.

A coughing roar shook the ground, folding everyone's ears back in unison; elf and umbrawolf alike. Rapid, heavy foot falls announced the dark figure that blurred past. The beast lunged at us.

Rafael was faster. He leaped, slamming into the rider and ripping her free. The sound was entirely too similar to flesh tearing. The umbrawolf staggered sideways, thrown off its attack. Air expelled from the rider's lungs in a harsh bark as she hit the ground. The Dragon fell with her, deliberately leading with that spiked pauldron. The traitorous elf's sternum shattered on impact. She died with a gurgling wheeze.

The umbrawolf jumped in the opposite direction, racing away from my Dragon across the clearing. He rose with the effortless grace of a dancer. Tendrils of bloody flesh clung to his left pauldron. The swirling grey beast rebounded off a rock wall, changing direction to launch itself directly at Rafael. It opened absurdly wide jaws lined with needle teeth as it lunged for his throat.

My hand flew to my heart with fear as the nonsensical part of my mind congratulated myself on the apt nightjar comparison. With such a gaping maw, the umbrawolf could easily swallow an elf whole.

The Dragon lashed out with a kick that caught the umbrawolf in its slavering muzzle. His talons ripped open horrific gashes, using the lupine creature's own momentum to drive it into the ground. With a squeal of pain, the umbrawolf thrashed on its side. It bled like any corporeal beast.

Using one foot to pin it in place, Rafael lifted the other for a single heavy stomp to the skull. The force popped one of the beast's eyeballs free from the socket, squelching between his long toes. My stomach turned, and I looked away. Despite my general tolerance for gore, eye injuries always sickened me.

The sounds of fighting died away around us. Had we routed this enemy so quickly, or was it a feint to test our strength? Other soldiers raced to us with swords drawn. As one, they stopped cold at the Dragon's bloody tableau. Nemohee gave a whoop, waving þeir sword cheerfully at my soulmate.

"Cheers, Red! Ye make it look easy," þey called.

"This one breached your line," he growled at the armored elves belatedly joining us. "Useless fucks." He flicked his foot at the umbrawolf's corpse, slinging gobbets of brain matter from his talons and eliciting gasps from the onlookers.

In the heat of the moment, I hadn't noticed the ring of wide-eyed, terrified stares aimed at Rafael. Most of them had never witnessed his fearsome strength in action. Norlissuin, riding a few paces behind me when the attack started, had dropped her scrolls in horror. Even the healers, inured as they were to the effects of violence, were visibly shaken.

The Dragon hefted the umbrawolf carcass over one shoulder as though it weighed nothing, impaling it on his already bloodied pauldron spikes to steady it. I'd expected the creature to dissipate into shadows, but it remained solid.

The fallen rider's helm had knocked loose with the fall, spilling dark hair in a pool around her head. Definitely not Silfanië, thank the gods.

"Rafael, you have our gratitude," I called out, louder than necessary to shift attention to me. "You've saved us yet again."

With a snort, he hoisted the body by the hair, preparing to toss it over his other shoulder. Nemohee glanced at each of us with raised brows. The rough handling of an elf's corpse sent another ripple through the crowd.

'Please don't mangle her body!' I shuddered. *'Especially not*

before the others.' The court's opinion of him had truly turned after his grisly murder of the smut book author.

Rafael huffed. "These people are incidental. I came to save *you*." '*Elves are so sensitive,*' he sent with a sneer in his tone. "If you had paid attention to my lessons, you could have handled this yourself. Put that armor to use."

That sent a murmur through the crowd, but I kept my focus on him. "I am only here in my capacity as a healer. You know that." '*Many of these people are not fighters! This is highly upsetting to them. Please don't make it worse.*' "Are there any here who recognize our fallen kin or claim her body for funeral rites?"

Rafael lifted the body, turning her face outward. Murmurs rose, but no one stepped forward. Frozen in their collective fear. The traitor was heartbreakingly young, and thankfully, no one I recognized.

Finally, Norlissuin tentatively asked, "M-may I examine her face? F-for my records?" Impressive courage.

The Dragon scoffed but motioned her over. She peered into the face of the corpse. Her finger shook only slightly as she touched the forehead, momentarily closing her eyes. Satisfied, she nodded to herself and scratched notes on the ever-present scroll, forgetting in the moment to be afraid of the imposing drake.

"My thanks, Lord Dragon. I do not recognize this individual, but I believe I've identified her family. If so, she is the last of the lineage."

"Hrrm. So none claim the body?" Rafael cast a cool glare across the crowd. No one stepped forward, and few met his eye. He gave me a disdainful sneer and stalked off, dragging the dead elf by the hair.

"You are bold, Norlissuin," I said as the crowd dispersed.

Nemohee laughed in agreement.

Her cloud of hair bobbed as she turned to me. "I am?"

"Aye, do ye ken what the drakes do with their fallen enemies?" Nemohee asked. With the historian at a loss, þey grinned broadly. "They sloch the bodies!"

"Forgive me. My grasp of hillspeech is patchy. Sloch?"

"Drakes eat the fallen dead," I translated.

Norlissuin swallowed hard, peering in the direction Rafael had gone. "Oh." She clutched her beloved scroll to her bosom.

"If it helps, I convinced Rafael to keep his people from devouring our own fallen, and instead take only the bodies of the enemy," I added. "He does not eat elves." Not anymore, at least.

Nemohee chuckled again at the look on the poor historian's face. "Fomorians taste of sickly sweet shit." Þey mimed tearing meat off a bone and spitting it out.

I glared at my friend. "Unhelpful, Nem."

"That is… Excuse me." Norlissuin wheeled away from us to bend over a bush and retch.

As the historian emptied her belly, I thumped the still-laughing Nemohee on the back of the head.

"WILL YOU allow me to demonstrate my gratitude for saving us?" I asked. "As a tribute?"

Removed from the others as always, Rafael sat methodically cleaning and checking his armor. The first rays of the rising sun cast curls of light over the moranga, which it greedily drank. He set aside his plackart with notably clean hands. There was no sign of the corpses.

Eight umbrawolves had comprised the attack: three felled by drakes, one by elves, the rest had escaped. We'd sustained some casualties—all elvish—and most of them newly arrived Lachanaur.

Attention fixed on me, Rafael straightened.

I stepped between his leather-clad thighs and sank to the ground before him, maintaining eye contact. Oh, to worship at this altar. My hands tingled, and I arranged myself more comfortably on the cushiony moss.

"Cúraniel…" His voice held a note of wariness.

I rested my elbows on his knees. "Might I speak my desires aloud?"

His mouth compressed into a line, but he stroked my hair. "Speak, then."

I ran my hands up the thick muscles of his thighs, careful to stop before he growled or grabbed my wrists. Leather mingled with the dracaena resin scent of his skin, spurring on my audacity. That, and the sizeable bulge between his legs.

"I greatly wish to suck your cock."

Rafael exhaled slowly through his nose, stillness passing over him in an almost physical wave. I rested my cheek on his leg. That same gentle hand caressed my ear.

"Why?"

"You know why. No part of your body is shameful, Dragon. You enjoy my climax." I traced lazy circles on his thigh. "I would return the favor." Daring, I bit my lower lip and peered at him from under my lashes. "At the very least, I would like to taste you."

He bent and kissed my forehead; the barest brush of lips over my skin, but it sped my heart. Hooking his hands under my arms, he pulled me up. His feet curled around my buttocks, supporting my weight, cock rising hard and hot between my breasts.

"Now you're teasing me." I tugged at the hem of his jerkin.

He caught my hands, breath quickening. "Over the clothing."

Never had such a benign phrase turned me inside out. My spine pulled taut, strung on the longbow of his body. A glance at his face revealed eyes burning with mirrored desire, but the shadows remained. He released my hands with a brow raise.

"Will you guide me?" I traced his jaw with a cautious fingertip. "I've no desire to overwhelm you."

The Dragon nodded once. I slid down far enough to brush my lips over the increasingly strained leather. Gods, I loved leather. The scent alone aroused me, and the way it molded to the body beneath…

A sharp intake of breath gave me pause. Rafael brushed my hair back, tracing the span of my ears. Maintaining eye contact as a bridge over the darkness, I skimmed the length of his erection with my lips, light as a moth's wing.

"Does this please you?" I pressed my thighs together. That minor contact had me squirming with need. "Shall I continue?"

Rafael's lips parted, eyes aflame, and he gripped my hair. "Yes."

His powerful chest rose and fell with the bellows of his lungs. I dragged my tongue over the leather. He trembled. What I wouldn't give to have this man come undone at my touch, in a healthy manner for once.

"May I remove your sword belt?" My fingers twitched with anticipation.

"Yes, but do not…" His gaze flicked away.

"Speak, beloved." Gentle, guiding him to comfort, I waited. If I must remain frozen in this position overnight to soothe him enough to accept my touch, so be it.

He rumbled, gathering himself. "Do not use your hands on my cock."

"I appreciate the clear boundary." I unbuckled the belt, sliding it from his waist onto the ground. To show my compliance, I rested my palms on his chest. Stretching down, I exhaled over his leatherbound cock. "Can you feel my breath?"

"Yes." Rafael tensed under me, muscles almost humming with anticipation.

Heat radiated from his body in caressing waves. Searing my skin, waking my own blaze. Gods, if only I could claw my way through those fucking trousers and choke myself on his cock until he finally spilled in my mouth. Until he painted my face and breasts. Instead, I laid the barest of kisses on the very tip, pressing through all the gods damned layers of wool and leather. He shuddered. I kissed his cock again, trailing my lips down to the base.

"Are you enjoying this?" Pressing my nose into the leather, I lapped at his heavy bollocks. His hand, tangled in my hair, weighed on the back of my head.

"Yes." A hiss through clenched jaws.

I glanced at his face, taking stock of his mood as I nuzzled and kissed his cock. Dilated pupils, almost rounded in their focus, darkened the flames of his eyes. A predator's intensity. Holding his gaze, I licked my way back to the tip.

"Use your teeth," he said in a breathy growl. "Make it hurt."

"Oh, my Dragon, still far more comfortable with pain than pleasure." I rested my cheek against his hard cock. "I don't want to hurt you!" Likely, I couldn't hurt him, regardless of my intent.

"Please." A tremor ran through the hand gripping my hair.

I turned my face to kiss the inside of his wrist. "As you wish." Gently, as I couldn't quite bring myself to bite, I grazed my teeth up and down his cock. His breathing grew ragged. Unbelievably erotic.

"Harder." His hand tightened, threatening to rip strands from my scalp.

An involuntary gasp escaped me as the pain shot straight to my clitoris. I clenched my fists over his chest, digging my fingernails into my palms to resist reaching for his cock. Or ripping his clothes away. Would he be more receptive if I offered my dripping wet cunt to taste while I worked on him?

A rumble rattled me. "Next time. Now, *bite.*"

Stretching my mouth as wide as possible, my jaws barely spanned his girth. Biting down met a tooth-breaking resistance, so I scraped with more force, working my way toward the tip. When I reached it, I nibbled experimentally. A growl vibrated through me. Encouraged, I nipped along the flared edge of the head. His cock throbbed, and he moaned low in his throat.

I lathed the leather with my tongue, soaking it, scraping and gnawing with my teeth to sculpt it around his magnificent cock. His thighs trembled. I clamped my mouth over the tip in anticipation, digging my teeth in as deeply as possible. Another pulse, and a third.

Rafael yanked me backward by the hair. Abruptly bereft of his heat, I landed on my ass with a thump as he curled in on himself.

"Dragon, are you well?" I scrambled upright, rubbing my tender scalp.

Folded in half, arms wrapped around his knees, he panted hard. The burning curtain of his hair obscured his face. "Yes." A note so deep it might have come from the heart of Vaeda itself.

"Show me your eyes." My belly clenched. Gods, not again. Was this reaction simply unavoidable?

He raised his head enough to reveal a lucid, blistering gaze. His breath hitched with the effort to still himself. Smoke curled from his nose and mouth. So close, and he had not panicked!

I released my own shuddering breath. "Did you enjoy that?"

"I did." He reached to trace my lips with his thumb. "But you will have blood on your hands this night."

"What—"

He stood, discreetly arranging his clothes, and stared down at me. A corona of heat distorted the air around him. A god of carnage or lust? With a wicked grin and a scarlet blossoming of scales, he shifted into his quadrupedal drake form. Darkness swallowed him as he loped away.

"Rafael," I called, to no answer. The bond told me he moved north at a rapid pace. *'Are you certain you're well?'*

'I am, but you have stoked an inferno within me. At present, I can only answer it with death.' His mind churned with violence.

I pulled back. *'Who are you going to kill? And what am I to do with your armor and sword?'*

'Have no fear,' he replied with evil humor. A roar shook loose the more precarious boulders around me, sending them tumbling down the hill.

I RARELY encountered Celebel during his waking hours, engrossed as he was in overall planning and strategy meetings with Feanim and various captains. Thus, when I came upon him drowsing on his back in our tent, I pounced. Not quite the grand tents and comfortable beds I'd enjoyed during our approach to Férioth, but far better than the exposed flight to Amrún.

Celebel slept in his usual undignified, open-mouthed sprawl. Absurdly endearing, and yet another perfect contrast to Rafael's tense, frequently interrupted snatches of rest with his back firmly against a wall. I drew that connection down to a tightly controlled trickle.

Startled awake by my kisses and caresses, Celebel sat up, rubbing his eyes. "Hello, what has you so worked up?"

His silky hair slipped out of its disarray, falling smoothly around his shoulders. I indulged in a moment of jealousy for his lack of tangles.

My hair was almost as straight, especially with the weight of it, but unruly in its thickness.

"Might I make use of your body?" I tugged the blankets below his knees and straddled him, stroking his lovely cock to wakefulness.

"You needn't ask." He laughed and rubbed his eyes. "I have a strong feeling I already know what drives you, but please enlighten me."

"I had something of a breakthrough with Rafael just now." I nuzzled his growing erection, and he moaned.

Secrets be damned, since Rafael had thoroughly broken the truce. Celebel needed to know my Dragon was indeed capable of growth. My Starshine panted as I licked the tip of his cock, sliding my hands over his firm belly.

"Not one person apart from me thanked Rafael for saving the healers from that umbrawolf, drake customs be damned."

Celebel's unfocused gaze said I was losing his interest. I slowed, kissing his belly. He heaved a sigh and tangled his hands in my hair. After Rafael's previous grip, my braids were hopeless.

My lips hovered over his shaft. "I offered to suck his cock in gratitude."

That snared Celebel's attention. "A most excellent display of gratitude. How did he react?"

"He somewhat allowed it! Through two damn layers of leather and that awful wool shirt he prefers. But the touch is the important part." I wrapped my lips around Celebel's cock and sucked, savoring the silky skin.

He sighed, caressing my ears. "Given that you are here working my cock now, I suppose it did not end the way you preferred?"

"Better than I expected." I withdrew my lips to stroke his shaft with my hands. "He did abruptly stop me, claiming he needed to kill something and the blood would be on my hands."

Celebel grimaced. "How charming. Shall I ask you to kiss my cock in same the way you did for him?"

I grinned up at Celebel, teasing the tip with the barest pressure from my jaws. "Not unless you're fond of teeth."

He blew out a breath, ears twitching. "Just when I think that great beast cannot possibly be any more perverse…"

"You wanted to know of progress. This is progress, and it will likely affect Rafael's behavior toward you."

"I would say, 'tell him I'm grateful'—ahh!"

I'd slipped a finger, slick with my arousal, into his ass as I returned to sucking. Forcing his full length down my throat until tears streamed from my eyes, his breath came faster and faster. I caressed his bollocks and his cock throbbed mightily. He cried out as he climaxed, spilling himself into my mouth. I reveled in the salty-sweet taste of him, drinking him down with greed. As he slumped back in the bed, trying to catch his breath, I took my time licking him clean.

"Shall I work on you now?" he offered blearily.

"I have precisely what I desired, thank you."

Chapter 49

IN my ignorance, I had assumed these battles would be like the others I'd witnessed; long amounts of time spent in preparation, culminating in one major clash that ended relatively quickly. Instead, when we finally met the enemy in the field, our soldiers were embroiled for days on end.

Winter storms pummeled the ground into freezing slush, adding a further veneer of discomfort to an already exhausting slog. Keeping the healers' tents clean of blood and gore was difficult enough without the added annoyance of sticky grey mud on every surface.

The healers worked and rested in shifts. I encountered neither soulmate, but my connections to both remained strong. I relied on that comfort as the trickle of patients burst into a rushing river.

The flood brought a log jam of crush injuries. Liriadis proved adept at managing the worst of these, and so I left them to her unless she requested my help. Tracking down every tiny bone shard was tedious work, demanding steadfast attention to detail.

My skills were better suited to address the next wave of unexpected trauma. A young Siltaur woman, one of Carafindrien's cadre of drake appreciators, stumbled, gibbering, into the tent on the arm of a lanky, sober-faced Lachanaur companion. I helped settle the woman onto a cot, where she thrashed and twitched uncontrollably.

"When we parted, she was lucid," the Lachanaur said. "We each closed with a traitor elf, then Fomorians drove us apart, and when we met again, she babbled nonsense."

I'd already yanked off her surcoat. "Help me get her out of this maille, I need to examine her. What is her name?"

"Laseryn. This is her first battle."

Þey heaved the smaller elf forward so I could shimmy the maille shirt over her head. The padding beneath was torn and dark over her lower left abdomen. I cut the laces and her companion pulled it away, revealing a shallow gut wound. It leaked tainted spirit with all the hallmarks of the cursed spearhead I'd removed from Rafael's side.

I snatched my hands away. "Do not touch any item stained with her blood. This is fell work, but I can treat it." Hopefully.

Her companion nodded, auburn locks falling over worried eyes. I shooed þem away with promises of updates and turned back to Laseryn. Sweat plastered her chestnut hair to her golden-brown forehead, and her green eyes rolled wildly.

"Laseryn, can you hear me?" Donning gloves, I dabbed carefully at the wound.

She mewled in response, blinking rapidly. The wound itself was a clean slash through the abdominal wall—fortunately too shallow to perforate the bowels—and only took a few moments to close. Unlike my experience with the Dragon, the sense of corruption only grew as the physical injury healed. I clamped down on my connection to him.

Offering a prayer to the Night Mother that Rafael wouldn't choose this very moment to barge into the tent, I swung my leg over the writhing elf's waist. My spirit probe found a pulse of acceptance.

"I must dive deep to save you," I whispered, and kissed her soft lips, parting them with my tongue.

She bucked mightily under me and nearly bit my tongue off. Blood pooled in my mouth. I exhaled hard, forcing the breath into her lungs, and drew heavily on my power to tamp down her instinctive defenses. The rhythm caught, and her heart settled with mine as we shared breath.

I delved into her mindscape. Into a forest fire burning out of control. Black plumes of noxious smoke choked me. Heat seared my skin. Trees fell, streaming fire. The flames roared, and I turned in a circle, straining my ears to locate my patient.

A child's thin cries came from deep inside the conflagration. Fuck. As I was, I'd never breach that wall of fire—symbolic or otherwise.

I visualized clouds and reached upward, snaring them to make calming rain. Only producing a trickle at first, I fed the thickening nimbus with my spirit. Not enough to strip me of protection, but not so little as to be ineffective. Finally, the growing storm burst. The ensuing deluge of peace doused the flames with a ferocious hiss.

Following the child's weeping, I picked my way over the smouldering ground, dampening the heat as I passed. The charcoal thicket grasped at my hair and raked ashen, painless lines on my skin. Burned out trees creaked ominously, and the occasional bough dropped with an echoing crash. Acrid ribbons of smoke stung my nose.

Laseryn hid under a bramble in the center of the ruined forest. A woman grown, she wailed with the voice of her younger self. She was unburned. I gathered her carefully into my arms, singing of the green beauty of my hill and mighty tree. Giving her hope to overcome the twisted spirit eating away at her sense of self. Ever so slowly, her eyes cleared and her voice matured.

I released her, withdrawing back into my body. She awakened, squeaking in surprise at the healing kiss we shared. I extracted myself from the embrace and climbed off her.

"Laseryn, please forgive me for the intrusive nature of this healing." I genuflected, lowering my eyes. "It was the swiftest and surest way to restore your mind."

My patient's throat worked as she found the words. "I-I...you are... My lady Cúraniel, I...please, my thanks," she finished weakly. A furious blush crept up her neck, tinging her ears scarlet. "I, ah, I have heard the Red Dragon is quite jealous..."

I waved away her concern. "Let me worry about him. Now, you need rest. Your companion was understandably distressed over your condition."

"Oh, Dostael! Are þey injured too?" She struggled to rise.

"Þey are unharmed. Rest now." I pressed a thumb to her forehead, guiding her into a restorative slumber.

Three more patients presented with the inflicted madness. Three more instances of a healing kiss and a taxing dive into a beleaguered mind. Exhaustion dulled my focus, slowed my hands. The day galloped past in a haze.

As twilight darkened the tent walls, the final madness patient was a burly Astolar. His eyes had rolled back, face and body frozen in a posture of horror. His hands hooked into claws. Thin, helpless noises whistled from his throat.

The initiating wound in his lower back had already been tended. He appeared to be in perfect physical shape otherwise. I climbed over him, sending my probe deep, asking for his acceptance.

Unresponsive. Gods, was he too far gone? No, there! A faint affirmative fluttered within. I pressed my lips to his, timing my breathing, matching his heartbeat…and couldn't sink past the surface. Crow, not again.

Pulling back the sheet covering his body, I shrugged out of my clothing. I laid atop him, skin-to-skin, and tried again. This time, when I matched his breath and heartbeat, I dove into his mind.

It was a slog, pushing through the cold, sucking mud of his subconscious. I found him paralyzed in the middle of a swampy morass. They were always in the middle. Hauling him bodily out of the muck was as exhausting as if it were physical labor. After an age of dragging him along, my feet found solid ground. I lugged us both to safety.

Holding him tightly, I willed my warmth into him, unfreezing his locked limbs and torqued muscle. Little by little, he softened, until finally he lay in a limp heap in my lap. Pulling from the mindscape, I warmed him until he smiled and extricated myself.

As I returned to my body, his hazel eyes snapped open. He seized me with surprising force, deepening the healing kiss. I allowed it, as the contact would help ground him. A stout cock pressed between my legs to bump against my vulva. He thrust, and I twisted my hips away.

I broke his grasp and climbed off the cot. If not for other considerations, I would have allowed him the comfort. As it was, I'd already risked too much.

"My lady, return to me." Bereft, his erection wilted. "I have never known such love—"

"Shh, it's merely an aftereffect. It'll wear off as you return to yourself." I pulled on my dress and wrinkled my nose at the smell.

Liriadis approached to direct me to the next patient. Thoughtless in my fatigue, I opened my connections once more.

Rafael launched a spike of rage straight through my brain, and I staggered.

'*What the* fuck *was that?*' he bellowed in my mind.

'*Calm yourself. Remember the cursed spearhead I pulled out of you?*' I held a hand to my temple to staunch the sudden headache. '*What you felt was my healing of patients stricken by that same madness. It seems the enemy is perfecting the method.*'

The soulbond hummed with tension as the Dragon approached like a growing hurricane. Liriadis observed me with open concern. My ears remained flattened, and I may have set jars down harder than necessary.

"My apologies. I'm managing an incoming drake tantrum," I said to her. '*Rafael! Absolutely do* not *terrify my patients.*'

'*You are MINE! I refuse to share your favor with any more of these fucking—*'

'*Rafael! Focus your ears, you stubborn, childish ass! I am not "sharing my favors", I'm saving people from inflicted madness. I derive no pleasure from this, I swear to you!*' Head in my hands, I doubled over and pelted him as hard as I could. '*Leave my fucking patients alone!*'

Liriadis laid both hands on my shoulders. "Are you sure you're well?"

I waved her away. I would not have the Siltaur healer make herself a target. Her brows drew together, but she returned to her work.

My head throbbed in time with my pulse. With no time to brew a tea, I shoved bites of lovage, angelica root, and mint leaves in my mouth, chewing frantically and hoping for the best. The bitterness sharpened my focus.

Shrugging a coat on over my blood-stained dress with trembling arms, I stepped outside as an ear-splitting roar ripped through the tent. Crow!

True to his sense of drama, Rafael dropped out of the star-strewn night. Landing directly before me with an impact that shook the nearby trees, mud spattered my clean coat. He roared again. The percussive force knocked me to the ground. I rolled on my side, clutching my ears at the stabbing pain. My hands came away speckled with red.

As the shockwave hit, screams pierced the air. Bottles of ointments and salves rattled off shelves, smashing and spilling precious ingredients. Loose powdered herbs whipped through the tent in a colorful hurricane. Cots and partitions fell.

Through the fuzzy ringing and throbbing ache, I perceived stumbling movement behind me. Panicked voices rose on all sides and I winced. How many burst eardrums would I need to mend?

"FUCK THIS," Rafael bellowed. "I WILL NOT ALLOW—"

"Fuck *you!*" I had no concept of my volume, but it tasted like a yell. Righteous fury lifted me unsteadily to my feet. "You will not harm my patients!" The world swayed.

His lips peeled back into that horrid grin, grey smoke billowing from his nose and mouth. "I will burn this entire camp to ash before I allow these ratfuckers to *defile* you." Violent crimson bled into his eyes.

I rubbed my pounding temples. A shame I couldn't summon a dampening field, if only for the benefit of the others. My hearing was mostly intact, though blurred as if someone had burnished the edges off the sounds.

Rafael loomed over me, snarling. Flickering light from the tent painted his face into a hellish mask. "How far do you truly think you can push me before I push back?"

"Then what will you do? Strike me?" Too tired to deal rationally with his possessive fury, I simply stuck my jaw out to make it easier for him. "You came here to vent your rage on my innocent patients, so let me focus your ears for you. Any blow struck to one of them is a direct blow to me. Go on then. Have at me."

He took a step back, wrath warring with shock on his face. I braced myself at the audible crack of his knuckles. Like the crack of an umbrawolf's skull.

"Why do you insist on testing me?" Rafael's shoulders tightened.

"Why do *you* insist this has anything to do with you?" I glared up at him. "This is the same healing method I've employed for thousands of years. It is by far the most effective for mending spirit wounds. Love and desire have nothing to do with it. You will *never* intimidate me out of saving a life, so either beat me bloody now and get it over with, or cease your growling."

The fight went out of him, and his shoulders slumped. "I swore I would never hurt you."

"You hurt me all the time, Rafael. You just don't use your hands to inflict it. Your jealousy hurts me. The way you lash out in rage hurts me. It hurts that you're pulling me away from patients and terrifying everyone. I'm exhausted, I have too much work still, and I've no desire to be ensnared in this argument *yet again*. So, do as you will, then leave me in peace."

"Never have I felt jealousy before meeting you." He cupped my face with both hands, talons caging my vision.

I flinched away. "You've always taken whatever you desired by force. Now, as you cannot force me to acquiesce while retaining my love, you don't know how to react. Is it possible the elves I healed today will develop feelings for me? Yes, it's common. I'm old, I'm beautiful, and healing creates an intimate bond." I held up a hand as his eyes narrowed. "It matters not, because those feelings will be unrequited. Do you understand?" I swayed on my feet but stayed upright. "Or do I need your permission every time I need to shit, in the event some innocent bystander might find me too sexy to resist?"

Rafael stared me down. I inhaled, pressing my bare toes into the freezing mud, and drew from the ground to replenish my fading strength.

"And if you find yet another soulmate?" he finally asked. "Am I required to tolerate that as well?"

"If I find another soulmate, I'll throw myself off a cliff." The very thought overwhelmed me. All I wanted was a nap.

"That is not amusing, Cúraniel." He tilted his head back and sighed as if beseeching the heavens. "You will be the end of me."

"I tried very hard to be the opposite of that, if you will recall," I huffed.

"Sheathe your tongue, woman."

"You first, Dragon." I strained to keep from sinking to my knees as we exchanged glares. "Shouldn't you be off bashing in Fomorian faces? Meanwhile, I'll warn you before I use that type of healing again.

And I *shall* continue, no matter how many temper tantrums you throw. You know how I feel about these threats."

Rafael hissed through his teeth, smoke wreathing us. At my back, all motion had ceased. The other elves' terror was palpable.

"Fuck off, Rafael. Fuck off or kill me. Those are your options." Hopefully, I sounded more confident than I felt. My heart pounded in my aching ears.

He shook his head slowly from side to side, clicking his teeth. The air wavered around him. Grass scorched and died where he stepped. The Dragon crouched, and I braced myself. But he leaped into the air, sprouting wings and scales, instead of attacking. He grew to his full-size dragon form, casting a false midnight across the camp.

I didn't realize I was shaking until Liriadis laid steadying hands on my shoulders. She healed my ears without a word.

I STOOD naked on the cliff edge of my hill. A chill breeze prickled my skin, and the Night Mother's twinkling robes blanketed the sky. In the valley below, a line of wretched people stretched as far as the eye could see. Elves, humans, even the occasional drake. Some screamed and wailed, tearing at their hair and clothing. Others shuddered in nonsensical dances. The most chilling stared at nothing, necks bent at odd angles. As I stepped forward to better see the awful tableau, they turned as one.

Myriad shining mad eyes speared me. The line surged forward. Climbing over each other, they scrabbled up the steep incline like ants. Faster than logic allowed, the grasping wave reached for me. I stumbled as I backed away, falling to the grass, and they were on me in an instant, crashing down in a tidal wave.

Surely, they would tear me apart! No, worse. A million hands sought my flesh, a million mouths kissed me, a million bodies grinding into mine. Screaming, I sought the Night Mother, crying out for her aid.

"This comes for you." Her bottomless eyes opened, and I fell into them, eager to escape. "Are you strong enough?"

"No! No, Mother! I do not have the strength!" I pulled my knees to my chest, floating in the abyss.

She swept her robe across the land, and every last wretch dissolved into mist.

I woke to Liriadis calling my name. Had I slept through the entire night? Tears pooled in the hollows of my ears and throat. I wiped them away quickly, hoping no one had noticed.

'There you are, finally! Are you well?' Celebel's worry tickled my mind.

'Not entirely.' I needed to push the confrontation with Rafael and the vision out of my mind to remain functional. *'I will find you when I may.'*

Marron sauntered into the healers' tents, bringing dawn's first light with him. It was almost a relief to have the normal amount of startlement over a drake's presence. Even the most direly injured patients scrambled out of his way, to which he responded with amusement.

Liriadis waved him past the triage line toward me. Compared to the green drake's muscular bulk, my people were delicate as fresh icicles in the sun.

"I don't eat elves. Too sweet," he said helpfully. They scurried faster. His scarlet eyes shifted to me. "You still live, eh?"

I completed the traditional greeting with, "No one has killed me yet."

The burly drake approached holding his right arm with his left. He glanced at the empty cot and crouched on the ground instead. Stray locks of deep green hair escaped the leather tie at the nape of his neck.

A stark dip marked where the cap of his right deltoid would normally rest—a severe dislocation in that shoulder. The entire area had swollen to almost twice its usual size. His sleeveless leather gambeson was shredded and soaked with blood on that side. I expected to find a broken humerus below that bloated, mangled joint.

"Green Marron, what have you done to yourself?"

He grunted. "A giant's thrown hammer, of all things." His slit pupils were a deep garnet rather than black, complimenting the bright ruby irises. I'd never noticed before. "The hulking pile of rocks was aiming for the Red, but as he suddenly winged off the field, it struck me instead." *Gods damn it, Rafael!* "Now, I can't fit my arm back in the socket." Stone ground over stone in his already-gravelly voice; the only indication in his demeanor anything was amiss.

No wonder we'd had so many crush injuries. I wished no suffering on an ally, but I was privately grateful a drake had taken the hit instead of an elf. At least I had a patient left to heal.

"May I palpate?" I asked. "I must lay hands to determine the extent of your injuries."

His external wounds had already closed. Herbs would do no good here, but I'd witnessed him heal far worse on his own. Over the tang of blood, the usual dragon musk had an earthy note like a rain-dampened forest.

"Poke away." Marron tried to shrug and the injured shoulder hitched, eliciting nothing more than a frown. He caught the sympathetic expression on my face. "The pain is nothing, but make sure the Red understands I'm not here seeking favors, eh? He's not the only jealous creature I have to contend with."

"I'll allow you to remain clothed if you'll keep me free of your mate's talons." I gave a rueful laugh at his snort and prodded the edges of the dislocation.

Marron's hide was pleasantly warm, more than an elf's but not so feverishly hot as Rafael's. The forest green, leaf-shaped scales stretched wide over the rapidly swelling joint, showing paler green skin underneath. Impact had forced the head of the humerus anteriorly in the socket, damaging the surrounding bony processes along with a pectoral tear and strained rotator cuff muscles. The neck of the humerus had extensive fractures, as well as some fragments. That he still had the arm was miraculous.

"I'll knit the bones together before I put the joint to rights."

"Whatever you need to do." Marron made as if to shrug again and caught himself, lifting only the uninjured shoulder this time.

"Stop that! Be still."

His eyes widened, and he obeyed. I placed my hands on either side of the break and poured my spirit into him, a rushing river seeking the lowest points. Focusing on guiding the ragged bone edges together, I reconnected the blood supply. Once the humerus was whole enough, I worked on the bony processes around the joint itself and repaired a few hairline cracks and the cartilage and ligaments.

The green drake watched me intently. "Interesting. I can feel the fragments moving. Normally, it takes ages for my flesh to expel them."

I nodded, focusing harder, coaxing the bones into a strong enough seam to tolerate the jarring shock of relocation. Finally, I directed the excess of fluids surrounding it to circulate back through his body, taking down the swelling. When I moved to repair the muscular damage, it was already righting itself.

Marron snorted. "I feel a sudden urge to piss. Is that your doing?" At a nearby intake of breath, he turned his head. "Calm down, you delicate blossoms. I'll not relieve myself on the floor like some witless beast."

I laughed. "It's the fluid circulation from the swelling. Has to go somewhere." I'd forgotten how his easy humor cheered me. "Does that arm feel solid enough to withstand shoving it back into place?"

The green drake squeezed experimentally along the site of the break with his uninjured hand. He flexed his right forearm and then, cautiously, the repaired biceps; corded muscle stood out under his scaly hide. I wondered, not for the first time, how his physical strength compared to Rafael's. Far more than raw muscle went into their hierarchy, but it played a significant role.

"Seems solid."

I trusted his judgement. "Because of your size, I'll have to bear hug your arm to put it back in place. It will be awkward, so consider this your warning."

He rasped a laugh. "Go on, then."

I wrapped both of my arms around his injured one, bracing it against my sternum, and heaved toward the joint as hard as I could. It moved in the right direction, but not enough.

"You lack the weight to throw behind it, eh? Here, you guide, I'll push." Marron gripped his injured arm below the elbow.

"Steady on, now push!"

Working together, his arm popped neatly back into the socket. Releasing the limb, I stepped back. He prodded the joint, experimentally lifting and rotating the arm.

"You work quickly." The green drake bobbed his head. Close enough to giving thanks.

"I wish all my patients were as easy as you." Gods, if only.

Marron chuckled. Rising to his feet, his head nearly grazed the top of the tent. I followed him under the stares of everyone around us. He paused at the entrance. With a knowing smirk, he made an exaggerated bow.

"Rest that shoulder for a day. Don't make me have to set it again." I tried and failed to imagine the challenges he must manage. No wonder he chose to remain calm.

His ruby gaze sobered. In draconian, he said, "When mates argue, each bites down on the other's shoulder." He tapped his previously injured trapezius. "We wrestle until one breaks the hold, then we fuck. Not for you, this method." His scaly brows drew together. "Beware his jaws, Moon Lady."

Was that an offer of support? Marron waved with his uninjured arm as if he'd said nothing out of the ordinary. I stared at his broad back as he departed into the brightening day.

Liriadis appeared at my elbow, wiping her hands on a rag. "I need a full report." She also watched the green drake disappear through the camp. "I assumed he'd be more trouble. Can they not heal themselves by shapeshifting?"

"Marron's remarkably even-tempered." A method not for me, indeed. "As I understand it, shifting might worsen injuries involving joints or bones, but it mends some types of soft tissue damage. Most of my knowledge is limited to what Rafael has told me."

She assessed me, nodding. "Yes…singing that tune, you must have a discussion with your big, scary red beast. I won't have him terrorizing anyone else, and I've healed more ears than yours today."

"I've had many such discussions." I rubbed my temples.

"Cúraniel, I don't have to tell you he's a violent man. I won't instruct you in your own song, but you know this will only worsen over time, yes?" Kindness glimmered in her bright hazel eyes. And pity.

The Night Mother's words flashed in my mind. "I know."

Chapter 50

EANIM waylaid me on my path to have that discussion with reached Rafael.

"I need you, come." His imperious tone put my ears back.

The annoying creature turned on a heel, clearly expecting me to follow. He led me through the camp to a relatively private clearing opposite Rafael's location. As usual, he'd spread maps and charts out over every available surface. I stepped around stacks of papers to sit on a mossy boulder.

"Would you like some wine?" Feanim proffered a bottle he'd dug out of a trunk.

"Whiskey would be more welcome. Why are you solicitous now?" Much as my legs ached with fatigue, I readied myself to leave at the first sign of contention.

He shrugged and poured himself a glass, admiring the amber liquid's glow in the morning light. Of course he used gold-stemmed wine glasses of such fine workmanship they had to be of Duedellen make.

"I've heard your latest issues with Rafael. The entire camp heard. Damned strong lungs, that one has."

"And you've brought me here for mockery?" I crossed my arms, bracing for the inevitably offensive impact.

"Will you calm yourself? I'm trying to help. No, I swear it!" He raised a hand to forestall my immediate protest. "We both know where this melody ends. The madness attacks are growing both in scope and breadth, and any of us might be stricken. Currently, you're the only one capable of treating the affliction. Can you teach your ability to others? We need a contingency plan in the event you are incapacitated."

"I've barely had a chance to breathe, let alone teach, but yes, I'm able to train others in my methods. It's a matter of how many have the capacity and willingness to learn, but that's a song for the future." I'd last attempted to teach my skill at Leyûduin. Many grasped the theory, but few had proven willing to risk their bodies and none their sanity.

Feanim took a long sip of wine. "I've spoken to Rafael this morning, at length, about his outburst. Don't pin your ears like that. I let him cool down first; I'm not suicidal."

I shifted the piles of papers and journals out of my way, pulled off my boots, and dug my toes into the cold dirt. "I would like that wine, after all."

Feanim smirked his infuriating smirk and poured me a generous glass. I accepted it with a 'continue' gesture and took a deep draught.

"For all his age and the legends surrounding him, Rafael is remarkably naïve about relationships."

I nodded. "He is. Every change is a new challenge. At least he hasn't attacked anyone over this current conflict. Yet."

"Indeed. I've attempted to explain to him what I went through. How I recovered and found Nimthil, all that. It's been a slow process, breaching his walls."

A sharp laugh escaped me. "You have no idea."

He frowned at the interruption. "As I was saying, I've spoken to him here and there about these matters. He mostly ignores me, but he was so overwrought this morning I think I finally reached him. He gets absurdly twisted up about you. I've never encountered anything like it."

"And you told him what? I'm not worthy?" Far too easy to imagine.

"Your words, not mine. No, focus your fucking ears. I told him I've never met any two people so mutually obsessed with each other. It's almost disgustingly cute."

"Obsessed, eh?" I refused to give him the satisfaction of acknowledgement.

He grinned. "You've made your connection to him the bass line of your personality, and you haven't known him a century. Yes, *obsessed*. I note the way you study him whenever he's near. You're pulled to him like you've been summoned. He does the same with you; tracking your every movement." He mimicked staring around the clearing. "Poor Cel went and got caught in the middle. He's never done well with truly headstrong personalities, but you two lunatics are an entirely new melody. That's a conversation for another time, however."

"Celebel can handle his own affairs, thank you."

Feanim raised his glass at that. "I recognize there is a strong possibility I may be stricken with the madness, eventually. If you're the only one capable of healing me, I don't want your mad fucking drake lover to pull my head off for it."

Ah, there it was. "So, this is all self-serving."

He gave me a sideways look. "Who else should it be serving? An ancient fucking dragon who throws jealous fits like an adolescent? Yes, it's self-serving. Rafael seemed to at least listen, though he's not precisely accepting of my words. I pointed out how many lovesick little youths follow you around like a shadow, yet you never swivel an ear to them—though your expression says you're oblivious to it. He should take it as a compliment rather than a threat, as you're actively choosing him."

Lovesick youths? Had he mistaken Xyxs' admirers for mine?

Feanim waved the topic away. "Your position is precarious. You're not officially Rafael's mate, so you have no power over the drakes, and you're not married to Celebel, so you have no standing with the elves without your lineage behind you." Eerily similar to my statements to Marron. I frowned, but Feanim blithely ignored my reaction. "You're actively choosing to be ostracized because of Rafael. And his issues with sex? You're far more patient than I could ever be."

So very many arguments with the Dragon about jealousy and trust, and so little overall progress. Perhaps hearing the same concepts from someone not directly involved would have an impact.

I sighed. "I never intended to make Rafael jealous. Celebel was a complete surprise. I saw him in my visions, but I never expected these events to happen the way they did. After I'd already met and bonded with Rafael, I thought perhaps it would be a different connection entirely. I regret causing either of them pain, but especially my Dragon. He's had so little comfort in his life. But I cannot allow my people to suffer when I have the power to alleviate it. It's difficult to convince him this isn't born of sexual desire."

Feanim nodded thoughtfully. "He would not allow me to explain the nuances of elvish sexuality."

"I can imagine."

"You truly fucking love Rafael, eh?" His shoulders shook with silent mirth. "I told him only an utterly smitten lover would tolerate his gods damned impossible ways."

I laughed. "I do truly fucking love him."

"You know he'll probably kill you one day. This conflict with Cel will explode when the war ends. Raf's been unhappy about coming to heel, but at least he can murder to his heart's content in battle. What will happen when he no longer has a clear enemy to attack?" Feanim's eyes stabbed into me, green glass shards.

I turned perpendicular to him, giving his stare a smaller target. "Rafael claims I'll be the death of him instead."

"Can he die? Mayhap he'll grow tired of it all and transform into a mountain range like his father." The Duedellen examined his glass and refilled it.

I accepted a refill as well. The wine was quite good, but the thought of Rafael becoming one with the bedrock soured the vintage on my tongue.

Feanim crossed his legs, one boot bouncing. "An unpredictable asset has no value in battle. If Rafael disappears from the field on a whim, as he did yesterday, it renders all my strategies useless. We took casualties because of him. If Marron's mate—was her name Vaerra?— hadn't felled a stone giant by herself, we would have lost."

"Fucking hells. Rafael complains of my methods while sending me more patients." Where did it end? "You must have smoothed his scales after your own confrontation. I wasn't sure if he'd ever speak to you again."

Feanim sighed heavily, setting down his wineglass. "Nim had some stipulations for getting married, thus I've attempted to right some perceived wrongs. She cares not what Raf thinks so long as he isn't actively trying to kill me. But I thought it best to start with him, since his actions affect everyone." Surely, the Duedellen didn't dare call him "Raf" within his earshot.

"Thank you. Your sexual proposition highly unsettled him. You're exceedingly lucky he reacted as he did." Were we becoming friends? Surely not.

"In retrospect, I never should have grown so complacent. You'll have to break him in before I try again." His eyes glittered wickedly.

I only shook my head.

Feanim swirled his glass, peering over the rim. "He turned me down flat when I apologized, though I made no other offer. He also threatened to take my eyes and ears if I ever propositioned him again. It's as though he experiences no sexual attraction outside of this intense fixation on you."

"Because he's not attracted to you?" I couldn't resist the jab, but at least Rafael had taken my advice and established some clear boundaries.

Feanim snorted. "You recall his reaction to Carafindrien. Similar body type to you. He ought to recognize that much. She's one of the most beautiful elves alive."

"She is, and certainly did nothing to deserve being thrust into danger. Not everyone has the same fetish for redheads as you." I'd almost forgotten that malicious act. My mood darkened. Feanim so casually put others at risk.

"True. I should have picked a Talithiri woman." His ears twitched as he examined my face for a reaction. "Perhaps Silfanië—"

"I'm in no mood for your goading." Setting the goblet down so I wouldn't throw it at him, I congratulated myself on my newfound self-control.

I hoped my sister had slapped his smug face at least once before she defected. With a pang, I also hoped she still lived. Severing the lineage also meant losing my connection to her, a choice I'd never regretted until the moment I'd found the talisman earring she'd deliberately left behind.

I turned my thoughts away from my silver sister. "If Rafael hadn't been so horrifically abused, who knows what might have been. Drakes are simply different in their sexual expression. Few take more than one mate throughout their lives. They also mate for power, and he refuses to let any of them have power over him."

"Yet he offers it freely to you." Feanim's mossy eyes held a bright edge.

"Rafael is a constant 'thorn in the nest', as his people say, but he loves me." I looked down at the beautiful wineglass now cradled in my lap. "Despite everything, we don't grant him enough acknowledgement for strictly adhering to his word. With all the shows of temper he's had since his arrival, he hasn't killed a single elf who didn't attack or betray him first. In that way, he's more trustworthy than our own."

Feanim's ear flicked. "Hmph, true enough. Do you realize your ability to bind the fucking Red Dragon to a simple promise probably makes you the single most powerful person in this world?"

NEMOHEE ALSO intervened on my way to Rafael. Despite the blood-steaked armor, þey were remarkably whole. The round buckler þey carried, now slung over one shoulder beside þeir helm, boasted new chips in its edge. That offhand resting on the pommel of þeir sword belied þeir casual posture.

"Have you finally made it through an entire fight without taking a bash to the head?" I teased.

Nemohee's answering grin was brief. A somber expression fell over þeir face like a curtain. "I ken where you're headed, and I'm wanting ye to ken we're all worried. I like Red well enough and all, but that bloody temper of his is getting worse. Unacceptably worse." Þeir short ears twitched.

"I can handle him. And this is far from his worst. He's only louder and more public about it than usual."

"You're not telling me he speaks to ye like that all the time?" Nemohee snorted in disgust, ears flattening. "I can't accept that, Cúraniel. Nor can Celebel. Worry sets his ears."

I kept walking. "Celebel has more reason to worry than most, but we're attempting to rewrite that verse."

Nemohee blocked my way, gripping my shoulders. Might as

well have been Rafael himself pinning me for all my struggling protests accomplished. I hadn't the energy to fight another battle.

"Nem, come now."

"No. Not a soul in this world roars and rages like that what doesn't eventually lay hands. I can't do a damned thing against his might 'cept spit in his eye if it comes down to it. But I'm wanting ye to ken I'm happy to have a go."

The earnesty on þeir face struck me to the core. "Nem, I appreciate the urge to protect me, but it's unnecessary. Rafael doesn't want to hurt me. It's only his inexperience with these types of emotions. I'm trying to help him understand, but it's fraught."

"I ken ye love him, but 'tis closing yer ears to his faults. No one should treat a lover in that way. 'Tis not loving. Fecking abusive, is what." Þey stuck out a stubborn jaw. "Should I go on and tell him off myself?"

"Don't you dare go yelling in his face. He likes you, but you know full well he'll strike you down. Please do not force me into that position." I chewed on my lower lip, smoothing my dirty shift. "If it improves your mood, Feanim spoke to him already."

"It does not." Nemohee's pointed nose wrinkled. Þey didn't budge, squaring þeir shoulders and digging þeir fingers more thoroughly into mine.

"Come now, Nem. I must try to resolve this."

"If ye can't convince him to stop fecking yelling at you, I'll do it. Or die trying." Silver eyes flashed. Pointed teeth bared.

Night Mother, grant me an end to the dramatics. "No one's allowed to fucking die on my account. Now kindly release me."

Nemohee finally stepped aside with a loud huff, gripping the hilt of þeir blade with a meaningful look. "I will be in earshot."

"We'll use a dampening field, rock head. I'm done with having the entire camp know my personal strife."

"Mmhmm." Þey trotted along behind me anyway, puffing out þeir chest to look as threatening as any elf could compared to a gods damned dragon.

Chapter 81

NEAR a path overlooking the gorge, Rafael sat writing in a journal with his back against a gnarled fir. His hair and eyes burned. Bright midday sun cast a harsh shadow beneath him, though it did nothing to warm the stony ground under my feet. I sighed in gratitude that he wasn't clad in that loathsome armor; I'd almost expected to find him perched atop a pile of bodies. The dampening field buzzed as I approached.

"Tell Nemohee to fuck off," he said without looking up.

I backed out of the dampening field. "Nem?" I called over my shoulder, keeping my ears and eyes on the Dragon. "Rafael wants you to keep your distance."

Nemohee spat some choice epithets in Rafael's direction, but þey moved away, deliberately stomping. Þey wouldn't go far, but it should be enough to appease him.

The dampening field tickled my skin as I approached again. "There, þey've gone."

Rafael continued to scratch notes with his quill. I settled beside him, taking care to stay out of his reach should his temper flare. No need to prove Nemohee right with my foolhardiness. Despite the tension, I still couldn't bring myself to fear him.

Silence grated on my already raw soul. "Will you look at me?"

The quill tip paused, hovering over the page, but the tight line of his mouth didn't waver.

"Rafael, please."

He snapped the journal shut. With an exaggerated show of setting it down, Rafael glared down his long nose at me. He knew very well how I hated that imperious sneer.

"Feanim said he spoke to you," I ventured.

The Dragon exhaled slowly. "He believes I am unreasonable."

"He's not alone." I clapped my mouth shut too late to stop the words from spilling out.

Rafael's sneer deepened. He stood as if the ground's pull had no effect on him. I followed. He'd not intimidate me with his height for this conversation.

The Dragon paced in a tight circle. From the way his muscles twitched and rippled, he moved about mostly to give his pent-up rage an outlet. Nemohee's words pressed on my mind. Rafael was spoiling to hurt someone.

"Is it unreasonable to want my lover, my *soulmate*, to remain as loyal to me as I am to her?" His eyes sparked with challenge.

I barely avoided a groan. "Must we continually sing this same refrain? None of this is born of desire. I want no others taking liberties with my body, but I cannot leave them to suffer. I will not. Unfortunately, the physicality is intrinsic to the healing." My eyes welled with tears. Equal parts exhaustion and emotion. "Do you truly think so little of me?"

My reaction gave him pause, and I pressed the advantage. "The entire camp is enmeshed in our turmoil now, thanks to your roaring. Everyone is frightened witless. Why do you think Feanim spoke to you first? Nemohee offered to be a living shield because þey're convinced you'll kill me. Even Marron dropped in for healing on his shoulder. He surely could have managed by himself. Your behavior disturbs everyone except you, since yours is the only opinion that matters. You're so fucking powerful none can touch you. Might makes right, so continue your tyranny." I braided and re-braided my hair to give my anxious hands something to do other than wipe the furious tears from my cheeks.

"What would you have me do? Lie down and offer you my throat? Debase myself?" The dark growl wrapped me in his volcanic spirit.

I sagged against the spindly tree. "Seems you want my throat. Why did you claim you'd never ask me to change myself to be more acceptable to you?"

Rafael halted, eyes searing into me. I refused to meet his gaze. He wanted a fight, and I had no more will to grant it. Silence stretched between us, bowstring-taut, humming with tension.

Finally, he rumbled an exhale from deep in his chest. "Feanim claims you are obsessed with me." His voice held an odd note.

"Feanim is correct for once. I spend an outsized amount of time worrying over you. How you'll react at any moment. Who will be angry with me over something you did. How you'll next hurt me. All the troubles you create for Celebel and everyone else. The ever-present threat of your rage…" I tossed my hands up. "You don't want to be here. You've made that abundantly clear. I wish I could simply love you without complication. I wish I could truly heal you. I wish…" Tears choked me. I hugged my arms. "What will happen when this war is over? Will you force me to break my own heart? Rip my soul asunder?"

The heat of his sudden proximity startled me. Gone was that violent potential, revealing the familiar aura of my beloved.

"May I?" He opened his arms.

Too weakened to resist, I let him fold me into an embrace. Against my better judgment, I buried my face in his chest, allowing myself to find comfort in his warmth against the chill air. The urge to accept his offer to carry me back to my hill, to my Great Tree, and forget this cursed war, threatened to overcome my good sense.

"Why do you love me?" he murmured into my hair.

"At times, it's as clear as star song on a cold, new moon night. Others, I lose the melody. You make it unbelievably difficult, you know."

"I know." The rage had bled from his eyes, leaving a lingering melancholy in its wake.

My heart softened. No! No unearned forgiveness. "I will not back down, Dragon. Are you sure my love is worth enduring these ordeals to be here with me?"

He closed his eyes. "The only surety I have had since meeting you is my absolute truth: I do not wish to live without you."

"Then you should know, if you continue yelling at me about meaningless healing kisses with strangers, you'll lose me forever."

Rafael snorted. "You yell at me constantly."

Perhaps it was a cultural difference with how the drakes challenged each other. Perhaps he simply did not understand.

I took a deep breath to tamp down the irritation. "*I am not a* physical threat to you. You could kill me with the flick of a wrist. Slinging banter is not the same as bellowed threats of violence. Do you truly wish me to live in fear of you?"

"No." His voice dropped to a whisper. "I have lived in fear."

At the tremor in his hand, I took some small pity on him. "Then you do understand the difference. This type of healing will only grow in demand and become more taxing in the future. What will you do then? Imprison me?"

He cupped the back of my head with one hand, pressing my face into his chest again. "This...*relationship* has been the greatest challenge of my adult life."

"I'm in accord with you there. You are one great gods damned challenge." I rested for three of his triplicate heartbeats and wiggled against his hold until he released me enough to meet his eyes. "Don't you *ever* fucking yell at me like that again. Do you realize how gods damned loud you are when you're angry?" I poked his chest. "You're banned from the healers' tent, you bloody menace. If you need healing, I'll come to you. Your rage is not who you are, Dragon. Don't let it consume our relationship. There is no salvaging it if you do."

Rafael exhaled slowly, the rumbling breath rattling my ribs. He dropped his arms with a hardening expression. "It seems you wish to do whatever you desire without consequence."

Groaning, I sank to the ground. So close to hearing my melody, but his pride still closed his ears. "Fucking hells, Dragon. Have you listened to *anything* I've said? Your jealousy hurts because it means you don't trust me. You don't believe me when I say I love you." I wanted to curl up and sleep until the conflict blew over.

"Your actions do not support your words."

I slapped the ground. Better than slapping him, and less likely to break my hands. "What if I demanded you give up fighting in order to be my lover? That you had to take the healer's oath and completely abandon your old ways? Would you do it?"

His glare should have set me alight. A muscle in his jaw jumped as his teeth clicked together.

"Absurd, isn't it? I wouldn't ask you to change a fundamental part of yourself, but you're asking it of me. I am a healer. It's not merely what I do, it's who I am. Intimate contact is a minor aspect; I do not actively seek it."

"So you have claimed. Many times. What is your point?"

"My point is Feanim was right—*gods* I hate admitting that—you *are* unreasonable. You're asking me to change who I am for you. You're always in my head unless I force you out, so you *know* the truth of my words!" I matched his scowl, shivering in the wind.

Smoke curled around his lips as he exhaled through his teeth. "Shall I take my leave? Perhaps return in a century and discover who is left standing after this war of fools?" His voice was dangerously quiet. The words fell like stones on my heart.

"I wondered when you'd return to your signature move. Fleeing emotional turmoil instead of working through it. Like a fucking *coward*." The tips of my ears burned, the flush creeping across my face. Damn my pale skin, making it so obvious.

"You rely utterly on my might, yet do not blunt the edge of your tongue." The smoke lingered around him, tendrils curling like his hair, like a crown.

"Efficient sidestep of my question. If you cannot strong-arm me, you'll simply leave me here to die, is that it?" Anger alone kept me from slumping. "Is this truly about healing or is it your jealousy of Celebel?"

"I fantasize about torturing that thieving *hthrakkga*."

"Ah yes, he's a thief because I'm your property. You're acting foul for the sake of it. There is no heat in your breath, Dragon."

Punctuated only by his occasional rumble, the silence yet again strained between us. I refused to be the first to drop my eyes. Though he'd notice the slight quiver in my lower lip, I held my head up. I desperately missed the days when I wasn't so beholden to him, when he didn't tally every slight and favor in his eternal mental ledger of grudges. Was it worth all this strife to hear him freely admit his love for me?

Rafael watched my thoughts crawl across my face, keeping his a hard mask. "I feel Celebel there in your mind, connected as I am, though his presence is lesser." He forced the words through a heavy, growling chorus. "Hrrm…at least I know he cares for you. This healing shit is so casually done. As if offering your body to strangers matters not at all."

"Because it doesn't—"

"*It does to me*," he snarled. "This healing, this work you have done with me, is intimate beyond anything I have ever experienced. Yet, you cheerfully toss it at any weakling who begs pity."

There was the terrified child cowering under his matted robe of hair, weighed down with layer upon layer of trauma. The one I could never quite reach.

"I've never delved half as deep into anyone's mind as I have yours. Working with you *is* different, Dragon. I'm only pulling these patients home. I'm not touching any of their old trauma, nor am I putting myself at such risk as I do with you. You nearly *ate my soul*." I sucked in a breath, steeling myself. "Tell me, how is using my body to heal my patients any different from your use of your body to fight and kill?"

Rafael bared his teeth with a thunderous growl, the wind whipping his hair into a blazing halo.

"Save the intimidation unless you plan to strike me." If he raised his voice now, even a little, I would leave him forever. My soul trembled and my heart clenched like a fist, but I could no longer tolerating such behavior. How many times had I teetered on this brink? Nemohee was right. "I will not be forced to fear my own lover."

He saw the truth writ plain on my face, in the set of my ears, and relented. "I would never—"

"You fucking *liar!*" I shrieked, voice cracking higher. "How many times have you sworn you would never hurt me? Yet here you are, mauling my heart. Again!" I folded, covering my face in my hands with a shuddering sob. "I'd rather you be honest and punch a hole through my spine versus stabbing me straight through with your words over and over, claiming no harm done!"

A hiss of indrawn breath. Rafael fell to his knees. He grabbed me, dragging me into his lap as he pressed his face into my cleavage, arms clamped around my waist like a vise. I struggled feebly against him.

"Release me, Jax." The weariness rolled over me in a wave. My vision greyed at the edges.

He shook his head with another growl, his voice slightly muffled by my breasts. "Never!"

"If this is so impossibly difficult, why not kill me and be done with it?" The words flew from my lips before I could stop them. "Just as everyone assumes you will."

Rafael snarled in response, the force of it rattling my bones. "Do not *ever* fucking say that to me again."

"Or you'll abandon me to my fate? Do it then, if you're so inclined. I'll cower no more under your threats."

"For you, I have broken myself in ways I never thought possible. Granted you power I swore I would never allow. Yet here I am again, fallen at your feet. You own me as surely as if you have placed a collar about my neck."

His voice was so raw my arms wrapped around him without conscious thought, stroking his hair and teasing out the tangles in his curls. He sighed and burrowed his face further into my bosom.

"Oh, Dragon. I want no power over you, and I hate being at odds. But you must stop allowing your fears to dictate our relationship. There's no way out of this quandary unless you can accept all of me." I traced the pointed tips of his ears, hidden under that thick mane. "Including the physicality of healing. Including Celebel. I have no more strength for fighting. Threaten me again, and you will lose me forever. You say you don't want to live without me, but I can't live like this. I know you can be better. Please choose that path, because you're destroying us both."

He was silent for so long I thought he'd chosen to ignore me. In the distance, crows squabbled over battlefield remains. How fitting.

Finally, he said, in a ragged voice, "It hurts. I do not want their hands on you."

"I'm sorry for the pain I've caused you. For the pain I must continue to cause. I wish we had been able to discuss those patients beforehand, but it all happened too swiftly." I kissed the crown of his head. "I love you, and I hope you believe me."

"I have read many accounts of love and thought them all fanciful nonsense until the day you told me of *him*. Until you actually left." Rafael sighed like a mournful wind through an empty valley.

"Fate snares us no matter how we flee."

"Hrrm. All this time, rage has kept me alive, kept me…safe. Just as it destroys everything I touch." His arms tightened. "I know no other way."

I closed my eyes, sinking into the buzz of his resonant bass. Exhaustion weighed my arms, and my hands slowed their ministrations, settling on his shoulders. I rested my chin on the top of his head. Gods, I'd missed holding him like this. There was something sweetly vulnerable about the way he sought comfort in my bosom.

"And yet," he continued, "love is more destructive, even as it rebuilds me in ways I cannot anticipate. Ah, I would knock the sun from the sky for you, but mastering myself is another matter. You are patient, my dove." He pulled back to look at me with concern. "You are also shaking with fatigue."

So I was. "I am at the very end of my strength." It came out as a whisper.

Rafael sat up, gathering me tenderly to his chest. "Then take mine."

Chapter 82

RAFAEL released me with reluctance at dawn. He hadn't moved a hairsbreadth all throughout my slumber, as though I might shatter at a harsh breath. Gone was the destructive crimson rage in his eyes, replaced with melancholic blue. I admired his thick lashes, so dark red they appeared black in most light. His pupils constricted to knife slashes in the sun.

I dashed my teeth against his unrelenting mouth, and he opened to me. A kiss born more of a need for unity than sexual desire.

"I will always love you, no matter what may come. But that is no allowance for abusive behavior." I nipped at his lower lip. "Do not force me to leave you." Reaching up, I tugged his chin down to look at me. "You hold equally great power over me, you know."

Something flickered in his eyes, too fast to identify. His gaze pressed into my back as I departed.

At Celebel's mental prodding, I sent him every memory I had of the confrontation.

'*Not quite as horrid as the rumors, but far worse than it should have been,*' he sent, anger and fear humming along the connection. '*Are we to have these cyclical jealous outbursts until we all lay dead?*'

A highly annoyed Nemohee burst from the gnarled woods to swat me on the back of the head. "Fecking hells, Cúraniel. Ye could have at least told me ye were unhurt!"

"Ack, I'm unhurt, I'm unhurt! Glad you removed your gauntlets, crow. We argued in circles for a while and finally came to…some form of accord. I was so done in after, I simply fell asleep."

"Ye do grace a good bit better than before." Þey pinched my cheek in a parental fashion, and a whiff of whiskey stung my nose. "After all that noise, 'tis a miracle ye can let yer guard down enough to nap in his presence." Disapproval dripped from þeir words.

I sighed. "Rafael can be remarkably soothing when he's not a raging blighter. He loves me, but he twists himself up."

Nemohee eyed me, ears flattening. "That was a good bit more than twisted up."

"Fair." I sighed. "No excuses. It's simply all he's ever known. He's learning, but it is a fucking arduous climb."

Before I could ask if þey had any whiskey left, þey offered a flask with a knowing smirk.

I uncorked it and took a deep, grateful swig. "You aren't hiding coffee about your person too, are you?"

Nemohee barked a laugh. "C'mon then, let's put ye to rights."

Þey hooked an arm around my waist and half-supported, half-dragged me back to the main camp. Celebel emerged from the tent as we approached. He wore a loose white shirt, unlaced at the throat, and tucked into a long, pleated black skirt. Effortlessly elegant, even with his sleep-tousled hair.

He rushed to embrace me, and I clung to his neck.

"Gods, Cúraniel. I cannot bear any more of this." He kissed my ear tips.

"Nor can I," I whispered into his shoulder.

"Awright, ye'll need to take better care of this one," Nemohee bellowed, flattening Celebel's ears. "She's been off having an all-night shouting match with the Bloody Drake. Get her some coffee and food." My dear friend never had quite mastered volume control.

"No surprise there. It's always either fucking or fighting with those two. Fighting this time." Celebel ignored my glare. "I'm relieved to find you whole." He pulled three stools from the tent, along with a small tray table, and we settled ourselves.

"I feel like a moth-eaten tapestry left in the rain." A yawn punctuated my words.

Nemohee heated the water with deft Lachanaur fire summoning as Celebel ground the coffee beans. A powerfully wistful longing for my hill gripped me. Would I ever meet my neighboring villagers again?

"I'm staying for this chat." Nemohee planted þeir feet in a solid stance when Celebel cast a sidelong look in þeir direction. "Have a go and shift me if ye have a kinch with it."

"I wouldn't dream of chasing you away," he said mildly.

He handed over the ground coffee and Nemohee set about brewing.

"I'm not some overgrown child needing nursemaids," I grumbled, and they both glared.

"It's not your ability to care for yourself worrying your loved ones. It's that foul-tempered red shadow of yours." Celebel's lips twisted in a grimace. "Once again, he has harmed more than you and I. That battle was precarious, and he has much to answer for."

"Rafael didn't precisely make any promises, but I believe he heard my melody. I've never attempted to cure jealousy. None of my books mention how to do it." I rubbed my forehead, the ghost of another headache rising. "Nem, medicine up that coffee, would you?"

My friend dumped a healthy portion of whiskey into my cup and topped it off with coffee. Þey handed it over with a grin. I reveled in the scent of it and swallowed half the cup in one go. Celebel produced oat cakes from a parchment-wrapped package. I dipped one in my coffee and shoved it in my mouth.

"One would never know you were raised with courtly manners," Celebel said drolly, and Nemohee snorted. He sipped at his coffee and nibbled delicately on an oat cake, dark brows raised in irony.

"Fuck off, both of you. Rafael has tweaked my ears over the same."

My lover's expression grew serious. "I felt certain he wouldn't actually lay hands on you, but I can't say all the shouting is much of an improvement. How are your ears?"

I twitched them. "Healed by Liriadis, Night Mother bless her. Rafael ruptured my eardrums with all that bellowing, but I didn't tell him that. He would have focused on the injury instead of the actual problem."

Rafael, eavesdropping in my mind, recoiled at my words.

'Yes, you're a truly abusive blighter sometimes. We will speak later,' I sent.

Celebel frowned. "And he somehow missed this injury to you?"

Meekly, as if I was the one who'd committed the offending act, I said, "He...often loses himself in his rage."

"Fecking hells." Nemohee set þeir coffee mug down hard, sloshing liquid over the side. "That is in no way acceptable. I'll rain on his wildfire right now." Þey leaped to þeir feet. The brilliant sheen in those silver eyes showed off the leanan sidhe influence, as did the sharp canines on full display. "He's not the only one what can give a good bite!"

"Nem, please don't. I finally have him calmed, and I don't want to worry about you."

Nemohee glared at me and said, in deliberately enunciated, proper elvish, "Fuck that. Cúraniel, I love you, but if you think I'll allow that oversized lizard to get away with busting up my best mate's gods damned ears, you've gone and lost your bloody senses."

"What if he—"

"I. Do. Not. Care." Þey stomped off before I could say anything else, white-knuckling the hilt of þeir sword. Frost crackled under þeir boots.

"Dûemer, protect my foolhardy soul-sibling," I whispered.

Celebel wrapped me in a blanket and his arms. I hugged him gratefully.

'Nemohee is furious with you,' I sent to Rafael, hoping to outpace the problem.

'I am well aware.' Almost sedate. *'The little monster is already raging at me. Vaerra gave me a tongue-lashing this morning as well.'*

Vaerra had come to my defense? *'Don't you dare lay a hand on my friends!'*

'You would never grant me another day of peace if I did,' he retorted, his tone sharpening. *'The criticism is valid. I have...acted poorly.'*

Surprise perked my ears.

"Well, is he having a meal of rage-spiced Lachanaur?" Celebel's overly casual question brought my focus back.

"No. He actually seems to be listening." I clamped down on my mental defenses, in case Rafael took umbrage to anything Celebel had to say on the matter. I hadn't the energy to deal with another overwrought confrontation.

Celebel pretended to drop his mug in shock. "For all this time, all I had to do was draw back Nemohee and fire þem at his head? Gods, what wasted efforts."

I laughed and shoved him. "I'm as baffled as you are, but I appreciate the unexpected change. Marron's mate went after him as well, apparently."

He gestured in Nemohee's general direction. "How does someone that thoroughly unpleasant charm everyone around me? It certainly feels calculated."

"Are we starting this again? I thought you wanted him to cooperate." I leaned away from Celebel, tugging my blanket along with me.

Earnesty shone in those sky blue eyes. "Do you truly not perceive it? Or are you willfully closing your ears to what he's doing? Rafael befriended my closest comrade, despite all odds, and yours, and somehow these other drakes he frequently harms. It's as though he's built a parliament of favors to back him against any ill will from you. He's *toying* with our very lives. All of us could lie dead at the end of this, and he hasn't a fucking care so long as he gains from it."

I listened until he ran out of fervor. "If I accept your words as truth, what do you expect me to do?"

He dragged a hand furiously through his hair. "You've made it abundantly clear. Nothing Rafael does is unforgivable, so long as he never quite steps over the lines you've drawn. He certainly loves to scuff and redraw them farther and farther. There are no true consequences for his behavior, nothing that could keep him in check."

"There never have been, dear heart. No soul in this world can force him to do anything truly against his will."

"You might, if he genuinely believed he would lose you." Celebel's voice chilled.

"The last time he genuinely believed that, drakes died." I blew out a breath. "Rafael stood by us when our own court wouldn't. He saved our lives at Seregond, and again in the spider caves. He's won many battles in our name. I know he creates difficulties, but those actions must count for something."

"You defend him reflexively! Will you put your feelings aside for a moment longer and truly listen, please? Think of the effect Rafael's recent behavior has had on the entire elvish camp. Can we trust him to stand and fight when we need him? How many died due to his whims? How many patients will feel safe in your hands now?" Celebel was right, and I'd been ignoring that ugly reality. "Gods, his expression when you goaded him to strike you—Do you think he considered it?" The dark slashes of his brows pinched together.

"I'm sure he did. It's his usual method of conflict resolution. At least he's finally accepted you as a permanent fixture. It's new people interacting sexually with me that's upset him."

Celebel plucked a dead leaf from my hair. "Have you any idea how frustrating it is to witness his abhorrent treatment of you and have absolutely no power to stop it? I feel worse than useless." He busied his hands with cleaning up the coffee, wringing a cloth over and over an already-shiny pot.

"Though it may seem otherwise, I don't enjoy being so beholden." I bit my lip. "He threatened to abandon us to the war."

Celebel slammed the pot down and I winced, hoping it wasn't dented. "This is precisely what I mean. Your Dragon uses every opportunity to force all of us to dance to his wretched song."

"He was only blowing smoke. Quite literally. He backed down in the end, as he has with almost every other fight between us." I swirled the dregs of my coffee, wondering if I had the energy to pour myself another cup.

"How noble of him." He tugged a lobe.

"Celebel, please. I've had more than enough confrontation. I spent all of yesterday shouting down an angry drake!" Tears threatened again, sharp and fierce. "Did you close your ears to the verse where I threatened to leave him? I cannot truly express to you how much that hurts. I spent so many years longing for Rafael to conquer his pride and accept his feelings for me. Before I met you, he might visit me at most once a season, and usually for only a few days. Sometimes a single night.

"I wanted him so badly, our meager seven dozen years felt like the longest age in history. Now that I have him in no uncertain terms, the contention has been unending, wearing down my very soul." My heart fluttered in my chest, tattered as the rest of me. "Understanding why he reacts in such extreme ways makes it no easier to bear."

Celebel tossed the rag aside and took me into his arms. I pressed my face into his shoulder, listening to his breath, his steady heartbeat. He stroked my ears.

"My love, I am certainly in agreement. It's one thing for your Dragon to rage at me. It's another entirely for him to target you," he murmured into my hair. "I cannot imagine the wrath he would visit upon my person if I'd bellowed at you in the same manner."

"That's a compelling song." I yawned again, my body begging for more rest. A tremor of fatigue ran through me. "I need to return to the healers' tents." I attempted to rise, but Celebel trapped me firmly in his arms.

"You need rest. The circles under your eyes are deep enough to drown in." His nose wrinkled as he sniffed me. "And you need a bath."

Celebel led me into the tent. He combed the knots and debris out of my tangled blanket of hair as I scrubbed away the accumulated filth with spongy moss. Scrubbed away all the tears and anger until my skin pinked and the bucket of water turned dingy.

He sang as he worked, a sweet song of starlight, and braided strings of chiming bells into my hair. When he kissed my ears, I was sorely tempted to initiate more, but good sense won out over my frustrated libido for once.

I helped dress Celebel in his armor, caressing him as I did. His eyes sparked with the promise of future favors. He wrapped a fresh dress around me, smoothing it over my curves. The casual eroticism of our relationship bolstered me in continually fascinating ways. We left the tent together—and stepped into another dampening field.

Rafael sat by a newly lit cook fire, poking it with the toe of his boot. Sparks jumped, landing harmlessly on him. Nemohee lurked at his back, arms crossed tightly over þeir chest with a glint of defiant triumph in þeir eyes, as though þey'd herded him to us by force. Perhaps þey had.

"What—" Celebel started.

I glided in front of him to forestall the inevitable conflict. The Dragon looked up at me with a rueful twist to his lips. That he sat lower than my eye level held significance. His hair had returned to its original blood red, his eyes flickered with gentle flames, and he wore no armor. On the surface, at least, he signaled he hadn't come for a fight.

"He's got sommat to say to both of ye," Nemohee prodded.

"This one exhausted an impressive vocabulary of curses in more languages than I would expect." Rafael cast a brief glare over his shoulder. "Þey managed to make a logical point. Eventually."

"Yer damn right."

"Nem, hush," I said.

Rafael had never appeared so uncomfortable, and yet truly repentant. Especially as an uncomfortable Rafael frequently metamorphosed into a violent Rafael. Humility settled on him like a poorly fitted cape.

He exhaled a rumbling breath, studying his hands where they rested loosely on his knees. "I…owe you an apology." Strain marred his voice, as if forcing the words up from deep within. My lungs froze. Celebel's guarded stillness behind me pounded a drumbeat in my head.

The Dragon's eyes flicked to mine, his arched brows drawing together. "I should not have allowed myself to lash out at you."

"Rafael—"

"No," he said. "I have hurt you. Intention matters not; I am forsworn."

Celebel caught my arm before I could rush to the Dragon's side. He blocked my way with his body, echoing my earlier move with an added, surprising turn to face me and give Rafael his back.

"Do not heedlessly forgive him as you always do," Celebel said, garnering a sharp glance from Rafael behind him. The Talithiri Consul held himself regally still, belaying the simmering anger under the surface. "You rush to smooth over his awful behavior as though the harm he inflicts upon others matters not, so long as he is contrite with you. He has only to act forlorn and you fall at his feet. Set aside your emotions for once and note the manipulation here. Please."

He addressed Rafael directly. "That outburst at the healer's tent was abusive, and I will hear no further excuses for it. Cúraniel was hardly the only one with damaged ears after all your roaring, not that I'd expect you to care. This is all a fucking game to you."

Over Rafael's shoulder, Nemohee nodded along with Celebel's words vehemently enough to throw þeir candle flame hair into disarray. That gave me pause. Embroiled in both my frustration with taking the blame for Rafael's actions and concern with his trauma, I'd been oblivious to the impact on those around me. Celebel must have spoken to Liriadis in the interim. What else occurred out of my earshot? Would the healers allow me back in their presence?

The Dragon rose to his feet with a deep rumble, putting the top of Celebel's head level with his broad shoulders. So much for contrition.

"What else is war, but a game? I am not here to address your concerns," he said to Celebel, with considerably less venom than usual. Perhaps there was hope, after all.

In the event that famous temper flared, I took a step around Celebel, reaching out with a flat palm. Rafael caught my hand, turned it, and kissed the inside of my wrist. The warmth of his lips tingled all the way up my arm. The heated look he gave me made everything else tingle. Damn him, I couldn't repress my smile.

Standing between them sent pleasurable frissons over my skin, staticky and sensitive. At once brittle and immeasurably stronger, I drew upon my soulmates' energies. Rafael's presence had the usual maelstrom of controlled power, but Celebel's was remarkably unyielding and solid. Enmeshment in both spirits made me lightheaded, almost giddy. The rest of the world melted away with dizzying speed. With an effort like running through deep water, I grounded myself. If only I could act as a conduit between these men. If only I could guide them into crossing that void themselves.

Rafael's velvety growl brought me back. "I am also not here to fight. For once." His viperine gaze flicked to Celebel and back to me.

"What assurances do we have you will not repeat the same atrocious behavior the next time she must perform a task you dislike?"

Celebel persisted.

To me, the Dragon said, "If I allow your little *nekarrazi* to strike me, will you consider it fair?" He smiled, not quite showing his teeth.

I immediately pulled my hand away and rubbed my temples. "You were doing so well."

Celebel's guarded readiness was palpable behind me. Rafael's eyes glittered wickedly, and the campfire flared. Nemohee chuckled under þeir breath.

Crow, not again. "How would that be helpful? Nem, don't encourage him."

"Ack, sorry. Red, yer a right humorous blighter when ye've a mind to be." The Lachanaur fixed a false scowl on þeir face, pursing þeir lips.

"Emphasis on 'blighter'. Do you swear not to retaliate if I coat my blade in dragonsbane first?" Celebel's flat tone clearly indicated he wasn't serious, but his words chilled me. They had the exact opposite on his intended target, whose fiery eyes lit with evil glee.

"Ah, he *does* have some flame." Rafael removed his cloak with a flourish, dropping it to the ground. Opening his jerkin and unlacing the neck of his shirt, he bared the center of his chest. Stretching his chin upward, he made himself vulnerable. He was enjoying this far too much for my comfort. "Go on, strike me down. Right through the heart." He tapped the area with a talon. "It has nine chambers; be sure to give your sword a twist." Talons swept upward in pantomime. "I will not stop you. Make a name for yourself, little princeling."

"Fucking stop trying to bring about my vision of death with your gods damned dick-dueling." I pushed against the Dragon's immovable chest.

"Now that, I *would* like to see," Nemohee said with a cackle.

Rafael glared, and Celebel bit back a surprised, tense laugh.

"For research purposes, o' course," þey added helpfully. "Comparative anatomy."

"Nem, get ahold of yourself. Gods damn it, Rafael. If you're trying to cheer me, you're creating the opposite effect." I bent and snatched his cloak from the ground, shoving it into his hands.

He rumbled with amusement, pulling the laces of his shirt closed. "What would you have me do?"

"Apologize to Celebel. You're deliberately antagonizing him again, and you said you wouldn't." I wanted to slap him, but it would only heighten his aggravating mood. I nearly tugged my earlobes off of my head instead. Not enough whiskey in the whole of Vaeda.

Rafael was all sharp-toothed innocence. "I presumed he would enjoy the opportunity to strike me unimpeded."

"Can I hit him?" Nemohee chimed in. "I mean, if Celebel isn't apt to take his shot …"

"Do you think you are able?" Rafael turned to give the Lachanaur a challenging sneer. His malevolent humor was almost worse than his fury.

My fingers itched to bounce the coffee pot off both of their skulls. "Cease this melody now, Nem! You too, Dragon. Gods save me from obnoxious redheads! Go cheerfully beat the life out of each other if it makes you happy. Why did I have to be surrounded by bloody *fighters*?"

Celebel's hands closed on my shoulders. "Easy, my love. I have no intention of taking him up on his offer. Rafael, you are an insufferable, arrogant prick—"

"You flatter me."

"—but I will do nothing against Cúraniel's wishes. You claim you want to make amends for acting terribly. Instead, you're determined to upset her again."

The Dragon sobered, his taunting smirk melting away. "Hrrm, I am loath to concede to you, yet I am at a loss. I cannot undo what has been done."

"You could start with an apology for trying to goad Celebel into a fight," I said sourly. "Utterly counterproductive. You too, Nemohee. He needs no encouragement from you to be an ass."

"Awright, I told him he was apt to lose ye forever if he didn't make a genuine apology for hurting ye like that. And he owes Celebel the same," Nemohee said. "After I cussed him good, that is. He took it surprisingly well."

We all looked at Rafael expectantly. His mouth twisted in distaste and he ran a hand through his hair. Interesting. He didn't often express embarrassment, as he so rarely felt any shame. A bold pair of mourning doves entered the edge of the dampening field, pecking at the barren ground. Gods, not another omen.

"I never meant to cause you harm," he said softly to me.

"And yet—" Celebel started.

The Dragon held up a talon. "And yet I have. Again. I am…hrrm, not practiced in making amends."

I raised an eyebrow, stepping aside, so he faced Celebel directly. The Consul folded his arms, and Rafael's hands twitched. For a moment I feared the Dragon would lunge. He sighed heavily instead.

"Hrrm, very well. I regret my recent actions." He leveled a hard glare at Celebel.

Celebel put his ears back. "Is that the extent of it? Would you realize your actions were regrettable if Cúraniel hadn't been distraught?"

I stepped between them again. "Cel, don't antagonize him in return. It is unfair to punish him for following the melody you directed." Turning to Rafael, I said, "Would you at least swear not to rage about my healing methods? Failing that, if you simply *must* vent your wrath, will you take it far afield? For my part, I'll attempt to give you more warning."

He held out a hand. I accepted it, allowing him to pull me into his arms.

"Done," he said.

I rested my head on his chest, listening to his slow heartbeat. Wishing I could pull Celebel into his embrace with me. Rafael rumbled with distaste, but otherwise contained his reaction. The doves cooed.

Celebel drummed his fingers on his arms. His eyes flicked to the Lachanaur waiting behind us. "Nemohee, would you excuse us?"

With a significant quirk of þeir mouth at me, Nemohee left the dampening field.

As though coming to some reluctant conclusion, Celebel sighed and smoothed his hair. He addressed Rafael directly. "You and I have focused exclusively on our differences, at the expense of the major commonality between us."

Rafael exhaled through his nose, tensing. I squirmed out of his arms.

"Peace, please. This is not a proposition," Celebel said. Damn. "We must find some way to harmonize. This relationship is unique in virtually every aspect. If you should desire a sympathetic ear, may I offer mine?"

The Dragon coughed a startled laugh, frightening the doves into flight. "Shall I fall, weeping, into your arms?" He waggled his fingers at Celebel. "Perhaps braid each other's hair? You elves love that."

Before I could scold him, Celebel intervened. "Gods, you truly share a song with Feanim, you sarcastic blighter. If you wish for any of this," he jabbed a finger at the three of us, "to improve, you and I," he pointed Rafael, then himself, "must strike an accord. A true accord. What would such a thing require?"

I held my breath, not daring to hope.

"What do you want from me, Celebel?" A dangerous spark danced in Rafael's eyes. The proper name straightened Celebel's spine like an arrow. My ears quivered. "Power, protection, knowledge?" A taloned hand swirled. "Enlighten me. Let us make a deal."

Celebel almost tugged a lobe, dropping his hand at the last moment with an exasperated chuckle. "Must you answer every question with a question? I'll have no more deals struck with a Háramorn. I seek only a mutually beneficial way forward. We are bonded, regardless of either of our feelings about it."

Rafael looked at me, appraising. I willed him to relent. He touched my cheek with a knuckle, and I leaned into his hand. A minute twinge in our soulbond, and something ever so slightly relaxed.

"Hrrm. Speak, then."

"If we are to protect her, we must present a united front," Celebel said. "I recognize my part in the court's betrayal. If I'd protected Cúraniel as she protects you, and if you and I hadn't had such discord, Férioth may have ended on a different note. Perhaps, with time, I might have changed the court's melody of you."

My palms tingled. Was this hope's manifestation? Rafael did

not move or blink. His usual rumbling breath quieted. The Dragon had a habit of turning his head slightly while listening without rancor. It removed the challenge of his direct stare. With that aquiline nose, it had the effect of a hawk studying a mouse.

"I ask not for your favor," Celebel continued. "Only that we may be true allies for her sake. And for both of ours. Our entire camp is well aware of your displeasure at the current state of affairs."

Rafael snorted. "Make your point."

"That very displeasure caused significant damage to our efforts. Lives were lost on the field when you abandoned your position." Celebel held up a hand at the growl of protest. "Yes, I know well how you care not for the opinions of others. Especially those you consider beneath you. But if you care at all for Cúraniel's wellbeing, you should reconsider. Others' reactions to you consistently hurt her, and this is where we may help each other. I will guard your interests if you guard mine. Those harmed by your most recent actions likely will not hear her, but they will listen to me."

"And you would not intervene purely for her sake?"

"I am ill-suited to mummery. My influence will extend farther if the effort is genuine." Celebel sighed, tucking his silken hair behind an ear. "Rafael, I am offering to support you. All I ask in return is a cessation of hostility and some manner of reciprocity. I care not what form such reciprocity takes, only that it exists. Is that acceptable?"

Silence stretched between them.

Celebel drummed his fingers, and finally said, "What would you have done if I'd raged at Cúraniel the way you did?"

The Dragon's gaze trained on me. I pushed every bit of longing into my eyes. My ears drooped, and I tugged at our soulbond.

"Not the sad eyes," he muttered, returning his attention to Celebel. "As you say, I must make amends. Your 'mutual beneficence' is acceptable. For now."

With a rush of elation, I threw my arms about his neck, hopping to kiss his cheek. Rafael rumbled in resignation. But I caught the faint smile pulling at the corner of his mouth as he turned away.

From behind me, Celebel laid a gentle hand on my shoulder.

I covered it with mine. "I plan to address the healers as a group, for what small good it may do." My stomach soured, and I clutched at my belly. Too much emotion.

"I will accompany you," he said.

Nemohee emerged from the woods, following the Dragon. His long, loping stride forced the shorter Lachanaur into a trot to keep his pace. Þey punched him in the arm. He immediately shoved back, sending þem sailing across the path and crashing into an uninhabited tent. Nemohee howled with laughter as þey struggled free of the tent branches and canvas.

"Yer a right blighter for that," þey yelled, dashing after him.

Chapter 53

HE healer's tents crawled with activity. Liriadis directed the packing and break down. The Consulate had given the order to move by nightfall in order to reach our objective. Most of the assistants—as well as several healers—avoided me, despite Celebel's intervention.

Liriadis had backed Celebel's speech to the others, forming the bridge that allowed me back into the group. Her straightforward approach cut through the protests when she pointed out I was the only one capable of healing the madness attacks. No one answered her call for volunteers to replace me.

"Never a moment's rest." She wrapped a delicate celestite crystal. "Your song is back on key, though."

Around us, elves carefully bundled herbs, bandages, and tools, and organized them into traveling trunks. Cots and worktables were disassembled, lanterns stowed, blankets folded. My stomach dropped until Liriadis pointed out where my items were mixed in with the rest.

"You run an efficient practice," I commented. "The Consulate should honor you for everything you've done here."

"I don't need honors. I only want more of ours outfitted with proper armor." She tossed her long braid over her shoulder.

"Liriadis, thank you. I don't know why you've invested such trust in me, but I appreciate it." Without her support, I would have been utterly shunned.

She startled me with a hug. "Your spirit shines in your eyes."

Why was I weeping? The shorter elf rocked me in her arms, patting my back like a child, and I sobbed harder.

"There now. Release that stagnant spirit. You've taken on a great burden with balancing that horrid beast and Lord Celebel—who is impossibly jealous of all the attention and care you give your drake. Oh yes, it marks the Consul when he believes no one takes note. Not to mention how you're offering your own flesh to heal this madness."

I sniffled into the shoulder of her tunic. Celebel, who turned heads everywhere he went, felt jealousy? Frustrated, disheartened, and often absolutely infuriated by Rafael, but jealous? Celebel had been disdainful when he'd first learned I was bound to a drake—and was so put off by meeting the man himself—it had never occurred to me note jealousy in his actions.

Certainly, Rafael would recognize that weakness and use it to his advantage. I couldn't deny the Dragon's manipulative tendencies. They came as naturally to him as breathing, but I never doubted his love for me. As stifling as a chokeweed at times, Rafael never wavered in his devotion. Not in his rage, nor when he lost himself in madness. Could I say the same for Celebel?

Rafael's endless need, his desire to 'burn the world' for me, drove him to decisions he never would have made on his own. Did I need his need for me just as greatly, or was it, as Celebel had said, some subtle influence? Ever since the Dragon had confessed his love, he'd essentially placed a collar around my neck. Ironic, that he'd accused me of doing the same to him.

Despite my often-explosive fights with him, I'd never admitted to anyone, least of all myself, the profundity of his power over me. If I truly would forgive him anything, was I endangering others with my leniency? Certainly, Rafael had made far more concessions than anyone else. He had demonstrated tremendous growth, despite the rocky path we trod together. Despite the ever-present specter of trauma haunting his steps.

And yet, I couldn't deny his escalating violence. It set my teeth on edge. No matter how mournful Rafael felt in the aftermath, no matter how he tried to atone for his actions, he was a clear and undeniable threat.

'*When he kills you,*' Celebel had said.

When. And then all of Vaeda? With only my safety to consider, I trod fearlessly into the path of Rafael's rage. But to pin the fate of the entire world on my continued wellbeing, regardless of the circumstance? How long could I bear it?

On the other side, what had my relationship with Celebel become? Almost a purely sexual connection recently, as he was more often frustrated by me than not. He spent more time complaining about Rafael and my actions than he did actually talking to me. In some ways, Rafael had honored their agreement far better than Celebel had, as Celebel had no compunctions at all about trying to convince me to sever ties with my Dragon.

Celebel raised valid points. I *knew* he did, and yet… Surely, he felt tremendous pressure in his role, and his belief in a just world had been shattered, but I had never agreed to be more than a healer in this conflict. I could not help him with statecraft, strategy, or planning, and yet he had expectations he'd never voiced. Perhaps I'd been too selfish to consider them. Did crafting the Pîntellum count for anything?

Finally, a sweet note in the silence, this new accord with Rafael. Oh Dûemer, please let it last this time! I hardly allowed myself to hope. Not yet.

Liriadis gave me a squeeze, ears twitching at the storm of emotions rampaging through me.

"If we are winning, why do I feel this sense of loss?" I whispered.

"Have you ever been to war?" She released me from the embrace to hold me at arm's length, appraising.

"This is my first." So isolated was I, conflict never reached me. A luxury.

"It is always so. The cost is great no matter the outcome. So much loss, so much grief. The soldiers congratulate themselves and the rest of us are left carrying the burden. Make your peace where you can."

WE SET up our tent late in a moonless night after a long march. Icy ground and scarce trees made growing tent branches difficult, so we simplified as much as possible. I paused long enough to admire a smattering of meteors before crawling inside and curling up next to Celebel.

Learning to sleep in armor had taken tedious practice, but the

Pîntellum allowed for some minor comfort. Lying flat on my back with my arms at my sides proved the easiest position. Crushing fatigue helped.

Wind whipped my face, filling my wings as I navigated the air currents with ease. It smelled of snow on the way, of drakes, elves, and prey in the meager forest. Drakes circled nearby. The mountains took on strange proportions as my vision brought details into sharp focus, sweeping over the landscape for signs of enemies.

Celebel sat bolt upright in our bed, shaking me awake. Dim shapes moved in the darkness. He raised a witchlight lantern, summoning its glow. A slow-creeping carpet of shiny black bodies filtered through the tent flaps. As one, we leaped to our feet.

Rage transformed Celebel. He laid about with his sword, slashing and stomping the spiders. Screaming at them. I followed suit, but instead of swinging blades, I threw heavy books from my pile of research materials. The resulting splats were satisfying, although I felt bad for my books. I silently promised to give them a thorough cleaning when this was over.

A ruckus drew us outside. Elves everywhere flailed under a growing surge of chitinous bodies. Their chittering cries froze my blood. Celebel caught my arm, thrust my crescent blades into my hands, and dragged me out of the tent.

We dashed to protect the noncombatants. An unarmed Lachanaur man fell under the weight of a wolf-sized spider, seizing as long fangs pumped venom into his shoulder. I lopped the head off of the beast too late. The victim's body stilled, his spirit departing.

One of the younger elves I'd rescued from the madness, the Astolar who'd sparked Rafael's jealous outburst, sprinted out of the darkness toward me, arms outstretched. Unsure of his intentions, I backed away as he toppled forward at my feet, screaming. Multiple spiders clung to his back, fangs embedded deep in his spine. I dropped and ripped the spiders away, trying in vain to send my spirit into him and pull the venom out.

The continuous waves of spiders granted us no respite, and Celebel made no sound other than the whistling cuts of his sword.

I wasn't fast enough. My former patient fell limp in my arms as his heart shuddered to a stop. I brushed his sweaty blonde hair back from his brow and lay him on the ground in a hopefully dignified manner. Twice now, his lack of Pîntellum-reinforced armor had dire consequences. All that conflict over a life I couldn't save in the end, but I did not regret the effort.

No time to mourn. A shrill cry drew my attention to where Pirinlach swung a lantern about like a cudgel. Norlissuin cowered behind her. Only their tent backed them. Celebel beat me there, carving his way through the eight-legged monstrosities. I raised my blades as a massive spider reared up in front of me, pedipalps wriggling with menace. A flash of flame made my eyes water, and my crescents met only air.

"Spiders burn," Rafael bellowed, and spat a thin stream of fire over my shoulder. I flinched, but his aim was true. A spider dropping from an overhead tree branch by a thin cord of silk shrieked and sizzled away.

He snatched both blades out of my hands and licked them. Before I could ask what the fuck he was doing, he breathed and ignited the cutting edges, handing them back to me. He plucked Celebel's sword from his hands, who let out a squawk of indignation. Rafael repeated the action and returned the burning blade to its bewildered owner. Then he spat flame in a tight arc around us, incinerating the approaching spiders.

"Save the healers," I begged.

"Yes, yes." A horse screamed in the distance. "Before you complain, I sent Boshkt to protect your precious mounts." He shooed us back and breathed a thin ring of fire around the historian's tent. It burned steadily in the grass, trapping the couple in place but also keeping the encroaching spiders away. Norlissuin peered around her lanky soulmate's shoulder and made eye contact with the Dragon.

"That flame will not endanger your books," he said.

"Much appreciated, but how do we leave?" Pirinlach asked. No nonsense, like Liriadis.

Norlissuin sucked in a breath. "Piri, don't be rude. The *Red*

Dragon saved our lives!"

Rafael snorted. He strode off toward the healer's tents, eye-searing flashes of flame marking his passage. I kept pace with Celebel in the Dragon's wake. Probably the safest place to be, though the spiders were quick to fill in the gap. We slashed and burned our way through.

Lámirië dashed to Celebel's side, loosing flaming arrow after flaming arrow with blurring speed, and stabbing with a shortsword at close range. Other elves collected around us, instinctively following their Consul's lead. We made a loose formation. A burning beacon in the night, Rafael paid them no heed as he targeted the thickest enemy wave. Spiders scorched on contact, legs curling in as they crumbled to ash.

A distant squawk sounded like Abrrys. Spider hisses mingled with cries of pain and fury. Drakes grunted and snarled around us, illuminated by the occasional belched flame. The endless clicking of legs hammered at my skull.

Shadows resolved into a massive red and black drake, casually strolling through the chaos and snapping up spiders in his jaws.

"Xyxs! Flame kills!" I shouted over the din.

The massive drake boomed a laugh. "More fun to bite."

He whipped around to catch a shiny black body in his long jaws, popping it like a grape. His tail swept others away, flattening them. A few elves trailed cautiously behind him—perhaps new lovers?

Nemohee and Feanim appeared in the gloom, fighting back to back. How had that alliance formed?

"That's twenty-three! C'mon, ye're slacking," Nemohee crowed.

Feanim broke ranks to skip over the carapaces of the larger creatures, stabbing and slashing as we went. "Oh, fuck off. The little ones don't count!" They danced around us, enjoying themselves as much as Xyxs had.

"The spiders target you," the Dragon called over his shoulder to Celebel. I refocused on the scene at large. He was right. The bulk of the spiders followed us, thinning the onslaught everywhere else.

"If I draw them into that hollow, can you trap them there?" Celebel pointed downhill with his sword to a sunken area, maintaining admirable composure. "Then I'll run for the healers' tents."

Rafael paused mid-spider-crushing. From his brow raise, he'd been about to suggest that very thing. "Yes." Was that a note of respect? He turned to the others. "You lot. Meet him on the far side. Stay off of the ridge."

Celebel sprang forward, whirling and slashing his way to the designated area. The other elves dashed off at a full sprint. I struggled to keep pace, guard myself, and pay attention to my soulmates.

Rafael's silhouette lit up. Serpents of flame surged from him, undulating in either direction, swallowing spiders as they moved. Soon, a burning wall encircled the hollow. Closing Celebel inside. What was he about?

The ground rumbled, and the center beneath Celebel's feet rippled and bowed upward. He rolled away, springing into a ready stance. Legs like spears pierced the moss carpet, and a spider of nightmarish proportions emerged. Pedipalps swished, and the monster turned twelve shining eyes on Celebel. Smaller spiders surged around him.

"There you are, you leggy fucker." Rafael roared. "Go, elf. I will part the flames for you."

Gods, that would take some trust. Celebel sprinted up the hill, scrambling over boulders as efficiently as the arachnids chasing him. Lámirië picked off the closest of those, aiming over the fire. As promised, the flames parted like a curtain and Celebel burst through the wall of fire unburned. The spiders at his ear tips crisped on contact.

Soon as the elf cleared the circle, Rafael leaped at the gargantuan spider. It hissed like a newly opened steam vent, front legs slashing the air. I lingered to watch, but a firm hand clamped on my arm. Lámirië dragged me away at Celebel's command.

Another blaze caught my attention. One of the main healer's tents had caught fire. Celebel glanced at me, and we bolted as one. Liriadis stood outside, directing more of her ire at the burning tent than the attacking spiders. We cut down a few before they could reach her.

"An assistant panicked while slapping spiders away and caught the tent with a torch." Liriadis gestured with a short spear, muttering curses.

I blew out a relieved breath. "Oh gods, I'd assumed one of the drakes—"

"We have far more control than that," Vaerra's raspy voice cut in.

I turned in time to see her rip a spider the size of a horse in half, tossing away the pieces. Celebel coughed in shock.

"My apologies, of course not. We—ah, we appreciate the aid." I'd almost thanked her and had to bite my lip. Fortunately, she couldn't see my face and ears inside the helm.

"You'll repay us in kind," she said. "Bitten, a few were, before the alarm was raised."

"These creatures can bite through your scales?" Liriadis was appalled.

"Only the larger of spiders, and the softer of us." Vaerra whirled and caught a cat-sized spider drifting in on a tether of silk, clawing it apart in a burst of ichor.

Celebel directed our soldiers to support the drakes. As they ringed us, he removed his helm and sang a clear note, sending his spirit to the skies. I removed my helm as well and joined his song, adding my spirit. We drew clouds together over the burning tent. At the crescendo, the miniature storm burst, blanketing the flames with rain. The fire sizzled out.

Celebel leaned against me. Such a small expenditure should have been simple, especially given his previous display, but his heightened emotions rippled through our connection. The appearance of the giant had shaken him. I touched my forehead to his, grateful for the skin-to-skin contact. Sweat and Pîntellum residue made it slightly sticky.

"The Red returns." Vaerra pointed with her chin.

A weird, roiling, black-edged flame cut a clean swath through a shiny blanket of spiders. It sheared off limbs, thoraces, and abdomens like a blade through silk. The infernal flame. In a blink, the seething mass thinned. The hissing voices of the spiders diminished. The clicking intensified, then quieted.

Rafael strode from the darkness, eyes glowing. "The queen has fled." With a grunt, he pulled a broken-off fang out of his shoulder. Like a spear, it was nearly the length of my entire arm. "The rest will follow." He waved away my immediate concern.

"A shame you couldn't kill her, with such quality bait," Celebel said with a wry twist to his mouth.

My Dragon only blinked. "Ancients do not burn easily, but she must molt to regrow the legs she has lost. Should gain us some spiderless moons." He scowled at the still-burning fires dotted across the camp and raised a hand. The flames curled in on themselves, winding back and traveling in a thin stream to dissipate in his palm.

"That's a useful trick," Liriadis said, just as Celebel added, "No wonder you're a master smith."

Rafael held a hand out to me, and I gave him my blades. For lack of a better description, he *pulled* the flames away from the edges. He repeated the process with Celebel's sword.

He rumbled thoughtfully. "I appreciate the armor you wear." It was the closest he'd ever come to actually thanking Celebel.

My ears twitched, and the Dragon studiously avoided my eyes. Celebel made a noise of bemusement.

"We'll handle the envenomations here. Go help the drakes," Liriadis said as Feanim limped up, loudly demanding attention.

Nemohee strode along behind him, humming cheerfully.

I followed Rafael and Vaerra to where Grenyk lay on its side, panting heavily. A pair of deep fang marks already festered under its burly arm. Crow, had the *viigsakh* encountered the queen? Pulling off my helm and gauntlets, I waved my hand across the fallen drake's face. No response.

"Watch it doesn't bite," Vaerra said.

Rafael positioned himself at the brown drake's head. I placed my hands on either side of the puncture wounds, feeling for the severity of envenomation. My awareness traveled through the interstices.

The tissue damage was already extensive, but not catastrophic. It would be excruciating with the amount of swelling and rapid necrosis. I concentrated, pulling at the traces of venom to draw it out in small bits to spare the vessels, rather than intensifying it all in one place.

Each time I drew from the brown drake, I funneled the venom

into the ground beside me. My stomach soured with the work, but it passed quickly. Once I'd cleared enough for the drake's breathing to ease, I moved to the next patient.

Xyxs sat with an impossibly swollen tongue lolling from his jaws like a fat purple slug. Saliva dripped in a constant stream. He bobbed his head when he saw me. slinging drool.

Rafael kicked him in the ribs, knocking the much larger drake over. "Fucking fool. Inside your mouth is soft," he said in draconian. "Hatchlings learn better than you."

"Leave him be." I spoke draconian as well, moving between the Dragon and his cowering target. "Lesson enough, that pain."

Xyxs mumbled in effusive agreement.

"Lower your head." I motioned for him to open his jaws.

He complied gingerly, nostrils blowing heavy breaths. Quite a lot of pain, then. He hadn't reacted this much when he'd had a spearhead lodged in his wing joint.

"No biting."

He opened his jaws wider, raising his craggy brows in earnest. With a quelling glance at Rafael, I laid my palm on the drake's mottled and bruised tongue. If he bit down, he'd take my arm off at the elbow. I focused on sending my spirit into the multitude of small punctures speckling the surface. Must have been minor spiders. Enough to cause swelling and pain, but no real tissue damage. I pulled the venom out in three big motions and shook the queasy tingling out of my hand.

Thus freed, Xyxs clacked his jaws, scraping his tongue along the roof of his mouth. While he was distracted, I wiped my hand on the grass. We moved to the next supplicant.

A smaller blue drake with a similarly swollen foot; a green and blue with multiple bites on his hands; another brown, banded like sardonyx, with nasty bite to the neck. I worked as quickly as I could with my flagging energy. Boshkt bobbed his head as I passed. It harmonized a drake with acidic venom would fare perfectly well during a spider attack.

The last was a black drake whose glossy scales reminded me uncomfortably of the shining chitinous bodies of the spiders. It had taken multiple bites and yet was still conscious. It watched with intense green eyes, and I got the feeling it was very young. Was it related to Lubber? When I pressed on a tender area, it hissed at me. Rafael immediately caught it by the throat with a deep snarl.

"Don't eat my patient, please," I protested. "We've discussed this."

"Your patient can show some respect." His growl buzzed in my skull.

"My patient is in pain. Leave off."

"Soft," he snarled in draconian to the black drake.

The poor thing dropped its gaze. There was no more hissing, not even when I directed Rafael to lance an overly swollen knee joint with his talons. The young drake bobbed its head at me as I finished, fitting my hands back into my gauntlets—mostly to avoid accidentally touching my Dragon's moranga armor.

"I expected worse," I said as he escorted me back to my tent.

The tip of my sabaton caught in a hole, and I stumbled, dropping my helm. Rafael caught me, hooking an arm around my waist.

I steadied myself. "Gods, I must have drawn on more spirit than I realized."

He snagged my helm with a dexterous foot and returned it to me. Damn his flexibility! Sheepish, I accepted, though I was in no rush to put it on again. Breathing the night air without the membrane's filter and freeing my stuffy ears was a blessing.

'*Would you fuck another drake to save their life?*' The question nearly made me stumble again. Rafael's posture hadn't changed, but he gave me a sidelong look.

'*In the context of the madness attacks?*' Would certain drakes be more likely to set him off than others? He watched with raptorial intensity whenever I interacted with Xyxs... '*Yes, I suppose I would if there were no other way to save them. Certainly would not be my primary intervention.*' I tensed, waiting for the backlash.

Silence from him had my ears training on the crackling of flames and the soft murmur of elvish voices in the distance. Drake feet crunched on slushy snow. Night insects quieted as he moved past, picking up their song once he was safely away.

"Rafael?"

His shoulders rose in a deep inhale. *'It would create more... complications.'* Everything about him created complications. *'You are mated in all but ceremony. If you lie with another before my claim is finalized, you declare new intent to claim.'* He gave me a significant look, each movement of his head trailing bright streaks in the darkness from his burning eyes.

The air went out of my lungs. *'Thus creating a situation where you may have to fight and kill my patient?'*

'You understand.'

'Then, I will find another way if it comes to that.' I frowned at him. *'You could have simply declared as much.'*

'You dislike it when I issue decrees, yes?' That look turned sly.

"You are exhausting at times." I swatted his shoulder, secretly grateful for his calm. "This is one of those times."

Chapter 84

OSERALON came into view like a bad dream, slowly flickering through a haze of flurrying snow. Perched upon the end of a granite extrusion, nearly a small mountain itself, it overlooked a wide, horseshoe-shaped valley carved by ancient glaciers. The walls of Oseralon stood upon the edge of the sheer granite drop for most of the elvish city's perimeter, giving the impression of a fortress of towering height. The gate faced the southern range where rugged slopes and ravines connected the mountains with the granite extrusion. A small river wound through the land, eventually tumbling off the cliff's edge.

Once sunken and now thrust back into the light by geologic upheaval, its bulbous guard towers boasted a constellation of long-dead giant barnacles and corals. Like far too many empty eye sockets and questing digits, frozen with age.

Scars of the battle which destroyed the city still clung like unshakeable memories. Sections of the western walls had caved in, exposing the chambers within. Only half of the towers remained, with debris littering the base of the walls near the gate. The stone around the gate itself bore deep gouges, rendered by the talons of a true dragon—Adacanir, the Great Destroyer. The remnants of the city stood as a testament to its majesty, as the destruction did for the power of its enemies.

Unlike Amrún, it had no bridge or moat, but a wide causeway spanning the ravine right up to the gates, a vestige of a more welcoming time. It would at least make breaching the city less complicated.

Rafael and Feanim looked for all the world like a couple of ill omens crouched together at the edge of a granite promontory surveying the fortress. I laughed to myself at how Feanim mimicked Rafael's posture. Celebel was off organizing troop movements and had sent me to ascertain the next moves.

"Marron will lead the breach," the Dragon was saying. He pointed to a few draconic figures stealthily approaching the western wall. "If it is as empty as it appears, there will not be much opposition."

"Empty?" We'd battled all this way for an empty fortress?

Feanim scowled, but Rafael acknowledged my question. "The attacks along the road were delays to permit the enemy to flee. We will search this place before we give chase. This one insists there are 'powerful spirit weapons' hidden in its catacombs."

"What if it's a trap?" Apprehension tightened my belly.

"Obviously," Feanim scoffed, as Rafael said, "It is."

"Beredhel is well aware of Rafael's presence," the Duedellen continued carefully, waving a hand at the Dragon. "It best harmonizes to lay a trap of our own rather than risk entering this place."

Rafael huffed. "I intend to spring this one. Let us discover the strength of your brother's bite. Assuming he is more than a phantom."

"And if he imprisons or incapacitates you?" Feanim yanked a lobe in frustration.

Once more, I agreed with Feanim against my will. The vision of Rafael in chains, dragged into hellfire, played heavily in my mind.

The Dragon smiled with the promise of violence. "Then I will be impressed for the first time in many, many years. Fear not. *Dear old Father* crushed this city once. I can certainly do it again."

I shivered at the withering hatred in his voice.

The treeless terrain, with its snow-covered, haphazard boulders, meant the approaching drakes were mostly undetectable from inside the fortress. Clouds hung heavy in the sky and snow billowed across the landscape, further cloaking their movements.

"Marron opening the gate is the signal to join." Rafael slid down the granite, finding his footing by digging in his taloned feet. The screech of claws on stone made my ears twitch. He tapped the top of my helm. "You will remain here."

I followed them to the rest of our company. We passed Xyxs moving in the opposite direction. He nudged my shoulder with a meaty paw.

"You fighting?" He spoke draconian, as always. "Armor and

blades. What flame does the Red's mate spit?"

Rafael snorted. "She fights with words."

"And my magic pussy." I clanged a fist off of my armored crotch.

Xyxs roared in laughter, forcing me to clap my hands over my helmeted ears, but I caught Feanim's snicker. Rafael merely squared his shoulders.

MARRON MET Rafael at the gate with a shrug. They'd met minimal, easily overpowered defenders. The place was mostly deserted and had already been stripped. The drakes ransacked every room, every holding cell and hallway, and came up with nothing. My Dragon confirmed their observations himself.

I watched through Celebel's eyes, wrapping him in my presence like a protective cloak via our bond. As Rafael had commanded, I sat safely hidden away with the others outside the fortress.

The invading drakes took one traitor elf alive. The big warriors were less than gentle with their prisoners, much to Feanim's annoyance. He and Celebel traversed the courtyard and through a dark hallway. Despite the curving, organic lines, its stark walls and oppressively small windows prickled the back of my neck. All of it made more claustrophobic by the crusted evidence of former sea life and the odor of mildew. Sound echoed strangely.

Feanim led the way down a winding stone staircase to a reasonably well-lit space for what appeared to be a dungeon. Stagnant air carried the weight of dank rot. Witchlight lanterns cased in iron hung from the low, arched ceilings, illuminating the cells lining the walls and a prisoner held bound to a chair in the center of the room.

The captured elf, another pale Astolar, struggled against his bonds. Sickened spirit bleeding from the prisoner's eyes made my skin crawl. That same creeping sense of wrongness defied my ability to pinpoint it.

A rumble alerted us to Rafael lurking in a shadowy corner. His eyes never left the prisoner. Celebel's eyes never left him.

"You will tell us what we require, or you will suffer," Feanim informed the traitor.

"Necessary torture?" Celebel asked in furtive sign. "We lose ourselves."

I agreed silently, lending him my support. Why was torture becoming the standard instead of the last resort?

"We haven't the time for such trite squeamishness." Feanim drew the moranga dagger from his belt with a gloved hand. "I need answers about the state of this stronghold and my brother's next moves, and I need them now."

Feanim took a menacing step toward the prisoner and jumped as Rafael's taloned hand landed on his shoulder. Clamping down, he neatly maneuvered the smaller man out of the way. The Duedellen's ears flattened. Likely, it was the first time Rafael had ever voluntarily touched him outside of a training exercise. The Dragon's message was obvious, and my stomach sank as he approached the prisoner.

With a swift motion, Rafael seized the hapless elf's face in both hands, tilting it upward and forcing the prisoner's jaws wide open. Leaning in close enough to kiss, he breathed an inky black smoke directly into the mouth of his victim. The elf's body arched.

Rafael forcefully exhaling into the opened mouth of a bound elf did things to my body that definitely didn't make me proud. Damn my treacherous libido. Celebel's displeasure radiated through the bond. I swallowed hard and redirected my focus. That type of smoke was unfamiliar. Perhaps I'd never know them all. *No, do not think of how it must feel from the inside.*

The prisoner's eyes rolled back and he convulsed.

Feanim's expression of horrified fascination mirrored mine. Celebel gripped one hand with the other, trying to steady them. Hard enough to whiten his knuckles. Panic rose in him and he looked away from the scene.

I pulled away as much of it as I could, sending soothing energy. *'Easy, Starshine. This is not what Rafael did to you. Rewrite this melody in your heart. Feel the stones beneath your feet, the roots and mycelium in the ground below. Center yourself.'*

Celebel released a shuddering breath and stilled. Calming him had a ripple effect on my distress, and my constricted chest relaxed.

Rafael's victim went abruptly limp, like a marionette with the strings cut. He forced the elf's mouth open a second time and inhaled deeply. The smoke climbed back out of the prisoner's jaws. The Dragon drank it in.

He looked over his shoulder at Feanim. "I have everything." His dark voice boomed in the starkly silent room.

With a casual flick of his talons, he sliced cleanly through the prisoner's throat to the spine. I bit back a tiny screech as blood spurted from the elf's ruined neck and his head lolled to the side. Beyond healing, that wound. Celebel shared my nausea.

"Why did you kill him? We could—" Feanim protested.

A taloned hand jabbed toward the dead elf.

"That," Rafael said, pinning Celebel with a blistering glare, "is harm."

Celebel said nothing, but his tension rose again despite my best efforts to calm him. Fucking hells. The Dragon swept out of the room.

Feanim stared after him. "Why the fuck was that so *sexual*?"

RAFAEL MOVED with an eerie ease of familiarity through the corridors, leading the Consulate deeper into the bowels of the fortress. Feanim peppered him with questions he largely ignored.

"There is at least one Neksarim in the catacombs guarding these vaunted weapons," Rafael finally said. "Beredhel's trap. He left them behind as bait."

Dread rippled through me.

"At *least* one? The last time you took on a single Neksarim, you were unconscious for days after." Celebel prodded, backed with my approval.

Rafael flashed a toothy grin over his shoulder. "That was a warm-up."

Feanim snorted, echoing my sentiment. Gods, my Dragon was far too enthusiastic about this prospect. Something about his comment plucked at the strings of my mind. What had been different about the previous demon? I could not place the note.

Xyxs joined them. He reported to Rafael that Marron had already left to manage the disgruntled drakes who'd expected to raid the place for treasure. The red and black drake had remained behind to assist with whatever traps awaited. Feanim translated for Celebel. His draconian had vastly improved.

Xyxs lumbered along behind the others. He had to duck to avoid cracking his head on the ceilings and door jambs, though they were tall enough for even Rafael to clear with ease. With his wings tightly furled, the red and black drake was still too broad to allow anyone to walk by his side. How would he would fare in a demon attack in such tight quarters?

Despite the company, I flinched at every creak of a hinge and unaccounted thump on the floor.

'*Stop that. You are making me nervous,*' Celebel chastised me.

My vigilance helped distract me from thoughts of Rafael possessing that prisoner. I kept it carefully hidden away from our connection, safely wrapped until I could examine those feelings.

After descending a nigh-endless flight of stairs, the Dragon stopped before a large, iron-bound door. Wards of containment gleamed along its frame. They sparked to life at his touch.

"Stay here until I clear the room." He switched to draconian. "Xyxs, guard the door."

With a hand on the latch, Rafael listened intently. Weird hissing leaked through from the other side, along with a spine-tingling whine. Making brief eye contact with Xyxs, he slipped through the door. Xyxs blocked the warded portal with his body.

The previous whine ratcheted up to an ear-splitting screech. Celebel and Feanim cringed, flattening their ears, and huddled close out of instinct. Heavy impacts shuddered through the walls, flaking the mortar from the ceiling. I caught flashes of twisting motion and urged Celebel to peer past the hulking drake. He refused to move in that close. Xyxs shifted from foot to foot. Muscles rippled down his back with anxious readiness.

Crashes. A glimpse of swirling, sickening madness. Weird hissing. Another heavy impact. A coughing roar shook the room. The abrupt stillness that followed had my heart galloping in my ears.

At some signal I couldn't perceive, Xyxs moved aside. Rafael stood alone in a vaulted, cavernous chamber, dispassionately dismembering a spherical conglomeration of limbs and faces. He worked methodically, wrenching each of the various heads free. With the only light source coming from the door behind me, I could barely make out the far walls, let alone the finer details of the demon's body. The ceiling disappeared high above our heads.

Rafael dropped the broken pile of limbs at his feet, where they burst into black-edged flame. Choking dark smoke dissipated into the dimly lit chamber, leaving only char behind. He shook himself and straightened, gesturing for the others to stay back. Was he simply masking the effects of the fight?

"*That's* a Neksarim's true appearance?" Feanim asked. "How solid. I thought they were more like your kind, with bodies of smoke and fire."

Rafael leveled a derisive sneer at him. How *dare* Feanim compare him to some *lesser* demon. An anxious giggle bubbled up from my throat to Celebel's silent dismay.

The fingers of his gauntlets chimed against his armored arms as Celebel drummed. "You appear no worse for wear."

The Dragon huffed. "This one was weak, inexperienced."

A wave of dread rolled over me, and everyone froze.

'*Something's wrong. Something is—*' I stammered obvious through our bond as Xyxs barreled into the chamber.

"Under the floor!" the big drake bellowed in draconian, his impossibly deep voice buzzing in my head even through the connection.

The floor heaved, fountaining upward in a spray of shattered flagstones. Rafael swatted a larger chunk of stone away from the door, deflecting it from the elves.

A gargantuan, distinctly dragon-shaped head broke free of the floor and caught Xyxs in its daggered jaws. Teeth closed on him with a sickening crunch.

Chapter 88

I SCREAMED as the monstrous dragon shook Xyxs with the vigor of a terrier worrying a rat and tossed him aside. Stretching nearly from wall to wall, the head kept rising until it collided with the ceiling. Celebel coughed the dust from his lungs and gazed upon our new adversary, allowing me to search for some sign Xyxs might yet live.

Weird purple flames flickered in otherwise bare sockets, gaping over hollowed cheeks. What few ragged scales stuck to the snout flashed shades of deep, bluish purple in the dim light. Desiccated flesh hung in tattered strips from the underside of its jaw like a macabre beard.

A lichdragon! If its head was any indication of the rest, this one was almost comparable in size to Rafael's massive dragon form. Giant moranga rings pierced the skull and held it loosely onto a long, curving neck made of mostly bone and gristle.

The head. Something about it… The fight that brought my troublesome Dragon into my life. His broken body…and her headless one. Oh *fuck*.

The lichdragon's front claws broke free, each easily longer than I was tall, scattering more debris. Rafael's body distorted, face elongating, blood red scales sprouting from his skin. He rapidly filled what little space remained in the once-cavernous room.

"*FLEE*," the Red Dragon roared as he shifted.

The lichdragon roared back, a choking blast of moldering grave cry. The force of it tumbled the elves backwards. Celebel gagged at the overpowering stench of death. Foul enough to turn my stomach through him.

He and Feanim raced through the halls, up the stairs, out to the courtyard. The main building burst apart behind them, violently birthing a swiftly growing scarlet dragon. A dragon of bone and sinew erupted from the courtyard itself. Locked in deadly combat, they bit and clawed each other.

Rafael's tail felled a guard tower. Celebel and Feanim dodged through a deadly shower as massive stones, chunks of mortar, and fossilized corals landed with percussive impact. Still gaining size, my Dragon leaped into the air with a mighty beat of his wings. The resulting wind shear hurled the fleeing elves forward.

With a decaying screech, the lichdragon followed. The two great beasts collided in an echoing boom, snarling and snapping. Hot blood rained in an arc, sizzling and burning where it landed.

Celebel stole glances at the sky each time the thunderclap of wings grew closer. The lichdragon bore up on tattered, rotting pinions that should have been far too fragile to keep her aloft, and yet, to my dismay, she was remarkably agile.

'*Fuck, fuck, fuck! That is Byxldurr, the War Crow. She's the drake who nearly killed Rafael when we first met! How the fuck did they bring her back from the dead? Because she was very dead. Thoroughly dead. Her fucking head was missing!*' I babbled out of shock, words tumbling over images.

Rafael's gutted, broken body. The long climb to the Great Tree. The closest he'd come to death in all his ages of life.

'*They clamped it back on, did you see? Giant moranga clamps holding her head in place.*'

I pulled back into myself, shaking out nerveless legs. A dragon roared again—Rafael—and the ground shook. Cursing my lack of athleticism, I leaped and vaulted over the pitted landscape, sliding on icy moss and scrambling over nebulous, snow-covered lava formations in my desperation to reach my soulmates.

When finally I reached Marron, the two Consuls had already arrived. I clung to Celebel, desperate to touch him, to ascertain his safety. He held me tightly.

Feanim signed to the other Consul and peeled off for the elvish camp at a sprint. Gods, Rafael was right. The little blighter was *fast*.

"Fucking hells, Marron," I cried.

"Fucking hells, indeed. Looks like Byxldurr crawled out of the grave to be a thorn in all our sides again." He shielded his eyes against the sun to watch the raging aerial battle.

As usual, he was far too calm about the situation, even as he ushered us to a safer distance. I stumbled along behind him on trembling legs as the shock set in. Overhead, the unmistakable *pop* of huge jaws snapping shut wrenched my heart.

"Xyxs! He's still in there. She bit him almost in half!" I blinked rapidly at the sudden tears, and the green drake cocked his head. "He…I don't think he survived." I sniffled, wiping my cheeks. Gods, I'd barely known him, but he'd been a friendly, cheerful presence amid the court's pressing hostility. Easier to focus on my sadness rather than the abject terror of the fight raging over our heads.

Celebel squeezed my shoulder in sympathy. "He was courageous, yes, but surely we should be taking cover instead of chatting?" He glanced at the sky.

I forced myself not to follow his gaze.

Marron continued as if Celebel hadn't spoken. "Got him, eh? Witless boy, he always did charge ahead." His brow furrowed. "Are you *crying* over a drake? You didn't mate-claim him as well, did you?" He rubbed his scaly, green chin.

"No!" Startled, I nearly choked on those tears. "He's surely dead!" It wasn't the first time I'd wept over a drake, and it surely wouldn't be the last.

Marron shrugged. "Most likely, yes. Byxldurr always did have a tremendous bite."

A shield-shaped scale the size of my torso hurtled to the ground between us. I jumped back as it slammed halfway into the rocky soil, spraying snow. The oil slick sheen of colors dancing over the bluish purple might have been lovely in other circumstances. Between that and the feathered wings, no wonder Byxldurr had been named War Crow. No, I refused to think of Rafael's gutted body. He would prevail. He *must.*

"That doesn't bother you?" I asked.

"Xyxs dying?" Marron shrugged again. "We all die in battle, eventually. Likely would have killed him myself one day. He was growing a bit too strong, and more than a little too cocky for my liking."

Tapping his talons on his arm, he amended, "Well, all of us die except *that* one." He jerked his head toward Rafael's dragon form, now wheeling overhead as he traded echoing blows with the lichdragon.

Each time their bodies collided in a great thunder, Celebel and I winced and ducked. Strangely, neither dragon used fire. The last time those two behemoths clashed, it had disrupted the weather patterns for moons, causing destruction for leagues in all directions. I hoped it wouldn't reach that feverish pitch again.

Marron's gravelly voice brought me back to the present. "We all told Byx claiming the Red was suicide, but she never listened to any voice outside her own skull. She found some nasty trinket meant to do him in, but even that failed. Though, unless she bites his head off and absconds with it, you'll be there to set him to rights."

The sudden sharp look in his ruby eyes made my gut churn. It didn't escape Celebel either, as he maneuvered between me and the burly drake.

"Is that a threat?" Celebel asked quietly. His hand tightened on the pommel of his sword.

Marron cocked a brow, and a ripple ran through his thick arms. "Do you want it to be?"

I'd never quite appreciated his sheer bulk until that moment. Gods, with Rafael engaged with the War Crow, we were completely vulnerable. Calling him could be the distraction that killed him, but I had no desire to test my armor as Feanim had either.

The ground shook with the force of both dragons' roars, throwing us all off-balance and neatly breaking the tension. A shuddering crack, followed swiftly by another, echoed through the canyon, and the lichdragon abruptly spun off. Flapping hard, she rose into the clouds. Rafael gave chase.

"He appears to be winning." I locked eyes with Marron.

"Looks that way," the green drake agreed carefully, scratching his square jaw. Scale rasped against scale.

My Dragon circled down from the sky with a bony appendage clamped in his long jaws. Landing hard on the ruined fortress, he collapsed inward on himself. Ignoring the protests, I broke away from

Celebel and dashed through the half-destroyed gate.

Rafael was standing, though gore and black ichor covered him. Blood dripped in a steady *plink, plink, plink* to pool on the broken flagstones at his feet. A nasty gash ran from his hairline straight through his left eye and down to mid-thigh on that side. Behind him, the lichdragon's severed foreleg rested on the crushed remains of an outbuilding.

Despite Rafael's wounds and obvious exhaustion, with a limp that spoke of a broken femur based on the swelling and the way he moved, he dragged a huge body along by the tail. My heart dropped to my feet, and tears threatened again. Splintered bones jutted through black-tipped red scales at odd angles. Leaking blood that no longer steamed, Xyxs was most definitely dead.

Rafael began to speak, stopped, hacked, and coughed. He spat a dark clot of blood on the ground where it hissed and sizzled.

"Fuck." A wheeze rattled behind the word. "She got my fucking eye." Annoyance rather than anger.

"Oh, Xyxs." I clutched my hands over my heart with a sniffle.

"Death conferred no more wits to Byxldurr than life did to Xyxs. She saw red scales and attacked. This fucking fool took the bite meant for me. Sheared his spine and punctured straight through his heart. Should burn him in tribute, I suppose." Rafael swayed slightly on his feet, hitching Xyxs' tail over his shoulder for a better grip.

"Did you catch Byxldurr?" I went to his injured side. "Let me tend your wounds."

"Only her leg." He gestured to the moldering limb. "And not here. I have no desire to dig my way out."

I followed him, and the cold, bloody trail left by poor Xyxs. Not even a badly broken leg slowed Rafael's normal pace. Stubbornly indestructible creature. There must be extensive internal bleeding as well. Interesting choice to reform in that body without his armor. Perhaps he could also hide it in shadows, like he did with his other clothing.

Rafael paused before the gates, leaning against the wall just out of sight of the others. He let the corpse slip from his shoulder. I rushed to his side. Any sign of physical weakness from him sent a screeching alarm through me.

"Heal my left lung." It came out in a gurgling wheeze. No wonder he'd left off the armor.

I opened his jerkin and tugged his shirt free to slide my hands under it. One palm on his left pec and the other on his side; sure enough, the lung had collapsed under crushed ribs. The touch also revealed a perfect set of deep puncture wounds outlining a bite to that shoulder.

I pushed spirit through the injured lung, easing the blood out, forcing the perforated membranes closed, and knitting the broken ribs. My spirit expanded through the branching pathways, re-inflating the organ. Breathe in. Breathe out. Rafael coughed once, twice, and turned his head away to hack up another considerable glob of blistering blood. The ribs needed more attention, but he waved me away.

"Good enough." His voice was stronger, and he did not bother to wipe the blood from his lips. I stepped back as he rearranged his clothing and picked up the corpse once more.

As soon as we cleared the gates, Rafael flung the body away like it stung him to touch it. Facing the corpse, he took a deep breath, throat swelling. He exhaled a bluish-white flame, nearly invisible in the daylight, to blanket Xyxs. The body caught fire immediately, scales crisping and shriveling in the intense heat.

Drakes, including Marron, gathered around us, watching the blaze with solemn eyes. They each plucked a single, small scale, mostly from the backs of their hands, and cast it into the blaze. A curiously touching tribute to the fallen warrior. Other drakes had died without fanfare, and certainly no acknowledgement from Rafael himself. Was it due to Xyxs' standing, or his sacrifice?

Elves sang to their dead. Any who'd held regard for the fallen elf in life wove their songs through the dead's lineage and deeds. One ancient's funeral process had lasted most of a moon, though most elves' rarely took more than a day at most. In contrast, the drakes were unusually silent, except for the occasional scale rattle and their rumbling breath. I shed a few tears despite my Dragon's hard glare, his one good eye overly bright against the blood masking his face.

Curiously, the blackened bones remained after the last of the flesh popped and sizzled away. The char helped to mask the stench of burning drake, but I wouldn't eat meat again anytime soon. Marron kneeled by the skull. When he wrenched the lower jaw free, an involuntary gasp escaped my lips.

Rafael laid a hand on my shoulder, steadying me. "It will be fashioned into a weapon; the highest honor we confer upon the dead." He wiped another tear from my cheek, examining it on his finger. "Hrrm. You weep more for a fallen drake than for your own kind."

"I'm shaken as much as mournful." The truth sang in my words as I spoke them. "I'd thought of the clan heads as invulnerable. Greater than death. As you are." Though it had never been evident to me which clan Xyxs had led. The mix of colors threw me.

The Dragon huffed. "Not at twenty generations removed from a true dragon and lacking demon blood. He was surprisingly strong, however, given his parentage."

I tried and failed to imagine Xyxs's parents.

Satisfied with the cremation, Rafael turned and strode back through the gates. He gestured for me to remain behind. I waited, anxiety mounting, until he re-emerged, this time dragging a bony, severed forelimb many times his size.

'*Left arm is weak too,*' he sent in a grumble. He must have been truly fatigued not to heal it himself.

'*Of course it is! You took a bad bite to that shoulder. If you would let me tend to you—*'

Rafael tossed the massive bony appendage toward the gathered drakes. "Byxldurr lives again," he called in draconian. "Her scent is now this death. You will inform me immediately if you detect her."

He departed without a backward glance, heading toward the camp. The drakes abandoned their bone collection, each approaching the limb to scent it. Marron's ruby gaze followed me as I trailed along after Rafael.

Chapter 56

RAFAEL crested a ridge just beyond the others' sight before his injured leg gave out. His flaming hair dimmed to red. I propped my shoulder under his arm, helping him back to his feet. Snow flurried around us, melting on contact with him.

I had no desire to carry his heavy carcass all the way to camp, so I guided him into one of the many lava tube caves dotting the landscape. With a quick burst of expelled flame, Rafael verified nothing waited for us in the dark pyroduct. He raised a dampening field, and we moved deep enough to avoid detection from the surface. Once secured, I sent a quick mental message to Celebel, explaining everything. He answered with support.

The Dragon shed his jerkin and shirt as he settled down with his back to the rough, crusted wall. As much as I wanted to help restore his eye, that femur was more pressing. At my guidance, he cut away the leather trousers. Remarkably, he offered no resistance, and I kept his lap covered with his discarded shirt.

"Gods, are you in terrible pain?" I ran my hands over the deep, mottled bruising and steaming wounds on his chest, soothing the flesh.

"Hrrm. Your touch helps." Pupils dilated almost round, his breath came shallow and rapid. Definitely in pain.

"I apologize for this. Brace yourself."

I guided the edges of the broken femur back into alignment. He followed the movement and gripped his leg with his good hand. Together, we gave his thigh a sharp jerk. Normal patients often fainted during bone setting. Like Marron, Rafael merely watched me work.

I dropped a kiss on his uninjured cheek. "You have a terrible habit of pushing yourself to your absolute limits simply because your body allows it. We'll all feel the repercussions someday. Sleep now. I'll keep watch."

He grunted, too exhausted to argue for once. With his mind intact, my work was straightforward. I grumbled to myself about his stubborn belief in his own invincibility. I would never recover from witnessing how he'd put weight on a previous compound tibial fracture. He treated hideous injuries as nothing more than a minor inconvenience. I poured spirit into his mangled leg, working my way up from there.

By the time I reached his ruined eye, his breath had slowed to the cadence of sleep. A delicate, finicky process, healing ocular injuries went far more smoothly with a slumbering patient. Taking my own advice, I ate a hardtack biscuit and a few of the chanterelles I'd stowed in a pocket of my coat.

Convincing his body to produce aqueous humor when it would rather burn everything to a crisp was no simple task. At least restoring the optic nerve was easy enough.

I drew on the cold of the cave, funneling it through my hands enough to prick with frostbite. Finally, his recalcitrant body cooperated. That eye would be horribly bloodshot for awhile, but it would heal. I shook the ice crystals from my hands. How his eyes, or truly any delicate membrane, functioned in that volcanic furnace was beyond my ken.

Sheltered from the worsening snowstorm, I held him as he slumbered, his head tucked under my chin. With Byxldurr's reappearance, could we truly win this war? If not exactly complacent, perhaps I'd been overly confident in Rafael's seemingly unassailable might.

How the fuck had Beredhel found the power to resurrect a drake who'd been dead for nearly a century? And convinced her to fight for him? Did he hold some fell sway over her?

Far too soon, Rafael stirred, rumbling and tightening his arms around me.

I stroked his hair. "Hush, Dragon. You need more sleep."

He pulled my breastplate and plackart free, sliding down to bury his face between my breasts. I relished the heat on my skin.

"Though I enjoy your caresses, you must eat before you do anything else." I kissed the top of his head. "'A bird can't fly on one wing', as the folk near my hill used to say."

He turned a baleful eye, his good one, to me. "Spread your legs then."

"Feeling better, are we?" I tugged at his hair. "And no. You're still covered in blood and undead dragon goo." How was it possible twice now I'd been forced to rebuff his advances while he was functionally naked?

Rafael rumbled and stretched, pressing me flat to the rough ground as he burned away the aforementioned goo. "Fucking lichdragon. I have not encountered one in many ages. The last was significantly smaller and weaker than Byxldurr." Nose wrinkling, he gave me a look of disgruntled vexation. I'd expected more concern. I should have known better. "Of all the fucking people."

"I feared for you! I haven't forgotten the aftermath of your last battle with her." Saying it made my heart pound. "What made her flee?"

"She was slower, less coordinated. Probably acclimating to the state of her body. That Neksarim was meant to weaken me for her attack." He stretched a second time, arching his back like a cat, and the absurd flexibility of his spine again struck me. I congratulated myself for my restraint in not taking a peek. Rafael propped himself on his elbows, looking down at me. "She has surely allied with Itreynith. This fight begins in earnest now."

Celebel was right again; Rafael had indeed been entertaining himself. Gods, given what I'd witnessed on the battlefield, what constituted actual effort?

"How's the eye?" I traced the outer edge of the socket with a careful finger. All the burst blood vessels blended the edge of his iris with the sclera.

Rafael blinked experimentally, and the pupil contracted and dilated in concert with his good eye. "Serviceable." His mouth twisted. "I have studied necromancy. It took incredible power to not only raise Byxldurr but turn her to that little blighter's influence. I must discover how it was done."

"Are you truly more annoyed about your lack of understanding than facing a significant threat?" That response was so typical, I had to laugh. Studied necromancy, indeed.

He kissed my forehead, and I twined my arms about his neck. When one hand drifted over my breast, I stopped him.

"Food first."

He growled and shifted his weight to glare at me. "Never thought you would *insist* I kill humans."

"That isn't what I'm saying and you know it, you horrible beast. You need sustenance, and there are better nutrient sources than people."

"How would you know what I need?" The Dragon purred in my ear. "*I* think I need to hear you cry out in ecstasy. It has been far too long." A hand slid up my thigh.

With a heave of my hips, I rolled him off of me and sat up. "There! You're weakened. I could never do that under normal circumstances!"

Rafael grinned, flashing his teeth. "I like to give you the illusion of control." He pinned me flat again, holding me firmly to the ground with the pad of a single finger pressed into my shoulder.

I sighed, exhaling through my nose. "Yes, fine, you're very strong. Will you please find some food? You may kiss me as much as you like when you return."

He rose, scooping me off the ground, and kissed me thoroughly enough to take my breath away. When he set me down on slightly wobbly legs, he held me at arm's length, appraising his work. My ear tips flushed hot.

"You're terrible. I love you." I rewarded him with a rueful grin. "Don't kill and eat any humans or otherwise wreak havoc."

"How you test me, my dove." The thin light filtering from the cave's entrance ringed his hair like an infernal halo. "I do love you. Minimal havoc it is." His eyes glittered in the dark as he bent to kiss me again. "If you are not in this exact spot upon my return, however, I shall wreak havoc such as the world has never seen."

"You make the sweetest threats."

"THAT BLOODY dragon fight destroyed what was left of the place. We found not a single note of the artefacts we sought." Celebel passed the wash rag across our shared hot spring. "We'll return to Amrún now. No need to keep pressing."

I flicked an errant dried crust of blood from my shoulder and sank deeper into the water. Sediment of aqua, rust, and marigold streaked the natural pool, brilliant against the bleak landscape. Fat snowflakes evaporated on contact with the steam.

"That bloody dragon fight scared me." I stretched my neck.

"Is this lichdragon such a threat? Your Dragon defeated it easily enough."

"It was a harder-won fight than Rafael let on." Overhead, the stars glimmered through a wooly cloud bank. "Even he admitted Byxldurr's reappearance marks a concerning key change. If another Neksarim had appeared…" I shivered.

Celebel rubbed his forehead. "Might I wash and braid your hair? So much of our time together has been driven by these crises, and I know not if that will ever change." At my murmured assent, he turned me and eased my braids loose, running his fingers through my voluminous hair. It floated around us, inking the ripples in the water. He worked a cleansing tonic into my scalp. "Hmm. Where is your braid knife?"

I blinked and pulled the small dagger from its hidden sheath. After the spider incident, I carried it at all times as a backup. "Do you have a sudden thirst for bloodplay?"

He laughed and took the knife from my hand. Separating a thin silver lock, he held his hair taut and sawed through it at the root.

"Cel, what are you—"

Weaving the lock into a tight braid, he held it aloft. "I'd like to plait this into your hair, if I may. As a youth, I watched my fathers exchange locks and braid our lineage pattern into each other's hair, and always wished for a love like theirs."

My heart and soulbond sang at the sweetness. "I'd be honored."

He set to work with a comb of carved jasper speckled like ocean foam. Humming as he worked, he extricated the strand of pearls and worked out my tangles. "Your hill was a pleasant dream from which I woke too soon. I feel such remorse for subjecting you to these horrors. Perhaps we should return. If we are to die, let us be surrounded by beauty and peace rather than isolation and despair." Pensive fingers danced across my shoulders.

"Cel, I made my choice. It is as it must be. If this means the Great Tree lives on unscathed, I consider it worthwhile. We must simply seek more of these quiet moments together." I laid my hand over his, willing away the pit in my belly. "Do not listen to melancholy's drowning song."

He kissed the tips of my ears. "Forgive me, Moonflower. It is only wistful musing. I am well."

"What would your fathers think of all this?"

"They were scholars and avowed pacifists. Simple enough to ignore strife outside the impenetrable walls of Velúara; complacent under my grandfather's long shadow." The comb glided across my scalp, parting my hair in thick sections.

"What blissful ignorance." I bit my lip. "Ah, sorry. I do not mean to criticize."

"No, no, you are correct. My fathers, for all their good intentions, reinforced the flawed ideals you broke your lineage to escape. Out of necessity, I learned swordplay from El—" He swallowed. "From Eledom." Gods, the sorrow in his voice.

"You mustn't blame yourself for his defection." Blame only fed resentment, and we'd had more than enough of that.

Celebel sighed and embraced me from behind. "I'm ruining the braid tension."

"You've ruined nothing. Did you fathers teach you to burden yourself with the world's ills?"

He kissed the back of my head. "Father Elairon lived a charmed life, but Father Célesor hailed from Ilitherin. I cannot fathom what he would say about the Dragon in our midst, let alone my particular entanglement. Likely only frosty stares and 'suitable' partners thrust upon me with regularity."

My ears swiveled to catch every word.

He pulled sections along the side of my head tight, weaving in the pearls. "My fathers forged their soulbond. Without having experienced the travails of a soulmate bond, I might not have otherwise believed the extremes it has forced upon me."

I risked throwing off the braid tension and tossed a glance over my shoulder. The dark slashes of Celebel's brows drew together, but no storm clouds rested on his brow. With a gentle tap on my cheek, he turned my head forward.

"Legacy is a strange thing, is it not? Elaris built Velúara. I could never hope to achieve such a feat, but perhaps achieving a new melody of peace is enough." The tugging at my scalp slowed.

I took hold of his hand, tugging it over my shoulder, and pressed it to my lips. "You, personally, have made peace with the Red Dragon himself, and you're saving our people from certain doom. That is far more than any elf in living memory has achieved."

"If we survive this certain doom, I'll accept your accolades. As for peace, that is a melody yet to be sung." Celebel lifted the bulk of my braid and let it spill forward over my shoulder across my lap.

My breath caught. He'd plaited my hair in the Elhalanros pattern, incorporating both the pearls and the shining silver lock.

"I need a bit of practice keeping the tension even at such length, but it's lovely on you." His eyes shone. "Will you braid mine?"

Chapter 57

"**S**URELY your princeling will be upset with you for bringing me here." Rafael had a wicked glint in his eye as he examined the interior of the tent.

Sexual frustration threatened to suffocate me. "Celebel once offered to let you fuck me in his bed, so I'm taking him up on that offer. But it means you must fuck me. Now remove your clothes."

He crossed his arms. "Pushy little thing. Why should I heed your commands?"

"Because I want to worship your body." I shrugged out of my gown as his growing heat filled the small space. "Because I can make you feel sublime."

He rumbled, lips curling, and carefully laid his sword belt to one side, pulling off his leather jerkin.

"The shirt too." I pointed to the floor.

"So demanding."

I loved the way his abs flexed and lats flared as he lifted the shirt over his head. Unable to resist, I hooked my fingers under the waistband of his leather trousers. He let me pull him forward. I ran my tongue over the hard lines of muscle, biting his nipples, making him hiss. I held his eyes while I pressed his growing erection between my breasts, using my hands to squeeze them together around his leatherbound cock. He moaned, gripping my hair with both hands. Inching backwards, I drew him toward the bed.

"Sit at the edge there," I commanded.

He smiled down at me, brushing the pad of a thumb across my lips. Obligingly, he turned and sat. I pushed his knees apart. Raking my teeth over the straining leather, I also ran my nails up his inner thighs. He tilted his head back. Rumbling encouragement, he loosened the ties of his trousers. I pounced on the opportunity, grabbing the laces in my teeth and pulling, releasing his glorious cock from its confinement.

Gods. If I could take his fist, surely I could take his cock, but the spines! My cunt ached in anticipation.

His eyes closed in bliss. Cautiously, I experimented with his tolerance. One long, expelled breath over his cock made it twitch. Another made him grab my hair again, pressing my face into him. I drank in his scent, rubbing my cheek against his hard flesh, savoring the experience.

"May I?" I asked, poised to press my lips to his shaft.

He answered with a low growl, extinguishing the witchlights. As his cock throbbed, I kissed him lightly, up to the tip and down to the base. His talons traced circles over my back, sharp enough to make me tense, but not quite piercing my skin. The tent flap rustled as I flicked my tongue along the length of him. Ever so slowly, I took him into my mouth, jaws straining around his girth. He hissed again.

Lips brushed the small of my back and familiar hands glided up my sides.

"Continue," Celebel whispered in my ear, sending a thrill through my spine to my aching clit.

I spread my legs to give him better access. Celebel's erection slid back and forth against my cunt. I moaned around Rafael's cock in my mouth, trying to press my hips back into Celebel without losing my grip. I'd never been so overwhelmingly aroused in my life. Wetness flooded down my legs, puddling on the floor between my knees. Arching my back—

'CÚRANIEL! FUCKING STOP!' The roar in my head not only knocked me out of my delicious dream, it also shook my bedroll so hard I nearly rolled off onto the cold tent floor.

I couldn't help myself. I dissolved into laughter. The furious thundering in my head threatened to escalate to migraine levels.

'Rafael, gods damn it, stay out of my head. You can only blame yourself for flipping a log and finding a worm!'

'You are the fucking worm!'

Laughing only angered him further. My face was aflame, and my head pounded in tandem with my heartbeat. How unfortunate Celebel was not here to witness this.

'*Fuck off!*' Rafael snarled in my mind.

'*I was trying to!*' I tugged uselessly at my earlobes. '*If you weren't such a prude—*'

'*I will burn that fucking—*'

'*You'll have to burn me as well, you big blighter. Why don't you come over here and fuck me into submission?*' I slapped the bedroll in frustrated lust.

Celebel's braid had held up well to the travel and subsequent thrashing in my sleep. I tucked in a single stray end and witchlights flared as I reluctantly dressed. Crow. What a waste of a truly exquisite sex dream.

THE SOULBOND'S tug led me to the top of a steep hill. Not as large as my home, but I struggled to catch my breath. I'd expected to find Rafael at the peak, looking down over the camp from the sharp overhang, but he was absent.

"Hiding from me now?" I called. "Don't you wish to hear more about my dream?"

'*Leave me in peace.*' His tone was a snarl.

I paced around. The bond told me he was near, but where? "You have no right to act thorny; you did this to yourself!" Reflexive, the urge to poke at him. "Where are you hiding?"

A deep growl started at my feet and rattled the pebbles across the ground. The sparse trees twitched and danced.

"Rafael, please. It was a harmless sex dream!"

An enormous scaly head rose above the overhang. Blood red and framed with spines, two long, white horns crowned him. Rafael in his full dragon form. Crow. A giant reptilian eye turned toward me, burning with fury. Suddenly I was very, very small.

"**I warned you**." The voice reverberated in my head, rattling my bones.

My vision filled with teeth. A blast of hot breath threw me to the ground. Scooting backward on my ass, I wasn't fast enough to avoid his jaws.

"Rafael, what the *fuck!*" I cried as he scooped me into his mouth.

His teeth closed, effectively locking me inside. Stunned, I glanced about my new prison. Each needle-pointed tooth stretched taller than my full height. His dentition fit together so closely only the barest light trickled in. The heat made it difficult to breathe. Thank the gods he hadn't eaten recently. Carnivore breath on that scale would have killed me outright.

Celebel's concern swirled through our bond.

'*Peace, Starshine. This is some new game of his,*' I sent. '*I will block you out so you may rest.*'

'*As you wish. We depart at sunrise.*'

The inside of the Dragon's mouth was drier than I'd expected—if I'd ever thought to expect such a thing. I stood and nearly slipped as it was. His tongue lay still. At its base lay the levered opening of the tracheal adaptation that allowed him to breathe fire.

Enough dragon temper tantrums. I wedged my shoulders against his gums, trying to squeeze my way out. Hopefully, the discomfort would budge his jaws. He closed his scaled lips in retaliation, blocking out the light completely.

"**Keep pushing. Perhaps I will swallow you and be done with it.**" Each syllable wrapped me in impossibly deep sound waves, felt more than heard in the frissons of my skin, the drumbeat of air shivering in my lungs. The movement of his tongue and stubborn jaws put me in mind of standing on a ship's deck during a squall.

"You fucking blighter! Release me this instant!" I kicked the root of a tooth as hard as I could without hurting my foot.

"**I am the fucking Red Dragon. And you are an impertinent little shit begging to be taught a lesson.**" The words rolled over and through me, lighting the ever-present flame between my legs.

Gods, Rafael could fuck me to death with the power of that voice. Did it count as yelling? No, I was a willing enough participant in this transgression. As I considered my death wish, his tongue slithered around my waist and dragged me away from his teeth. I shrieked and punched at it.

"Do you truly mean to eat me over a dream? Fucking hells, Dragon." I panted out the words. "If I am no longer allowed my sexual fantasies, you may as well put me out of my misery. Or, if you're feeling charitable, you could drop me in one of those bizarre human cults that despise female orgas—"

'Shut your disrespectful mouth, Cúraniel.' The physical thunderclap of a growl knocked the air from my lungs.

His tongue tip jabbed at my mouth. I clenched my jaws, but he shoved it past my lips, effectively drowning out my cursing. He rolled me with that muscular tongue, sliding it between my legs. My body's immediate arousal angered me further.

I hammered at his tongue with my fists. *'Release me right now, you fucking beast!'*

'You must be punished.' Rafael's tongue undulated between my legs.

I cursed myself for the throbbing of my clit. The Dragon knew perfectly well how my far my carnal curiosity extended; our treacherous soulbond bared my desires.

A coughing laugh echoed in my head, so I kicked at him as well. His tongue abruptly withdrew from my mouth and unwound, allowing me to regain my footing. Then the tip thrust hard between my legs, lifting me into the air.

I cried out. My weight forced his tongue deep inside me, stretching me to capacity. Beyond capacity. I clamped my internal muscles as hard as I could and wrapped my legs around the invasive appendage as he lifted me. Reaching the roof of his mouth, I braced myself with my palms, struggling to find a handhold.

"Too big! It's too big. You'll tear me," I pleaded through teeth clenched around the delicious pain. "You'll split me in half!" But oh gods, how my arousal sluiced down my legs. I spared a hand to pinch and roll my nipples.

'Have you not begged for this very thing?'

True, but I refused to admit it. He'd never demonstrated any willingness to engage with me in this form.

The Dragon's tongue twisted and thrust. Fuck, he truly meant to split me apart. My traitorous body responded with mad lust. I whimpered as I writhed, impaled on him. He let me drop, a little at a time, just enough for me to land hard on the tip of that destroying tongue. My thighs quivered, burning from the effort of holding me in place. The sweet strain brought me hovering at the brink of climax.

"Let them sing of my death," I panted, sliding my hand down to flick my clit. "Who else has departed Vaeda in such a way?" Demolished in the dark, sweltering cavern of the Red Dragon's vast maw.

'Shall I release you now?' The taunting tone infuriated me further, somehow also driving my desire to greater heights. He slowly lowered his tongue until my toes skimmed over the bottom of his mouth.

My defeat was imminent. "Gods, please continue."

'Beg.' His tongue slid out of me.

I stumbled as I landed on the floor of his mouth. "Are you fucking serio—"

That damned tongue whipped out, cracking me hard across the buttocks and knocking a startled yelp from my mouth. A welt rose immediately as I rubbed my sore ass.

"**BEG.**" The word slammed into me.

"You…ugh, crow! Fucking hells." I clasped my hands in supplication. "Please fuck me. Punish me as you see fit, oh grandest and mightiest of catastrophes…and scourge of my fucking life."

"**Insolence.**" His tongue lashed out again, this time connecting with the backs of my thighs as I turned away from the blow.

"*Ouch*, damnation! Forgive me, or eat me, or whatever else you plan to do. Just fuck me first, please. Please!"

An amused cough knocked me forward. I braced myself against his teeth as his tongue thrust into me again. Impossibly huge. Impossibly forceful. Sipping desperately of the cooler air leaking through the minute gaps in his teeth, I barely avoided a swoon. His tongue rammed into me over and over. The orgasm built again, strumming up my spine. Pain built into a delectable pressure that threatened to sweep me away forever.

It crested, and I screamed my throat raw, collapsing against the spear wall of his teeth.

THE INCONSISTENT light disrupted my sense of time. Celebel queried, understandably concerned. Rafael's mind was closed to me despite my best efforts to pry.

Every movement of the Dragon's head created earthquakes, no matter how slowly he did it. He cushioned my falls with that damnable tongue. He also fucked me mercilessly with it, regardless of my half-hearted demands for freedom. I couldn't hide my appetite from him, not in such proximity.

"I enjoy consuming your orgasms in this way," he purred, after my latest ruinous climax.

I jabbed at his gums again, tempted to pull open the old cuts I found there, but it would only encourage him. The thought of wading knee-deep in scalding dragon blood held no appeal.

"Yes, you are suffering greatly." That laugh again, taking my breath away with the heat.

"I am quite weary of being damp and overheated."

"Are you now?" His tongue snaked between my legs again, and I skipped away from it, hopping on one foot to regain my balance. **"Never has playing with my food so entertained me."**

'Release me, you absurd hedonist!'

A furious voice called from outside his jaws. Celebel. My heart jumped in apprehension.

"Rafael! Bloody Wyrm! You great fucking monster, release Cúraniel this instant! You've held her captive long enough!"

I fell sideways as the Dragon moved and crawled to peer out of his teeth. Fortunately, he had peeled his lips back. Celebel stood far below us. He looked impossibly small from this vantage. A light drizzle fell, darkening the ground.

"Who are you to make demands?" The Dragon uncrossed his front paws, flexing his talons meaningfully.

Celebel startled at the voice booming through him. "What of your claim not to harm her? Surely, she will need food and water, and to make water of her own, unless that's another deviancy of yours. We are striking camp, and I shall not leave her to your caprice any longer."

I did indeed have a pressure in my bladder I'd been ignoring. Blessing my efficient body, I was grateful not to be a human, what with their constant need to pass waste. It gave me an idea.

The Dragon snorted, knocking me off my feet again with a toss of his head. A horrible, drawn-out screeching noise flattened my ears. He'd raked his talons over the bare granite. Thunder rumbled in counterpoint.

"I'll piss in your mouth if you won't release me." I kicked his gums again.

The floor dropped out from under me as the Dragon suddenly lowered his head. I tensed, expecting him to attack Celebel. Instead, light momentarily blinded me as his mouth opened. He draped his tongue over his jagged teeth as a sort of walkway. I climbed up and over, blinking in the sun, and chilled by the winter air on my thoroughly saliva-coated skin. Celebel's eyes widened.

"I need a century of baths." I slid down. As I reached the tip, Rafael flicked his tongue and launched me into the ground. A liberal caking of dirt joined my saliva coating. "You wretched hellbeast!"

With his long, wedge-shaped head propped on one paw, Rafael looked down at me with a distinctly amused expression.

I wiped my face. "Fucking gods damned, cursed, rotten, sky crocodile!"

Behind me, Celebel hummed, and the rain picked up. Almost a blessing, despite the cold.

Rafael snorted, a blast of hot air. **You should thank me for all the orgasms.**

I bit my thumb at him, and he shook his mane of scales. Tilting his massive head back, his throat swelled. A telltale glow stoked in his great maw as he turned to Celebel. I shrieked in genuine fear for my unprotected soulmate. The Dragon exhaled...

Through his nostrils instead of his mouth. He blew a vast cloud of pale smoke. The same smoke from holding his flame too long in his mouth, searing the softer tissues. It reeked of charred flesh.

Celebel gagged, coughing hard and doubling over. I hacked and choked along with him. Eyes streaming, I staggered to his side. Celebel glanced up, red-rimmed eyes bright with fury, and he made a strong skyward gesture with both hands, singing a pure note. The power he pulled down tingled along my skin like approaching lightning.

The Dragon's malicious laugh ricocheted off the granite.

The sky ripped open like a cut wineskin, and freezing rain drenched us all. Rafael's eyes flashed dangerously as he drew his wings over his horned head, backing further under the overhang. Frigid as the sudden downpour was, I welcomed rinsing my skin. The rain ceased as abruptly as it began, clouds dissipating into a clear, blue sky.

"Fuck. You," Celebel spat, along with a wad of blackened phlegm.

"**Blame your irreverent soulmate**." Rafael laughed another booming, hacking laugh, and shook the water from his scales, dousing us in a second shower. He turned his head, tucking his snout under a wing joint.

Celebel's ears twitched, mirroring mine as we absorbed the Dragon's statement. *Your soulmate*. Elation rose on the updraft of hope.

Chapter 58

Celebel

IT began as a distant rumble. Overhead, boughs creaked and shook, creating flashing patterns of the light. Pebbles danced around my stallion's hooves as the vibrations grew. Dust plumed, making Helicos sneeze and my eyes burn. I cursed the impulse that had led me to drag the moisture out of the area in retaliation for the Red Dragon's goading.

"Gods, now what?" Beside me, Cúraniel twisted in her saddle as shrieks came from the back of the line, both elvish and draconian.

Elves scattered away from a massive tree as it fell. It landed across our ranks with an explosive impact, spraying bark and limbs, and effectively split our party in twain. Gods, was anyone injured? Riding through densely packed woods spread our ranks thinner than I preferred, but at least it helped them evade the falling obstacle.

Helicos quivered but held firm in his position. I patted his neck in appreciation of his discipline. Iruwher danced in place, blowing, as Cúraniel tried to calm the bay courser.

"Scolopendra," came a familiar bass bellow. The Dragon had deigned to join us.

What in the bloody hells?

Another dragon trumpeted in alarm. The ground rose and fell as if Vaeda itself heaved a sigh. A mighty wave rippled up the path, flinging all of us into the air. Horses screamed, drakes bellowed, elves cried out. I leaped clear of the saddle as the helpless stallion landed badly and stumbled to his knees.

Nimble Iruwher kept her footing and her steadily cursing rider seated. Eerie, fluting howls twined through the trees. Umbrawolves. Odd; they would be at a disadvantage in daylight with most of our forces out in the open.

"Is he hurt?" Cúraniel slipped to the unsteady ground to assist.

Helicos rose, snorting and shaking his mane as I ran my hands over his legs in fear of finding a break. Lameness now would leave him vulnerable to the shadowy wolves closing in.

"Thank the gods for the fortitude of elvish horses. He is whole," I said, drawing my sword.

All around us, elves examined their steeds and assisted each other. It warmed me to spot a brindled brown and black drake lifting a fallen limb from the dazed rider and destrier trapped beneath it. More so when elf and equine appeared mostly unscathed.

The drake turned and flung the bough at the first umbrawolf to break through the tree line. Knocking the beast flat, the scaled warrior lunged forward and leaped upon the trapped rider. Draconic jaws closed around the rider's head.

The Dragon swooped down from the sky in his winged man form, landing beside us. He turned and leveled a devastating kick at a passing umbrawolf. Those cruel talons laid open the beast's side. It fell with a whimper. The drake spat fire and burned away monstrous wolf and rider alike.

"What the fuck is a scolopendra?" Cúraniel demanded.

"The worst fucking creature in all of Vaeda." The Red Dragon wore a snarl in place of his usual scowl, carving his severe features into a hellish mask.

Another rumble shook the trees. As one, we turned to witness a new horror erupting from the ground near the back of the column. Massive purplish-blue pincers impaled a yellow drake and kept rising. A segmented body of deep red followed. Endless flame-bright legs stabbing the air as the creature surged upward. It towered over trees, hills, and dragons alike; slim, but impossibly long. And unbelievably fast. It flung the drake free of its pincers and snatched a blue dragon from the sky.

My lady shivered. "Spiders burn. Surely a giant centipede will as well?"

"Not these," said the Dragon. "Take your people and flee to the bedrock." He pointed to a lofty granite outcropping. "I will attempt to hold it off."

Attempt? Had the legendary God of Carnage ever doubted his superior fighting prowess? Had the War Crow's return shaken him so greatly?

I seized Cúraniel's hand, and we fled for the high ground. We gathered others as we passed, sending the horses toward the eastern mountains, and prospective safety. Umbrawolves snapped at our heels, picking off stragglers. Nemohee appeared, cutting down a riderless umbrawolf as þeir roan galloped past. Others took up the fight and formed an effective rear guard.

Screams crescendoed in a symphony behind us. The hissing and clicking of spiders paled in comparison to the behemoth at our backs. I resisted the fearful urge to turn, focusing my strength on climbing the sheer wall before us. The hale among us ascended first, working to haul our injured up the cliff with ropes. I breathed again once the last few elves were safely at the top.

Below, the scolopendra wreaked havoc with whiplash speed. It burrowed through the ground as if swimming. The creature breached repeatedly, each time with violent force. A rainbow of dragons swarmed overhead. They swooped, saving their fire in favor of fang and claw screeching over the centipede's carapace, mostly to no effect.

The Red Dragon waited until the monster was almost upon him to transform. Had he done so as we'd fled, he surely would have crushed any remaining elves in the area. Cúraniel clutched my arm so hard she would have left bruises if I'd been unarmored.

The scolopendra descended, pincers wide, as Rafael's body distorted and expanded. His great jaws closed behind the creature's head just before it skewered him. Rolling on his back, the Red Dragon kicked with his hind legs; a giant cat eviscerating its prey.

Trapped, the massive arthropod swung its equally pincered tail as a cudgel. The resulting collision with the Dragon's side echoed across the nearby canyon. I was not the only elf who cowered and covered their ears.

Writhing, the scolopendra regained its traction and ripped free of the Dragon's bite. Bright purple ichor splashed where legs tore away.

It disappeared beneath the earth again. The Dragon regained his feet, blood steaming from punctures along his side. He moved with halting awkwardness, gathering himself for a leap into the air. It took a few attempts to clear the ground, nothing like his typical fluid movements.

"Is he well?" I asked.

Cúraniel frowned, gaze growing distant. "Rafael says scolopendra can paralyze even a dragon with a direct bite," she said with rapt horror. "They secrete venom from tiny stingers on their legs as well. Fucking hells."

The scolopendra reappeared, hurtling upward. It aimed directly at the Red Dragon's belly. Cúraniel gasped, grabbing my arm. I tensed and braced for the inevitable. As its indigo pincers opened wide, a green blur slammed into the monster from the back.

Marron, in his dragon form, bore the nightmarish creature down, staying well clear of its snapping pincers and jabbing legs. They landed with a concussive blast that flattened the nearby trees in all directions. The green dragon bit and shook the scolopendra. The Red Dragon wheeled and landed on its flailing tail. Gods, that creature was almost long as the two of them combined.

The centipede rolled, nearly flinging off the attacking dragons. Claws screeched on armored exoskeleton and jaws clacked together as the drakes battled to maintain their hold. Vaerra slamming into the monster's midsection with an echoing impact. A burly brown dragon, built like a living boulder with a horned snout and tree trunk legs, charged into another exposed section of the scolopendra's flank. The collision knocked the combatants sideways.

Marron's wings stretched over the land. He bugled a strange, muffled cry. The land responded. Waves of earth rose on either side of the dragon, rolling inward. He thrust his head beneath the surface, shoving the scolopendra deep. On the creature's opposite end, the Red Dragon did the same. The brown dragon backed away and slammed into the scolopendra again.

At some unspoken signal, the dragons took to the sky, though the brown one glided away rather than truly flying. Rolling waves of earth bore the scolopendra down. Circling in a tight formation, each dragon breathed continuous flame. Subtle at first, a glow suffused the ground beneath them.

Other dragons joined them; yellow, shining black, and the serpentine silver. Their combined flame melted the rock into a bubbling cauldron. Its brilliance stung my eyes, and I averted my gaze. Crackling pings of obsidian resonated at the far edges. Gods. *Like plates breaking.* Had the children—

"Oh, clever," Cúraniel breathed, and I risked a glimpse.

A blue dragon, Tyldain, called down a drizzle of rain upon the boiling lava. Frustrated at the minimal response, the dragon screeched and lashed his tail. Smaller dragons joined him, an ocean of blue, silver, and grey wings. The drizzle intensified to a proper rain, but far from enough to harden the molten ground. It swelled, threatening to release the monster beneath. A pincer breached the surface.

Curse my horrid timing to dehydrate the area, just as we needed a storm. No more unleashing my temper without considering the consequences first. I had to rectify my mistake.

I pulled my helm off, shaking out my hair and aching ears, and raised my arms for attention. "Lend me your voices," I called, and sang a rising scale to summon the rain. "We must aid the dragons!"

No small risk, joining spirit in that manner. History spoke of those who never returned to themselves after such enmeshing of power, choosing instead to release their souls into the shared song. Greater and more pressing was the risk of the scolopendra's renewed attack.

My people funneled their spirit through me. Cúraniel harmonized with her rich alto, then Feanim's sharp tenor rose. Nemohee with þeir powerful contralto. Lámirië's soprano. Each new voice added focus and power as our song grew. I had a pang as nearby vegetation withered, lending its moisture to our cause, and vowed to return and replant this place after the war.

We raised a mighty chorus, pulling clouds from the very spirit of the world, cold from the stars themselves. Together, we lent our strength to the blue dragon, weaving our song around his calling.

He squawked in surprise as our power enveloped him. With a glance at us, he beat his wings harder, faster, whipping the newfound sleet into a true ice storm. We sang louder, swaying in unison, and the dragon added his mountainous voice. Other drakes picked up the melody in a thunderous bass line.

The crackling grew louder as the surface cooled, adding a new counterpoint to our melody. Drunk with the sheer force of it, I lost myself in the music. Higher, deeper, clearer, all-encompassing. The whole of Vaeda sang with us.

Finally, the blue dragon lit upon the blackened ground, utterly spent. His body shrank to an azure speck in the freshly cooled lava field. One by one, the other dragons landed, shifting into their smaller forms.

I sat heavily, winded. Some elves had swooned, overcome with the vast spirit. Healers, more practiced in such power weaving, moved from patient to patient, coaxing them to wakefulness. A handful remained still. I winced. That loss rested upon my shoulders.

"It does not." Cúraniel settled beside me, having completed her rounds. "Whether you'd called the rain away earlier or flooded the entire valley, the drakes could not hold that creature on their own. If it had attacked again, if it had felled Rafael, we would all be lost." She stroked my hair, and I leaned into her touch. "That was amazing."

As I opened my mouth, her eyes unfocused.

"Rafael needs me," she signed. "Paralysis."

I laid a gentle hand on the back of her neck. "Go to him. And give him my thanks, or however you offer gratitude. I cannot fathom the casualties if he had not warned us of that monstrosity's approach. Thank Marron too, if you encounter him. He was the one who truly saved us."

She grabbed my face, pressing an emphatic kiss to my cheek.

THE WAXING moon silvered the botryoidal polyps of cooled lava as I wandered through the scar. Collectively exhausted, we'd made a hasty camp on the granite rise, gathering ourselves for the remainder of the journey. The drakes ringed us, sleeping heaped in piles of snoring scales. I wished to be alone with my thoughts in relative silence, or perhaps to assure myself the scolopendra was indeed imprisoned.

Though a chill wind howled across the meadow, the fresh pumice under my feet provided steady warmth. The occasional pop and ping had me jumping at shadows.

Marron advised the obsidian encasing the creature would not hold indefinitely, thus we should not tarry overlong in the area. Despite his ominous warning, the drakes' cooperation in containing that horror released a knot of tension in my lower back. Marron had supported me well enough at Velúara, but this was the first I'd witnessed drakes truly working in concert. Perhaps there was a glimmer of hope with my stalwart rival.

Shadows gathered far afield, drawing my attention as they rose. I drew my sword. Umbrawolves again?

"Celebel Elhalanros," called a voice from the hooded figure coalescing before me. Hollow, it rang both familiar and strange. 'Elh'lanros,' it pronounced my lineage, as one long-acquainted.

Leaning on a blossoming staff, the figure pushed the hood back. Moonlight limned regal features now haggard. A once-warm brown face greyed unto death. Dented golden bells hung from tattered braids. I clutched my chest, gasping with the pain of recognition.

"Araglin! Oh, Araglin." I ran to embrace my lost friend, to kiss his cheek, to welcome him home. "Gods, I'd thought you lost!"

"Stay back," he cried, raising his arms. "You are not safe."

His words hit me with physical force, and I skidded to a halt, my sabatons scraping on the pumice. I appraised him, truly seeing him for the first time.

Burning coals took the place of his kind, dark eyes, now sunken into sockets like pits. Skin wrapped so tightly across his starved frame, he was more skeleton than living elf. Tattered ears drooped, shorn of earrings, and his once-meticulous braids hung in frayed disarray. Of his golden velvet robes, only rags remained.

"There are powers at play here you do not yet understand. I beg only your ear." Araglin raised the staff clutched in his right hand. A bulbous bloom of pointed petals, shaded lavender by the moon's gentle caress. The Protean Staff.

How had he come to possess it? Why did he appear before me now? What could possibly diminish him in this way? My back tightened with dread. I longed to barrage him with questions, but I signed formal acknowledgement and took a knee.

"I bring firstly a warning." The thin, carved out quality of Araglin's formerly rich voice constricted my chest. "Beredhel approached the court through Feledhor as his agent, offering us promises of restored greatness. I meant only to broker peace. Why should elves war against our own kind? Beredhel was universally beloved before his disappearance. Surely, we could reconcile our differences, thought I.

"Oh, my dear friend. I was such a fool. When the others changed allegiance, they did so out of pride. Never did I suspect they would enact violence upon our kindred. Worse, I never suspected Beredhel capable of the most vile treachery. Not only against his brother, that invitation was a trap for us all.

"Beredhel does not seek restored grandeur. His goal is the absolute subjugation of Vaeda, and he uses the consumed spirit of elves to power his machinations. Those who seek succor with him are slowly severed from the shared song, turned, and compelled as the Fomorians are. Worse, he consumes their very soul to create weapons of despicable design. This foul work he accomplishes so slowly, none are the wiser until it is too late."

He raised his arms, ragged sleeves fluttering in the wind like the wings of a dying moth. "I was the first. Fool that I am, I met Beredhel in person before you ever brought the Red Dragon to my hearth. He laid hands upon me, presenting me with a ring to promise peace. That very ring siphoned my spirit over time. What he stole from me, he forged into the primary madness weapon."

I started. "The spear that struck the Red Dragon all those moons ago?" Did he know of the corrupted gestation trees as well? I bit back the urge to tell him everything.

"The very same. Each weapon inflicting such a wound to the psyche requires a soul, but he made a mistake with the prototype. My song was too powerful, too uncorrupted. Thus, he could rip away only part of it. That weapon was flawed, but he was too eager to snare the Red Dragon's power for his purposes. The forging left me as I am now." He gestured at himself with a bony hand. "Dead and yet alive. Starving, always starving." Araglin's too-bright gaze dropped, along with his volume. Shame tightened his voice. "My only sustenance is the spirit I glean from other elves."

Tears sprang to my eyes as I leaped to my feet. "Oh, my dear Araglin. Surely, we will unravel this curse upon you, to make you whole once more. Please, you must return to camp with me. Cúraniel is a powerful healer. If she can cure the Red Dragon of his inflicted madness, surely she can restore you."

Araglin shook his head, emphatic enough to whip his tattered ears. "No, no, sweet Celebel. It is not safe. When the hunger rises, I cannot control myself. I have done far more than enough harm. Do not ask me to endanger the others any further. Even now, that starvation gnaws at me, compelling me to attack and drain you. I am made a monster."

"This cannot be," I cried. "You were ever the gentlest among us, the most temperate. I rebuke your claim of monstrosity!"

I lunged for his robe, grasping only night.

My friend backed away, eyes flaring wild and fierce. "I have no right to beg your forgiveness, though I desire it with all that remains of my being. Please, take this artefact I stole back from Beredhel as a token of my goodwill. I will aid you as I am able from the shadows. Save them, Silver Star. Save the turned elves before it is too late. Before they have no remaining souls to save. Farewell."

"No, Araglin, please! I have so many questions. We can save you, I know it." Sobs wracked me. "Please, allow us to try!"

He melted into mist, leaving only the Protean Staff behind.

To be continued in
Book 3 of The Soulbound Song

Acknowledgements

THIS book presented challenges I never could have overcome without my friends, family, and community. Writing and publishing truly is a team effort and I love the collaborative process as much as I do the drafting. Here's to growth and lessons learned.

My sister Charlotte: You've supported me through every step. I'm so happy you've discovered a love of reading. I love you always, big sis. Even if you still don't like fantasy books.

None of this would be possible without my husband Henry's ongoing support. An integral part of what makes Vaeda feel so real, you're a plot hole-seeking missile and an endless font of creativity. Thank you for weathering the storm with me.

To my alpha and beta readers, thank you for patiently wading through more of my chaotic early drafts. A.E. Cosby, thank you for helping me with sign language grammar, nerding out over music together, and being a constant inspiration. I don't know where I'd be without your friendship. Jennifer Kay, thank you for always being down with whatever nonsense I throw at you. O.H. Phukdischidt, thank you for your continual belief in me. Juan York, thank you for wading through all the romance to give me insightful critique—and for the page holders! Jess Duncan, what an absolute blessing to reunite with you, old friend. Thank you for all the encouragement. Winter, thank you again and forever for lending your perspective to bring Nemohee to life.

To my incredibly patient editors R.N. Barbosa and Yarnwyvern, thank you for all the therapy. And the enabling. I'm so lucky to call each of you a dear friend. Barbosa, you helped me shape this story from a clump of old drafts and random snippets into beautiful cohesion with your wisdom and humor. I am forever in awe of your writing prowess. Yarnwyvern, thank you for listening to my endless rants while you polished this beast of a manuscript into a shining gem.

Ruthie Bowles, thank you endlessly for the sensitivity reading. You have an absolute bouquet of talent. Maddy Armstrong, thanks for the consultation on distilling, tolerating my never-ending deluge of special interest babbling, and helping me survive being a fellow Armstrong. Savannah Rose, thank you for the info on raptors and your incredibly inspiring nature photography. Fawn, I am forever grateful for yet anther gorgeous cover. Watching your artistic skill and talent grow is an absolute honor.

To my readers and Soulbound Singers Discord members, thank you forever for being a constant source of motivation. Your enthusiasm for this story and acceptance of my chaos gremlin self bolsters me in ways you'll never know. Maybe the real treasure was the memes we made along the way.

Finally, to Hekla, aka Hex, thanks for purring at my side through the whole thing. And the occasional squeaks and bites.

In Memoriam: Mike Houlihan. Fly high, friend. You are missed.

About the Author

C.A. Chaplin resides in California with her husband, her black cat, and still too many carnivorous plants to count. Her writing is the culmination of degrees in psychology, gemology, Traditional East Asian Medicine, the unpacking of purity culture, late-diagnosed autism and ADHD, and a life spent dreaming of dragons and elves.

To learn more about the Soulbound Song series, please visit: https://www.cachaplin.com/